THE FARRIS CHANNEL

THE SIME~GEN SERIES from The Borgo Press

House of Zeor, by Jacqueline Lichtenberg (#1)
Unto Zeor, Forever, by Jacqueline Lichtenberg (#2)
First Channel, by Jean Lorrah and Jacqueline Lichtenberg (#3)
Mahogany Trinrose, by Jacqueline Lichtenberg (#4)
Channel's Destiny, by Jean Lorrah and Jacqueline Lichtenberg (#5)
RenSime, by Jacqueline Lichtenberg (#6)
Ambrov Keon, by Jean Lorrah (#7)
Zelerod's Doom, by Jacqueline Lichtenberg and Jean Lorrah (#8)
Personal Recognizance, by Jacqueline Lichtenberg (#9)
The Story Untold and Other Stories, by Jean Lorrah (#10)
To Kiss or to Kill, by Jean Lorrah (#11)
The Farris Channel, by Jacqueline Lichtenberg (#12)

Other Jacqueline Lichtenberg Books from Wildside:

City of a Million Legends
Molt Brother
Jacqueline Lichtenberg Collected: Book One: Science Is Magic Spelled Backwards and Other Stories
Jacqueline Lichtenberg Collected: Book Two: Through The Moon Gate And Other Tales of Vampirism

THE FARRIS CHANNEL

SIME~GEN, BOOK TWELVE

JACQUELINE

LICHTENBERG

THE BORGO PRESS
MMXI

THE FARRIS CHANNEL

FIRST EDITION

Published by Wildside Press LLC

www.wildsidebooks.com

DEDICATION

To the souls currently living as Salomon, Ernest, Naomi Gail, Becca, Paul, Deborah Ruth, and Julia Summer. Whoever you may be when you read this, know that you are loved, respected, admired, and cherished.

CONTENTS

ACKNOWLEDGMENTS 9

THE STORY OF THE FOUNDING 400 13

CHRONOLOGY OF THE SIME~GEN UNIVERSE 17

PROLOGUE: "Now Is the Time!" 19

CHAPTER ONE: Fateful Decision. 21

CHAPTER TWO: Fort Tanhara 28

CHAPTER THREE: Fort Rimon 49

CHAPTER FOUR: Reluctant Farewell. 64

CHAPTER FIVE: Irreversible Damage 81

CHAPTER SIX: Consequences 107

CHAPTER SEVEN: Fort Hope 124

CHAPTER EIGHT: Confessions. 151

CHAPTER NINE: Winter Initiatives 165

CHAPTER TEN: Opinions. 181

CHAPTER ELEVEN: Expedition 199

CHAPTER TWELVE: Chance. 219

CHAPTER THIRTEEN: Reversals 233

CHAPTER FOURTEEN: Disillusionment 252

CHAPTER FIFTEEN: Grave Digging 263

CHAPTER SIXTEEN: Grave Robbing 283

CHAPTER SEVENTEEN: Zeor 303

CHAPTER EIGHTEEN: Wayfarer. 321

CHAPTER NINETEEN: Healing 339

CHAPTER TWENTY: Forty-Nine Days. 351

CHAPTER TWENTY-ONE: Reception 374

EPILOGUE: The Last Sectuib 388

NAME THE VILLAIN CONTEST 390

THE NAZTEHRHAI AMBROV ZEOR 391

ABOUT JACQUELINE LICHTENBERG 403

ACKNOWLEDGMENTS

I never intended to write this book about the founding of the House of Zeor. But as *Star Trek* fans became immersed in the Sime~Gen universe, at first via the first novel, *House of Zeor*, then the first award winner, *Unto Zeor, Forever*, both about men who headed up the House of Zeor, they kept asking questions about the House of Zeor, the Farrises, the concept *Sectuib*, and how it all happened.

Being *Star Trek* fans, they wrote stories to argue for their own answers, Sime~Gen fan fiction stories. That body of fan fiction is now much larger than the professionally published novels, and available online for free reading via Simegen.com.

Jean Lorrah was particularly curious about how the channels ever became channels, and kept asking, none of my answers putting the matter to rest for her. Finally she wrote up a piece of fiction that incorporated my answers to date, gave it to me at a *Star Trek* fanzine oriented convention. She then posed more and more questions. Which I answered until I got laryngitis.

So I did what any self-respecting member of science fiction fandom would do, I told her to write her story up as novel. She did. It was terrific (she was already a professional writer, not to mention a Professor of English—she could write, oh boy, could she!). So I presented it to my editor at Doubleday, and they bought it. That novel is *First Channel*.

Thus Sime~Gen has two main entry points which are crafted to let you absorb the complex background by osmosis, without pausing as you read the story, *House of Zeor* and *First Channel*.

House of Zeor is for veteran Science Fiction readers, especially *Star Trek* or Vampire Romance fans who love to be challenged by a very different reading experience. *First Channel* is for general fiction readers who may be a little leery of science fiction, or who prefer to start reading a "series" at the "beginning."

All of the Sime~Gen novels have a love story at the core of the plot, and some, like Jean Lorrah's *To Kiss or to Kill*, are Romance Genre. *Unto Zeor, Forever* is a "doctor novel romance." My ambition is to have a Sime~Gen novel in each of the recognized genres, to illustrate how Science Fiction is not a genre at all.

Despite being published as a Series, Sime~Gen is not a series, but a Universe. The novels are not all about one character, though if you pay attention you may find certain souls that reincarnate, having learned one lesson and now face yet another new lesson.

The Sime~Gen novels were framed as the story of The House of Zeor and the impact of its legend on the course of human history. It's the story of a group of loosely affiliated souls who struggle with issues bigger than they are and apply various philosophies to their problems in different eras and epochs, including eventually space colonization.

All the previously published novels can be read in any order, and should be re-read in different orders to get the most out of them. They are re-readable books, books which reveal something new with each re-reading.

This novel, *The Farris Channel*, about the founding of the House of Zeor, assumes the reader has read a few of the previously published novels and needs answers to questions.

So here I must acknowledge all those who asked these questions that led to this novel. They number in the hundreds.

I must also acknowledge the contribution of Jean Lorrah who wrote *First Channel* and *Channel's Destiny,* the two direct prequels to this novel, chronicling what happened when Rimon Farris discovered the trick of "channeling" and how this eventually led to the founding of something as odd in human history as a Householding. Those two novels made this novel absolutely necessary.

Now Jean is more interested in writing about her musician characters, Zhag and Tonyo, who appear in the short stories in *The Story Untold and Other Sime~Gen Stories* as well as the novel, *To Kiss or to Kill*. If you pay attention, you'll find prior incarnations of those souls in *The Farris Channel*. The descendents of Zhag and Tonyo and the film/video industry they found, have as profound an impact on the course of history as the House of Zeor does.

But there is another story set chronologically between *Channel's Destiny* and *The Farris Channel*. We call it "Companions," because it's about the Gens of Fort Freedom and their role in the burgeoning growth of the Fort until it becomes such an irritant to the junct Territory that the Fort is destroyed, the survivors scattering to form the Forts you will read about in *The Farris Channel*. Because *Companions* has so much explosive action, flame-and-glory writ large, we are debating whether would make a better screenplay than novel.

Jacqueline Lichtenberg
June 2011

THE STORY OF THE FOUNDING 400

As the list of Sime~Gen novels grew over the years, it was becoming very difficult for new fans to scrounge up copies of the Sime~Gen novels which were scattered across various publishers in hardcover and mass market paperback. So one of the editors of the Sime~Gen fanzine *Ambrov Zeor*, Anne Pinzow, who happened to work for Toad Hall, a publisher at that time, sold the idea of doing reprints of the novels along with a large, new novel.

But publishing was in dire flux (so what else is new?) and Toad Hall did some figures and decided the new novel needed a pre-publication subscription sale of 400 hardcover copies before they could publish it. We had been selling about a thousand copies of each of the Sime~Gen fanzine editions, so we thought that would be possible.

Jean Lorrah and I went to the fans, who at that time mostly connected with us via snailmail, though we had begun moving online to Simegen.com. It took a few years to get signed pledges from each of 400 people saying they'd pay $25 for a hardcover copy of *The Farris Channel*. Signing up also gave you the chance to have a character in the novel named as you'd wish. Some of those names have been used here.

By that point, the publisher had closed up shop. Even though *The Farris Channel* was mostly written, it wouldn't get published.

But by then, we were well ensconced online, and with a form

people could sign to join the 400 (list faithfully kept by Ronnie Bob Whitaker and Karen MacLeod). We forgot to take the form down from the Web. We ended up with over 500 subscribers, but no publisher.

So once again, we were shopping Sime~Gen around. We had a screenplay on the market by Anne Pinzow (yes, she's a professional at that, too), and Jean was working on an e-book novel for the Romance e-book market. Fans were still writing Sime~Gen stories and novels and cooperative fiction (a kind of online gaming). New fans were introduced via the fan fiction, scouring online bookstores for used copies of the published novels.

Meisha Merlin approached us with a good offer, and we signed a deal with them for omnibus reprints and new novels, and they brought out the first volume, *Sime~Gen: The Unity Trilogy*, with a genuine trilogy of novels—*House of Zeor* by Jacqueline Lichtenberg, *Ambrov Keon* by Jean Lorrah, and *Zelerod's Doom* by Jacqueline Lichtenberg and Jean Lorrah.

Those three novels are all about the same characters living the same lives, re-engineering society around them.

I wrote *Personal Recognizance* for one of those omnibus volumes and rewrote *The Farris Channel* to Meisha Merlin's specifications.

But Meisha Merlin folded before they could bring out any more novels.

Then, at a convention, Robert Reginald, who runs the Borgo Press imprint of John Betancourt's Wildside Press, approached us out of the blue. They wanted the novels.

We worked a deal, but it took a few years to get all the technicalities in place. Wildside already had two of my reprint novels, *Molt Brother* and *City of a Million Legends* successfully marketed as e-books and paperbacks. They were releasing reprints and e-book editions of Jean Lorrah's *Savage Empire* Series. In addition, they've done collections of short stories by each of us. Now finally, with this volume, polished for this new market, they will have all the Sime~Gen Novels extant in print simultaneously.

All this has taken so long that we lost touch with many of the Founding 400+ subscribers who want this novel, and one fan in Australia has set up a SimeGen Group on facebook to try to connect with them. The List of the 400 is appended to the end of this volume.

If you know any of these folks who have lost touch, please tell them *The Farris Channel* is now available.

CHRONOLOGY OF THE SIME~GEN UNIVERSE

The Sime~Gen Universe was originated by Jacqueline Lichtenberg who was then joined by a large number of Star Trek fans. Soon, Jean Lorrah, already a professional writer, began writing fanzine stories for one of the Sime~Gen 'zines. But Jean produced a novel about the moment when the first channel discovered he didn't have to kill to live which Jacqueline sold to Doubleday.

The chronology of stories in this fictional universe expanded to cover thousands of years of human history, and fans have been filling in the gaps between professionally published novels. The full official chronology is posted at

http://www.simegen.com/CHRONO1.html

Here is the chronology of the novels by Jacqueline Lichtenberg and Jean Lorrah by the Unity Calendar date in which they are set.

-533—*First Channel*, by Jean Lorrah & Jacqueline Lichtenberg
-518—*Channel's Destiny*, by Jean Lorrah & Jacqueline Lichtenberg
-468—*The Farris Channel*, by Jacqueline Lichtenberg
-20—*Ambrov Keon*, by Jean Lorrah
-15—*House of Zeor*, by Jacqueline Lichtenberg

0—Zelerod's Doom, by Jacqueline Lichtenberg & Jean Lorrah
+1—*To Kiss or to Kill*, by Jean Lorrah
+1—*The Story Untold and Other Sime~Gen Stories*, by Jean Lorrah
+132—*Unto Zeor, Forever*, by Jacqueline Lichtenberg
+152—*Mahogany Trinrose*, by Jacqueline Lichtenberg
+224—*"Operation High Time,"* by Jacqueline Lichtenberg
+232—*RenSime*, by Jacqueline Lichtenberg
+245—*Personal Recognizance*, by Jacqueline Lichtenberg

Sime~Gen:
where a mutation makes the evolutionary
division into male and female
pale by comparison.

PROLOGUE
"NOW IS THE TIME"

"I, Xigram Klairon Farris, Last Sectuib in Zeor, commend this narrative to the permanent record of the Zeor Archives."

A subliminal stir wafted through in the vast amphitheater packed with the members of Zeor. Xigram faced them from the stage and spoke in measured tones. He knew they saw an elderly man, white haired, frail, with the typical black Farris eyes, and a sufficient hint of the Zeor Farris nose, lips, chin.

In one hand he held a magnificently bound volume from which he was about to read. The formal cloak of the Head of this, the Last Householding still functioning in the galaxy, draped his shoulders. It was the bright blue of Zeor, with the distinctive black edging of the Farris, the hem thrown back over his shoulders to expose the white lining designating the Sectuib. All the primitive, time-honored and hallowed symbolism was echoed in the garb of everyone in the audience.

They all knew they were about to hear the very private, never before transcribed story of the Founding of Zeor. They had all grown up on this bedtime story, and the amphitheater's ambient vibrated with the warm, secure feeling of childhood's bedtime.

But this telling would be different. This time they would hear it told as the Sectuib in Zeor Received it from his predecessor and Delivered it to his successor. This was the real story, not the fairy tale. Today, they would all Receive Zeor and take it away to give to the galaxy.

The stage behind the Last Sectuib was set with the archeological treasures of Zeor. Foremost was the remains of the stone on which the names of the first martyrs had been inscribed. Around that oldest symbol of Zeor were arrayed the plaques and monuments that had been added to the Memorial to the One Billion over the centuries. A huge glowing image of Zeor's stylized dagger symbol dominated the background.

The Lamp had been lit within a bubbling fountain's pure water brought from Earth for this ceremony. Over the last ten days, the Roll of Martyrs had been read by the Officers of Zeor in a round-the-clock marathon before an audience that was never less than a third of the crowd Xigram now faced.

Xigram Klairon Farris took a deep breath, gathering himself before plunging across the point-of-no-return. For once he had recorded the full, unedited narrative into the Archive read aloud before Zeor in his own voice as he had Received it, he would extinguish the Lamp of Zeor for all time.

Zeor has served its purpose; the Vision has been made real for all humanity. So why, then, did his throat close up tight over the words? *As the narrative instructs, this must be my last duty or my soul, the souls of all who have ever been ambrov Zeor, will never know peace.*

He swallowed hard and began as thousands of parents for thousands of generations had begun.

> "This is the Ideal of Zeor.
> "This is the Heart of Zeor.
> "This is the Spirit of Zeor.
> "This is the Reality of Zeor."

He opened the great volume he had written with his own hand and began to read in a voice strangely not his own:

CHAPTER ONE
FATEFUL DECISION

Del Rimon Farris, ranking channel in Fort Rimon, rose behind his desk as people boiled through his door and more pushed in behind.

He had never had so many shouting people cram into his office before. In such a babble, he strained to understand what they were yelling about.

Simes and Gens alike, those who had come here to homestead with him, and the refugees they'd taken in, all emitted clashing emotional fields which charged the ambient nager with determination, maybe rage, and all of it directed at him, personally, pounding his Sime senses.

As close as he could figure it, the refugees desperately wanted to avoid another disaster such as had destroyed their homes and left them begging Fort Rimon for shelter. The Fort Rimon natives wanted to defend their homes from the refugees' panic.

Del Rimon eased down into his desk chair, braced his elbows on the arms, and calmly laced his fingers and tentacles into an arch. Acutely aware of the painting of Fort Freedom that hung on the wall behind him, framing him in two generations of tradition as he sat there, he worked to spread calm through the room.

Benart, a big Gen who was Fort Rimon's chief record keeper, edged through the crowd to sit on a tall stool at the corner of Delri's desk. He took up a slate on which he usually scrawled notes of meetings. His muscles tightened, his chalk screeched jerkily across the slate.

Fear will be the end of us all. Panic will destroy us.

Del Rimon's Companion, a supremely talented Gen, focused steady attention on Rimon. That let him work on the emotional turmoil with his special channel's talent. He made eye contact with several key individuals, one after another, and they began helping calm the ambient.

With that bit of local quiet, he zlinned the distance beyond the building. Far outside their little walled compound they dubbed with the grandiose name, Fort Rimon after Del Rimon's grandfather, smoke plumed from behind the hill that separated them from Shifron, the local junct town.

Even from within the shielded office, Del Rimon Farris was sure he was zlinning the death of the town of Shifron at the hands of a huge mob of Freeband Raiders. Surely Fort Rimon would be their next target.

Divided internally by this dispute, whatever it was this time, the Fort would fall more quickly than Fort Freedom, the original Fort, had fallen.

They didn't have much time.

Del Rimon rose from behind his desk, motioned his Companion aside, apologized to Benart with a nod, then stepped up onto his desk as he gathered his nager about him. With the extra height, he let loose a silent nageric snap that spread harmlessly over their heads. The Simes who could perceive the nageric signal fell silent immediately. The Gens noticed the Simes staring at Del Rimon and turned to see what had happened. Silence enveloped the room.

He stepped down from the desktop. He felt all the other channels in the room finally getting a grip on the ambient, and he realized almost his whole channeling staff was here.

"Xanon, what exactly is this all about?" asked Del Rimon in soft tones.

Xanon edged forward. "It's still about Clire. I mean again. This has to be settled, now, Rimon."

Del Rimon did not let the habitual "Call me Delri; I am not

my grandfather," escape his lips. It was a lost cause.

Instead, he enunciated slowly, so all those used to different accents would understand. "Aipensha has had her say, and Lexy and I agree with her. Clire should take an early transfer now, and that decision should be based solely on her current medical condition not put to a vote of the channeling staff. As a pregnant Farris, Clire should not be placed under this kind of stress, especially not when the Fort is expecting an attack soon. We'll be working the whole channeling staff to exhaustion after the battle. I don't want Clire in Need at that time."

The crowd pushed back to let Xanon stalk toward Del Rimon's desk. Xanon was a short man, a channel who had arrived with the Fort Butte refugees, but though he had a fair talent for the channeling arts, he had little trained skill, a fact which escaped him.

Xanon waited while the ambient nager settled to a tense but calm flow of invisible energies. Then his strong baritone rang through the room. "It doesn't matter that her name is Farris. She has violated a primary regulation of Fort Rimon and must accept the punishment any other channel would be subjected to."

He turned to face the group. "The Farrises all agree that this Farris woman should not be disciplined for undermining Kolenan's conditioning ultimately causing two deaths. Isn't it odd that the only people who happen to think she's too delicate to take a little transfer deprivation because she *might* be two weeks pregnant are her relatives?"

Suddenly everyone was talking at once again, Aipensha, Lexy and Clire hitting a perfect soprano chord as they protested, "...is pregnant!"

Clire's not related to me. Not closely anyway, thought Rimon. Clire might be a descendent of his grandfather, or maybe great-grandfather, but even she didn't think so. Rimon wasn't sure if Clire's baby was actually Garen's. *Practically no chance it's my child.* But the timing was right for it to be his own.

Through the noise, it became clear about a third of the people in the office accepted the Farris judgment that Clire was indeed pregnant, and the other two thirds were mortally offended by the automatic deference accorded Farrises by those born and raised in Fort Rimon.

The Fort Rimon natives were outnumbered by the refugees who had arrived from the failed Forts this last year.

As Rimon drew breath to shout for silence again, his Companion, Bruce, stayed him with a gesture and bellowed, "Silence!" His powerful Gen nager undulated into nauseating waves of invisible energy fields that grabbed every Sime's attention. Then he stepped out from behind Del Rimon's desk, dampening the waves and glaring at the assembly as silence fell.

Tall, lanky for a Gen, with a craggy tanned face, he was the senior Gen of Fort Rimon with a medical expertise that had gone unquestioned even by the new arrivals, probably because his last name wasn't Farris.

He had to look down to meet Xanon's eyes. "Farris channels really can zlin in sharper detail than other channels. I've seen them call a pregnancy within hours of conception! I'm not exaggerating. Some of you could zlin a pregnancy within two weeks too, but not in a Farris channel. Aipensha and Lexy are Delri's daughters, but not related to Clire. Clire arrived with the first refugees from Fort Intalace, and now she's the sole survivor of that whole Fort!"

"What difference does that make?" shouted someone in the back.

"She'd be ranking channel in Intalace, if anyone had survived. Her baby is heir to Fort Intalace," argued Bruce.

A woman's voice rose. "If that baby actually exists! Xanon's right. Two people died because of Clire's much vaunted Farris judgment. Any of the channels in this Fort, pregnant or not, would be subject to justice. It's not much of a penalty considering what she did."

Xanon took that as his cue to pace back to Rimon's desk and lean across it. "Clire deserves to be executed, but your Fort Council called it an accident and imposed only a four day transfer deferment and only for two months running. I intend to see that she gets it and learns her lesson. Farrises are not above the law."

The nageric buzz of agreement filled two thirds of the room while Rimon's own people, huddled at one side around Clire, became very still, waiting for his decision.

He met Clire's eyes, but spoke to Xanon. "A four day deferment *would* probably kill her child, and if that happens, very likely I wouldn't be able to save Clire."

Xanon kept his back to Clire. "Of course you'd say that to protect another Farris. Or could this possibly be your child, a double-Farris child?"

The nageric silence turned ugly.

He admitted she's pregnant!

Clire's nager was wrapped in an icy wall about herself. Kahleen, Clire's Companion, used her Gen body's field strength to make a protective wall around Clire.

Clire's eyes held a bitter warning. She was a proud woman, a mostly self-trained channel, with no inherent loyalty to Fort Rimon. "What could the identity of the father have to do with whether the child and I will be allowed to live?"

Chaos erupted again, and Rimon sighed, exchanged glances with Bruce and settled to wait it out again.

Del Rimon wanted to use all the authority of his hereditary position in the Fort to rule in Clire's favor. However, to the majority of Fort Rimon's current residents, that would prove that Farrises made decisions by personal whim and favoritism.

We can't survive the coming battle with this ripping my channeling staff apart.

Before he opened his mouth, Clire knew his decision.

Her eyes declared him enemy while her nager turned to stone. He had promised to protect her and he was about to break that promise. *I won't break that promise, not really. I'll save her somehow.*

Cramming his emotions down inside where none of the non-Farris channels in the room could zlin them, Rimon said, "Then let's put it to a vote as Xanon has asked."

They had just about the entire channeling staff in the office. They could settle it right now.

He stood up and addressed the room. "Here is what we will vote on. The Fort Council has levied a non-lethal penalty against Clire Farris. However, the Farris channels agree that penalty might result in the death of her and her unborn child. The Farris channels agree the penalty should be deferred until her child is born and weaned. Meanwhile, she should start taking early transfers now to protect the development of her child.

"The question: does the consensus of the Farris channels overrule the decree of the Fort Council in channeling matters as has always been the custom in Fort Rimon?

"Benart, call the roll and record the vote. I will then take the result to the Fort Council for a final decision."

Benart reached down for a clean slate from the pile by his foot, and started the roll call.

As Del Rimon expected, all the Fort Rimon natives voted to abide by the Farris perceptions. He saw the newcomers counting as each vote was announced, not trusting Benart.

To Rimon's surprise two of the newcomers abstained. Benart announced the result. The resentment against Rimon had produced a death sentence for Clire and her child. He knew that the newly elected Fort Council, composed mostly of refugees from Forts with no Farrises, would not overrule the channeling staff vote against the Farrises.

How will they feel when we bury Clire and her child? I won't let this happen. When it became obvious Clire was indeed pregnant, they'd say she became pregnant after the Fort Council's decree in order to duck the penalty, knowing the other Farrises would protect her.

He gathered himself up to accept the regrets of his people before they went back to work side by side with the guests who had taken over Fort Rimon and made it their home. "Clire, I will not let this happen. Know that. Believe it. Kahleen and I will not allow this."

"I need transfer now, Rimon. Don't do this to me. I've already waited too long."

"You have a few hours yet. I'm calling an emergency meeting of the...."

Raid alarm drums thundered and outside cries of "Wagons approaching!" rose as the ambient stirred into a practiced defense drill.

Wagons? Freeband Raiders don't attack with wagons!

CHAPTER TWO
FORT TANHARA

Solamar Grant was first to spot the riders coming toward their wagons from the Fort gate. The Fort ahead of them was so close he could zlin its ambient nager. It had to be Fort Rimon, it just had to, and the Fort had sent riders to help them.

Grant was riding beside the lead horses of Fort Tanhara's lead wagon, filled with their sick and injured. He was alternately zlinning the fraying harness of the right lead mare in the four-up, and dropping back to help herd the two cows and eight sheep that had survived the five months of travel from the remains of Fort Tanhara.

He kept flicking his attention toward the Freeband Raiders who were gaining on them.

The Freebander riders chasing them had come across a low hill that masked something big burning, a town maybe. Now they were gaining steadily, gaining much too fast. *Must have stolen the town's horses.* Freeband Raiders' horses were always in bad condition, except right after they'd been stolen. RenSimes who had turned Raider stole what they wanted, used it and discarded it, never giving a thought to upkeep.

The wagons couldn't go any faster. They weren't on a trail or even a beaten path across this mountain valley. Every rock, hole, and hummock twisted and strained the tack, the wagon wheels, the wagon chassis. The drivers were zlinning the ground ahead to pick the best course for the wagons. They couldn't go one bit faster, and it was too slow.

If we don't make it, everything I've worked for is lost. All these people will die. Maybe Fort Rimon will die too. Mentally, he told the harness to hold, the horses not to founder, the Gens in the wagons not to panic. *We have to make it. We have to or the world may be lost.*

His father would have scoffed at him for being melodramatic. His father had never grasped the scope of the Farris channel issue the way his grandfather had. He repeated it out loud. "We have to or the world may be lost."

One of the young Gen women rode up beside him and shouted over the din of rattling wagons and pounding hooves, "Sol, can you zlin them yet? Is that Fort Rimon up ahead? Are those riders coming at us juncts?"

"Can't tell for sure yet!"

"But you're our best channel!"

I'm no kind of channel, were the words that leaped to his mind and pushed at his lips but he swallowed them back. He knew she meant he was the most sensitive Sime with the Tanhara refugees, which was true. *With luck, they'll never have to know more than that about me.*

He focused and zlinned again now the riders ahead were closer. "Those riders are renSime, nonjunct, so that has to be Fort Rimon." *It just absolutely has to be!*

"Get the Gens mounted and ride for the Fort—that'll lighten the wagons. Get all our Gens behind that line of Fort riders and don't look back. Don't do anything to distract those Fort renSimes. They're here to deal with the Raiders for us."

He felt her protest ignite her nager. She was no Companion, but when her attention alighted on him, he felt it. With two tentacles, he gestured her to caution.

In response, she put her attention on the horizon beyond the Fort. Then, like the Fort Gen she was, she obediently pulled her horse up and dropped to the rear wagons, calling for their remounts which were already saddled and strung behind the wagons.

Soon everyone was shouting for the Gens in the wagons to

mount up. In small groups, they began to ride for their lives, and for the life of the Fort. Both Forts.

Solamar did the one thing that might betray him to the Forters as an outsider. Without consulting anyone, without even telling anyone what he was about to do, he rode out ahead to meet the riders from the Fort—*Fort Rimon, it has to be.* A real channel would stay behind, well defended and safe. A real channel was a non-combatant. A real channel didn't take stupid risks.

But to Solamar's Sime senses, it no longer seemed like a risk. What he zlinned now matched what his even more reliable intuition told him. Fort Rimon's crack combat team was riding out to defend Tanhara's refugees from the Freebanders chasing them.

The Fort's stockade lay at one end of a fertile valley, far from the junct village behind the hill at the other end. It was far enough from the steep sides of the valley that attackers couldn't shoot down into the Fort, and it was on a slight rise that provided both protection from mountain floods and a tactical advantage in defending their walls.

Surrounded by tilled fields, almost completely harvested now, and by terraces on the hillside—orchards, trin tea plants, and, yes, grape arbors, the Fort appeared secure and prosperous.

It looked exactly as it had been described to him when he'd taken on this mission. It zlinned right, too except there were way too many people in that Fort.

As he balanced his weight forward, urging his horse on, he let go of his ordinary senses, letting himself drift into hyperconsciousness, the Sime's hunting mode. Gen nager flamed bright enough to sense from miles away, if you were sensitive enough and knew how to zlin for greatest distance.

Closer now, the Fort ahead leapt into stark relief to his Sime senses, a towering vortex of powerful selyn fields. Even as he approached the line of riders coming toward him, the vortex over the Fort collapsed in on itself, turning quiet, intense, focused.

The source of that invisible brightness more intense than the sun was to the naked eye had to be the Fort's Companions, trained to work with the channels. The Companions' brightness dominated the glow of the higher-field Gens, but as he watched, it all diminished. No doubt the Gens had withdrawn underground, leaving the renSime defenders on the walls. Oddly though, it seemed a number of low-field Gens were still outside the shelters.

No, it wasn't just a few low-field Gens. It was a lot of low-field Gens plus a few channels who where managing the nageric fields. They had used the Gen nageric power to shape a silent, invisible message to the Sime attackers who could read those fields.

It was a message of supreme confidence, and a total absence of a sense of being threatened.

Solamar had expected that when the last Companion was underground, the channels would follow them into the shelters, joining the children and most of the ordinary Gen donors.

But they hadn't.

It was drilled into every denizen of the Forts that renSimes are expendable. The Gens, the Companions and the channels are the life of the Fort, just like the children.

That drill was the only reason that Fort Tanhara had any refugees alive to flee the collapse of their defenses. Because the channels and Companions had been safe, they had healed the wounded. Freeband Raiders were only renSime, with maybe a few captive Gens.

Solamar had joined Tanhara only four days after that last devastating battle. Lending his talents to the healing effort, he had been accepted as a channel without question, and he had let them believe he was a refugee from Fort Faraway which had been completely wiped out.

As far as he knew, he was indeed the last survivor of the Fort Faraway refugees who had been heading for Fort Rimon. He wasn't about to watch Tanhara and Rimon go down too, not after leading these people all the way here.

As one of Fort Tanhara's channels, Solamar knew he had no business riding ahead like this. But none of the renSimes was mounted on a horse that could make it.

Nearing the oncoming riders, he drew up and let his chestnut mare breathe while they approached. He manipulated the ambient nager to identify himself as a channel and turned his horse to face the Tanhara wagons.

When the lead riders came abreast of him, Solamar leaned forward and whispered into the horse's flickering ears, "All right, Trilli, time to run again." His weary mount took heart and, still blowing hard, fell into the pace of the Fort Rimon defenders.

Solamar went duoconscious, so he could see the renSimes around him as well as zlin for their leader. He found the one with the most disciplined and confident nager, a woman mounted on a fine black stallion—*good thing Trilli isn't in season!*

Moving in close, he shouted an explanation of the pack of Gen riders now approaching from the lumbering wagons of Fort Tanhara. The renSime gestured her understanding with three tentacles of her left arm and signaled her riders to spread out, leaving a gap in the middle of their line to allow the Fort Tanhara Gens through.

Solamar noted how quickly the gap between Tanhara's rear wagon and the lead Freeband Raiders pursuing them had narrowed.

Freebanders had no allegiance to any junct town or government, no law governing their actions. All they wanted was to capture plenty of Gens. All they ever did with Gens was Kill them, savagely stripping the Gen of selyn until the Gen died of the shock.

Freebanders craved nothing in life but the massive, fear-magnified deathshock of Gens. They didn't Kill to live like the town juncts; they lived to Kill.

The Fort Rimon formation split in a very crisp, disciplined drill. The leader yelled at Solamar gesturing, "We'll delay the Raiders. You circle your wagons around our gate. Our people will cover you from the walls. Get your people inside. Sacrifice the wagons. Got that?"

Solamar gestured his understanding with two tentacles, grazing her nager with an affirmative flick of his field.

The renSime tossed him a ferocious grin that sizzled through his nerves igniting something wondrously warm deep in his belly.

She shouted, "I do love ordering a channel around! Go!"

With a hearty laugh, Solamar went, wafted on a nageric zephyr breeze of acceptance, admiration, and delighted interest. Every cell of his body returned that interest. He cast his eyes to the heavens. *A renSime? Isn't my life complicated enough already?*

The first of the Tanhara Gen riders, some with children mounted in front of them, several carrying infants, and one with a newborn, pounded through the gap in the renSime line. His own Companion, Losa, rode in the middle of the group carrying a baby in the crook of her arm, controlling the horse with her knees. His life might well depend on Losa's survival.

Solamar cleared the Tanhara Gens and pulled out in front of the Fort's renSime contingent to race flat out for the wagons.

Shouting and gesturing, he explained the plan with nageric emphasis as the wagons roared past him.

Despite it being beyond his authority to give tactical orders, the Tanhara renSimes driving the wagons set to implementing the Fort Rimon plan.

The cattle and sheep were cut loose. Now that they were inside the valley, the exhausted animals wouldn't stray far, especially with the dogs herding them. That left the chickens, a few goats, more dogs and some cats, and a dozen geese, in the wagons.

Most of their riding stock had gone ahead with the Gens, leaving all the Tanhara renSimes riding in the wagons, driving them, or mounted on the few horses left. The lead wagons with the wounded also carried most of the channels and Companions to care for them.

The trailing wagons bristled with renSime defenders ready to die for Tanhara if necessary. The last wagon held two hopelessly ill Gens and an elderly channel, ready to sacrifice their lives to give the others a few precious seconds to escape.

Several renSime passengers took positions beside the drivers with arrows at the ready, an unusual weapon brought from out-Territory. Tanhara had been forced to master it during their flight when they met Freebanders who used it to pick off channels and Companions from a distance. One Band had chased Tanhara across two Territories and learned better than to get too close.

As Tanhara readied for the fight, the Fort's riders passed the wagons at full gallop, speeding to intercept the Freeband Raiders.

They crossed the edge of the tilled fields. Now they rolled over the stubble of harvested wheat fields. The ground was softer, slower, but rock free. Speed picked up. *We're almost there. We're going to make it.*

Zlinning their prey about to escape into the stockade, the Freebanders spurred their horses mercilessly. They wanted those Gens who were fleeing ahead.

Solamar saw one of the Freebanders' horses founder. The junct Freebander, a scarecrow figure of skin and bones clad in rags, leapt clear of the horse and ran, augmenting his speed by burning extra selyn. Even without a horse, he was still closing on the rear wagon.

Solamar dropped back to the rear wagon just as the Fort Rimon renSimes met the oncoming line of Freebanders.

The Rimon renSimes picked off the leaders with throwing knives, arrows, and bullwhips. The horses and Simes thus downed tripped several more Freebanders. The pile-up slowed the rest of the attackers. Most leapt off their horses and continued on foot.

The Rimon renSimes regrouped and caught up to the last wagon.

The lone runner on foot had now been joined by those unhorsed. Burning extra selyn, they were more desperate than ever to get at the Tanhara Gens.

With a quick scan toward the Fort, Solamar realized that most of the Tanhara Gens were going to make it to safety. But the last wagon was in trouble.

Solamar rode for the Freebanders, gathering his concentration. He grabbed hold of the junct's personal fields with his own, and yanked hard.

The handful of juncts closing on the rear wagon went down. *Oh, shen. They're dead!*

He hadn't meant to Kill, but juncts could be so fragile, especially the malnourished and dissipated Freebanders.

The leader of the Fort's renSime troop turned to him and saluted with four tentacles. Even at such a distance and through the surging ambient, he felt her astonishment and approval. But she was also irked at him for not riding on to the Fort gate. She ordered him away with a gesture.

Solamar turned his horse and galloped for the head of the wagon train, feeling his mare laboring with fatigue. He leaned over her neck and told her, "Just a little farther now, Trilli, and you'll get a good meal and a warm barn to sleep in." He shifted his weight encouragingly.

As the wagons climbed up to the Fort's gate, Solamar swung onto the lead wagon's left rear horse near the failing tackle he'd spotted earlier.

They reached the top of the rise where the area in front of the gate was broad and flat. The gates still stood slightly open.

Solamar gestured the renSime driver to circle right, easing the strain on the failing harness juncture.

They led the first ten wagons into a semi-circle around the gate, and headed the lead wagon straight into the wall of the Fort. Zlinning to judge the right moment as he gentled the skittish horses, Solamar climbed onto the wagon tree and pulled the pin.

With the horses separating from the wagon, he rode the tree, steering the horses along the wall toward the gate, letting the wagon tongue drop as the driver stood on the brake.

The wagon stopped with the tongue only a stride short of the wall.

RenSime drivers and passengers scrambled off the slowing wagons, and freed the horses. Tanhara channels and Companions pulled the stretchers out of the lead wagons, and helped the walking wounded. The moment everyone was clear, each wagon was tipped over barricading the still open gate and the smaller door beside it.

The older children and everyone else wrestled the panicked animals, people, stretchers, and crates of screeching birds toward the open gateway.

Beyond the barricade, on the far edge of the harvested fields, the Freebanders had regrouped and were now pounding toward the Fort behind a large contingent on foot.

Solamar was certain these Raiders were just a contingent split off from the larger horde that had destroyed whatever town was burning behind the distant hill.

Have I found Fort Rimon only to lose it?

Through the gate opening, Solamar zlinned the Tanhara Gens with his own Companion, Losa, a white-hot glow among them. *The Rimon Gens didn't all go down to the shelters so they'd be there to help our Gens.*

Behind Solamar, at the barricade, both Rimon and Tanhara marksmen took positions on the overturned wagons and laid down a barrage of arrows that stopped even the Raiders who were in the grip of Killust. Solamar didn't have time to be shocked at the Rimon use of the bow.

Meanwhile, the Fort's mounted renSimes attacked and harried the Raiders, buying time as the next fifteen wagons pulled into a circle around the first ten. That left three wagons outside the makeshift barricade.

Tanhara refugees struggled to salvage their possessions at risk of their lives.

Rimon defenders swarmed out of the Fort shouting orders to cut the draft horses loose and scatter them down the path into the confusion of attacking Raiders.

Against the flow of defenders coming out to help, Tanhara

animals, people, older children, all burdened with whatever they could carry, all shouting advice, yelling orders, and trying to keep track of their loved ones, clambered over the toppled wagons, boiled across the narrow space and poured through the Fort gates struggling toward safety.

The smaller gate door was barely wide and tall enough to get one horse through at a time. The last of the four-ups that could squeeze through the Fort gates cleared, and the huge gates began slowly closing.

Over five dozen prime draft animals were driven down the hill into the swarm of Raiders.

As the gates closed, some stretchers had to be abandoned, the wounded carried over someone's shoulders. The channels struggled to control the ambient, dampen the panic, and scrambled to get into position where he could help. Solamar dismounted and pulled Trilli into the stream of frantic people entering the Fort.

More than two hundred adults, kicking at the chickens and geese, dragging the goats, calling their dogs, towing and carrying children, crammed through two narrow openings to join the mob of Gens and other children they had sent ahead. Many tarried outside the shelters in mounting anxiety for their loved ones while Rimon's Gens urged them to go below where it would be safe.

The channels managed to keep the local ambient muted, unattractive to the attackers. Solamar finally in position, joined his efforts to theirs. He boosted one of his patients onto Trilli's sweaty back, a renSime with a broken leg. "Just a few steps," he assured the man, "and you'll be in a solid bed, no more jostling, no more wagons."

He split his attention between his fainting patient and the battle forming at the barricade. The Fort's riders arrived at the barricade and leaped from their horses to the overturned wagons. The Freebanders arrived right behind them, pounding at the defense line, and dying.

Death filled the air, the small deathshocks of selyn-depleted renSimes forming a wave of background noise under the potent ambient.

Then the Freebander's fire-arrows began to rain onto the wagons. Sheets of fire leaped for the heavens. Screaming panic shattered the ambient lanced with burn-pain and pulsing horror. The world turned black, red and white.

Solamar plunged himself hypoconscious, struggling to cut off his awareness of the ambient, once again wishing he were Gen. Gens didn't have to feel everyone's pain as if it were their own.

Again, Gen pain split the ambient, this time a Companion's burn pain sizzling like lightning.

An instant before his awareness shut down, Solamar zlinned several Raiders off in the distance lanced by the incredible shock of that Companion's pain, fall from their horses and lay twitching.

Raiders didn't use fire as a weapon because it could do more harm to them than to their targets. *What is going on here?*

Drenched in sweat, shaking, he coughed in the smoke and dust, suddenly hyperaware of the smell of singed flesh, the screams of the horses, the stench of fear. He let himself drift duoconscious again, still leaning all his weight into holding his horse's nose down, keeping the animal from bolting into the mass of humanity ahead of him. He rejoined the other channels trying to control the ambient. The burned Companion was being carried into the Fort. Raiders would soon learn not to use fire as a weapon against Forts.

Above them, from the top of the stockade wall, arrows arced into the massing Freebanders, peppering the ambient with the pain of each hit. Despite his effort to avoid it, Solamar zlinned each plume of selyn rushing out of a junct renSime already near Attrition.

Some of the Fort's renSime defenders packed in around him as an escort. "Quickly! Channels to the underground shelter!"

The people and animals ahead of Solamar jammed together, trying to make room for those still coming through the big gate. Solamar turned to watch it close behind him.

Freebanders leaped through a sheet of fire from one of the wagons, over the heads of the defending archers, landed in the midst of the churning mass of refugees and headed for the gate. Just inside Gens were still crammed into the mob pushing through. More Freebanders were coming over the burning wagons.

Solamar's escort turned toward this new menace, and a moment later the wave of Freebanders came at them in a flying wedge, slashing their way through with long, heavy bladed knives.

True to form, the lead Freebanders in the attack were all close to Attrition, the point at which their bodies would run out of selyn. They were dead if they didn't get a Gen to Kill within the next few minutes, draining the Gen's life force to replenish their own.

Bleeding renSimes fell all around while Tanhara defenders grappled with the Raiders.

Then the flying wedge of Raiders was past Solamar, into the seething mass of humanity inside the Fort. The miasma of deathshock spread like a poisonous fog within the walls of safety.

Screaming, howling and slashing, another wave of Raiders leaped through the flames of their own making, some of them with their clothing on fire.

Solamar zlinned a knife flying through the air. He lunged toward the target, one of his own escort, planning to push him aside.

The knife thunked solidly into flesh. The tip sliced into heart muscle. The man died standing up. Solamar landed on top of the renSime corpse and sprawled in a tangle amidst trampling feet.

Trilli bolted into the mass ahead. Someone caught the reins, and that was the last Solamar knew about the horse and his patient.

Hands and tentacles pulled him to his feet, his green shirt and tan riding leathers drenched in the guard's hot blood.

He was only a few steps inside the gate when it thudded shut.

Five renSimes levered the huge crossbar into place. Tanhara refugees were still pushing through the smaller door fleeing the mass of Raiders behind them.

The ambient was a strident, paralyzing, sense-deadening pressure against his whole body. And then suddenly—it wasn't.

A towering nageric presence penetrated the ambient, dominating everything nearby with a fine but massive precision.

That has to be a Farris Channel.

In the bubble of controlled silence, his head cleared and he searched for the channel. *There!* Right inside the door. *He shouldn't be out here! It's too dangerous.*

Too stunned to protect his own senses, Solamar zlinned right through the wooden Fort walls. Another larger group of Raiders came boiling over the wagons in a howling mass of raging Need and unbridled Killust. The defenders retreated before them. *They'll surely take the Fort. We've destroyed Fort Rimon!*

Solamar stood, transfixed by failure.

A strong, bony hand suffused with that massive Farris nager grabbed Solamar's hand and shoved it against the rung of a ladder. "Up!"

Solamar climbed, pushed by the Farris, and in moments was standing on top of the Fort wall beside an older man who pulsed with that peculiarly overwhelming nager. The Farris channel. In the midst of battle.

The Farris was tall, hawk nosed, with the typical black hair, brows, and eyes, dimpled chin, high cheekbones that Solamar had seen only in drawings. Definitely Farris.

"Zlin there!" A nageric prod directed his attention to the view over the wall and down into the boiling mass of hand-to-hand combat around the overturned wagons. The defenders were being cut off and systematically destroyed by the Freebanders. Six wagons were on fire.

A group of Freebanders pushed one of those burning wagons up against the Fort's wall. On top of the wall, a squad of renSimes hurriedly deployed a trough from the cistern at the corner to a point above the burning wagon and sluiced the fire with water, wetting down the wall too.

As Solamar stared, two more Fort renSimes were overwhelmed by Raiders. *We're going to lose this Fort too.*

A male voice off to his left called, "Rimon, we've got to get that door closed!"

"Not yet, Jhiti!" answered the older Farris channel. "We still have people out there." Even as he spoke, more renSime defenders beat off Raiders and retreated through the narrow opening of the door. Two more Raiders followed them in. There were more defenders still out there fighting.

So this is Rimon Farris! No wonder he has such a nager.

Then Losa's searingly penetrating nager shattered the ambient. The Farris whipped around to gaze down into the stockade's yard. Unconsciously, Solamar spun in sync with him.

Losa had been cut off from the hatchway leading down into the shelter. Raiders surrounded her. She had given Solamar transfer only five days ago. As brightly attractive as her nager seemed, she didn't have enough selyn to withstand being attacked by so many renSimes.

Two of the Raiders slashed at her with their long knives, toying with her fear. Blood spurted as she backed up, selyn energy pluming forth from the wound making the Raiders grin. Solamar's whole body went into healing mode, reaching toward his Companion to staunch the loss of selyn with his own body's fields, even though he was too far away.

It was what channels did—heal wounds, fight disease, bring Gens and renSimes to peak of health. More than instinct, it had become for Solamar a total way of life as he pushed and pulled the Tanhara refugees toward the legendary Fort Rimon, where they were all going to die.

"Snap out of it!" commanded the Farris.

"They know what she is!" protested Solamar transfixed. "They'll murder her and try to strip her dead body of selyn." Below in the yard, the two Raiders stalked Losa, attracted by the pluming selyn they could zlin. It was just one small skirmish in a yard full of fighting, running, chaos and dying.

The Farris glanced from Solamar to Losa. "She's your Companion."

"Yes."

"Help me get the Raiders' attention!" the older channel commanded grimly and turned to the yard below.

Suddenly the ambient around the Farris was pure Gen— bright, hot, incredibly enticing. Solamar joined the effort to create the illusion of two great Gens hidden visually from below by the guardrail and part of the water tank but nagerically obvious.

"Good, now a little fear for spice, like doing a disjunction lure. Follow me."

It was remarkably easy, just like dancing with an expert. In counterpoint, they swirled and pulsed with fear, using the channel's unique control of the body's nageric projection to seem to be Gen to the senses of the Simes below.

Solamar, tired, aching, terrified and desperate, let himself float on the Farris nager, let that ineffable power sweep through him, using his body as an extension.

One by one all the Freebanders in the yard, and even those still fighting the defenders outside by the wagons turned toward the spot above where two replete and terrified Gens waited to be Killed, to be savagely stripped of all their selyn energy.

The Raiders would see only two heads, one black haired, one blond, and maybe a bit of shoulder, not enough to tell Sime from Gen visually. But every renSime, Raider or not, zlinned those two deliciously terrified Gens and so they knew they were seeing two delicious Gens no matter what their eyes might report.

Now, even the Fort renSimes were responding to that projected Gen fear, only they did have an idea of what was actually going on. Freeband Raiders fed on Gen fear as well as selyn. The Fort Simes never Killed, never craved fear, but got all their selyn through their channels. The Raiders had no clue what a channel could do with selyn fields.

Losa's attackers ignored her, but she just stood panting,

swaying on her feet, dazed from loss of blood, unable to take the moment to run. There were so many people, so many bodies, so much blood, there was no way to run.

Two other channels caught near the entry to the underground shelter also paused, halting their guards from hustling them into safety below, and joined Rimon's effort. One of them was a Farris, but Solamar couldn't zlin which one. He just felt another massive, dominating nager emerge into the chaotic ambient.

Suddenly, the courtyard was pulsing with four huge, golden Gen presences. Rimon joined them all as he had joined seamlessly with Solamar, and created a junct's greatest fantasy.

The renSime defenders looked upward, waiting for a command.

"Now what?" Solamar asked the older channel. "If your renSimes attack, we'll lose the Raiders' attention."

"When I signal, quickly shift your showfield to renSime."

Solamar zlinned the Fort Rimon renSimes outside, creeping toward the Fort wall, trying hard not to disturb the Freebanders' fascination with the "Gens" above. In the yard, the defenders shifted to clear a path between the Raiders and the still open door beside the main gate. Then Solamar understood what the older channel planned and real fear spiked into his showfield.

That galvanized the Raiders, and suddenly five of those outside armed with long, ugly bullwhips, hurled themselves at the palisade wall. One whipmaster, standing on another Raider's shoulders, lashed his whip around a spike at the top of the wall, and suddenly two Raiders swarmed over the whipmaster and started over the wall at the "Gens."

All along the catwalk, Fort renSimes closed in from both sides to protect the channels.

"Now!" shouted Rimon Farris.

Rimon's order seized the four of them in a nageric pulse and wrenched their showfields from Gen to renSime.

To all the Simes within zlinning range the "Gens" had disappeared.

The two Raiders climbing the wall paused, shocked to find

no Gens awaiting them atop the wall, shocked to find two Simes standing where two Gens had been, shocked to be attacked from both sides by renSimes they hadn't been able to zlin through the massive "Gen" fields.

Jhiti tackled one of the Raiders, and at that second, the other leapt for Rimon, a dagger in one hand, screaming, "Wer-Gen!" sure he had zlinned a Sime turn into a Gen then turn back into a Sime.

Solamar stepped into the hurtling body, grabbed, turned and flipped the renSime, aiming to fold him over the top of the wall and leave him hanging there. But the Raider was hardly more than an animated skeleton. The body arced high over the top of the wall, and the Raider tumbled screaming, "Wer-Gen!" and was abruptly silent.

The ambient was so roiled with deathshock, Solamar wasn't sure that he'd even felt the man die.

In the yard below, a shout went up, "Wer-Gen!" And suddenly all the Raiders inside and outside the Fort were screaming, "Wer-Gen!"

The circle of attackers around Losa closed on her once more as they broke and ran for the gate followed by all the other Raiders in the yard.

Jhiti bellowed, "Don't let any of them escape!"

Defenders leapt to obey, spreading the order as they ran, blocking all avenues of escape for the animated scarecrow figures.

The Raiders, driven into a small clump, retreated into the center of the yard, toward the entry to the underground refuge. Losa stumbled toward that beckoning safety, caught up with the crowd of Gens, children and Fort Rimon non-combatants dodging rearing, screaming fire-crazed horses and knots of Raiders on the hunt, formations of disciplined renSime defenders of the Fort and piles of dead bodies.

One of the Raiders, at the point of death by selyn Attrition and desperate for selyn hurled herself at Losa's back. A Sime woman, a Farris, broke out of the knot of those cramming through the hatch to the underground refuge and peeled the Raider off Losa offering the Raider a selyn transfer.

Even at that distance, across the choppy sea of warring nageric fields, Solamar zlinned that Farris channel working to drive selyn into the Raider's wasted system. Raiders could not accept selyn in the peaceful, collimated flow a channel offered. Raiders needed to burn a Gen to death by taking their selyn.

The Raider died trying to Kill that Farris channel woman. The other Raiders converged on the Farris and she went down under the heap of scrawny bodies. The other defenders were unaccountably slow coming to her aid, and when they'd yanked and tossed the skeletal bodies off of her, she rose, staggering. Her nager was so pale Solamar could barely zlin her presence.

Losa, still bleeding blood and selyn, yanked herself free of the renSimes who were trying to help her into the shelter and plunged toward the Farris woman, stepping on the piles of bodies, staggering as dead flesh shifted under her boots. Off balance, she gave one last lunge toward the Farris, offering all her selyn in a Companion's instinctive response to a channel's Need.

The Farris turned. Solamar saw it all in slow motion, flash-burned into his eyes, his memory forever. His own Companion whose selyn was meant only for him, his source of life on earth, offered it all to a Farris channel, with no frisson of fear or even caution. No Farris would Kill. Everyone knew that.

The Farris handling tentacles, four on each arm, twined themselves around Losa's Gen forearms. The Gen arms were so inviting without tentacles but rich with swirling selyn fields.

Time had stopped for Solamar as his thighs bunched as if to propel him off the wall in a mad flying leap toward his Companion.

The Farris woman's lateral tentacles emerged at the sides of her arms, two slender pink-gray organs with no real strength, rich in nerves that could draw selyn from the Gen body, drawing a month's life into the void of a Sime's Need.

Solamar felt strong Farris hands clamp rigidly onto his shoulders, pulling him back from the suicidal leap.

The Farris woman's lips sought the necessary fifth contact point as her four laterals seated themselves against Gen flesh. Losa turned her face toward the woman in Need, offering her lips, the best, most nerve-rich contact point that gave the channel the best possible control of the speed of selyn draw.

And it was over.

Losa dropped dead at the Farris woman's feet.

Solamar was only dimly aware of his body drawn back hard against the trembling Farris channel behind him. Shock held him rigid. The noise of battle receded. The boiling chaos of the ambient nager, riven by his Companion's deathshock slammed into his nerves, his mind, his emotions, his innermost self.

Outside, the retreating Raiders, scrabbled over the wagons to flee the only thing they feared more than death by selyn Attrition, the supernatural wer-Gen and forced transfer from a channel.

Behind them, Jhiti pinned a Raider to the planking and broke his neck. Solamar remembered he had intended to take that Raider down himself, had planned the move in fact, and forgotten all about it in an instant. That death was near enough for Solamar to feel it against the general background of death and dying, but it barely registered under Losa's searing, shattering deathshock.

Jhiti looked up to find Rimon still alive, holding Solamar back from the edge of the wall. Jhiti straddled the corpse and yelled, "Rimon, what are you thinking? You two shouldn't have done that! You shouldn't be up here at all."

Guilt suffused the ambient, quickly damped under the channel's control. "Yes, Jhiti, I know. We'll discuss it later. See what can be salvaged from the wagons and round up the rest of the stock these people brought before the Raiders get them. We've got a winter to face soon." To Solamar, he said, "This way. We have work to do."

"Work...." repeated Solamar in a whisper.

"She's dead. I'm sorry. I've lost a Companion to Raiders too.

We've lost a top channel in this. Maybe you and I can still save some lives."

"Save lives...." Solamar heard himself repeat those words, but his mind couldn't understand them.

In the yard below, the hatch to the underground shelter opened, and people swarmed over the refugees, separating the animals from the people, sending riders out into the gathering dusk to collect the animals that had been cut loose, and other squads out to chase the retreating Raiders and to hunt for survivors.

As he followed Rimon down the ladder into the yard, the fire brigade dragged two donkeys into the yard and hitched them to the well's wheel. Before long water was flowing. Solamar heard some renSimes and Gens banging pot bottoms and calling all cooks to the cookhouse. If nothing else, the Gens and children had to be fed.

The Fort Rimon channeling staff swung into practiced motion, separating the injuries into type and severity, and rushing them off to treatment. The Tanhara channeling staff was swept into the organization as if they'd lived in Rimon all their lives.

As Rimon Farris ploughed through the courtyard, one arm around Solamar's shoulders, order was left in his wake. The Fort Rimon organization made this major disaster look like a routine drill until Rimon got to the hatchway to the underground shelter where the channels had set up their main hospital.

The Farris channel cast about among the bodies, the seated wounded, the milling and the dazed. Finally he snagged a Gen man who was clearing bodies. "Where's Clire?"

The man stopped, emitting grief laced with fear. "She's gone."

"She didn't die. I'd have...."

"No. The Raiders got her. A squad followed them to rescue her, but they haven't come back. I've been here the whole time. I'd know if she'd been brought in. She's not down there." He gestured to the hospital. "Lexy is though. She's working on

Aipensha...she was alive last I heard."

It was Solamar's turn to support Rimon's weight as shock took all the strength out of his knees.

Solamar sought his internal time sense, so reliable in any Sime. It had ticked off the seconds while his mind had stopped and now it told him nearly an hour had passed while they worked across the yard from emergency to emergency.

The Gen explained to Solamar, "Lexy and Aipensha are his daughters. Aipensha was trampled by a horse trying to catch Clire...."

Rimon bolted for the hatch.

CHAPTER THREE
FORT RIMON

I'm too late.

Rimon knew it the moment his head cleared the stairwell. Lexy's nager dominated the long, narrow space lined with stacked cots, filled with the desperately wounded, the smell of wet earth, lamp oil, blood and death.

Aipensha's nager was nowhere to be zlinned. Lexy was bent over a bloody pulp of a dead body lying half on a cot near the back. He knew the corpse had been Aipensha before he got there.

He grabbed his living daughter away from her sister's body, held her tight. His only living daughter.

A chasm opened inside him and swallowed him whole.

He clung to Lexy, letting his nager penetrate hers, soaking up her pain, giving her the peace he didn't have. His gut insisted his life had ended. He couldn't tell his feelings from Lexy's, and, for that moment, he didn't care.

So many. I've buried so many. I've lived too long.

Gentle hands came, bundled Aipensha's body in a blanket and cleaned up the puddle of blood. The hands belonged to the new channel whose wondrous skills had saved the Fort. Now he graced the dead with dignity.

Finally, two Gens took Aipensha away. Rimon clung to Lexy with one arm and reached out to stop the blond man. "What's your name?"

"Solamar. We're Fort Tanhara. What's left of it."

There's not much left of Fort Rimon either. We've lost two Farris channels today. But he couldn't say that. It wasn't "two Farris channels" that they'd lost. They'd lost Clire and Aipensha, probably because he'd ignored the oldest of their rules and exposed himself to the battle. His daughters had followed him out, and Clire would not have let herself be left behind despite pregnancy and Need.

No. Right now, it was two channels that were lost. A strategic loss. A scheduling problem.

With that thought the agony of the wounded rushed in at him. They could still be saved.

He stepped clear of his daughter and addressed her as his number two channel. "Lexy, you take this end of the shelter up to number thirty. Solamar, you take the middle up to number sixty. The bunks are numbered on the sides, see? I'll take the far end. I'll send a Companion to work with you." *As soon as I find out who's dead.*

Holding himself very stiff and hard inside, Rimon threw himself into organizing the hospital and treating the worst of the wounded.

It was routine work at which he'd had decades of practice. He used his superior sensitivity to pair up channels with Companions and assign them to patients they had the skills to help.

Here, in the press of life and death crises, everyone did what he told them to and looked to him for the next task. There was a rhythm to it that let the work flow through him far beyond the point of deadening exhaustion and into that clear space where nothing existed but the task at hand.

One by one, the wounded were treated and carried off to quieter places to heal. Rimon was relieved when Kahleen arrived.

Kahleen had her masses of auburn hair braided into a crown on the top of her head. She wore a shapeless infirmary smock over thick sweaters that did nothing to hide her comely young figure from any Sime's senses. Her nager, schooled to the high precision demanded by the Farris channels by years of work with Clire, was tarnished with sorrow but held in steely check. Rimon compared her with Solamar then gestured her toward the blond channel.

"His name's Solamar. He shouldn't be working alone."

Bruce arrived, just as tense as Kahleen and just as disciplined as he slid into his routine Companion's position by Rimon's side. Rimon asked, "Dayyel, Iriela, Fengal?"

"They're all fine. Fengal stayed in the shelter."

Fengal, Bruce's son-in-law, was a channel and his renSime daughter, Iriela, was pregnant, due this month. *Fort Rimon has a future. We just have to get there.*

"That's a relief. I'm all right, so you should trade places with one of the trainee Companions down there." He gestured.

"You sure? Hate to leave you with this."

Rimon nodded, not taking his attention from stopping the bleeding under his hands. "Go. I'll see you later."

Bruce went, slicing through the nageric haze as smoothly as when he'd arrived. Bruce had survived uninjured. Bruce would give him transfer when the time came. Rimon brought his attention back to the wound he was healing.

The Gen Companions of the channels needed skill and stamina to assist in managing the selyn fields around their patients, twisting and tilting the field gradients to spur the patient's own body to heal, supporting the channels as they gave emergency selyn transfers to the most severely injured. One lapse in the Companion Gen's concentration could spell death for the patient or devastation for the channel's sensitive nervous system. Bruce was one of the best. His replacement...not yet.

Life on the trail, and even after building Fort Rimon, had given Bruce and the older Fort Rimon channeling staff more than enough practice. Rimon set himself to transmit some of those lessons to this new trainee and keep his mind off Aipensha and Clire.

Through the night, Benart, master scheduler, brought down Companions who had slept, shooed others up to bed. Bruce and

Rimon directed the shift changes, improvising pairs creatively to keep the healing work flowing. Aipensha and Clire were not the only casualties on the channeling staff, and though Simes required little sleep, the Gens did.

Sequestered in the underground chamber, Rimon had no direct awareness of the work going on above them in the Fort. He just knew the survivors were collecting the corpses, putting out the fires, salvaging what was left of the wagons, preparing for the cold of the oncoming night, and somehow finding accommodation for the new arrivals in the already far overcrowded buildings.

Just before dawn, it had become very quiet in the underground shelter. Only three patients were left. The others and the staff in charge of them had moved up to the more capacious infirmary building where fire had taken out only part of the roof.

Whenever the hatch into the underground shelter opened, Rimon heard the hammering, the groan of the water wheel, the scrape of logs being dragged as reconstruction began. On one puff of cold air, a hungry Companion accompanied by a crowd of renSimes came down the stair, bodies aching, throats raw with smoke. But the Companion had apparently had some sleep.

"Delri!" she called when she saw him. "Lexy said we'd find you down here. We're supposed to bring these patients up now because there's room in the infirmary. Lexy says you have to get ready for the memorial at dawn."

"Are they going to be ready for a Memorial now?" Suddenly Rimon was acutely aware of his blood crusted clothing and the fact that "room" in the infirmary probably meant as many more deaths as discharged patients. "With the graves that is?" His throat was a little raw too. He was not going to cry for Aipensha now. He swallowed hard.

"Rimon," said Solamar. "Those two you've been working on can go, but this one can't be moved again. I was just resting a bit before trying to bring him around. I'd appreciate some help if you can spare the time."

Bruce had rejoined them a few hours previously and now was working with Solamar while Rimon had one of the youngsters from Tanhara by his side. The girl seemed to have been trained by Solamar "What did you say your name is?"

"Uh, well, I don't think I did say. Rushi."

That broke her concentration on Rimon's fields. "Rushi, you go with our two patients here, then get something to eat and take a nap before the Memorial service. We'll want you fresh and ready to work by noon. We're going to require someone of your solid skills."

The renSimes grabbed stretchers while Solamar and Rimon held the selyn fields steady. The two patients were raised out of the shelter and the small crowd departed leaving Bruce and the two channels to consult on the last of the critical patients.

Solamar's clothing was likewise bloody and well soiled from the hard ride in to the Fort, but his hands and forearms were spotlessly clean as were Rimon's. Both of them used the last of the clean water to scrub their tentacles while they discussed the patient, a badly wounded Freeband Raider who hadn't died in the battle.

"I don't think he'll make it. He couldn't have been Raiding very long, Rimon, or should I call you Delri?"

"I'm not the Rimon this Fort is named after. That was my grandfather. I'm Del Rimon. People who've known me all my life call me Delri. Most of the newcomers here just call me Rimon and everyone else does that too sometimes."

Solamar handed him the sliver of soap remaining and continued to scrub lather over his arms. "This young fellow can't be more than a month past changeover. If we can save him, he might disjunct."

Thinking of the future. Good psychology, but Rimon wasn't ready for that. "Any idea what happened to him?"

"Nobody knew when they brought him in a couple hours ago. They found him wedged into a space under a pile of dead horses. I've pretty much dealt with the internal bleeding. The concussion is a wait-and-see problem, but it should clear up if we can get a transfer into him. Still he hasn't come around yet, and that's a very bad sign."

As he scrubbed, Rimon zlinned the unconscious youth behind him. "Bruce?" Rimon gestured with one wet tentacle and the massive Gen nager moved so Rimon could zlin the whole body. The other channel had indeed dealt with the internal bleeding, and a nice job he'd done too. Cuts and abrasions had been cleaned of infection, small details efficiently handled.

"I'd guess he's unconscious more from the nageric shocks in the ambient during the battle than from the concussion. Imagine what burns feel like to a Raider in Need!" Rimon studied the youth. "You're right. If we can get a transfer into him, he just might make it." The boy was thin, but not skeletal like the older Raiders. His light brown hair was long and filthy, lice infested. "Malnutrition, but not very advanced. Still that'll make every-thing harder."

"Ever saved a Freebander in this condition before?"

"No, but my father did once or twice. He kept me out of it, so I don't know how he did it. I was too young. The girl died in a Raid right after she disjuncted so I never got the whole story. Of the last two Raiders we've treated here, one died and the other ran away and set the barn on fire as a diversion. None like this, though."

"Tanhara had about the same experience."

They looked at each other as they toweled dry. Two of the three best channels in the Fort were about to hurl their last remaining strength into a lost cause, strategically a very bad administrative decision. And they both knew it. And they both didn't care.

Bruce took the towels and as one, the two channels closed on their comatose patient, both well aware that the Companion wouldn't have it any other way either.

Rimon felt the other channel shifting his secondary system to project a showfield.

The channel's unique physiology with two selyn circulation systems allowed them to create interference patterns in the selyn fields around their bodies, showing the world a physical condition that wasn't actually true. Using the secondary selyn system to project a showfield, a channel could seem to be renSime or Gen, as they had done to trick the Freebanders. However, another channel could zlin right through the façade.

Rimon felt how Solamar's deep weariness was far worse than his own. He wasn't a Farris, with the ultra swift Farris recovery time after the effort to give or take selyn, but though he lacked Farris sensitivity, he had an exquisitely honed precision to his field work and some other harmonic qualities that just felt good to Rimon's ravaged systems. He chose not to mention the other's fatigue and simply added his strength to their joint projection.

Bruce moved into place once the two channels had crafted a working field around the patient. "Am I right?"

Rimon flashed him a grin. "Perfect as always. This will be the last for tonight, then you can get some sleep before the funerals."

The return grin said it all. They both knew neither of them would get any sleep. "I'll make the first try," said Solamar. "That way you can watch to see what goes wrong and maybe we'll succeed on the second try."

Rimon wondered if this man's optimism would get on his nerves eventually, but for the moment it seemed right. *You have to look up to see the stars,* as his father used to say.

Rimon flicked a tentacle in assent, and gripped the fields. Solamar responded by insinuating his own fields through and around Rimon's, creating an interlaced grip the like of which Rimon had never experienced. Again, it felt right. Comfortable. Secure. He'd never had anything like that with a non-Farris before.

Solamar edged onto the cot beside the frail body, cradled the renSime's arms in his hands and extended his own handling tentacles, two on the top and two on the bottom of each arm.

The strong handling tentacles curled around the renSime's arms searching out the youth's tentacle extensor nodes. Retracted, the tentacles lay sheathed beneath the skin, mere ridges from elbow to wrist.

As Solamar applied precision touch to the extensor nodes, reflex caused the youth's handling tentacles to extend, but there was no strength in them, no direction, no grip. The lateral tentacles, normally sheathed at each side of the arm barely peeked from their orifices. They were moist with ronaplin, the selyn conducting secretion necessary to make this transfer of selyn work.

Rimon braced himself, knowing how the youth would resist what Solamar was about to try and how dangerous that resistance would be for the exhausted channel who already seemed like a friend. Solamar's whole attention remained on the Raider as he too gathered and braced himself, and Rimon felt that penetration between them deepen. It was almost as if he, himself, were prepared to shove selyn into the Raider's depleted body.

Now.

Abruptly, Solamar waxed high field Gen and rammed adrenalin pumping fear into the fields.

The youth arched back in shock, body bowed nearly in half, and his tentacles whipped around Solamar's arms. The laterals extended, moist pink-gray tiny by comparison to his handling tentacles and found their place between the interlaced tentacle grip. As the contact seated, the Raider lunged forward. Still unconscious, he sought the necessary fifth contact point with his lips, and Solamar obliged, bending low to touch his lips to the boy's.

Rimon zlinned the flash of the first spark of selyn drawn from Solamar's body and then the fields went wild as the Raider's Kill conditioned system rebelled against the channel's freely offered selyn.

The Raider needed to rip selyn from a resisting Gen, forcing that Gen to give up life, taking not accepting the gift of another month of life.

Rimon moved closer flicking aside Bruce's apprehension. Bruce moved with him, steadying down into full concentration, holding the fields steady for Rimon, so Rimon could watch every detail of the abort as if his own body were channeling selyn to the Raider.

The selyn that had begun flowing from Solamar's secondary system to the Raider did not cut off abruptly. It was more like a piece of woven fabric tearing, one thread at a time, and with each thread's snap, selyn whipped back into Solamar. The backlash produced a rapid-fire burning sizzle that crackled through Solamar's nerves and induced the same painful burning sensation throughout Rimon's body.

One second, he was watching, and the next he was into the transfer abort, taking it all into himself. His Sime perceptions flared blazing white, then suddenly he was standing in his father's treatment room, the log walls hung with heavy rugs to cut the drafts. Each colorful hanging held a poignant memory, a scent of home and love.

His father was bent over a scrawny Freeband Raider who was bleeding onto one of the treatment couches. The girl looked as lice infested and malnourished as the Raider boy.

"Delri!" snapped Zeth Farris. "Pay attention now. Zlin this carefully. You won't get a second chance." His father bent to create the fifth contact point, lip to lip, initiating selyn flow into the Raider's debilitated system.

Delri zlinned, each ebb and whiplash reversal of the selyn flow his father commanded, the dodge and weave against the Raider's abort reflex, the interlacing with fear like a delicate spice, the slow bleed of selyn into those raw nerves conditioned to accept nothing but a Kill.

He zlinned it all. He understood it all, and even believed it while knowing that Raider had arrived long before his changeover into an adult with the ability to zlin.

* * * * * * *

Solamar felt the searing agony of the abort backlash, the reflexive spasm of every muscle in his body. His heart squeezed shut and wouldn't move. His lungs emptied and wouldn't fill.

His hands clenched, his throat closed. The effect was all too familiar to him, but he was only peripherally aware of his body.

His mind awoke in a cozy room filled with neat counters over cabinets closed with curtains, open cupboards and several beds on high pedestals. There was a fire in the hearth, colorful wall hangings and matching rugs, several fat candles. He'd never seen the place before, but it sang of home, love, security.

A Farris man bent over a scrawny, filthy renSime girl, driving a transfer into her behind a shimmering haze of the impenetrable Farris nageric wall.

On the other side of the bed, just barely zlinnable through the working channel's nager stood Del Rimon, transfixed by the scene before him.

Solamar blinked.

He lunged to a sitting position on the cold packed dirt floor of the underground shelter, head and gut screaming that he was falling, falling forever and landing would hurt.

Bruce knelt beside Rimon who was prone on the floor, and all Bruce's formidable attention centered on his channel. It was almost as if there were no Gen in the shelter at all.

Finally, Solamar's diaphragm unlocked and he dragged in one long, sobbing breath while his eyes began to blink again, and his heart thud-thuttered into motion. A thought formed among the ice crystals clogging his mind. "What have I done?"

He was unaware he'd said it out loud until Bruce whipped around, the searchlight of Companion's attention sweeping across Solamar, assessing his condition, then flicking back to Rimon. "Solamar, help me!"

Solamar found he could indeed move. Their patient was still comatose, apparently not much worse for the aborted attempt at getting selyn into him.

Solamar got his knees under him and crawled across to Rimon, setting aside the blossoming headache. Unconscious, the Farris was much more readable. "Not as bad as it looks," he told Bruce as he dusted off his hands and wiped them on his shirt. "Give me some space here."

Bruce widened the disciplined cone of his concentration and Solamar moved in to cradle Rimon's forearms in his hands, extending his own laterals to make a brief contact. As he'd suspected, the problem wasn't physical. Rimon had leapt out of his body and was still standing in his father's treatment room in another time.

Solamar took a deep, steadying breath, then another, extending his consciousness, reaching for that long gone room and its vibrant occupants. "Rimon—Del Rimon Farris, you must come back now."

Three times he called, and the third time he heard a forlorn, "Father...."

Rimon fell back into his body, terrified beyond measure by the falling sensation.

Solamar gathered the jerking, twisting Farris up, turning him over and folding him into a bracing hug. "You're all right. We're all unharmed. Nothing here to be afraid of." He kept murmuring reassurance until he felt Rimon's awareness center downward and finally make contact with Bruce's reaching nager.

Those two are perfectly suited. He wormed himself out of the way to let Bruce work on his channel with that neatly meshed precision one could only admire.

"You all right?" asked Bruce over his shoulder, his attention never wavering from Rimon.

"Sure. Nothing much more than I expected except Rimon caught the edge of it at just the wrong angle and it really knocked him over."

"He doesn't do that often," muttered Bruce and went to work supporting Rimon's effort to breathe normally and get his internal selyn flows collimated again.

In Solamar's experience, Farrises could be incredibly tough, soak up the most improbable abuse to a channel's dual selyn system, and shrug it all off, then fall down unconscious at the most minor fritz in the fields. Bruce was no doubt used to the routine. However, the Gen didn't know what had really ripped through this Farris.

Solamar retreated against the cot with their unconscious patient. Sitting on the dirt, he lowered his pounding head to his knees and wrestled his own fields back into order, very carefully avoiding any thought of Losa and how she would have smoothed the process for him.

Kahleen is as good. Better even. I'll be all right here. He repeated it until he almost believed it and resolved to think about what he'd done to Rimon later. *It won't happen again. He'll be all right too.*

Barely two minutes later, Rimon struggled to his feet, giving Bruce a hand up and apologizing profusely for fainting. He paused to zlin Solamar, and waited while Solamar relaxed his showfield, inviting scrutiny.

The Farris attention swept through him like a warm light, then Rimon offered him a hand up. "You almost had it there. I think I can do it on the next try." Seeing Solamar's worry, he added as he turned to the Raider, "I'm fine. Bruce is miraculously good at this. We practice a lot, though not on Raiders."

Solamar met Bruce's gaze, but the Gen's attention stayed wholly focused on his channel. *Kahleen will be that good, too.*

Rimon edged onto the cot and took the Raider in transfer position in one smooth motion. A bare moment later, it was over and the youth's body was seething with rich selyn and starting to heal itself.

Rimon stood and said to Bruce, "This kid has a long way to go, particularly with the concussion, but he should regain consciousness in an hour or two. Stay here with him and I'll send someone down to relieve you before he wakes."

Bruce nodded. "I could use some rest. You gave me a good scare there. I'm glad Solamar could help."

With a vast grin, Rimon turned to Solamar, gathering him up with a gesture. Together they moved toward the far end of the shelter. Rimon spoke to both of them as he sidled down the narrow aisle. "So am I. One second I was watching the Raider abort, and the next Solamar was shoving my fields back into order. I would have expected a crashing headache, but I'm fine."

Solamar found himself facing the wall of cabinets at the far end of the shelter. "Where are we going?"

"Upstairs." Rimon shoved a lever up and dragged the rack of cabinets forward exposing a stairway. "Channeling staff is housed right over this shelter, just in case of emergency. We have to get cleaned up, find out what's going on, and get ready for the funerals."

Solamar followed Rimon up and directly into his office. It was a spacious room with a high ceiling. The hearth was ablaze, and the window let in dull gray sunlight. Someone was rummaging through a file cabinet, and someone else was stacking slates on the large desk.

Rimon strode in asking questions: who was assigning quarters to the arriving channels, was the damage report ready, who was arranging the funerals, where was the casualty list, and was there a selyn ration assessment yet. The answers flooded in as more people rushed into the office supplying information punctuated with more questions: where is this person, where is that person. All too often the answer was "dead." The name Clire peppered the answers.

After a few minutes Solamar found himself escorted to a room in a wing jutting out behind the office. Nageric silence descended as they entered the short hallway. The split log construction of the main part of the building here gave way to fitted stone walls, opaque to most selyn fields.

His escort, a young child, chattered tensely, "This is where all the channels sleep most of the time. Most of the Companions live right over there with the channels' families. We're still really crowded. We're going to build a whole lot more buildings in the spring, well even more than that because now there are all these Tanhara people."

"Where are the Tanhara channels housed?"

"Oh, here and there. Benart is making a list. You're supposed to sleep here this morning until we find you a place. This is Rimon's room," he said opening a door. "I just brought in a bucket of warm water, and I'll be getting another as soon as it's hot, so go ahead and bathe. Rimon said you should find something of his to change into. Just chuck your clothes out here and I'll see they're burned."

Solamar gazed down at what he was wearing. Blood caked and crusted sleeves and thighs. Rips sliced this way and that, often joining two or more wear holes he'd grown used to on the trail. A few cuts, bruises, and some scrapes adorned his exposed skin. His hair felt like greasy spikes.

A little stunned at the efficiency and hospitality of it all, Solamar nodded. It had been months since he'd stood inside a building, and then it had been hardly more than a ruin. "Thank you very much. I'll get cleaned up."

"Benart said to send Kahleen in to you as soon as she wakes. Is that all right?"

"Yes, that would be fine. Thank you."

The boy cocked his head to one side. "When I grow up, I'm going to be a channel. Would you teach me?"

Taken aback, Solamar could only smile. "Well, if the Farrises want me to, I will do all I can."

"You think you should do what a Farris says?"

"Well, usually, but certainly where training a channel is concerned."

Suddenly the child grinned more brightly than ever. "Welcome to Fort Rimon. I'm BanSha. We're going to be great friends."

He scampered away laughing.

Solamar gazed after him, feeling his own smile fade slowly as he puzzled over that odd conversation. Then he went into the comfortably appointed room.

Though he understood this was not Rimon's home, but only the room where he slept when he had to be close to the infirmary, it felt like a home. There was a magnificent quilt hung on the wall over the head of the bed, an ingenious thing created from what appeared to be a baby's quilt in the center, surrounded by tightly woven ultra fine silky black angora fabric. By touch, it seemed the quilt had been stuffed with wool fibers and stitched to a backing just as fine as the front.

The only image on the quilt was a long triangle topped with the arc of the moon's horns with an odd third peak in the middle. It was made of a single piece of bright blue cloth on a field of what had probably been white at some time. The baby's quilt was worn, scuffed and much mended while the rest of the quilt was newer. The material was top quality, the stitching perfect and the thing had to be worth a fortune beyond its sentimental value. Just touching the corner infused him with a sense of awe.

Aware of the passing of time, he went to rummage through Rimon Farris's closet and drawers and make himself presentable, feeling decidedly awkward about invading the privacy of his generous host. It was as if the symbol on that quilt was a ward, guarding the man's privacy.

He became very sure he shouldn't be here at all when he found a gorgeous jeweled belt of familiar expert workmanship tucked into Rimon's sock drawer. *He trusts strangers so easily.* He ran the supple leather through his fingers and examined the stitching. It could easily have been made by Solamar's grandfather. His father would have been able to say for certain. Solamar's own skills at reading objects had never equaled his father's. He returned the belt and took some heavy wool socks.

He changed into the awkwardly fitting clothes. He'd have to find the Tanhara people and discover who was left alive, find the Dispensary and get to work, find—well, Kahleen probably knew all the answers.

CHAPTER FOUR
RELUCTANT FAREWELL

Rimon didn't see or speak to Solamar again until the funerals. The Tanhara channel had been gone from Rimon's room when Rimon arrived to wash up, gone from the Dispensary when he arrived to check on things, gone from the hospital when Rimon came to follow up on those he'd treated. Someone said they'd seen him heading for the stables with Kahleen in tow, and Rimon imagined her silent protests. She hated horses. Or rather, they hated her.

So, just before noon, when he saw Solamar standing on the boulder they used for a podium at the edge of the cemetery, Kahleen nowhere evident, Rimon barely recognized the man. He was clean, well barbered, neatly dressed in clothes that almost fit, clothes from Rimon's own closet, boots from someone else and a wide-brimmed hat he didn't recognize.

Rimon climbed the steps carved into the side of the boulder and took his place beside the top channels from each of the Forts whose refugees now lived in Fort Rimon. Their Companions and the three people from the Fort Rimon Council who had survived the Freeband attack made a crowd.

Everyone turned toward him as he slid into the group's complex nageric field. Bruce was late, but that was just as well. Rimon didn't relish the idea of Bruce's grief pounding into the ambient nager. Bruce's nageric field was the only one that could pierce Rimon to the core. He looked around, waiting for Lexy.

It was not noon as originally planned. The sun was lowering

swiftly in the leaden winter sky. *Might snow before dawn,* Del Rimon thought bleakly.

Jhiti moved up behind Rimon and offered, "Losing Aipensha is a terrible blow. Everyone loved her."

He drew Jhiti up beside him. Jhiti was one of the three surviving Fort Council members. He was a renSime with organizational talent who had taken charge of their defenses. "Yes, her loss is a very serious blow," Rimon answered steadily. *I never should have ventured out of the shelter. She only followed my lead.* "Still, overall we were very lucky this time, thanks to your endless drills."

Rimon carried three large slates with the names of the dead which he would have to read, some of whom had been the leaders of the group so adamantly opposed to letting him direct the channeling staff transfer schedule, sparing Clire and her unborn child on his own judgment. *If I hadn't let them vote— vote!—on Clire's medical condition, she wouldn't have been in Need. She wouldn't have Killed.*

Rimon knew, all the channels knew, that even if they got her back now, they could only hope to save her child. She herself would be doomed to a horrible death.

He sucked his gloom in and hid it deeply inside. "Jhiti, your crew did a remarkable job on the cisterns or we'd have nothing but ashes for walls now if any of us even survived. Whoever heard of Raiders using fire-arrows!"

"They must have picked it up from some town, maybe from Gen Territory. It isn't just that they want our Gens. They hate us. They all hate us."

Jhiti looked back at the Fort where a stream of people still trudged down the steep hillside toward the gathering group. "We'll have to build new walls anyway. Have to enlarge the compound. With Tanhara here we're in a bad way for shelter, stables, water, everything."

Rimon heartily agreed. Part of the acrimony he'd been facing from the various factions was from simple overcrowding. Simes, sensitive to the life-energy fields of others, the emotions of others, were never meant to live so close together. "I want to get the foundation for a new wall dug before the first bad freeze. We can cut logs and erect them even during the winter, but we can't expect to dig efficiently after the ground freezes."

Jhiti agreed with a flick of his nager. "I'll want to put the new wall at the very edge of the drop-off to the valley floor even though that may be an irregular oval. It will be a little easier to defend, and it appears we'll grow to fill the whole space and have enough people to defend that much wall. People were sleeping under the weavers' looms today."

"We'll have to hold Fort Council elections again," replied Rimon heavily.

"I don't think that's a good idea," said Jhiti. "But if you say so, Benart will get it organized. With all these new people, it'll be complicated."

"Benart is trying to inventory feed for the animals and figuring rations for the winter. He's delegated the channeling schedule record keeping to Val so he can straighten out the supply problem." With so many strange channels trying to work together, it took an experienced channel to keep everything moving, so Val had to add Benart's record keeping and communicating tasks to her usual job of assigning the channels' work schedules. The new arrivals were in no condition to help yet.

Jhiti only sighed. "Like I said, elections don't seem a priority."

To Fort Rimon natives, maybe it isn't, thought Del Rimon, but every decision he made without Council backing would be chalked up to some strangely twisted motive and by spring the Tanhara folks would be taking sides, splitting and fracturing the temporary unity forged during this emergency. He supposed the distrust of him arose because none of them could zlin him, Lexy or Aipensha well enough to know how he really felt about things. *Not to mention how I just ignored the Fort rules, climbing the walls during an attack.*

He swallowed hard and tried not to think of Aipensha as he watched people gather at the edge of the ever-growing cemetery, grouping themselves around the flat boulder as they had too many times recently.

He scuffed at the boulder's surface, noticing that someone had chiseled it flatter here and there.

Just after noon, they'd held a brief ceremony over the mass grave of the Freebanders. Raiders never collected their dead.

The dead stock animals had been stripped of all useful parts and the remains buried down past the fields.

Four more of the injured had died, so the ceremony had been delayed to dig the additional graves.

Now three long, neat rows of new graves had been opened with a few others scattered about next to previously deceased family members. Some of those graves were for tiny bodies. Eighty-six had died, including the Tanhara dead, plus a hundred ninety-two Freebanders. And Clire.

The bodies were laid out beside their respective resting places, shrouded in plain cloth. Rimon heard the rhythmic tap of hammers doing emergency repairs of burned sections of the Fort. Guards were posted on the walls, and around the cemetery to protect the path back up to the stockade in case of another attack.

Several search parties, foraging parties and scouting parties were out. Rimon had seen to it that all those missing the funeral had volunteered to do so, and not because they couldn't yet face their grief.

Finally, Rimon saw Lexy and Kahleen coming down the hill. He stepped up front and signalled the musicians. They struck a low, long chord of howling grief, a cry of bereavement, the traditional opening to funerals.

Rimon grabbed the ambient nager to inject his own sick loss, anguish, shock, and ragged disbelief into the emotional atmosphere, working them toward the catharsis they'd been suppressing since the previous day.

He had watched Clire Farris Kill Solamar's Companion, Losa. His daughter, Aipensha, had been trampled to death trying to save Clire from her kidnappers. Neither would have been outside the shelter if it hadn't been for his disregard for the oldest of Fort laws.

Solamar stepped up beside him, and joined as they had when the two of them had stood upon the Fort wall and become a beacon of blazing Gen nager for the Raiders. Only now, they raised grief, shame, remorse, guilt and all that went with being unable to save a loved one.

Kahleen joined Solamar, dressed in her best and flipping her unbound auburn hair behind her shoulders. Lexy slid against Del Rimon's other side, her field work impeccable, blending her channel's nager into theirs seamlessly. She took a moment to mutter, "The selyn audit is finished. Tanhara lost a lot of renSimes, so they're arriving here Gen-high. We'll have enough selyn to support the workers and get the new buildings done. The Companion situation looks good too with Aipensha...."

She just plain blew the fields to pieces sending shards of flashing emotion slicing through the crowd. In that split second, Rimon was undone.

He turned in front of Lexy, grabbed her tight to him, rolled so his back was to the crowd and tried to block all Lexy's Farris nageric power from the crowd while he rocked against the hollow pain they shared.

It's not your fault, Father.

It was a whisper on the wind, an icy twist to the ambient. He looked over Lexy's bent head with eyes and Sime senses. At the edge of the graveyard, near the Farris plots, mist oozed from between the tall evergreens. Against that mist, made of that mist, shrouded in misty nageric clouds, stood Aipensha clinging to Zeth Farris, her grandfather.

Behind her gathered rank after rank of the dead. Rimon recognized many from the names on the slates he held and others from his own distant childhood. The wraiths whispered as if singing to the music. "It was not your fault. You saved the Fort. Live now, grow stronger."

Aipensha's voice led them, her accent, caroling her irrepressible joy in life. His father's voice blended with hers. Behind Aipensha the chorus chanted her words, an echo that passed back to the farthest rank under the trees, in the depths of growing shadow. "Father," she sang. "Del Rimon," sang the others. "Rimon Farris!"

A stiff breeze whirled through the valley, rattled the trees, dispersed the tendrils of mist as if they'd never been. The musicians fell silent.

Kahleen and the other Companions on the boulder beside them had moved to contain the raw nageric outburst.

Rimon, still sheltering Lexy, turned to the gathered mourners to see what they had made of the mist turning into people who spoke as if chanting to the music of grief. The audience looked up at him with no trace of awareness of what he'd seen. *Seen not zlinned* he realized. There had been nothing to zlin. There had been nothing there.

Beside him, Solamar whispered, "Who was that?"

Solamar *saw that? I don't believe he saw that.* "Aipensha. My daughter. Zeth, my father. Others who died yesterday, or years ago. They're together now."

Their eyes met, and he knew Solamar had seen.

While he stared at Solamar, Lexy pulled herself together, hugged him one last time and stood away. The three channels once again orchestrated the tenor of the ambient nager in a more staid fashion.

Nevertheless, they had shared their naked grief and guilt with everyone there, heaping it on top of what others felt. Rimon was ashamed.

He began the ceremony. "We gather to bid farewell to eighty-four of the finest people who have ever lived and two of our children. They gave their lives so that we could go on and realize their dreams. We stand as one with them all, carrying the responsibility they so ably shouldered."

He brought up the slates. The light was dimming fast now, the air cooling. First came the Tanhara dead, and leading that list was Losa, Solamar's Companion.

Solamar had to be prompted to step forward and say a few words on her behalf while she was lowered into her grave, and the attendant, a Tanhara Gen, began covering her over with reluctant strokes of his shovel.

Before they'd finished, Rimon read the next name, and very quickly Solamar picked up the rhythm of it. Rimon went through the dead of the other Forts among them, each with a channel to speak for them, and finally came to Fort Rimon's own dead. Benart had listed Aipensha last, right after Clire, or Rimon would never have gotten through his part of the eulogies.

By the time Aipensha had been lowered into her grave, they were standing in the dark, a full moon on the horizon. Still the sound of shovels echoed. They couldn't walk away from these graves only to fall to bickering again. The world inside this Fort had to unite against the groups arrayed against it from outside. Rimon spoke.

"Fort Intalace was the first to be overrun. Clire Farris arrived here with four others from Intalace who gave their lives defending Fort Rimon leaving her the sole survivor. Intalace was destroyed by the juncts of the town they had settled near.

"Fort Butte was defeated by drought and a bout of plague and sought refuge here last year.

"Fort Unity, a large and thriving community, attracted the attention of the territory junct government and was taxed to death before floods and mudslides wiped out their crops. Freeband Raiders, accidents and disease nearly took them all before they arrived here this last spring.

"Fort Veritt was almost wiped out by raids from the Gen army because they settled too near the Gen Territory border and the local Sime town wouldn't turn out to protect them from the Gens who thought Fort Veritt was the source of the raids into Gen Territory. Most of the Veritt refugees here still have nightmares about the last Gen raid that caught most of their channeling staff in the open and burned down their Fort and all its crops.

"Fort Tanhara," he gestured to Solamar, their ranking channel, "I'm told was overrun by Freeband Raiders and town juncts who worked in concert to destroy the Fort. That is the most frightening development so far.

"The town juncts and Freebanders hate us more than they hate each other. They hate us because we don't Kill our Gens. They hate us because we are not addicted to Gen pain and fear and death, not dependent on the Kill to garner enough selyn to live for another month, not junct. They hate us because we are perverts.

"Freeband Raiders have never been any kind of organized menace. Here in the mountains, they've never been more than small packs of wild animals that swarm over any unsuspecting road party. Now suddenly they're mounted, and they shoot fire-arrows to destroy our buildings, cooperate to scale our walls.

"Our scouts report the town of Shifron has been attacked by a very large, organized band of Raiders. A small part of that band split off and chased Tanhara here wanting their Gens for the Kill. Theory is they have taken the town's Gen Pen and are settling in for the winter. Scouts report the town's ordinary junct population has fled south."

Rimon paused to let that news sink in. From Shifron the Freebanders could raid Gen Territory for fresh Gens to Kill during any break in the weather. The Gen civilization out there allowed no Simes to live among them, and kept a standing army to enforce that. But to selyn starved Freeband Raiders who often Killed two or three times a month instead of the normal junct's one a month, Gen Territory was filled with herds of Wild Gens, not people living as best they could in a harsh environment.

If there was no break in the weather, those Raiders would come to Fort Rimon for their Kills. By spring, perhaps the more peaceful, disciplined junct residents of Shifron would return with the Sime militia to take their town back.

Shifron had been making a good living between furs, lumber and pine nuts. They'd want their town back.

"Rimon Farris," Del Rimon said, "my grandfather, the first channel, discovered how to avoid Killing Gens, how to take selyn from any Gen and transfer it to any renSime, letting the Gen live to produce more selyn. Most of you are the fourth generation of this dream of a world where no Gen has to fear the Kill and no Sime has to fear dying of Attrition. But in only four generations, we are failing."

The only sound was the rhythmic snick-hiss-thud of the shoveling.

"Our failure stops today. Today, over the open graves of our parents, children, siblings, and loved ones, we pledge ourselves anew to my grandfather's vision.

"Fort Rimon will survive this winter, and by spring we'll be bigger, stronger, and better than ever. Come spring, we'll clear more land, plant and prepare for the following winter. And we will help the citizens of Shifron take their town back from the Freeband Raiders. Shifron will have no reason to ally with the Raiders against us."

They might do it anyway, thought Rimon. "To achieve this, we must re-unite these six Forts!"

"Seven," interjected Solamar.

"What?"

Projecting his voice to the crowd, Solamar said, "...these seven Forts united. I am the last survivor of Fort Faraway. I arrived at Tanhara just after their last battle."

"What happened to Fort Faraway?" asked Rimon loudly enough for everyone to hear while he masked his renewed grief. *Faraway gone too!*

"Forest Fire. Just before harvest, a huge firestorm swept down the canyons driven by fall winds. We rode ahead of the fire and then made for Tanhara. We survived junct towns, Freebanders, wild animals, even a Gen army patrol, and then plague destroyed us last spring. I made it to Fort Tanhara with two children and my Companion, but they died within a few days."

Rimon zlinned that there had to be a lot more to that story than Solamar was telling.

"Seven Forts United," proclaimed Rimon. "We will be as one, solid, strong, and vital. Our walls will not be broken, our hearts will not weaken."

The shoveling fell silent, the diggers standing to attention beside the fresh graves. With dense clouds rolling over the surrounding mountains, Rimon signalled the musicians for the final tribute so people could file past the graves, winding through the graveyard to visit each of the fresh piles of earth, murmuring their farewells then starting back, each walking alone in the dark, heading up to the small door in the wall on this side of the Fort.

The Simes lingered to help the Gens who didn't have the Sime ability to zlin through darkness. The Gens gravitated to the Simes who could use the invisible selyn-glow of the Gen bodies to discern the path back to the Fort. They didn't separate themselves by their Fort of origin.

* * * * * * *

Solamar was exhausted. After the funeral, he had done a stint in the Dispensary giving transfers of selyn to fatigued renSimes in Need because they had been augmenting, using up extra selyn during the battle or its aftermath so they could work faster and stronger. It was nearly midnight and this was the first moment he'd had to breathe since they'd first spotted Fort Rimon with the Freeband Raiders chasing them.

He'd sent Kahleen, a truly remarkable woman, an exemplary Companion, to get some sleep and knew he had to rest a bit before letting himself grieve for Losa.

He pushed open a wide door in the side of the Dispensary building, a long, flat fieldstone building with a slate roof. It let him out into a space next to the wall. The patrollers atop the wall noticed him immediately and saluted nagerically. He crunched on through the ankle high snowdrifts, hands tucked inside the cloak someone had loaned him.

The Fort was so crowded, it seemed there would be no place for even a moment's solitude to just let his nager expand without fear of hurting someone. But with the snow and cold wind, he thought perhaps the cemetery would be deserted, so he walked along the wall to the small door. The cemetery would be a good place for dark thoughts.

He heard the donkeys trudging around the well, though it was out of sight across the compound. He'd seen two wagons filled with kegs of river water parked by the stables earlier, and some of that hammering in the distance was the repair crew working on the well outside the walls. *How long will the water last with all these people?*

He heard a second pair of animals being led out to the well. He walked past the building that housed Rimon's office, the infirmary, and sleeping quarters for the channels. Someone was emptying chamber pots into the privy pit behind the infirmary. Sanitation. Feed for the animals. It was going to be a very hard, very busy winter and he was already too exhausted to think.

Near the door out to the cemetery was recent construction, rows of family housing right across from the wing of the infirmary. Piles of dirt, split logs for the walls, and detritus surrounded the new buildings. Tonight, each one was accommodating three times the number it was designed for. People were tending crying children, nursing headaches, avoiding nightmares, trying to grieve silently.

He waved a tentacle in greeting to an old man sitting on the steps of a new house whittling what looked like a toy.

The small door in the Fort's wall was barred with three hardwood planks and guarded by two young renSimes.

"Tuib, the order is that nobody is to go out until dawn after the scouts return. All the gates are shut."

Of course. "Yes, that's good. Thank you," he said as he passed by without breaking stride. A little further on he came to a stair and mounted to the top of the wall where guards paced, zlinning the distance.

He came up to the first one who stood with his hands tucked up in his sleeves and asked, "Mind if I walk the wall for a while?"

"You're that new channel from Tanhara," the renSime identified. "I'm Filo. Sure, go ahead as long as there's no Raiders out there. How far can you zlin?"

Channels could zlin much farther than renSimes, but some channels were more sensitive than others.

"There's nobody this side of that ridge." Solamar indicated the low hill between the Fort and Shifron.

"Then it's all right for you to be up here."

"Good," he told the guard. "I just wanted to breathe fresh air, move a little." Outside the Fort walls, horses were tethered to a line, and a large herd of sheep was watched by four dogs and two renSimes. He'd heard people talking about the main herd of sheep being wintered in a nearby canyon at the edge of the valley. Some loose cows had snuggled up to the lea of the wall. Tanhara's stray chickens roosted under the bushes around the Fort's hen house.

"You just want to zlin the distance instead of the wall in front of your nose?"

"That's the idea." Solamar didn't mention how easily he could zlin through the Fort's walls.

"Guard duty has its good points!" agreed the man. "Just mind that ice where Jokim spilled his tea. Kick the snow down where you find a drift. Someone will be up to shovel it soon no doubt. Everyone's sleeping in shifts because there's no room, so plenty are working even now."

"They're talking about new buildings already."

"Been building for months. Now with Tanhara added, we're hauling river water from the irrigation canal for tonight and we won't be able to do that all winter. They're going to start a new line of privies tomorrow morning and another new well."

"Tanhara is very grateful for your hospitality and sorry for the losses our arrival has cost."

The guard gathered himself, nager shaded with grief. "We'll get through this. Rimon will see us through it. I have to get on about this patrol. Just let us know if you zlin anything out there, then get down fast. We dare not lose any more channels."

"I'll do that."

The guard headed off toward the woman patrolling the next section of wall, and Solamar turned in the other direction. He circled back, walking over the arch of the gate leading out to the cemetery

Just short of the privies, halfway to the next guard's beat, he stopped and leaned against the outer rail to stare out into the night throwing his attention into the lonely silence out there.

The ambient behind him felt crowded. At least nobody was actively paying attention to him now that the guards had zlinned his presence.

A crack in the clouds let moonlight through, sparkling off the snowflakes drifting on a light breeze. He let himself go hyperconscious, shutting out awareness of sight, hearing, smell, touch and taste and focusing on the selyn fields interacting to form the ambient nager. He scanned the wilderness seeking peace among the trees beyond the cemetery where he had seen the dead walking, summoned by Rimon Farris's grief and guilt.

He had intended to meditate then grieve for Losa before considering that development. *What have I done?*

Clearly, Rimon had not experienced anything like that vision before. Solamar knew that the kind of deep nageric interaction they had shared twice that day might have sensitized Rimon to planes of existence beyond the scope of most people's awareness, if Rimon had the talent.

Sudden expansion of a channel's awareness could be deranging or even deadly for one as sensitive as Rimon.

Why did I ask him who they were? The words had just flown out of his mouth, in simple curiosity, not to validate Rimon's perception. Still, it had been a dreadful error.

Behind him, a Farris channel nager slid out of the infirmary door, instantly spotted Solamar and headed for the stair next to the privy. Solamar greeted Rimon nagerically, but kept his attention on the landscape. Moments later, Rimon joined him at the high rail, breath puffing in clouds visible in a narrow shaft of moonlight.

They stood side by side, zlinning distant nothing, not thinking, just breathing quietly, letting awareness slide away. Solamar let the strong, steady Farris presence wrap him in quiet. It was almost as good as solitude.

Ever so slowly, they both surfaced to full awareness of their surroundings, with no shock of a new sudden emergency. Solamar thought Rimon would just let it stay that way, a restful interlude. But no.

"So," Rimon said at last, "you saw them too."

Solamar considered denying that, claiming ignorance, but a Farris would zlin right through any deception. "I thought I saw, well, they'd be ghosts, if they were your father and your daughter."

A frisson of anguish flickered around Rimon at the word ghosts. "Did you hear them speak?"

"Maybe. Maybe I just have a vivid imagination."

Rimon turned and inspected him visually as well as nagerically. "You do. You didn't imagine hearing what I clearly heard, seeing what I saw but couldn't zlin. Nobody else saw what you saw. Why?"

"I wish I knew. I don't generally go around seeing ghosts." Solamar shivered, and not from the cold.

"That's what it was? Ghosts."

"You said you recognized Aipensha. But she's dead. So what you saw was her ghost."

"You didn't see Losa's ghost, did you?"

"No."

"But...?" prompted Rimon.

"I wasn't feeling guilty about her death, just appalled, horrified, shocked, all the usual when someone you know and like, someone who's a part of your life, dies."

"I was feeling guilty."

"I know. I could zlin that much."

"You could?"

"Well, I don't get much from you," admitted Solamar, "your showfield zlins like solid stone most of the time, unless you're projecting. I can't zlin your primary fields. Still, when you were so upset, I picked up on some of it. I'm sorry. They were after all your ghosts, not mine."

Rimon grinned into a gust of snowflakes.

"Now why would that make you happy?"

"I have a theory that the people from the other Forts who've ended up here don't trust Lexy and me, don't trust our judgment because they can't zlin us clearly. Maybe you won't distrust us just because we're Farrises. Maybe they'll listen to you. Maybe things will get better here."

"Things weren't good here before we arrived?"

Snow spackled them while Solamar listened intently to Rimon's summary of events leading up to Clire's Killing Losa. "That explains a lot. Clire was a Farris. Losa was a good Companion for me, but not up to what a pregnant Farris would need."

"So you see, Solamar, we must hold new elections for a Fort Council to include Tanhara."

"I hope Tanhara can help unify these groups."

"We must become not seven Forts, but just Fort Rimon, one united community."

"Rushing to hold elections won't create that unity. We should hold elections when we've finished digging privies, wells, and post holes before the hard freeze. Right now, no one from Tanhara would know who to vote for, and the rest don't know who from Tanhara to vote for."

"That's what I thought when there were just three Forts here. It didn't work, and things have become worse."

Solamar took a chance. "Seven is a better number for this than three, more idealistic."

"A number can't be idealistic!"

"No?" He conceded with a shrug. "Perhaps not."

Rimon zlinned him, and Solamar dropped his showfield and opened himself to the Farris perceptions.

Then Solamar zlinned the Farris back, and was treated to a view of the depths of that formidable channel's soul.

Rimon laughed as he disengaged their fields. "Well, perhaps a number can be idealistic. Stranger things have happened today!" He turned to go back down the stair, then paused. "My father, Zeth Farris, saw ghosts too. They say it drove him to his death."

Solamar felt the apprehension in the man. He stepped forward and gripped the bony Farris shoulders. "You are forgiven by your ghosts. You are not imagining that. You couldn't have done anything else with Clire under the circumstances. We have to prevent such a circumstance from developing again. What began in Fort Freedom with your grandfather, is vitally important to the world. We will not fail." *That is my mission,* thought Solamar.

"You believe in ghosts," Rimon accused.

"Yes. Only...I'd rather that weren't generally known. No one in Tanhara knows." He'd been sworn to secrecy about what he knew, what he could do, before he'd been trained, and until now he'd never broken that oath.

"You believe in life after death?" asked Rimon.

"...uuuhhh...yes."

"It really is real," he half asked, half begged.

"Yes. We were not hallucinating. They came because you were hurting so very much and they love you. They had to tell you that they know it wasn't your fault."

"Yes. And they did that. So they won't come again."

"Probably not."

"Only probably?"

"I can't foretell the future."

"That would be a handy skill."

"Probably not."

Rimon laughed, a short, harsh, bark. "Good point. I don't want to know how I'm going to die, or when."

"It will be at the right time. That much we know."

"Do we?"

"Yes."

"You're positive."

"Yes."

Rimon scrutinized him in every way. "I believe you. I don't know why. But I do."

"Good. You won't discuss it with anyone else?"

"No. No, I won't."

It had the weight of a solemn oath. "I'll sleep better knowing that."

Rimon nodded slowly, still studying Solamar. "Take your turn in the room first. I'll catch a few hours right after dawn. I left Bruce tending a renSime who may be permanently crippled from his injuries. He's one of our best weavers. And I have to see to that Freebander we saved."

Rimon picked his way down the snow covered stairs, kicking the treads free as he went. Solamar followed.

Zeth Farris had died seeing ghosts. *Who would have thought!* Now he'd introduced Rimon to the idea ghosts were real. *I've made a grave mistake here already.* But dissembling to a Farris would only make things worse.

CHAPTER FIVE
IRREVERSIBLE DAMAGE

"Great timing, Delri!" greeted Maigrey with Gen cheerfulness. Rimon entered the channels' recovery room at the infirmary and closed the door behind him. Xanon's Companion continued as if Rimon had asked for a report, "Tuzhel just woke up and we eased him through his disorientation."

"Good! How bad was it?" He'd been very worried the Raider would succumb when the shock of disorientation hit. Any Sime had a strong awareness of where and when he was in the universe. When physically moved during unconsciousness, as Tuzhel had been, the Sime's awakening was fraught with the horror of knowing he was in one place while his senses told him he was in another. The fright could tax an injured system beyond recovery.

Nageric field manipulation by an experienced Gen or channel could realign the senses, but Raiders would rarely cooperate with the process.

"It was pretty bad, but I've seen worse," said Maigrey. "He let me help because he thought I was his mother. The confusion lasted long enough that I was able to get his mental feet on the ground."

"Good work. I was depending on you." Rimon said unnecessarily because Xanon listened exuding disapproval of all Freebanders, captive or not.

"After that," continued Maigrey, "we got him shaved and scrubbed down from all the infestations before we put him in the clean bed. End of the hall, left side. His old bedding's been burned. He's still a Freebander, but he doesn't look like it now, except he's too skinny."

Xanon's disapproval of Maigrey's admiration for Rimon filled the small space as pervasively as the smell of wet wool from Rimon's thawing, dripping cloak.

There was no one else in the room, though from the remains of a solid meal scattered across the sideboard, it seemed there had been staff here recently. This was where the Companions brought the channels to recover after a difficult functional, so there was usually food for the Gens who had to wait while their channels shook with fatigue.

Rimon met Maigrey's eyes and offered silent apology that he'd asked one of Fort Rimon's most diligent Companions to work with Xanon, a channel with too much ego and almost no skill.

Rimon ignored Xanon, flung his cloak onto a hook and stomped his boots free of snow. "Good. I talked to Solamar. He's that Tanhara channel who helped me on the wall. He'll take over here when I leave later."

Xanon's opinion of that was likewise clear before he said, "I can take that shift."

Rimon had always responded to Xanon's remarks with detailed reasons, but he now knew that no explanation would convince Xanon that he wasn't half as good a channel as Solamar, nor that Rimon could know that about Solamar after so brief acquaintance.

"Thank you, but Val has recorded the shift schedule and has sent Kahleen to get Solamar to eat. Maigrey, is Bruce still with Tuzhel?" Rimon zlinned Bruce's towering Gen presence near the end of the long hall, but no details. The Gen was concentrating deeply on his work.

"No, he finished doing what he could with Tuzhel's sores and went to sit with Sian who's right across the hall."

"Good. I'll see to Sian first, then I'll have a long talk with Tuzhel."

"There's no point, Rimon!" said Xanon. "He's a Raider! He must be from Gen Territory. He barely speaks Simelan, and wanted to Kill Bruce. We had to tie him to his bed! He's nothing but a wild animal."

Maigrey nodded. "He is from Gen Territory. His parents were Gen. That's why he speaks Genlan! His Simelan isn't all that bad. It's just accented."

"Did he say how old he is?" asked Rimon.

"No, but he says he's Killed three times. He's a little vague on elapsed time."

"You see?" said Xanon. "We shouldn't waste precious resources on this one."

"Xanon," instructed Rimon, "Tuzhel is a person, not an animal. If we can save him, we will. Policy."

"He'll betray us to the Raiders first chance he gets."

"He might. Though, if we don't give him every chance, we'll have betrayed ourselves. The Church of the Unity may not be a dominant force in this Fort as it was in Fort Freedom, but it represents our origins and its founder began adult life as a Freeband Raider. Then he helped my grandfather discover how to channel."

Rimon remembered the moment when Solamar had looked at him in the underground shelter as they prepared to attempt a transfer for this Raider. Never for one instant had Solamar considered *not* trying to help Tuzhel. It was not that the Tanhara channel was resisting the temptation to let the Raider die, but that he felt no such temptation. Maigrey and Bruce felt the same way and none of them were adherents to the Church of the Unity.

"Xanon, go check with Val for your schedule. I'm going to look in on Sian before talking to Tuzhel."

"Sian will never recover use of his left arm, or his legs either," declared Xanon. He wasn't glad about it, but it was as if an injury like that somehow diminished the value of the man. "Maigrey, let's see what Val has decided now."

Rimon tossed Maigrey a sorrowful look at having assigned her to Xanon. When the door closed, he took an apple from the sideboard and poured himself some tea, waiting for his nerves to settle after exposure to Xanon's abrasive selyn fields. He couldn't identify why the Fort Butte channel set his teeth on edge, but clearly it was mutual. *A lot of the Fort Butte people are like that!* Maybe it was that the Church of the Unity hadn't survived in Fort Butte. That made him wonder about Fort Tanhara.

Carrying his tea and munching his apple, Rimon walked down the corridor of the infirmary's second floor, zlinning patients in the rooms on either side, watching the various channels, some of whom he hardly knew, work with the selyn fields around the wounded, spurring their healing.

Usually, most of the first floor was offices, but now they were using all but his own office for patients. Val had commandeered his office for her big schedule board and they were running supply logistics out of there too.

He found Bruce in Sian's room at the end of the second floor hall.

The infirmary rooms were barely big enough for a narrow bed, a couple of chairs for the channel-Companion pairs working on the patient, a counter with a pitcher and basin, and normally well stocked cabinets. Tonight, the medicinal supplies were dangerously low, and the counters littered with used bandages. Soiled bedding was piled in the corridor, and the trash bin held scraps of ripening food, and bits of bloody refuse. A candle basket overflowed with candle stubs to be melted down for reuse.

"Sian," greeted Rimon.

"Delri, I was hoping you'd come by. That's why I kept Bruce here. Bait."

"You know I can find him from the other end of the flax fields."

"If he was mine, he'd never get that far away!"

"Great," observed Bruce. "Now I've got Simes fighting over me! I must be very skilled at sowing strife." Bruce tried for a glum nageric effect. It didn't work.

The two Simes shared a chuckle. Then Sian said, "No kidding

Delri. You're in Need."

"Not much," Bruce answered for him. "Only about two days. He hit Turnover the morning of the attack."

Turnover was the point, halfway through the month, when a Sime had used up half the selyn taken in that month's transfer. It was often accompanied by an alarming, sinking sensation, and always followed by the increasing awareness of life trickling away, of death approaching, of the Need for more selyn.

Rimon moved to where Bruce sat in one of the polished hardwood chairs. "Sian, we're going to make a long, slow, deep examination of your injuries and see if we can relieve some of that paralysis."

"Just give me my arm back. We can build me a loom that doesn't require feet."

Weaving was his art, his pride, and other than his children, his greatest joy. He was married to the master dyer of the Fort, a woman who had borne him four children. For him, life and weaving were all of one piece.

Rimon leaned on Bruce's fields. The Gen felt the nageric shift and brought his attention to focus on Rimon as Rimon focused on Sian. Rimon smoothly supplied the nageric support for Sian as Bruce withdrew. For a moment the renSime didn't even notice. Then he smiled and shook his head. "I never believe it when you two do that."

Grinning back and nagerically accepting the compliment, Rimon moved to the bedside and hitched one hip onto the edge of the bed, reaching for Sian's arms. "Let's see how much progress you've made."

"Not much. You got one transfer into me, but I don't think it'll work again."

"It wasn't fun, I know," Rimon finished the thought as he slid his hand under the flaccid arm, cradling the elbow. "Oddly enough your laterals aren't much affected by this injury."

A Sime took in selyn through the lateral tentacles that normally lay sheathed along the sides of the arms. Those tentacles were almost all nerve with little muscle. They were protected during a transfer grip by the strong, dextrous handling tentacles.

Rimon extended his handling tentacles to secure the grip, and pressed just so on the reflex node, forcing the renSime's laterals out of their sheaths. That wouldn't have worked if the paralysis were total. "Just relax and let me zlin your tissues."

Rimon twined his lateral tentacles around the two flaccid ones on Sian's left arm, and the two normal ones on the renSime's right arm. He felt the contact with Sian's nervous system open. Then he bent and made the necessary fifth contact, lip to lip, searching the nerve rich skin of the lips for the match that would allow his Sime senses access to the body before him.

Trusting Bruce's trained attention not to waver from him, Rimon completely let go of his awareness of touch, sight, sound, taste, and smell, then immersed himself in the purely Sime perception of reality, the shifting, surging, billowing fields of energy generated by the incessant motion of selyn through a living nervous system.

He narrowed and refocused, letting his awareness trace the selyn flows twining up and down his patient's arms. He zlinned the damaged tissue near Sian's shoulder joint. The swelling he'd zlinned before was nearly gone, but some of the nerve cells controlling the muscles were dying. Some were already dead, the faint glow of selyn extinguished. He narrowed focus again to separate one cell from another, almost impossible with nerve cells.

Delri spent so much of his time in this healing mode state of awareness that it had become a restful norm for him. As he worked, he felt tension dissipate and the surrounding room disappeared from awareness, and suddenly he zlinned how the nerve canal itself was intact, but only some of the nerve cells were recovering. Sian would have to grow new tissue there or lose the use of his arm. Or maybe not.

He switched his attention to the lower spine injury that had left both legs paralyzed. The situation there was worse, but it gave him an idea.

He dismantled the contact, brought himself to awareness

of his ordinary senses, thinking furiously, weighing risks he couldn't begin to assess.

He rose and paced in front of the workbench up to the small hearth where the fire had died to embers. Bruce followed him. Rimon turned and put his back to the faint warmth. He stared at Bruce.

"You," said Rimon to his Companion, "are still the best Companion in this Fort, the best I have ever found."

"Why does that sound ominous?"

"Because what I have in mind will work only if you exceed even your highest standard. This will be fine, fine work. Your unwavering concentration will be even more critical than ever. The risk...." He shifted attention to Sian. "The risk is death, Sian. This would be an all-or-nothing experiment."

The renSime pulled in a deep breath, his skin paling in time with his escalating alarm. "And the reward?"

"Maybe nothing. Maybe restoring most of the use of your arm, possibly restoring some sensation to your legs. I really don't know what will happen. Clire tried this on Garath, and you know what happened." He watched Sian absorb that while Bruce attempted to stifle his reaction.

Garath had been a renSime from Fort Butte who suffered a full paralysis of his right arm when a building collapsed during construction. He had lost all ability to draw selyn through his right side laterals.

Xanon and the other Fort Butte channels had failed to get a transfer into Garath. Clire, with Rimon's help, had attempted to induce healing in those nerves using a procedure she had only heard about.

Bruce said, "Delri, Garath died and you barely managed to save Clire, and that almost cost you your life."

"I remember," assured Rimon.

"And it took Clire nearly ten days to recover. Aipensha isn't here to save you this time. Do you want Lexy to watch you die?"

"Lexy isn't to be involved, no matter what. This is between Sian, me, and unavoidably, you."

Sian said, "No. We can't afford to risk you."

Rimon sat down on the bed again, motioning Bruce to take a chair. "Your injury is much less severe. Clire had never watched the procedure and was caught off guard by a side effect. I zlinned what happened. I think we can use this procedure, not so intensely, and still get some results for you. It's a judgment call, and not mine to make alone."

"Definitely not alone," injected Bruce glumly. "This is not a good idea."

"Will I be less at risk in four or five days?" asked Rimon, keenly aware of Need creeping up on him as every heartbeat used up selyn while every one of Bruce's heartbeats left the Gen's body surging with new selyn his tissues created. Need was what being Sime was all about. Gens were a lot more complicated.

Bruce sighed but didn't answer aloud.

Rimon asked Sian, "Are you willing to risk your life for the possible, partial, use of your arm, maybe a little improvement in the legs? Think about it for a...."

"I don't have to think about that. I'd risk anything. My family might have other ideas, but I wouldn't want you to tell them until it was over. They'd worry, and it would be wasted if it turns out all right. Everyone knows I've not much chance of surviving this."

"Oh, but you do, Sian, you do." Sian had four children to think about. "You could live for years in this condition, with maybe a little improvement with time."

In great stillness, Sian confronted that vision. Utterly still for more than a minute, he did think, hard. Then he shook his head. "No, that's not life. If you think this will work, it's worth it to me. But it's not worth any risk to you, Delri. I'm just not worth that."

Rimon held the ambient nager firm and steady and just returned the renSime's gaze, waiting silently.

Eventually, Sian took a deep breath and threw his head back to moan at the ceiling. "All right. I see your point. It's up to me to evaluate the risk for myself, what my life would be like if I say no. I can't say how it would be for you. Delri, what would you lose that's so valuable you'd rather not live without it?"

"Self respect. The knowledge that I've done my best, used all my strength to make the world a better place. Clire...no matter if we recover her and try to save her child, Clire is dead to us. This procedure is her legacy, the legacy of her Fort. It shouldn't die with her. It should be here for her child."

"Then," said Bruce, "you must bring Lexy in to monitor. Nobody else would have any chance of zlinning what you're doing."

Trapped by his own logic, Rimon sighed. He turned a smile to Bruce. "Agreed." *Gens!*

Sian laughed. Bruce looked bewildered then shrugged, and asked Sian, "Should I go get her?"

Sian looked at Delri. Sian had grown up under Delri's leadership of Fort Rimon and was now in his prime, master of the weaving craft, respected among the Fort Rimon natives. In the weaving shed, his word was law as was his wife's among the dyes. Almost half the Fort's buying power came from selling their linen and wool blends in their special bright colors. Livestock and food didn't bring in nearly as much.

"Yes, Bruce, go get her," agreed Sian. His nager rang with confidence and even joy. "Delri is going to cure me."

Delri, thought Rimon, *is not going to live without trying.* That was as far as he could go.

They spent the wait discussing the cloth supplies that would be required for their increased population, and how much would be left over for sale to buy the items they couldn't make for themselves. They ignored the difficulty that permanent loss of Shifron might cause. If the juncts didn't rebuild their town, the Fort would just have to go bartering down at Turen Gap.

The discussion was getting interesting when a veritable crowd arrived. Lexy came in first followed by her Companion, Garen, whom Rimon was not happy to see. Garen was Garath's brother and really shouldn't be involved in a repeat of the procedure that had failed for his brother. Yet here he was at Lexy's side, and obviously committed.

Behind them came Xanon and Maigrey making it six people and their patient crowded into a room just barely big enough for three.

"Xanon, out," ordered Rimon with the flick of a tentacle. "If you've nothing to do, go rest. Bruce! Garen, watch your fields."

Rimon grabbed Bruce's hand, turned around and edged back into his place beside Sian, dragging his Companion along, forcing Xanon and Maigrey out of the room. Maigrey gave a sheepish shrug as she herded her protesting channel out. Finally, the door closed, leaving Lexy, Garen, Bruce and himself with the patient.

As carefully as everyone had tried to protect the renSime from the massive shifts in the fields when so many channels were crammed together, they all felt Sian's relief as the ambient around him firmed up again under Rimon's attention. Rimon was acutely aware of how his fields dominated any environment, even with Lexy present, and did his best to soften the effect.

Rimon noted Xanon and Maigrey lingering outside the door. He traded knowing glances with Lexy. She said, "He's not going to leave. He heard Bruce say you're going to try Clire's Stitch."

"Not exactly."

"He's sure nothing can be done. But I think he came to watch you die trying."

"I won't," Delri told his daughter, his heir. He explained what he wanted to do, and then she had to examine Sian again.

She agreed there had been good progress over the last few hours. "It could work. But I ought to be the one to try it."

Oh, no! "I watched Clire do it, so I know what went wrong. Bruce wanted you here to watch it go right, to learn how to do it." He pointed out how this was Clire's only legacy to the Fort unless they could save her baby, which was less likely with every passing day they didn't get her back. And that did it.

"All right. Show me how it's done."

"Sian? Ready?"

"Just do it. Lexy, don't let anything happen to him."

"Lexy," countered Rimon. "Zlin me. Lock hard." He felt the rhythmic life pulse of her body fall into sync with his own. "Good, but whatever happens stay clear. Bruce. Hold steady and don't let the fields around me shift."

Rimon took his place on the side of the bed and in one, swift, continuous move he made the five contact points and sank back into that state of non-awareness of his physical surroundings. Leaning against Bruce's control of the ambient, he focused down into the renSime's cells, found the nerve canals, went deeper and found the individual cells trailing tiny connectors that almost touched.

He zlinned how the cells traded energy pulses, the dimmer, dying cells blocking more than they transmitted. Clire had shown him how to use selyn to stitch those nerve cells together, bridging the gaps left by dead cells, leaving behind an invigorated cell ready to divide again. The trick, she had explained, was to make sure the cell only divided once or twice, replacing the dead nerves and no more.

Delicately, concentrating wholly on what he was doing, Rimon imagined tiny threads of selyn energy, and allowed selyn to flow into the renSime to form those imagined filaments.

At first he knew he was just imagining how the selyn he was feeding into the renSime's system stitched the broken nerve connections together. Then he was zlinning a duplicate image of the renSime body, a hazy outline true in every detail superimposed on the physical body.

He focused on the duplicate, noting the severe gapping in the lower spine and the dim area near the left shoulder. He knew how it should zlin. He could zlin it as it should be. It was more than just imagination. It was as if he were creating a virtual image etched in selyn.

A frisson of startlement crackled behind him. In the pearly haze floated a glowing image of Solamar. "Rimon, what are you doing...oh, I...oh, Rimon!"

"You're not here. You're asleep," accused Rimon.

"Pay attention!" Two tentacles gestured and Rimon's attention snapped back to his patient.

The hazy image of the renSime's nerves outlining his body had shimmered into mist, but as soon as Rimon's attention focused, the image sharpened again, now brighter. A movement drew Rimon's attention to his right. *Aipensha!*

A swirling sense of unreality, then confusion and doubt, followed by fear shattered Rimon's concentration on his patient. His deceased daughter stood over his patient with him, but he knew that in reality his living daughter was holding the patient's fields steady. His body felt her strength, and felt nothing of Aipensha.

"Concentrate!" commanded Aipensha.

"Focus!" warned Solamar sharply.

Dizzy, Rimon brought his whole attention back to the interlaced lines of throbbing energy that composed a second body for his patient. He knew what he had to accomplish. He knew how the weaver's body should zlin. As he anticipated that result, it formed in the hazy latticework hovering over the weaver's body.

Exhaustion threatened his grip on the fields, but Solamar stepped up behind him and urged Rimon's tentacles to spread out, somehow lengthening to encompass the entire hazy image of the weaver's selyn circulation. "Down now, press down, rejoin the perfect image to the body."

With the last of his strength, Rimon kneaded the two images into a single whole. Everything wavered, but he kept pushing, and then something let go and he was falling.

He fell forever, too terrified to scream.

* * * * * * *

Solamar Grant jackknifed upright in Rimon's bed with a gasp and sat amid his blankets dragging air into his lungs, feeling the chill dry the sweat from his brow.

The fire was banked, the room lit only by bright Gen nager. Kahleen was curled up in a blanket on the settee near the hearth, sound asleep. Gens had to sleep more than Simes, and usually slept more soundly. Grant let himself pant for a while, assembling the memory of the dream.

He mopped his forehead, scraping sleep out of his eyes, and confronted reality. It hadn't been a dream. The falling sensation at the end was the surest giveaway, but the clarity of the memory was enough all by itself. He had accidentally wandered during sleep. He hadn't done that since childhood. Worse: he had wandered into Rimon's awareness, and Rimon had noticed him there.

None of that should have happened, and it was all his fault for opening Rimon's awareness while trying to get a transfer into Tuzhel.

As strength returned to his trembling limbs, Solamar wrenched the blankets aside and grabbed his clothing. *What have I done! What have I done now!*

He took time to gather Kahleen up and put her on the bed, spreading more blankets over her. She didn't stir.

Then he was racing down halls, augmenting to a slightly higher selyn usage for speed, dodging slow moving Gens and patients. He ignored shouts about rules against augmenting indoors, flashed around a corner, raced down stairs and came up to a tightly packed crowd in the hall between Sian's room and the room across from it where they had the captured Freebander, Tuzhel, confined.

Xanon and Maigrey were there, Xanon pacing, haranguing several other channels and Companions while Maigrey sprawled in a chair titled back against the wall, broadcasting boredom.

BanSha, the boy who tended Rimon's sleeping quarters, was struggling with a bucket, mopping the floor as he backed out of the Freebander's room. He couldn't be more than twelve natal years old, small for his age, with no sign of physical maturity yet.

Solamar grabbed the ambient selyn fields and tilted the

gradient, smoothing it out. All the channels except Xanon immediately adjusted and cooperated, bringing their alert attention to Solamar. When Xanon finally noticed, he turned and stared at the source of the distraction.

"Excuse me, I have to get into Sian's room to help Rimon. Surely you all have assignments?"

"No," started Xanon, but the others cut him off, and in moments the corridor was empty of all but BanSha who was staring up at him worshipfully.

Solamar spared him a wink as he crashed through Sian's door uninvited and, he realized instantly, unwelcome. Lexy flinched at the intrusion before Garen could block the field turbulence for her. She valiantly ignored her personal worry as she addressed the problem Rimon's oddly fractured fields presented.

Incongruously, Solamar's heart warmed with delight at her strength.

Rimon was supine on the floor beside Sian's bed, Lexy bent over him, Garen supporting her while Bruce worked on Rimon from his other side. Brilliant though he was, Bruce was applying the wrong treatment and Lexy knew it wasn't working, but not what to do.

Solamar slid into the ambient, shutting the door behind him. He knelt, cupped a hand on the crown of Rimon's head, extended tentacles and planted his other hand at his solar plexus. He grabbed hold of Bruce's rock steady field, whispered, "Del Rimon Farris," into Rimon's ear, then sealed the Farris channel's spirit into his body.

All the while, the refrain pounded through his mind, *"What have I done? Why did I do that?"* All the while, he knew. This man had touched him deeply. He couldn't let Sian die at Rimon's hands, but he couldn't let Aipensha manifest further in Rimon's life either.

Abruptly, Rimon gasped and grabbed at Lexy and Bruce, pulling himself up to a sitting position. Panting, he rasped, "I'm alive! This is real!"

"Dad!" choked Lexy, the ambient shattering with her relief.

She grabbed him and held on tight.

Bruce shuddered and turned away, curling his fields in on himself to keep from disturbing the Farris channels.

Garen grinned at Solamar, and let his celebration fill the room. "I don't know if you did that, Solamar, but I really thought he was gone!"

To avoid having to answer that, Solamar rose and went to the bed where Sian was still unconscious.

Rimon struggled to his feet, assuring Garen, "You and Lexy did a great job. You're a fine team, the two of you."

Wishing now for Kahleen, Solamar made a lateral contact with the weaver. The renSime's left hand laterals responded eagerly to his grip. He ran his attention all around the man's selyn circulation system, tracing out the paths that had been broken by the injuries. Selyn passed through all the nerves brightly, suffusing all the muscles and tissues with pure life. Healing now seethed through every cell in the man's body.

He broke the contact and let Rimon take his place, despite the protests of the crowd in the little room. Before Rimon could even hitch his knee onto the bed, Sian tossed restlessly and fought back to consciousness.

"Rimon!" Without thinking, the man raised his left arm to take Rimon's hand, then stared dumbfounded at his own arm. He noticed his legs had moved too. "Rimon!"

The channel grinned at his patient. "It appears you've made some improvement."

"Everything tingles," Sian understated.

Rimon said, "It'll probably get worse before it gets better. You've a lot of healing to do. I want you to get some sleep." The channel guided his patient down into slumber. "When they bring you something to eat, eat it, and no nonsense! I've put you through a terrible strain."

"But Rimon, it tingles!" sighed the weaver. "Tell my wif...." One more sigh and he was deeply asleep, oblivious to the increasing discomfort of his nervous system.

Lexy signalled Bruce to get Rimon out of the room, whispering, "I'll take over here. You get some rest. Then explain what you did. I couldn't zlin anything."

Rimon started to reply, but Bruce hustled his channel out of the treatment room. Over his shoulder, Rimon said, "And Garen, nice work. Very nice work. I hardly felt your presence when you were focused on Lexy. No distraction. No irritation. We'll talk as soon as there's time. I have some things to say about Gareth that you should know."

"I'd appreciate that," answered Lexy's Companion.

Solamar followed them out and closed the door, flashing Garen a grin that was knowingly returned. He was still sorting out the relationships among these people, and it seemed there was more between Rimon and Garen than the Companion's brother's death at Clire's hands. *I'll ask about that sometime.*

The hall was now clear, though the floor was still damp. The instant the door closed behind them, Rimon speared Solamar with a look that could melt stone. "What are you doing here? You are supposed to be sleeping."

From the other end of the hall, a new Gen nager joined them. Kahleen, pulling on a heavy sweater and binding back her hair as she walked, heard Rimon's remark and added, "Solamar, you snuck out without me!"

Solamar protested, "Snuck?!"

Rimon pulled Solamar's attention back. "I thought—I thought I...how could you...you were there! When I was healing Sian, you appeared...wherever that was!"

Bruce was jarred out of his Companion's staunch calm by that incoherent remark. "Rimon?"

"Snuck," stated Kahleen, going to work on Solamar.

Rimon impatiently hushed his Companion with a tentacle gesture, still glaring at Solamar.

Two more words from Rimon and people might start to think Rimon was losing his grip on reality. The Fort could not afford that.

Solamar blurted, "I must have had a nightmare." *Oh, no I didn't mean that!* "Not your fault, Kahleen, you've been terrific.

Really, I know you're still in shock over losing Clire, but I lost my Companion too and have barely slept since the funeral. We all have grieving yet to do. It's not Need nightmares that you could ward off. It's the loss."

She nodded. "I woke convinced I was late for a meeting with Clire. You'll grieve after your transfer." She turned to Rimon. "All the Simes will be having that problem during their first couple of days post-transfer. Don't consider yourself an exception."

"I won't," assured Rimon. "I don't, and neither should you. You shouldn't be here. You were sent to rest. Val expects people to stick to the schedule."

Projecting contrition to hide his satisfaction that he'd changed the subject, Solamar shrugged. "I just woke suddenly and knew I couldn't get back to sleep, so I came over to see if there was anything I could help with. I zlinned an uproar right through that door, so I went in to try to help. You must have felt me come into the room while you were unconscious. I'm sorry, but it was the smoothest field insertion I could do. Must have seemed like a slap in the face to a Farris."

Very, very quietly, Rimon cloaked the two of them in a rigid field that would be shutting Bruce out as well. With his back to everyone else, he accused Solamar in a harsh whisper, "You had *my* nightmare. I saw you while I was treating Sian."

Solamar agreed with a tiny nageric flick, muttering, "We can talk about that later. Privately." He couldn't let Rimon think he was going crazy. *What a mess.*

Rimon scrutinized Solamar deeply, then dispelled the wall around them and said aloud, "You're right, you did do your best and it wasn't at all bad. We'll practice that insertion technique later and you'll get the hang of it."

Solamar agreed nagerically and said, "You did something remarkable in there if Lexy couldn't follow it, so the Fort's record should be written up on that one in detail—now before you forget. Our Freebander is awake, so why don't you go record what you did while I...."

Rimon was already striding into Tuzhel's room leaving Bruce, Solamar and Kahleen to follow.

Bruce said, "I'll go break the disappointing news to Xanon that both our Farrises survived as did the patient who is much improved. He'll be so crushed."

Rimon stopped two steps into the room, turned and watched Bruce's receding back, his mouth hanging open, two handling tentacles frozen in mid-gesture. Solamar, too, contemplated the retreating Gen back, noting the way the Companion wrapped his fields around himself and ignored Rimon. It was the most eloquent picture of polite Gen outrage he had ever seen.

Kahleen said, "Delri, you should pay more attention to Bruce."

It was a diplomatic way of saying, in front of the Raider, that Rimon should not have shut Bruce out of the exchange with Solamar. He was really getting to like Kahleen. She was right. Bruce would have to be included if he could figure out how to recover from this disaster and explain to Rimon what had happened while he was healing Sian. Then, before his transfer with Kahleen, Solamar would have to make time to learn more about her. Maybe Clire wasn't the only great loss she'd suffered in that battle.

"I expect you're right, Kahleen," Rimon acknowledged. "Bruce will be back soon. Sometimes he needs a bit of time. What Companion wouldn't?"

Rimon turned to their patient who was watching them hyper-consciously, zlinning but not seeing or hearing. The Raider was focused on Kahleen, raising intil, the appetite for selyn, by basking in the Gen's nager. He wasn't actually in Need thanks to the transfer they had forced into him, but transfer couldn't satisfy Killust.

They're right. He wants to Kill a Companion.

Solamar focused on supporting Rimon as the Farris sat on the edge of the Raider's bed, plucking the restraints with a ventral tentacle as he forced the renSime to duoconsciousness, able to zlin and see at the same time. "Want these off?"

Tuzhel glared at Rimon but his attention was riveted on Kahleen. Rimon swiveled to glance at Solamar.

"Kahleen," said Solamar, "you should go on back to sleep." He focused his Need laced attention on her. She returned it with a warm clasp of support. She had every reason to hate the Raiders for what they'd done to Clire. Still, she couldn't find it in her heart to focus that resentment on this youth. She was the object of his Killust and returned that interest with overt hostility. If they were to get any work done with the junct, she had to leave.

With a wry grin, she departed saying, "Call me if I can help." The door closed gently behind her.

Solamar hid the surge of admiration that overtook him, but the Farris noticed it. Rimon however was now intent on the Raider before him. Swiftly, he released the restraints that held the youth to the bed frame leaving the junct renSime free to attack. He would, too, despite the pain from his partially healed injuries.

"Tuzhel, you couldn't Kill her because you couldn't take enough selyn fast enough to matter to her. She's a trained Companion. She has enough selyn to serve *this* kind of Need."

Rimon let his showfield project a channel's Need. Billows of voracious darkness filled the room with aching, screaming panic, deeper, blacker and darker than anything a Raider would have encountered and utterly paralyzing for the renSime youth. *Except for Clire's Need during that battle. That's what she'd have zlinned like close up.*

As quickly as it had enveloped the tiny room, the Need was gone. Tuzhel was left pale and sweating.

Wonder what Lexy made of that? thought Solamar swallowing hard against the echo of Need induced within his own secondary system. He hadn't moved swiftly enough to keep that nageric surge from spilling across the corridor.

Now he knew Rimon had wanted him there to control the spread of such nageric disturbance, and he'd nearly failed. Surely the Farris woman had felt the surge of Need he hadn't blocked even through the two doors separating them. An image of her being startled sprang to his mind's eye and he found himself smiling at the closed door.

Immediately, the door opened again and Bruce sliced neatly into the room's ambient, moving to stand behind Rimon with apology written all over his nager.

Tuzhel sat up and ran both hands and his handling tentacles over his shaved head, shaking and not just from the pain in his half-healed tendons.

Solamar thought, *Rimon is making a big mistake here.* At the same moment, Tuzhel whispered, "BanSha says channels can do anything. I didn't believe him. But he's right. He says he's going to be one. I want to be one too."

Rimon pried the clutching hands loose and nudged the youth's chin up, meeting his eyes, gently engaging his nager. "A person is born a channel, or not a channel. It's not something you can choose. You can choose to stay with us, to learn a trade, to live among Gens and never Kill again. No Sime in this Fort is allowed to Kill. It's a hard choice that only the bravest among us can make, especially after what you've been through the first few days of your life as an adult Sime. That would make the choice much harder. But if you really want it, we'll help you choose not to Kill."

Solamar heard Rimon's unspoken, *and maybe even survive it.* Disjunction for this youth would take at least six to eight months, and the last few months would be horrible agony until he broke the addictive craving for the Kill.

Eyes narrowed, the junct accused in a heavily accented, mixed patois, "This Fort a-gonna be smashed flat in the next raid, ain'it?"

"I doubt that," answered Rimon honestly. "Though many of us may die by violence before the town folks return to exterminate the Raiders. But that's only one reason Raiders don't live long. To Kill so frequently, you give up all the best years of your life. To gain some of them back, you must face the risks."

"Tuzhel," said Solamar, "BanSha didn't tell you about what

happens when a Sime who has survived by Killing tries to live by taking selyn from a channel?"

Rimon eyed Solamar but zlinned Tuzhel's reaction. Clearly the youth was as ignorant of disjunction as he must have been of changeover before it hit him and he matured into a Sime almost overnight after growing up expecting to be Gen like his parents.

Rimon turned back to their patient. "If we let you go and you return to the Raider band you were with, you will be dead within five years at the most. Probably you will die within two years. Isn't it true that the Raiders you have met are young? Have they ever told you of someone they knew who was more than six years past changeover?"

Tuzhel's eyes were fixed on Rimon now, and he was thinking hard. His head moved in a silent negative.

"How old do you think I am?" asked Rimon.

"Old. Older tha' I cn count."

Rimon held out both hands, with all eight handling tentacles extended. "Here's how many years since I was born." He closed his hands and retracted tentacles, then opened them again, then closed them and opened his right hand with handling tentacles extended. Closed that and held out three tentacles. "Do you know how many years that is?"

"Count tentacles too?"

"Well, yes, that's how we count."

After some cogitation, he said a number in Genlan that Solamar didn't know, but it seemed the youth could count, just not in Simelan. "That's older than my Da...."

The ambient shattered, but Solamar held the fields in the room rock steady, still braced against any unexpected move the Farris might make. Rimon controlled the ambient effortlessly while Solamar marveled at the recovery the man had made in just a few minutes after hurling all his strength into healing Sian. *Apparent recovery,* he reminded himself. He knew he couldn't zlin what was really going on inside a Farris, and Rimon was better than most at using his showfield to mask his inner turmoil.

"You Killed your father when you changed over?" prompted Rimon, knowing the answer.

Great, welling shame, horror filled the room and Rimon let it billow uncontrolled. Solamar followed his lead, not understanding, but sure that this junct would never choose the Fort lifestyle after being treated like this.

Bruce came forward and grabbed the scrawny, completely shaven young man and swept him into a warm embrace filled with Gen love. "Oh, that must have been horrible," he muttered, but his voice and nager carried immense sympathy. "It wasn't your fault, Tuzhel. We understand how these things happen by accident."

He held him, rocking back and forth as sobs burst from the young throat. "Weren' no accident. H-he, he hit me with a shovel. He wanna kill me...I...I...I didn't want to die! I should-a, but I couldn' wanna...."

Nobody in the room was about to correct his Simelan. He'd learn soon enough the difference between the Kill and murder.

Bruce murmured all the right things, then said, "Here you will never have to want to die, Tuzhel. Here you can survive, do good and be glad to live. There are a number of people here who had similar experiences. We're always ready to take in young people who get to us in time. And you are in time, Tuzhel. You can live."

That was more the message Solamar thought might work with a young junct. But the youth was having none of it. "I want to Kill you!" He squirmed trying to get a transfer grip on the Gen, but Bruce and Rimon manipulated the fields to create the illusion of shifting, moving contact points that kept eluding the junct until he gave up.

Bruce hugged him again. "No, you don't want to Kill me. You just want to satisfy your selyn Need," he contradicted, then looked over the youth's head at Rimon. "Nothing I could do would provide that for you. Besides, right now you're not in Need." He rose and backed away now that the storm of grief had abated in the typical First Year Sime's way of rapid adjustments.

Circling back to his position behind Rimon, he muttered a quick apology and returned to his primary job of keeping his attention on Rimon, letting the channel use his Gen selyn fields to work the ambient.

Rimon was eyeing Solamar again, speculation rife in that gaze but barely zlinnable in the ambient. "You up for a little demonstration, Solamar?"

Not sure what Rimon wanted, Solamar grinned confidently. Rimon zlinned his uncertainty and returned a serene confidence in Solamar's abilities. To the renSime youth, the ambient nager was a steady, evenly glowing field punctuated lightly by Bruce's throbbing glow.

As any Sime during the first year after changeover, the youth was easily distracted into studying selyn fields. Obviously, Rimon intended to use that trait for instructional purposes, but Solamar couldn't follow his thinking. What could you say to a Raider who knew his compatriots would be back soon, that nothing could be gained by the struggle to disjunct except an ugly death at Raider hands?

Rimon moved away from the bed with an air of judicious consideration then rounded on Solamar with a devilish grin and spoke looking directly into Solamar's eyes. "Tuzhel, zlin our fields closely now. I'll pretend to be you, at the final moments of the disjunction process. Bruce will be a Gen that you'd want very much to Kill. Solamar will be the channel who is ready to give you transfer, and in the end, he will give you transfer."

I will? Solamar thought very quietly to himself as he returned the confident grin of the Farris channel who wasn't fooled for a second. *This can't possibly work. What kid would choose to go through such agony for nothing?* Nevertheless, he nodded and took a position apart from Bruce as the Farris shifted the fields in the room totally captivating the First Year renSime's attention.

Smoothly, Rimon's showfield began to mimic a junct renSime in Need, voracious Need for Killbliss not just selyn, a Need unsatisfied for months.

Cooperatively, Bruce put all his attention on Rimon's imitation renSime and began to offer him transfer, as if he were ready to serve his channel's Need. Solamar brought his showfield up to create the impression of a Gen offering transfer to that imitation-renSime as any channel would prepare to serve a real renSime's Need.

Rimon responded by precisely mimicking the rising intil, the sharp, voracious intensity of a junct in Need hunting a Kill. Bruce's fields far out-shone Solamar's, even though Bruce and Rimon were more than ten days from transfer. Still from the renSime's perspective, Bruce must have seemed as if he contained all the selyn in the world.

To play his part in this charade, Solamar had to remain the lesser enticement, offering a mere channel's transfer, not a true Gen Kill.

Rimon upped the power and Bruce followed his lead with that amazing talent sometimes displayed by the Companions of the truly powerful channels. Solamar held steady while Rimon demonstrated the agonizing moment of decision that every disjuncting renSime had to go through.

Disjunction was not so much contained in the months of increasing, agonizing dissatisfaction with channel's transfer, the intensifying lust for the Kill, but in that final moment of choice at the end of all that suffering. Rimon had obviously taken many juncts through that moment and knew its every nuance.

Tuzhel, wholly lost in the selyn fields, moved closer, kneeling on the bed, pushing toward the scenario unfolding before him, attention flicking back and forth between Bruce and Solamar in time with Rimon's enactment.

Rimon moved toward Bruce, letting his very genuine Need for this particular Gen show through, but giving it a distinctive twist, the Need for Gen pain, agony and final deathscream, for the pure egobliss of the Kill.

Rimon reached for Bruce who offered his arms for the Sime's transfer grip, letting his deep-seated yearning for that transfer slowly turn to horror, revulsion and then terror as Rimon's tentacles touched him. It was just the response a junct craved from a Gen.

Solamar, aware the Raider could lunge for Bruce at any moment, did nothing but hold steady, being the channel he had never been raised to be, never been trained to be. That was a secret he had to keep from Rimon Farris, somehow, despite all the rest he'd have to tell him. So he threw himself into his role, dismissing his entire personal identity and becoming the channel Rimon thought him to be.

Rimon's attention flicked over Solamar, zlinning his fields. Then he lunged two steps toward Bruce, hesitated, then threw himself at Solamar.

Solamar braced one foot behind him, brought selyn up just as if giving a transfer and took Rimon's weight as their lateral tentacles entwined and Rimon went for the fifth transfer point, lip to lip. As the two of them went over backwards, Rimon actually drew selyn, his showfield projecting a relaxed, beautiful satisfaction, not Killbliss at all, but something better. The transfer completed before Solamar's shoulders hit the floor and Lexy flew into the room blowing the faked fields to smithereens.

"Dad!"

Rimon laughed, a free jolly laugh, throaty and relaxed, just as a newly disjuncted renSime might laugh. He looked up at Lexy and swept the fields back into the neutral wall of opalescence it had been before the demonstration.

Tuzhel sat back on his heels amidst the blankets, duoconscious again, staring at Rimon. "That wasn't real."

"No, it wasn't," said Rimon. "It was just very close. That's what it would be like, Tuzhel, hard, and very much a free choice that you and you alone would have to make."

Bruce pulled Rimon to his feet, shifting his own fields and attention to help Rimon adjust his fields, and Solamar rested the back of his head on the rug wishing Kahleen were there but feasting his eyes on Lexy from this odd perspective, zlinning her take it all in and adjust to the lack of a real emergency. *There is one gorgeous woman with a spirit like solar fire.*

He rolled over and got to his feet reassuring her, "Rimon decided to demonstrate disjunction crisis for Tuzhel." He turned to the youth. "Did a pretty good job being you, don't you think?" He held his breath.

Tuzhel nodded, "I wouldn' never have to Kill? I wouldn' feel like I have to?"

Rimon said with relentless honesty, "Maybe sometimes for a few minutes you might have that feeling. It would go away in the time you could hold your breath. Need just wouldn't ordinarily feel the same as it does to you now. But I'm not going to lie to you. Disjunction is a hard thing, maybe the hardest thing a Sime can do. If you were a few months older, you wouldn't be able to survive it. So you must choose now."

Tuzhel looked at Garen who had come in behind Lexy and closed the door. Even with Tuzhel kneeling on the narrow bed, the room was crowded. Tuzhel slowly nodded. He was scared, but he was game. "Yes." Something fundamental had changed in this lost youth. It wasn't a logical decision. It was more like a leap of faith.

More than a little amazed, Solamar let his genuine pleasure show. *The Farrises are just not like any other kind of channel.* He'd known that but he'd never actually *known* it. What he'd inadvertently done to Rimon while trying to get a transfer into Tuzhel the first time might have done irreversible damage to the Farris. *He's seeing ghosts, he's starting to work on the non-material body of his patients, and now he's struck this boy's soul. What next?*

CHAPTER SIX
CONSEQUENCES

"Bruce, I'm sorry," said Rimon the instant Tuzhel's door closed leaving them in the hall. "Kahleen was very upset with me...." *More like furious,* he thought, adding, "She was right to be."

Lexy, exuding approval of her father, said, "I'll go ask Val to assign someone to Tuzhel and see what she has for me next."

Garen started after Lexy. Rimon stopped him with a hand on his shoulder and held the Gen's eyes as he said, "You've raised a fine son, Garen. BanSha was the key that turned Tuzhel around. Your son will make a wonderful channel for this Fort. Go tell Lexy that, and see she gets some rest."

Garen beamed. "BanSha will be a big help once he changes over. His mother would have been proud." He took off after Lexy double-time.

Rimon turned back to Bruce, starting his apology again. "Look, I never meant to shut you...."

"No, it was my fault," replied Bruce with a shake of his head. He explained to Solamar as if Rimon were not right there, "Delri and I have been working together almost since his changeover. I just...." he shrugged, "well something's going on and Delri's not talking to me."

Solamar offered, "I'm sure Rimon will fill you in on everything that's been happening."

"Rimon certainly would," said Rimon, "if Rimon had the least idea what *has* been happening!"

Bruce laughed and explained to Solamar, "Strange, mysterious and unprecedented things always happen around Delri, Aipen...Aipensha and Lexy." He took another deep breath. "Even Clire. Every once in a while the events are just new skills arriving accidentally." He turned to Rimon with a sigh. "I miss Aipensha but Lexy is nearly mad with grief. Poor Garen. You don't want my nager spreading doom and gloom as well as annoyance all over the place."

Rimon had no answer for that. His own behavior had edged into the unconscionable and here his Companion, his dearest friend, was making excuses for him. Gens often did that. He met Solamar's gaze, exchanged Sime-to-Sime shrugs and Bruce chuckled.

At the end of the hall, a cart came squeaking into view, steaming lovely food aromas into the early morning air. Rimon, despite Need clamping down on his guts, found that he was hungry. *No, Bruce is hungry. I could eat.*

BanSha and one of the older girls named Bekka stopped the cart and began distributing trays to the patients still bed bound. Bekka was a sturdy child with brown hair and eyes and a soft gentle smile, always ready to help.

Rimon said, "Bruce, you're hungry. And Solamar, you're on shift now while I'm supposed to go rest." As he spoke another channel and her Companion came down the hall toward them with purposeful strides. "Isn't that one of your Tanhara channels?" asked Rimon, reminding himself he had a lot of people he had to get to know.

"Yes. I'll brief her on Sian and Tuzhel's progress and then see what Val has on the schedule for me, probably Collectorium duty this morning, Dispensary this afternoon."

Solamar strode toward the channel Rimon didn't know, grateful to escape. Rimon could zlin the fatigue Solamar was hiding well. He was keenly aware that he'd surprised Solamar by actually taking a transfer from him, even if it had been only half the selyn a renSime would demand. *Maybe I shouldn't have done that.*

But it had worked beyond Rimon's wildest hopes. Tuzhel wanted to join the Fort now. Later, when disjunction became arduous, it might be a different story.

"Come on, Bruce, I'll answer your questions over breakfast." He nerved himself up to telling his Companion about seeing ghosts and then imagining Solamar. Everyone knew Rimon's father Zeth had died ranting insanely about ghosts. Bruce would never look at him the same again. *It has to be done,* he told himself grimly.

He paused to offer a few words of praise to BanSha and zlin the boy carefully for signs of Changeover. There was nothing yet, so he led Bruce downstairs and out through the channels' on-duty sleeping quarters. They grabbed cloaks from the stand by the door, and using the exit at the far end of the wing, they made the short dash across the open in howling winds and blinding snow.

They entered the Dining Hall through the hot, steamy and bustling kitchen. Running around the clock, they served breakfast, dinner, snacks all the time.

As soon as they settled at a table in the corner of the dining hall, Benart came over with an armload of reports, chattering at top speed.

Inventories had been completed, and though they had a good selyn supply, they were going to run short of food before spring crops came in. Water and sanitation was already a problem but progress had been made on the latrines despite the snow.

Parties had been out cutting new logs for the larger wall, as well as firewood. Every hearth was now ablaze against the intense chill that had set in, yet most rooms were cold. Some of the new post holes had been dug before the heavy snow arrived. During the blizzard, the carpenters focused on carving new nails and bolts from the hardest woods, training the older children in the art. Wool they had intended to trade was being spun for winter cloaks, gloves, socks and blankets.

Space was a very serious problem. You could not keep so many renSimes packed so close to so many Gens without expecting an incident at some point.

Management decisions would have to be made, and enforced, and that meant a duly elected Council.

"Xanon has been talking to his Fort Butte followers," said Benart glumly. "You'd have thought that your healing Sian after Xanon gave up on him would count for something. Sian is going to walk again, isn't he?"

Rimon speared Bruce with a glare. "That remains to be seen. He's definitely recovering. He clearly wasn't as badly injured as it first seemed, as usual with nerve injuries."

Benart raised his eyebrows at Bruce.

Bruce said, "We'll see better tomorrow, but I think he's going to be able to weave again."

"May take some retraining, possibly some rebuilding of the looms, but I do expect he'll be able to weave if not walk, and might still be able to play the shiltpron," said Rimon. He thought it would come out better than that. *I have no idea what I did or how!*

Now it would be hours, maybe days until he could corner Solamar and get some answers, if the Fort Tanhara channel even had any answers.

"Well, Delri, even with Sian improving, the Butte people are listening to Xanon and talking to everyone. They even have some Fort Unity and Fort Veritt people agreeing. Now Xanon is saying that because you are such a good channel, you think you're good at everything and can tell everyone what to do about everything.

"Lots of people are assuming the food shortfall means we can't all survive, so this Fort has to decide how to deploy our resources. They don't trust Fort Rimon people to make decisions because we think you, Lexy and...well you two should have the final say. So they want a new Council without any of us, or our Church of the Unity people, on it. The Unity folks are behind you like a solid wall no matter which Fort they come from. But there's no Church left in Butte, hasn't been for a generation."

Bruce said, "I don't like this "Butte People" "Unity People,"

"Veritt People" versus "us." We can't survive in factions."

Rimon nodded. "True, but we will survive. I don't know why Xanon can't see that while the other Forts have failed, Fort Rimon has not only survived, but prospered. We're strained right now with the influx of all these people, but we were on track to manage the winter just fine until Tanhara arrived."

Rimon knew he had made a fateful error when he let a judgment call come down to a vote, a political decision about whether a fact was true or not. *You can't vote on facts.* If Clire had gotten the transfer he'd wanted her to have, when he wanted her to have it, she wouldn't have Killed during that raid. With her, their chances of surviving would have been excellent. "What's Garen saying? Clire is carrying his child." *Not mine. It won't be mine.*

"Garen hasn't been talking," laughed Benart. "He's been working with Lexy until he's cross-eyed tired." He shifted his attention to Bruce. "...and you know how a Companion is when working. They never say a word, don't even acknowledge your presence. You'd think they were part of the furniture without personality or opinion!"

Bruce passed a hand over his face and hung his head at this characterization. "It isn't an easy job you know!"

"He's just teasing," said Rimon. "Eat your stew. You still have dessert to finish." Rimon had eaten his fill of the beans, grains and roots in a few bites and was picking at a cracker, trying to look busy.

"Bruce is probably just as tired as Garen," said Benart. "Garen fell asleep in his soup right at this very table last night and Lexy had to wake him and find someplace for him to sleep."

Bruce said, "He's avoiding grieving, avoiding even thinking about Clire. He never wanted to get her pregnant, knowing how Farris women die in childbirth. He's in love with Clire, even now she's junct if not dead."

Rimon said, "He is, and Clire was falling for him." Garen had been all she talked about the one night Rimon was with her. "Clire's child is the only Farris of the next generation, so far."

"If she's still alive," said Bruce.

"There hasn't been any word?"

"Search party blew in an hour ago," reported Benart. "There's a major blizzard coming. They said they went as far as Shifron and zlinned her in the town. So she's there, a prisoner. Is there still time to save her baby?"

"Maybe." Wind howled. The storm had closed in, keeping the sky dark at dawn. "We have to get her back first. She knows she's going to die. I don't know what she feels about the baby, but she's got to be hating me."

"As soon as the storm's over, we'll send a team to bring her back," said Benart. "I've got volunteers already and Jhiti's sorting them."

The dining hall's outer door opened and a dozen snow crusted Simes left shovels and stomped into the entry, apparently one last work party that finally gave up digging the new latrine pits. It took two of them to push the outer door shut again while the others stood picks and shovels against the wall in the entry and pulled open the inner door to the dining hall.

For a few seconds, both inner and outer doors were open. The cold air blasted all the way to Rimon's corner and Bruce shivered, rippling the ambient with powerful Gen discomfort. Rimon joined with several other channels scattered through the huge room to blend the ambient nager around the newcomers and smooth out the goosebumps propagating through the ambient.

One of the workers noticed Rimon handling the fields and approached. He said respectfully to Rimon, "Jhiti wants you up on the walls." He gestured toward the stables. "They've zlinned something on top of the east ridge, and they don't know what to make of it."

"On my way," answered Rimon, rising as he flicked a tentacle at Bruce in a *stay* gesture, explaining, "It's cold outside and that's a long way to zlin. Eat."

On the way out the front door, he grabbed another cloak off the public hooks and pulled it tight as he slogged across the knee deep drifts to the stair near the stables.

There wasn't a Gen out here now, which made it hard to zlin anything. He almost crashed into the well housing. Even the donkey was off duty.

Zlinning to his left, he noted the school and all the family houses were filled with three times the number of people they were built for. They even had people housed in the factory building to his right. Ahead of him the stables held twenty people crowded among the animals.

It was too early in the year for such a storm, which boded ill for winter. They had to build more housing, and that meant building the new wall. He had rebuilt Fort Rimon in four different locations and knew what a mistake it was to put residences at the perimeter. They would have to build a bigger underground shelter and drill everyone in how to get to their combat stations. He, himself, would have to follow the rules next time, no matter what.

Jhiti zlinned him coming and sent two renSimes down kicking snow off the steps and holding out hands to help him up the icy treads until he could reach the guide rope.

He climbed to the walk, following Jhiti to the vantage point. "Delri, you're tired."

"We all are. There'll be time to rest come winter."

"I guess. Brisk fall weather, wouldn't you say?"

Rimon chuckled. "Should we consider moving?"

"Not again! We've got too much invested here."

"I wasn't serious!" protested Rimon fighting the wind's efforts to sweep him off the catwalk.

"I should hope not!"

Jhiti had helped rebuild Fort Rimon every time. If they hadn't moved so far into the mountains, the other Forts would have found them faster. More refugees would have survived.

"Delri, when was the last time you slept?"

"I got a couple hours yesterday. Bruce takes good care of me."

"Glad you didn't bring him out here," said Jhiti as he brought them around to face due east across the valley. He had to hold the hood on his cloak closed until he got his back to the wind. "I'm going to rotate shifts in one hour increments all night. It's just too cold."

"Good. Even half-hour shifts for those not used to these storms. Are there enough dry socks and gloves?"

"Zedros is still hobbling around from his leg wound, but he's got people working round the clock in the laundry."

Rimon had delivered the young renSime at his birth and watched Zedros grow into a fine manager. "So where is this mystery you want investigated?"

"Zlin Fremir Peak. Now follow the ridge down to the pass. If someone was coming through that pass when the storm closed, think where they'd camp? Zlin there. Am I imagining ghosts?"

It was a long way to zlin without a Gen anywhere out there and Rimon wasn't deep enough into Need yet to make it easy. "Give me some space, and I'll see."

The renSime backed off a few steps and focused his attention on his patrols, his back to Rimon.

Rimon closed his eyes, and went hyperconscious, letting go of all his physical senses to zlin the far distance. He made out the ragged side of Fremir Peak and knew how the pass snaked around it. With imagination he traced the path a traveler would follow through known landmarks and came to the shadow of a shadow that Jhiti had spotted.

The renSime had zlinned this only because there was nothing in the valley except the livestock huddled under the snow and some trees, plants and wild animals that didn't have a perceptible selyn signature. On the mountains edging the valley there was no life, except...*whatever that is.*

There was something there. Rimon studied the haze until it resolved for him. Then he studied it some more.

He scuffed over to Jhiti and reported, "Just a haze of selyn fields blurring around some boulders. I make it three renSimes, in bad shape, very low on selyn. No Gens. Maybe a horse or two. I don't think they're very healthy."

"Raiders?"

Rimon thought about that hard. He shrugged.

"Juncts from the town?"

"Why would they be coming down into the valley now?"

"Going up, out of the valley? Last refugees from Shifron?"

"Possible." He zlinned the distance again. "What I'm zlinning would also be consistent with three renSimes freezing to death."

"We don't have any scouts out to the east. All our own are accounted for, unless Tanhara had sent someone on ahead of them, or after missing livestock?"

Rimon decided. "Outfit a rescue party, but arm them well." He fended off suspicion he was zlinning the advance scouts of another failed Fort wandering in search of the mythical Fort Rimon. Or worse, the totality of the survivors. "I'll check with Solamar and Benart to see if any Tanhara are missing. In any event, even if they are Raiders or town juncts, we have to help."

"Six renSimes, ice climbing gear, food, bandages, dry socks. What else?"

"A channel. They're likely in Need. If they're injured, maybe a channel can heal them enough to get them down off that mountain. Send a sledge. Horses can wait at the foot of the trail. Get everyone back here before dark."

"You'd hardly know it was daytime out here now. I'll see if Val can spare someone who could work without a Companion, or should we take a Gen?"

Rimon pondered. "Volunteer Gen. Tell Val to consult Solamar if she requires a channel's judgment."

Jhiti took off around the catwalk calling to his guards, sending someone to break out a sledge. They hadn't been used yet this year, so it would take some preparation.

Rimon made his way down the stairs. They had guide ropes rigged all the way to the bottom now. He only slipped twice. He collected Bruce, talked to Benart, found Solamar in the Collectorium taking donations from Gens. There were no Tanhara unaccounted for. Rimon sent a messenger to Jhiti then let Bruce order him to sleep.

He would have taken that opportunity to tell Bruce about his ghosts, but Bruce fell asleep, fully dressed, sprawled across Rimon's bed. So he covered the Gen with two thick quilts and stretched out on the settee with a wool blanket and fell asleep zlinning his Companion. He didn't have a single Need nightmare, and was too exhausted for any other kind.

Around noon, feeling much refreshed, he left Bruce snoring and went back to his office.

He didn't know the Tanhara renSime he found sitting at his desk juggling assignments with Val's efficiency. Bekka, a cobbler's apprentice, and BanSha who couldn't get enough of hanging around channels, were cleaning up the litter from a meal. Channels and Companions were streaming in and out checking Val's assignment board and ironing out details with the man replacing Val.

On the board, he saw that Solamar was working Dispensary and Lexy was off shift. They would have to prepare some infirmary rooms for the rescue party. He studied the board and listened until he had a sense of what was going on then told Val's stand-in, "I'll work Collectorium for two hours, then check Sian and Tuzhel."

The man looked up, blinked and recognized, "Rimon Farris? Ah...." He scrambled through the slates on his desk looking for a note.

A familiar voice roared, "He just said what?"

A smaller voice answered, "He just told the scheduler what he would do, never asked, just told."

The room filled with Xanon's thinly feigned astonishment. The channel plowed into Rimon's already full office. "You should be ashamed," he proclaimed.

Rimon turned from the scheduler. The room full of channels, Companions, children, and messengers froze into nageric ice.

"For knowing my job?" asked Rimon.

The man at Rimon's desk thrust a slate at Rimon.

Xanon scolded, "For sending your own daughter into terrible danger for no good reason and without any authorization."

"My daughter?"

The man at Rimon's desk pushed the slate into Rimon's hand. "Lexy went with the rescue party. Read it."

Rimon suppressed his astonishment keeping the ambient level. He read the slate. It was a note from Lexy. "Dad. Sian's almost fully recovered. Tuzhel's spirits are high. All the other cases are under control, and I just did an hour in Collectorium. Besides, we don't have another channel on duty who could do three transfers in rapid succession and heal frostbite and who knows what else at the same time without hours in recovery. So I'm going with Jhiti to fetch those renSimes. Val isn't upset. Lexy."

Without letting his alarm show, Rimon asked Val's stand-in, "Did Garen go with her?"

"Yes. Jhiti wanted Garen and Lexy wouldn't let him go alone."

That makes sense! thought Rimon as he breathed a gentle sigh of relief. To Xanon he said, "What danger? Garen's with her, and he's the best mountaineer we have, Sime or Gen." Rimon couldn't count the number of times Garen and Jhiti had saved Lexy's adventurous butt when they were growing up.

Very coldly, Xanon enunciated, "A responsible leader does not send his best people out into a blizzard for no good reason! A responsible leader most certainly does not do such a thing without consulting those he's responsible to. You had no right to make that decision alone."

The sentiment in the room was equally divided. Those who agreed with Xanon were horrified at Rimon. Those who had confidence in Rimon's judgment were equally horrified at Xanon.

Xanon whirled and directed his outrage at those who disagreed with him. Rimon worked to keep the ambient level. Half the channels in the room pitched in to help him. The other half were too upset to think of helping.

The Tanhara renSime behind Rimon's desk stood and said, "Xanon, how can you possibly think Rimon would send any of us out in this blizzard for *no good reason?* Farrises really can zlin that accurately, and they don't lie to us about what they zlin. Sian's healed because of Rimon's ability, and Tuzhel will disjunct. If Rimon says there are three renSimes stranded out there, then there are, so Jhiti and Lexy will bring them in."

"And maybe they're juncts!" retorted Xanon, aware he was losing his audience.

"So maybe they are!" said the renSime. "But that doesn't mean they aren't people!"

"That's not the point," grated Xanon. He turned to the room at large. "The point is who has the authority to risk our lives? If we are at risk, we should be represented in the decision. We can't have just one person making all our decisions. Sending out a rescue party, attracting possibly hostile attention! That's a Council decision."

Val's stand-in said, "By then the poor people would freeze to death. You want that on your conscience? I certainly don't. When it comes to acting on what a Farris can zlin that nobody else can, the Farris must have full authority. Rimon wouldn't do anything to jeopardize Fort Rimon! Everyone he sent was a volunteer, including Lexy."

Someone near the door turned and left. Someone else followed. Next to Val's schedule board, one of the Fort Veritt men said, "Xanon, give it up. The Farrises really can do things you can't. Let them get on with their jobs, and me with mine!" He led an exodus.

More people arrived to check the board. Rimon turned to the renSime behind his desk. "Thank you for the eloquent defense! What is your name?"

"Dakin. I've always worked in scheduling for Tanhara, but I don't know most of these people. If you have a minute, I could use some advice."

"There are a people here that I don't know either."

They spent the next half hour sorting out Rimon, Unity and Veritt transfer schedules. Rimon was surprised how much he did know about the Unity and Veritt channels, and somewhat distressed by how his mind pigeon-holed all the people here by which Fort they had come from. When Val came on shift, everything was in order and she was delighted with her new assistant.

She glanced at the board and told Rimon, "Well, you'd better get to work if you're going to get all that done before Lexy gets back with three more patients. Maybe tomorrow you can have your office back."

"We'll be ready," promised Rimon. He just wasn't sure he wanted his office back. The way Xanon was talking, every decision would be challenged until they got this new Fort Council elected.

He put in an afternoon's work, in the Collectorium taking selyn donations from the Gens, in the Dispensary giving transfers to the renSimes. When Bruce turned up, the work went faster and easier. Rimon double checked the last of the patients and sent them home, though where they'd sleep nobody knew. After that he only had a few people coming in to have infections treated.

Rimon spent an hour with Sian. The weaver seemed to have recovered use of his left arm, and was only a little unsteady on his feet and effusively grateful.

Rimon sent Sian home to his family leaving Tuzhel the only resident at this end of the hall. Two partially disabled patients who couldn't rejoin the labor crews were teaching the Raider proper Simelan vocabulary and showing him how a renSime could adjust to the normal Need cycle.

Outside, the storm abated and the cramped bustle of the over-crowded Fort picked up. Inside, the channels' workload subsided to normal, and below normal. It was one of the few times in his memory when Fort Rimon had both enough selyn and enough channels to handle the work. It was disconcertingly abnormal.

At sundown, he left Bruce eating with his Gen friends and a group of Tanhara Gens and went to the east wall to zlin for Lexy. He climbed to the catwalk.

Oberin, Jhiti's second in command of security, welcomed

Rimon and pointed at Fremir peak. She said, "I can't zlin that far, but we haven't seen anything coming back over the snow all day. With all that white, they should be visible."

A shaft of sunlight pierced the heavy black clouds casting a rosette path along the snow, but there was no sign of the rescue party. Rimon paced a ways apart and zlinned the distant pass.

He distinguished the horses, a renSime waiting with them, and beyond halfway up the mountainside, at a camping spot he knew well, Lexy and Garen were clear.

Around them the renSimes who had to be Jhiti's guards were almost unzlinnable in contrast to Garen.

As he watched, a group of renSimes separated from Garen, moving down the trail so slowly they had to be carrying survivors.

Rimon told Oberin, "I think they're just now starting back. It'll be midnight or later by the time they get here. Keep your shift changes rapid as it gets colder, and now that the snow's stopped, expect another Freebander Raid. You can tell Val I said to adjust the transfer schedules around your guard schedule. The Watch is going to be critical for a while yet. Keep a squad ready to go out and protect them as they come in, or just go help if necessary."

"With enough people, I can do that. Only problem is, my guards have been assigned to digging. That will be starting again tonight. We have to clear this snow, build fires to soften the ground, and start on those post holes again. The Raiders won't attack a group of just renSimes, so we only have to worry about Lexy and Garen."

"I zlinned a lot of hatred in that band that attacked us. They weren't just looking for Kills. They wanted to destroy us, maybe take this Fort as their winter quarters since they destroyed Shifron so thoroughly." Arrows, particularly fire-arrows were not Raider weapons for good reason.

Oberin nodded. "That's what Jhiti said, too."

"The guards on duty have to be ready to fight efficiently at a moment's notice. I treated more than fourteen cases of frostbite today. I don't want to see any more. Send them in to change their socks and gloves as frequently as you can. Be sure they get some hot food between stints digging and sentry duty on the walls."

"Fourteen cases? Jhiti will be livid."

"Yes, he will."

Oberin zlinned her guards, already thinking hard. "I'll send a runner for you when they get close."

Satisfied he'd gotten his message across, worried about Lexy and their late night return, Rimon went back inside to socialize with the new channels, surprised at how disappointed he was when Solamar wasn't there. Even more grimly disappointing though was the way the dining hall was peopled by small groups separated by Fort of origin.

At last, he spotted a group of channels from Unity and Veritt huddled over hot trin tea and biscuits with a group born in Fort Rimon. They were near one of the blazing hearths that barely took the chill off the large room. That chill was emanating nagerically from the cold Gens.

That made Oberin's problem with stoic guards clearer to Rimon. The chill felt by the Gens, even inside the thick log walls and with hearths blazing, prevented most renSime guards on the walls from distinguishing the sensation of their own distress from nageric echo in the Fort's ambient.

He brought his trin tea to the channels' table and tossed the topic of ignored frostbite out to the group. Then he watched as they spun plans for dealing with the more severe winter to come. He learned more about the new individuals in an hour than he had since they'd arrived.

By the time he left the dining hall he was filled with renewed optimism about their chances of surviving. They had a superlative channeling team here. All they had to do was pull the renSimes and Gens together and the Fort would hum. Planning to discuss that with Lexy the moment she got back, he pushed to get their office space reorganized.

About midnight, Bruce came into Rimon's office where a

crew was moving Val's scheduling operation back to her room, which Rimon had cleared of injured Gens.

"Benart told me to tell you they might have the school operating at least part time using the dining hall. If we can get the children onto a normal schedule, everyone will be more productive. Oh, and Oberin wants you on the wall."

Rimon looked at the chaos around him. "Can't do anything until this is cleared out anyway." He headed for the door, felt Bruce's protest. "All right, come along. But change your socks, and grab gloves and a stocking cap."

Rimon was almost three days past Turnover, aching with Need which had Bruce's selyn production rate rising steeply. Chill carried on that Gen field, broadcast over the Fort from up on the walls, would be felt by every renSime. On the other hand, Bruce's anxiety as he waited inside, not knowing what was happening would be worse.

Bruce caught up with Rimon on the catwalk at the eastern edge of the Fort. Rimon put his arm around his friend's shoulders and enveloped them both in a firm nageric field. "She's not with them," he whispered, absorbing the Gen's shock. "Neither is Garen."

When Bruce's nager had leveled out, he let go and stepped aside. "Let me zlin."

Oberin took Bruce aside and distracted him while Rimon observed the snow covered fields.

The vast, flat expanse of drifted snow was lit by the moon shining through a crack in the clouds creating a ribbon of bluish light across the snow. The river made a flat, white ribbon on rippled white meandering down the valley.

Lexy and Garen were zlinnable, camped up on the trail through the pass, surrounded by an indistinct haze of renSimes. He knew the moment she zlinned him zlinning her across that expanse.

Well over halfway to the Fort, the sledge entered the shaft of moonlight, the renSime driver concentrating on zlinning the path invisible beneath the snow.

In the sledge, Rimon zlinned three renSimes. It seemed that Lexy had given each a good transfer, but Rimon was sure they were far from well. Without any detail at this distance, he was guessing, but knowing Lexy, he was sure.

A squad of Oberin's guards departed by the small door beside the gates. Rimon swept the surrounding valley, paying careful attention to the direction of Shifron, and found it all deserted except for the huddled livestock.

Rimon reported to Oberin and Bruce. "Jhiti is not with them."

Oberin sent word around the Fort's walls, but no one had to be reminded to keep their attention on the quarter they were guarding, rather than on the approaching sledge.

In time, the big gates were swung open to admit the sledge and horsemen, and the well practiced Fort Rimon welcoming committee went into action.

Rimon and Bruce took charge of the three strange renSimes, clearly non-juncts, Fort renSimes. The sledge and horses were swept away into the barn and the guards sent inside to warm up. In minutes, with the three strangers all talking at once, they had them installed in the infirmary rooms that Rimon had prepared.

They were scouts for the last survivors of Fort Hope now camped four days' ride east with search parties out in every direction searching for Fort Rimon.

Once that was clear, Rimon and Bruce locked gazes, knowing what Lexy planned. She and Jhiti were going after the rest of Fort Hope. As one, they set aside the frisson of alarm, the reflexive if unwarranted fear for Lexy's life, and went to work on the three patients she'd sent them.

CHAPTER SEVEN
FORT HOPE

One of the renSimes had a cracked bone in his right leg. The other had been badly clawed in a close fight with a bobcat, though his laterals were intact. The third was frostbitten and exhibiting symptoms of exposure.

The three took turns relating their story as they were carried to the infirmary. "It happened at the top of the last rise before the pass, just where you can zlin a trail under the snow," said the woman who had been clawed. "I knew that had to be the trail to Fort Rimon. The bobcat knocked Haben there," she indicated the man with the broken leg, "off his horse. Came at us out of the rocks. I went for it with my knife, but my hands were too cold and I lost my grip. Kreg threw his cloak over the beast's head, and we finally broke its neck."

She indicated the frostbitten renSime who added self-deprecatingly, "Stupid thing to do, but it worked."

"Sort of," corrected Haben, easing his broken leg as they maneuvered the three stretchers through the door into the infirmary hall. "Then we were stuck. Lost one horse to the cat's attack. It ran off the cliff. Kreg got us over the crest, away from the bobcat and dead horse, and made camp. Only, we were stuck. Kimra was unconscious and good as dead until Lexy came. I thought Kreg was dead the way his nager collapsed. Never zlinned anything so good as that Farris nager coming at us!"

Kimra was still weak from loss of blood. Haben, immobilized by pain, had lost blood too, and Rimon was concerned that Kreg's immune system seemed inactive. Gangrene was a real possibility there. Yet Lexy had done her usual superlative job so almost any channel in the Fort could have finished the work.

As they were about to separate the three renSimes, Kimra stopped Rimon. "Thank you for your help but we have to ask more. Lexy and Jhiti have taken our horses. With what they can retrieve from the horse that went over the cliff, they can make it to the camp. They've just got to have help bringing all the wagons, cows, horses, mules, sheep, dogs, children, pregnant women, sick, injured, wounded here. With this weather, I'm afraid of what they'll find in camp."

Rimon asked the one question he really didn't want to know the answer to. "How many people?"

"Two hundred sixty three counting the children if nobody's died since we left."

No way. There was just no place to put them. He turned, took a deep breath and called Oberin who had stepped in to give the stretcher bearers new orders. When she arrived at his side, he relayed what the scouts had said. Fort Hope was short on warm clothing, channels, Companions, but had broken wagons laden with excess food. Within minutes Oberin was organizing a series of parties to ride out and establish a chain of supply dumps and by dawn teams with wheelwrights, all their gear, and a few channel and Companion volunteers, moved out.

Oddly enough, it took until late into the afternoon, after most of the hubbub of departures had subsided, for the main explosion to begin.

Rimon was treating four frostbite cases at once, three guards he had brought to Kreg's room for efficiency. He was restoring circulation, cleaning out dead cells and triggering their immune systems in five minute rotations with Bruce coming along behind him, stimulating the renSime systems. They all sat with the frostbitten limb immersed in bowls of tepid water that BanSha refreshed at intervals. They joked about absurd scenes that might occur with the overcrowding after Fort Hope's arrival.

Rimon felt Xanon approaching but barely had time to pull out of the healing functional before Xanon broke into the room without regard for the fields, "There you are, hiding from the consequences of your actions!"

"Hiding?" asked Rimon whose field when coupled to Bruce's dominated the entire Fort for those who could zlin. Even when he was in a well insulated infirmary room like this one, he knew most of the channels could find him.

"I'm here to take over this treatment room from you. You're wanted by the new Fort Council. You have once again placed us all at insane risk without due process."

The two Fort Rimon renSimes and one Fort Unity renSime Rimon was treating began to object, but Rimon forestalled their outburst with a flick of his nager. The new Fort Hope patient was shocked.

"What Council?" asked Rimon.

"The one preparing to hold elections," answered Xanon. "Not that you ever pay any attention to what the people of this Fort are doing."

Bruce stepped in front of Xanon, field reflecting like polished walnut, cutting the lesser channel off from the renSimes. "The people of this Fort consist of the remnants of six, almost seven, failed Forts and the membership of one very successful Fort. The policies that have failed are not likely to be adopted by the owners of *this* Fort."

It was way past time someone had pointed that out, but Rimon hadn't wanted it to be Bruce or himself, and certainly not in public. "Xanon," said Rimon quietly, "Bruce didn't really mean that."

The Unity renSime said, "If Bruce hadn't said it, I would have. Rimon's leadership and judgment have spelled success for Fort Rimon beyond what any of the rest of us have achieved. You can't argue with that."

Bruce moved to let the two channels zlin each other.

Kreg said, "Speaking for Fort Hope, though nobody's authorized me to, I'd say it's enough he's a Farris. We did fine until we lost our last Farris channel in childbirth."

Xanon's cold stare made Kreg fall silent, nager very still. Xanon snapped to Rimon, "Ten minutes in your office," spun on his heel and marched out of the room, letting the door stand ajar behind him. Rimon scrambled to contain the turbulence in the ambient.

Two breaths later, Kreg ventured, "I guess things are a bit... complicated here?"

The Unity renSime observed, "They wouldn't be without Xanon. I don't know what's wrong with him."

"He's scared," offered Rimon. "He'll gain confidence as he develops as a channel. It's just that he won't accept tutelage from anyone yet, though I hoped he'd learn from Bruce."

Bruce flashed a glance at Rimon, then fixed his attention harmlessly on his own toes. "Sorry. I wasn't thinking how Xanon felt. A lot of people must be just as scared, just as determined to regain control in their lives."

"I started off wrong with him," admitted Rimon. "Maybe Solamar will get through where I haven't."

From the door Solamar said, "I doubt that. Xanon has already gathered that I trust your judgment and considers that a fatal flaw in my judgment."

Rimon shrugged. "One of us has to get through to him. You here to take this over?"

"No. Val has me in Dispensary in a few minutes. I dropped by your office to see if we could talk, but it was full of very upset people. Very full."

"Yes, exactly. Well." Rimon waved Solamar off with one tentacle. "Go on then. Val's madly juggling the schedule around the channels who went to rescue Fort Hope. She has to accommodate the new people Lexy will bring back." Rimon had counted on time to talk to Solamar.

"Lexy will be fine, Rimon. She did the right thing."

"I know. I knew that before I knew why she did it."

Solamar went to find Kahleen and get to work while Rimon did one more round of therapy on his frostbite victims. Then he sent Bruce to tell Val to send someone to finish up and check on Kimra and Haben so he could talk to this ad hoc Fort Council full of very upset people.

"Meet me in my office," added Rimon, "once you've got the schedule straight with Val. Remind her I'm due for Collectorium soon. Getting a Council elected will be good. Channeling staff has no business coordinating work crews."

His office was too crowded, even with the excess furniture gone. Xanon sat behind Rimon's desk.

All the other seats were full. There was even a Gen perched on the corner of his desk. Others stood.

Except for himself, there was no one from Fort Rimon. He barely knew them by name, though their medical histories rose from memory as he zlinned each nager in turn.

Rimon lifted control of the fields from Xanon, the only other channel in the room, and approached his desk chair. Xanon vacated the seat to stand beside the desk straining not to let his showfield betray his resentment.

Rimon sat and looked up at the crowd. Six renSimes and five Gens formed Xanon's appointed Council. None were master craftsmen, proven managers, or the sort of wise elders Fort Rimon generally put onto the Fort Council. No survivors of the old Council. None who had sat on Fort Rimon's Council in the past. They were all looking at him with grim distaste.

"Good," smiled Rimon into the ambient. "When will the election be held?"

The stunned silence quieted the ambient.

"We thought you would object," said one Gen. She was a general donor, not a Companion to a channel. Rimon had taken selyn from her on occasion. He knew her medical history and was sure he'd think of her name in a moment.

"But why? Organizing an election is a task that must be done, but nobody has had time. I'm glad you've banded together to take the initiative."

"You aren't going to tell us we should be out logging for the new wall?" It was a renSime at the rear. Rimon hadn't given the man transfer, but recalled seeing him in the Dispensary waiting room. He had a disk in his back that shouldn't be stressed so Rimon had told Benart not to schedule him for logging duty.

"Why?" asked Rimon. "Aren't you doing useful work right here?" He let the ambient reflect his trust.

Someone asked, "You *want* a new Council elected?"

"Of course. How soon can we get the polling done? We'll have to do it in two shifts I think. The dining hall won't hold everyone at once and you can bet everyone will want to air their opinions before the vote. Can we can start tonight, then let the day crew vote at breakfast?"

"That soon?" muttered someone on the side.

Rimon projected a disconcerted bewilderment. "Solamar said you've been in here for a while. Haven't you figured out a schedule yet?"

Xanon, striving to hide his discomfort at losing control of the new Council, tried to wrest the ambient from Rimon. Rimon paused, then glanced at him as if just noticing his bid for attention. He favored the channel with a smile. Making sure every renSime in the room noticed, he relinquished the ambient to Xanon.

Xanon couldn't handle the conflicting fields, so he ignored the increasing nageric chaos he'd created and said, "There will be a new and duly elected Fort Council when this Council decides to hold the election. What we want to know from you is will you ignore that elected Council? Or will you acknowledge its authority."

"We?" asked Rimon. "You're on this Council?"

Caught, Xanon had to backpedal. "Of course not. I'm channeling staff."

Rimon nodded, "Me, too." He let the chaos in the room continue to worsen while Xanon made a few clumsy swipes at organizing the fields again. "I don't generally have much occasion to interact with the Council. Here in Fort Rimon, the Council has always kept things running smoothly so the channeling staff didn't have to pay much attention." He looked at the people in the room. "Isn't that usually the way a Fort operates?"

General agreement disrupted the ambient.

In fact, in Fort Rimon, the Council usually consulted Rimon so their plans didn't disrupt selyn delivery.

Xanon still couldn't bring the fields together and it was getting on the renSimes' nerves.

Treating Xanon like a First Year channel just learning his craft, Rimon gently corrected the fields into a coherent ambient nager again without lifting them from Xanon's control. He clasped his hands and twined his tentacles, and smiled up at Xanon.

Xanon said, "We are taking precious time from our other duties to organize this Council because you, once again, took it upon yourself to implement decisions that belong to the Council and the residents of the Fort."

Rimon let the fields deteriorate again under Xanon's fumbling control and observed the far from unanimous agreement among this Council. Xanon's unhappiness with that response was clear to Rimon but not the renSimes.

Rimon addressed the Council. "We have an excess of channeling staff and more than adequate selyn supply, but can't make it to spring harvest on current food stocks.

"The Fort Hope people have a shortage of channeling staff and extra food they can't move because of broken wagons. Would this Council have voted against sending all the aid we could to over two hundred people also dedicated to the non-junct life? Even if they didn't have the food we'll require, could this Council vote to leave them to die in the harsh mountain winter without the proper gear?"

Despite Xanon's efforts the ambient shattered. Bruce opened the door as everyone spoke at once. The accusations leveled at Xanon interested Rimon more than the renSime reaction to Bruce slicing neatly into the nageric chaos.

As Bruce worked his way through the crowd to Rimon's side, Rimon learned that Xanon hadn't told them all the facts about the people they were about to take in. Xanon shouted for silence as Bruce arrived at the ideal spot to help Rimon contain the chaos.

Rimon blended Bruce's throbbing, ever rising Gen field into his own showfield, and very delicately worked Xanon's grip on the fields so that order once again emerged despite all the disagreements flying.

With nageric peace came an audible order. Finally one voice emerged. "Rimon, tell us truthfully. Did you know all that when you sent Lexy out there?"

"I didn't send Lexy," said Rimon. "She and Garen decided to go without consulting me."

Xanon accused, "She didn't consult anyone."

"Which is as it should be," agreed Rimon. "I found out later she went up on the wall to zlin for herself and found that after I'd evaluated the situation, one of the renSimes had gone nearly comatose from hypothermia. She realized they had to have a channel, and since we had the excess staff to cover everything, she went with Garen. It's what I would have done in her place, so why should she have done anything else?"

"If I've heard it once, I've heard it ten thousand times," said one of the Gens. "The Farrises are the most important channels we have. Why risk one when anyone else could have done the job?"

"What risk?" asked Rimon. He added what Xanon had failed to tell them. "Garen is our best mountaineer. I wouldn't risk Jhiti in this weather without Garen. Garen has spent most of his life in two mountain Forts growing up with Lexy who has never lacked an adventurous spirit. If she goes anywhere with him, I know she's as safe as she'd be in the Fort. Anyone from Fort Rimon could recount many tales as proof." *Far too many for a father's comfort.*

Once again Rimon showed Xanon how to organize the fields into a coherent ambient and left him in charge of the room again. He could barely contain his astonished delight when Xanon held the pattern longer this time.

Unfortunately for Xanon though, the renSimes in the room

couldn't fail to notice the lessons. It was coming clear to them why Rimon and not Xanon was in charge here.

One of the renSimes summarized, "So you unilaterally ordered the Fort Guard out to rescue three strangers, who might have been Raiders. Later Lexy just decided on her own to go, but now the channeling staff administration agrees?"

Xanon added, "The Guard is not under your command."

"No, the Guard is not under my *command*," agreed Rimon blandly. "I did not *order* the Guard out. Jhiti called me to *consult* because he knows I can zlin all the way to Fremir Peak on a quiet night. I reported what I'd zlinned. Jhiti, who *is* in command of the Fort Guard, listened, then assembled an appropriate unit to go to the rescue."

Everyone was talking at once. Again that was not what Xanon had told them. A Gen near the front said, "You can zlin all the way to Fremir Peak? I don't believe it."

One of the renSimes who had been zlinning Rimon's field management lessons said, "I believe it. Turned out to be just what he and Lexy said would be there, three renSimes in bad shape."

Rimon corrected Xanon's grip on the fields, a little more subtly this time, leaving the other channel to do more of the work. "So can we elect a Council tonight?"

Bruce startled, then steadied, but that threw Xanon's tenuous grip on the fields awry. Rimon helped him again and left him to manage alone. Bruce said, "Benart has too much to do to run an election now."

Rimon captured the attention of the renSime who had been studying the field management lesson. He was probably the steadiest, maybe the smartest one in the room. He seemed the sort of person who ought to be managing projects. Finally, he remembered the man's name. "Alind. Since Benart doesn't have time to organize the elections, would you take charge and get this done? Just ask around. Anyone can tell you where the election supplies are stored and how we usually staff the committee."

Rimon stood up and summoned Alind up to his place. "You

can use my office. I've got Collectorium duty." Rimon gathered Bruce with a wave of one tentacle and, giving the fields one more correction, left Xanon in charge. At the door, he turned and added brightly, "Thank you, Xanon. You've been very helpful."

As Rimon expected, it didn't take Alind long to discover how complicated Council elections would be. There were arguments over increasing the number of Councilors to eleven from the usual seven. There were objections to holding the election before all the Fort Hope people settled in and debate on holding a seat for them.

The election soon became the central topic over even Lexy's adventures bringing in the Fort Hope refugees, and Benart's adventures contriving to house them.

Nobody had yet proposed replacing Benart, Sian, Val or Jhiti and Oberin. As a result, the foundation for the new wall, an irrigation trench bringing water from the river up to the base of the hill, and the new latrines all progressed at a breakneck pace. Food, laundry, new knitted woolens, and channeling services ran smoothly, even though people argued about the Council situation while they worked.

The weather held, but the cold deepened. Rimon spent much of his off time pacing the catwalk around the walls, watching people work, fretting about their frostbite exposure, evaluating health and level of exhaustion, watching the older working children for signs of changeover, and zlinning toward Fremir Peak.

As he circled the walls, he saw the first logs being raised to mark the anchor points for the new wall, and piles of material marking where new houses would be built.

He rationed himself to one full circuit of the walls in the morning and one at night. Before descending from his vigil, he would stop, close his eyes, and dream about how the whole compound would look when the new walls were up and new housing built all around the new perimeter.

The plan called for dismantling the old wall and moving those logs out to the new wall, adding what new logs were necessary. To do it quickly took planning. Their experts had to range far into the western hills edging the valley, and up beyond the cemetery to get the logs.

With growing Need, Rimon had no patience for the detailed reports on his desk, so he spent more time on the walls. Around noon, eight days after Lexy and Jhiti had left, Rimon was on the walls zlinning Fremir Pass when he was rewarded with the appearance of two of Jhiti's guards.

Rimon was waiting with Oberin when the returning Guards brought word that another pair from their squad were a day behind them. Jhiti wanted two more guards to start out from Fort Rimon with answers to the messages these carried, creating a constant contact with the Fort Hope camp.

Lexy's messages asked for more clothing to be sent with the next dispatch. The rescue party, she reported, could repair all of the Fort Hope wagons and mount them on sled rails instead of wheels. All the wagons Rimon had sent after her had arrived intact.

With each new pair of guards arriving, Rimon got personal messages from Lexy of breathless reassurances that all was well and she was making good friends among the beleaguered channeling staff of Fort Hope.

Late in the evening, the day after Alind managed to hold the elections, filling all the eleven seats with Xanon's choices, Rimon was working Collectorium. Trying not to think about Lexy, he chatted with each of the Gens who came to donate selyn. Bruce worked the conversations with him, relaxing the Gen. It was how he had always kept up on the Fort's affairs, but now he took extra time with each donor he didn't know, discussing the Fort and what they felt would make them happy here.

His Companion would often disagree with him, argue to draw the donor out and let them see Rimon alter his opinions when new facts appeared. The two of them did the same with the renSimes they served in the Dispensary.

He and Bruce often enjoyed these conversations so much

they referred to working Collectorium as "resting."

Just before midnight, Rimon was taking selyn donations from the kitchen staff early shift and discussing the shortage of crockery and soap that would result when Fort Hope arrived while Bruce was napping in a corner. His Companion's field was so high, and so comfortably peaceful, Rimon felt relaxed despite encroaching Need.

He had just finished carefully siphoning off the donor's excess selyn when a Gen stopped outside the door, attention penetrating the thick wood with calm urgency.

"Come in!" called Rimon waking Bruce. The kitchen worker left as the Gen entered. It was Rushi, the young Companion Solamar had been training. Val had been using her as a midwife, broadening her training.

"Rimon. Bruce, Iriela is in labor."

The infirmary's most insulated, stone-walled rooms were used for births, so Rimon wasn't surprised he hadn't noticed. He grabbed for his cloak moving toward the door. Over his shoulder, Rimon asked Rushi, "You told Val?"

"Yes, she told me where you were working," she answered taking off after Rimon and Bruce

Together they crossed the narrow space between buildings, tossed their cloaks on the pegs by the door and went to the birthing chamber. Rushi went to Val's office.

The birthing room was a cheerily decorated, triangular space at the outside corner of the building, windowless except for a few vents near the top of the wall. It was supplied with two blazing hearths, and cabinets filled with supplies. The split log walls were faced inside and out with mortared river rocks arranged in swirling patterns.

The stone insulation swathed the room in a nageric peace disturbed only by the occasional nageric shriek of tissue forced to stretch beyond endurance. When a Gen was giving birth, all the stone wainscoting was required.

Today, Iriela's renSime nager, paled by the severe selyn draw of the fetus, barely touched the stone walls. Iriela walked leaning on Maigrey, who was still serving as Xanon's Companion. Today, though, Maigrey led Iriela around the worn track in the carpet. At least Xanon was not there, berating Maigrey for her every move.

Bruce went right to his daughter, keeping his attention on Rimon to shield her from his very ripe Companion's nager. He enfolded her in his love and his arms. Maigrey stepped back to allow Bruce to hug his daughter.

All Rimon's ultra-composed, always-ready-to-work, never-failing-in-pinpoint-concentration, Companion could do at the moment was mutter, "Rella, Rella, Rella, Iriela my wonder," while his nager filled the room with whirls of anticipation and immense respect. Rimon clamped down on the ambient. She needed this from her father right now more than she needed selyn.

The Gen was so confident of Rimon's skills he wasn't considering the danger the next few hours posed for his daughter. But then Rella herself had been one of Del Rimon's successes. Rimon felt his primary field and his showfield align perfectly under his best friend's fatuous joy.

He angled aside to zlin Iriela's condition. They had given her extra selyn just the previous evening, but her baby would be a channel and was already taxing her system for more selyn. She would be all right for a little longer.

While he was devising his strategy for this birth, Rushi came in with Iriela's husband Fengal, and Fengal's Companion, Aislinn.

Bruce turned with a great welcoming hug of joy for his son-in-law, a channel of considerable accomplishments but nowhere near Bruce's level. "Fengal! See, Rimon was right. We're going to meet our new boy in a few hours."

Fengal hugged him back. "I never argue with Rimon. He's always right."

The door opened again and Bruce's wife, Dayyel sidled into the overcrowded room. She was a Gen who'd been raised among Simes, but not a Companion. Her presence barely rippled the ambient, but it did complicate the fields.

Before Bruce's ever growing and searingly joyful nager could crush poor Fengal's control despite everything Aislinn could do, Rimon intervened. "We could use some working space here."

Maigrey put Iriela into the tilted chair beside the birthing couch and prepared to leave.

Rimon stopped her with a tentacle gesture while he said to Iriela's mother, "Dayyel, I know you just got word and want to stay and support Rella, but...."

"Say no more," assured Dayyel. "Rella, just do what Rimon says like we talked about yesterday."

Iriela started to answer, but drew breath as another contraction clamped down. Bruce stepped toward her, but Rimon caught him with a tentacle. "Bruce, go take care of Dayyel and your family until I call you. Guard the corridor. Maigrey, you work with me for a few hours so Bruce can do the grandfather's job in peace."

Bruce got the message even if most of the others in the room didn't. Their transfer was just too close now, so Bruce was too high field to be of use to his renSime daughter, especially when he was constantly blowing the fields to smithereens with spikes of joy while she was fighting what felt like death.

Bruce scooped his wife and son-in-law out of the room, saying "Fengal, you and Aislinn can find something to occupy Xanon while Maigrey does my job for me."

Rushi led the way out cheerfully remanding her patient to the channel for delivery and everyone trooped after her ready to start partying.

Suddenly the room was empty except for Rimon, Maigrey and Iriela. As the door closed Rimon brought his whole attention to focus on Iriela.

Maigrey, Iriela's lifelong friend, wanted to hold her hand and mop her forehead, but Rimon gestured her back to her Companion's duties. She couldn't do much for Rimon, but she was in better emotional shape than Bruce and much lower field so she wasn't raising Iriela's Need.

Rimon took the channel's stool next to Iriela and brought her contractions under his control, smoothing out here, balancing the muscular effort, encouraging selyn to flow there, examining for bleeding.

Then he captured her attention and directed her mind away from the effort her body was making. It was her first child, but she had been thoroughly prepared. Though she'd only been in labor for a few hours, her waters had broken and she was dilating easily. *This is going to be fast.*

Maigrey hitched herself up onto the tall stool behind the chair and focused on Rimon, firm, supportive, confident.

For Rimon it was all in his showfield. Inside he just wasn't all that sure. Outside the Forts, for a renSime or most Gens to give birth to a channel usually resulted in the mother's death because, unlike Gens and renSimes, channels drew huge amounts of selyn from the mother at birth.

No other children had a clue about whether they would become Sime or Gen at maturity. But channels knew their destiny. Certainly, Iriela's boy was going to be a terrific channel if his selyn draw was any indication.

Rimon's secondary selyn system was replete from his recent stint in the Collectorium. But would he be fast and smooth enough to get this much selyn into a renSime without the selyn energy burning her? Bruce's daughter.

During the hours that followed, he reviewed his successes and his failures. His own father hadn't been able to teach him much. He'd invented most of it by trial and error. Every time he fed Iriela more selyn, not transfer but just providing a sustained trickle of selyn, he worried.

Iriela's confidence grew as his waned. By the time they had her installed on the birthing couch, her upper body and arms strapped down so she couldn't move to try to satisfy any sudden spikes of true Need, Rimon knew this baby would need more selyn than his mother's renSime nerves could carry in the moments before birth.

This child had a top Companion for a grandfather and a

channel for a father. He would be a very strong channel, if he lived. Rimon knew he would have to get his tentacles onto the fetus before birth and infuse selyn into the child directly without burning the mother. He also knew all the times that technique had failed with renSime women.

"Maigrey, you've done a splendid job here. Now you're starting to tire. Go get Bruce for me."

Maigrey stepped back, wearily sweeping her attention away from Rimon.

"Go on," said Iriela. "Father would want to be...." The rest was taken by a low, open throated grunt that turned to a moaning groan.

"And send Rushi in," added Rimon.

Moments later Bruce and Rushi replaced Maigrey who very reluctantly closed the door behind them. Bruce's whole family was waiting in that hall.

Rimon briefed Bruce in clipped tones and half sentences. His Companion wrapped Rimon in his solid field. Rushi didn't have enough of a field to penetrate Bruce's nager, and Iriela was a selyn depleted renSime with her baby a pinpoint of concentrated selyn at her center.

Rimon had long since educated Iriela on what would happen if he had to use this procedure. She threw her head back gasping, "Do it, Delri. I'm fi...." and again her words dissolved into a groaning push.

Rimon cleansed his hands and tentacles in the basin Rushi provided, then worked his hands up around the baby's head. He felt his laterals slide through the hot blood and mucus, finally contact the baby's skin. He closed his eyes and focused wholly on his Sime senses.

Bruce's hold on him was so strong, he felt as if his body and all his Need with it were separated from his work with the fields now. He found the contact points, and met the baby's Need with a diffuse cloud of selyn, soaking the mucous with the energy of life.

The mother's body was consuming selyn voraciously,

bleeding selyn and blood, pluming gouts of selyn out with every contraction, burning selyn at augmented rates in the huge muscular contractions.

Thrashing wildly against the restraints, unconscious of her actions as her body went deep into selyn Attrition, Iriela was drawing selyn out of her own baby as Rimon infused the fetus with the energy of life. It wasn't enough selyn for her and her draw was burning the fetus's nervous system. He hadn't expected her to be able to reverse the normal birthing selyn flow. Sometimes a channel would Kill her unborn child to save herself, but not a renSime.

As the contraction eased into death, he withdrew his hands and, moved up to grab Iriela's forearms in a transfer grip, making the fifth contact lip to lip. He drove selyn through the mother's spasm-locked body and into the baby.

Iriela's heart started again, and the final contraction began. The baby's selyn draw peaked. Rimon felt the baby then, as he often felt his patients, not just as a body madly sucking selyn out of his secondary system, but a whole person wanting to live.

He fell into a rhythm, feeding first one then the other. He lost touch with the outside world, zlinning only the inward selyn flows.

* * * * * * *

He was standing before an odd brick edifice, radiating a powerful heat. He was a large, muscular Gen male in the prime of life. He knew metal was melting inside this huge furnace, and he knew this batch would come out to be the purest steel seen in a thousand years.

But even more exciting than that, he anticipated his wife's surge of glee after their next transfer. He was Companion to the most wonderful channel who ever lived, whose determination and unfailing optimism had rebuilt his House and the junct town around them. This new steel he was making would give her an invulnerable feeling and she would make all their dreams come true.

* * * * * * *

Delri! Delri, come back.

"I'm not going anywhere." Delri said to his father while he strained for the memory of steel making. The concept was so powerful, filled with solutions to problems, exquisitely simple and marvelously complex at once.

You are here and now. It is the child who will be then, long, long from now. You are not the child and you are not to be who the child will become. You are Del Rimon Farris. You are the hope for that future to be, but you must save this child in this now.

* * * * * * *

He was standing in a small, comfortably appointed house, gazing out at a lovely, neat row of houses. The area was surrounded with a high wall. It was a Fort, but like no other he had seen. The small houses were surrounded by whitewashed fences and neat rows of whitewashed stones. There were chickens, dogs, children, and a flock of geese. These strange people had lived there longer than he'd been alive, but they had welcomed him.

In this warm, welcoming living room, he was struggling to demonstrate a channel's functional to another channel. Delri recognized what he was trying to do, but also that the effort was crude and clumsy, badly executed. The other channel could not follow his field manipulation, no matter how patiently and slowly he repeated it.

"Rimon," said an elderly renSime who was watching them, "you can do this. I know you can. It is part of God's plan for us. You will not let us down."

And he knew he was Rimon Farris. He was himself, and he was his own grandfather, all at the same time.

* * * * * * *

"Rimon!" It was Solamar Grant, speaking silently in his mind again. *"Come back to the present now. Iriela Needs you. Her child is coming. Now, Rimon!*

Rimon fought the nightmare sensation, struggled to detach himself from Grant's attention and squirmed away, twisting and turning, and coming up in the dimly lit room, a few hours before dawn, safely in Fort Rimon's birthing chamber, firmly protected by Bruce's rock steady field.

As his awareness surfaced, he dismantled his transfer grip on Iriela. Bruce's grip relaxed in a vast, trembling relief. Quickly, he edged Rushi aside and moved to receive the baby, laving the half-born infant with an abundance of selyn. His mind, though, was somewhere in the distant past. Or was it the future? Nothing made any sense. Bruce encouraged Iriela to push now, push hard, just once more.

The squirming, slippery infant lay safe, alive in the cradle of Rimon's hands and tentacles. With one tentacle, he cleared the newborn's air passages, and with two others he encouraged him to start breathing.

He swaddled the baby in the warmed blanket Rushi handed him. He tucked the little body up on the mother's stomach to await the afterbirth. Iriela had barely caught her breath by the time Rimon finished the well practiced move.

Then Bruce and his daughter were gasping and laughing. Bruce's nageric spike of relief and happiness penetrated even the massive shielding of this room, and Maigrey and the whole family crowded in before the afterbirth was cleared.

Their pure joy vibrated the walls, rumbled through the earth, shook the distant tombstones in the cemetery, stirring Rimon's ghosts, thrashed through the trees, and Rimon saw the grape arbor spring into full bloom in seconds.

Bruce looked at him oddly. This was not a moment Rimon could bear to spoil for his Companion. He drew his showfield tight around himself, and gave everyone a warm, happy smile that was perfectly genuine.

"Rushi, you finish up. No complications evident at all with the afterbirth. Iriela, you and Fengal have a fine, strapping healthy baby boy to raise into a channel this Fort will love. What's his name to be?"

"We told you," said Fengal, doing his best to help Rimon work the fields in the overcrowded room. "He'll be Wade, after Bruce's great-grandfather."

Rimon couldn't imagine how he'd forgotten. This was to be the family's long planned tribute to Bruce's family's out-Territory origin. Only it seemed wrong somehow. This boy should have a name starting with an S.

"Good, I'll tell Benart to enter him in our Record," he said, looking at his hands. "After I clean up, that is."

Rushi started for another basin of water and soap laid by for this purpose, but Maigrey opened the door for him, and they watched him flee the scene with vast puzzlement. Their bewilderment grew when he sternly gestured Bruce back into the room and kicked the door shut behind him.

It happened again. And this time he wasn't seeing ghosts, he was becoming ghosts and returning convinced he was someone other than himself. *I have to tell Bruce, but not now. Oh, not now. Let him have this moment.*

He went about his duties for the rest of that morning, trying to drown the memory in more urgent affairs, trying to convince himself he could perform any channel's functional and not drift off into some insane vision.

When Bruce tried to join him, Rimon waved him off to attend his family. They would talk soon enough. That awful confession would preempt Bruce's happiness.

Rimon worked until noon, then took one of his now habitual breaks to pace the walls and zlin Fremir Pass. First, he spent a few minutes watching the younger children playing in the yard. They were supervised by adults from different Forts; the children were mixed too. The youngest were marching and chanting a vocabulary song, spelling out difficult words. Another group was playing the popular ring-toss game called *Zeor*. You'd never know they were from different Forts.

Then he spotted the third pair of guards to arrive. They carried a long report from Lexy. It was only two days before Rimon's scheduled transfer, and his concentration was not what it should have been. He read the report three times before he understood it.

Lexy detailed what had happened to Fort Hope, most of which everyone knew from the scouts' story. After the last of Fort Hope's Farris channels had died, a series of decisions went wrong and a harvest came in very short. In desperation, they had sent a party to trade with the out-Territory Gens, relatives of Simes who had arrived at Fort Hope after changing over out-Territory. Traditionally, the Forts had always kept ties with Gen towns across the borders near them. This time, that policy had backfired.

A nearby Sime town had housed a garrison of Licensed Raiders, Sime government sanctioned troops that harvested Gens out-Territory. Licensed Raiders carefully limited their take of Gens to avoid depleting the local supply or triggering a Gen army action against the Territory.

The Licensed Raiders got word of Fort Hope's illegally trading in their hunting ground and organized an all out attack on the Fort, razed all the buildings, murdered a third of the Simes and carried off a few dozen Gens. The ones who were not Companions would eventually make Choice Kills to be sold at auction.

The survivors set out for Fort Rimon, expecting to acquire another Farris channel, and re-found their Fort in a safer place. Only Fort Rimon was no longer where it should be. It had moved.

Following directions the locals gave them, they had to destroy some diseased horses, fight off Freebanders, and survive a tornado. They found another abandoned Fort, but there they lost people to a fever.

Setting off following yet more vague advice, they encountered some out-Territory Gen merchants who had strayed across the border with four wagons loaded with corn, oats, wheat and beans. Suddenly they found themselves in a pitched battle.

The Gens, not realizing they were in Sime Territory, not comprehending that Simes could truly intend to help them find their way back to Gen Territory, turned on the Fort Hope people as if they were Raiders and fought to the death. The last three of the Gens raced their horses over a cliff instead of risking being Killed by marauder Simes.

The battle did so much damage to the Fort's wagons and horses, that, figuring they had to be very close to their goal, they cached most of their own food supplies as well as all that survived on the Gens' wagons, in a cave and continued searching for Fort Rimon.

When the trail petered out, the terrain provided no clue to where a group might settle, and there were no more towns. So they camped and sent scouts in every direction looking for clues to where Fort Rimon might be. Then the early winter storm hit the open camp with devastating force.

All of that confirmed what the scouts had told everyone, but Lexy had made a new decision.

Since the Fort was already short of food, and the Fort Hope people had a large number of Gens who would have to be fed through spring, it was imperative to bring in that cached food from the cave before winter closed in. The Fort Hope people were from the southern plains and had no idea what the mountain winter would be like, or how long it would be until a crop could be brought in.

Lexy was sending the majority of the Fort Hope members, starting with the most injured or disabled, to Fort Rimon along the trail established by Jhiti's Guard detail. Those who could ride would be mounted, and a few wagons would be used for the injured and the Fort's possessions.

The empty wagons would go with Lexy, Garen, Jhiti, his Guard troop, and some Fort Hope renSimes, to where they had cached the food. It might take a couple of weeks, but they'd bring the food that Fort Rimon now had to have.

Moving wagons over the ice crusted snow would be slow, maybe impossible over the Fremir Pass. Lexy asked Rimon to send help to get the people over the pass even if the wagons had to wait for spring to be brought over.

This time there was nothing in Lexy's letter except business, everything from details on patients she was sending him to an inventory of skills and resources that Fort Hope was bringing them. Her plan was a good one. She was doing exactly as he'd have done in her place.

It never occurred to him to share Lexy's report with the newly elected Council before showing it to Oberin who took immediate action.

Hours after Oberin's guards were dispatched, Xanon, Alind and several others stormed into Rimon's office bursting with outrage. "You had no right to authorize this scheme of Lexy's!" roared Alind, head of the new Council.

But it was Xanon whose outrage filled Rimon's office. "...and certainly not to withhold her report until we heard about it from that Raider you're trying to educate."

"I didn't authorize anything, and he's not a Raider anymore. Tuzhel has chosen disjunction," corrected Rimon.

Alind insisted, "You shouldn't have replied. That was for the Council to do, and we've voted against her idiotic scheme. There's too much risk of getting snowed in way off there. We can't risk her that way."

Everyone's afraid, Rimon summoned patience. "She wasn't waiting for authorization. By the time my reply gets to her, Lexy will be on her way back with the wagon loads of food. The guard carrying my reply will take four more days to get back to the camp, then several more days along Hope's backtrail before she reaches Lexy."

They wasted another hour of Rimon's time berating him for not handing the message over to the Council immediately, then tried to take the report away with them.

Rimon argued that it contained the details on the patients who would arrive starting possibly as early as tomorrow. He wanted channeling staff to read it.

After he let them all read the message, even Xanon could see his point. Alind went to order Oberin not to show messages to Rimon anymore, but to bring them directly to the Council.

It was almost midnight by the time Rimon had finished briefing and mobilizing the channeling staff to receive patients. Oberin reported that the advance party of Fort Hope had topped the pass on foot. Fort Rimon wagons were waiting for their sick and wounded at the bottom of the trail down from the pass with people there to help.

Benart had the redeployment of resources well in hand, though they were desperately short of blankets and winter clothing. Rimon had contributed the blankets from his bed and taken down the old quilt from the wall over the bed. It was as warm as three blankets and would do until they could make more. All over the Fort, other people were taking down treasured old quilts and loaning out blankets. They would all manage.

Once again, Rimon found himself pacing the catwalk around the walls, noting the progress of the incoming refugees. Having memorized Lexy's message, he was distantly aware he was obsessing on Lexy because he missed Aipensha. *Because I'm afraid.*

He knew after his next transfer with Bruce, he'd have to cope with a surge of grief such as he hadn't experienced since his wife had died. He could feel that welling bubble of agonizing, lonely grief lurking deep inside him, but walled away by the insistent pounding of growing Need.

At my age, he thought morosely, *I should be used to Need walling me away from my feelings. Only I'm not.* The moment his transfer was over, all that deferred emotion would sweep through him. He knew it would happen, and he also knew he'd be utterly surprised by it. He always was, and this time would probably be the worst of a lifetime. *Postsyndrome,* he thought, *isn't always filled with grief. So why are the grievings the ones I remember so clearly?*

He faced the grim truth. He was old. He'd lived a full life, loved a fine woman passionately, shared fabulous Postsyndrome times with her, had wonderful children who fulfilled all his wildest expectations, avoided terrible disasters, saved many, many lives, worked with one of the greatest Companions who ever lived, and enjoyed grand good health...until now.

But he was old. Too old to be leading the rescue Lexy was leading. Too old to fight every day and all night too. He wanted rest, security, grandchildren like Bruce's. He wanted to sit back and enjoy the Fort he'd built, and rebuilt so many times. And what was he getting? His mind was deteriorating like his father's had. There was a good reason people didn't trust him with their lives anymore.

Intellectually, he knew that was just Need talking. Need left any Sime depressed, anxious, short tempered, a walking gloom factory haunted by nightmares and without appetite for anything except selyn.

Need aside, he also knew he was losing his mind. He had to tell Bruce. Soon. Lexy had to take over. She knew it already. She was out there doing his job.

Aipensha!

The surge of grief had none of the piercing, shattering stridency he knew would come after transfer. That it could reach him now showed just how bad this was going to be. He had to talk to Bruce and he only had two days to do it. He'd put it off now for eleven days and he was out of time.

That was made abundantly clear by the incident this morning at Wade's birth. He didn't want to think about what had happened. *I have to tell Bruce. I have to.*

At this very moment, his Companion, nagerically the brightest Gen in the Fort, was clearly zlinnable in the dining hall with his wife, children, cousins, in-laws, celebrating the birth while Rimon paced the wall. Bruce hadn't had much good time with his family since Clire arrived with the Fort Intalace survivors and Fort Butte right behind them. The Gen deserved his celebration.

He could zlin Bruce so clearly from where he was that he

really didn't feel abandoned by his Companion. Their selyn fields were locked in step. His subconscious felt secure. He had no personal or professional reason to interrupt the festivities.

Bruce's family didn't deserve to have this time spoiled by his self-pitying gloom and he just didn't have the necessary will to go in there and pretend to the joy he knew he would feel...one day soon.

Everyone in this Fort has a grief riding them, he told himself. *I delivered Bruce's grandchild this morning. I should be happy.*

Disgusted with himself, Rimon turned away from zlinning Fremir pass and deliberately walked around the wall to stand facing the cemetery, rubbing his own nose in how many other people had losses to mourn.

In the cloudy, cold, moonless dark, the cemetery was black on black shadow. The livestock had all been rounded up and fenced into shelters, the hen house enlarged.

Currently, the nightshift workers were digging post holes on the opposite side of the Fort, and the loggers were working way out beyond the cemetery. Behind him, inside the Fort, the factory was bustling. The wainwright was building more wagons, Sian was at his loom turning out fine wool cloth for underwear while his weavers made blankets.

The school building was inhabited by families, some three and four families to a school room, but the section of the building dedicated to laundry had three smoking chimneys. Laundry had become a round the clock endeavor.

Rimon faced outwards toward the cemetery and the logging crews far up in the hills behind the cemetery. He zlinned the hills cupping the cemetery like a treasure, yielding up the tallest trees of the hardest woods.

Will we all be buried in that cemetery? Will any of this ever have meaning?

Before his eyes, the dark grew misty, smeared with dizzy whirls, then lightened.

* * * * * * *

He faced a huge amphitheater with rows of seats stretching to the sky and beyond, more people than could ever be alive in the world at once.

He was standing behind a lectern holding a strangely bound book open in one hand. He saw Lexy, Aipensha, Benart, Garath, Bruce, his wife, his father, all his family and more he didn't know how he knew.

Behind him were arrayed a huge collection of great magical lanterns illuminating brightly colored, shining objects with what could only be selyn fields. *Lanterns can't do that.* Except... these did.

There was the symbol Slina, the legendary Pen Keeper who had befriended Fort Freedom, had woven into the quilt she'd made for Delri when he was born.

He recognized the rock upon which the names of the martyrs of Fort Freedom had been inscribed, crumbled and broken but still familiar.

He knew he was not on Earth.

He knew he was about to declare Rimon Farris's dream fully realized. He knew the long hard journey would finish not in triumph but in a success so absolute it wasn't recognizable as success. Nobody here had ever zlinned or met a junct.

He swallowed hard and began, as he somehow knew that thousands of parents for thousands of generations had begun.

>"This is the Ideal of Zeor.
>"This is the Heart of Zeor.
>"This is the Spirit of Zeor.
>"This is the Reality of Zeor."

He opened the great volume he had written with his own hand and began to read in a voice strangely not his own.

CHAPTER EIGHT
CONFESSIONS

"Solamar, where's Rimon?" asked Bruce's wife, Dayyel, as she served honey cake all around.

Solamar started to gesture east where Rimon spent so much time zlinning Fremir Pass, but Rimon wasn't there. Then he found the immense Farris nager, and gestured northwest. "On the wall." Rimon's nager was dimmed, focused outwards.

"Bruce," she said, "why don't you take him some cake. He may not want to eat any, but he'll know we're celebrating because of him."

Bruce was holding his new grandson on his lap, glowing with the joy of it all.

Solamar said, "I was going to go outside anyway, so why don't I take it to him? Kahleen, you should stay and eat. We have late shift tonight." It was long past time he talked with Rimon about what he'd done to the Farris when they forced that transfer into Tuzhel.

Kahleen, her mouth full, answered with a gentle nageric glow of gratitude.

Solamar added, "Meet me at the Dispensary then." He rose, gathered the cake, which Bruce's wife wrapped in a cloth, and tickled the baby under the chin. The answering gurgle captured his heart for all time. *Home. This is home.* It was an astonishing discovery he'd been making three times a day since he arrived.

Solamar wove through the sprawling party, saying hello to those he knew, accepting introductions to those he didn't. There were only a few Tanhara people at this Fort Rimon event, but Solamar was amazed how many of Rimon's people he already knew well.

The happiness in this room is intoxicating. He made it to the back door into the storage area, the exit nearest the building that housed channels' rooms attached to the infirmary. He crossed the narrow alley between buildings, went up past the room he shared with Rimon, on into the infirmary, past Rimon's office and out the door by the new latrine next to the stair closest to Rimon.

That was when he zlinned the anomaly. Well, no, not zlinned exactly. It was another sense entirely perceiving this. Where Rimon had been was only a vast whirling hole of non-energy, a holiday in existence, or a singularity where selyn stood still. It was the impossible made real.

Oh, no! Energized by frantic guilt, Solamar flew up the stair and raced along the narrow catwalk, praying, "No, no, I can't be the cause of this!"

He skidded to a halt and knelt beside the prone form on the walkway, the thick cloak covering the Farris body, selyn frozen in mid-pulse in both the channel's systems. Rimon wasn't dead. The selyn was not dissipating as it would from a corpse, yet not pulsing and circulating as with a living being. For Rimon Farris, time had stopped.

He knew it was an illusion caused by his point of view, but it seemed real. Closing his eyes, shutting down his own Sime senses, Solamar groped for the image of the world around him, limned in shimmering otherlight that was not energy or substance. He found it and the state of mind necessary to follow the thin silvery cable that still led from Rimon's body through the anomaly to where he had gone.

Solamar found himself in a huge amphitheater, filled with people listening to Rimon read. With all his training and experience in the realm of nowhere, Solamar still took far too long to realize Rimon had leaped into his own future self, reborn to a time when mankind spanned the stars.

It'll be all right, Solamar told himself, *if he doesn't remember this.*

Rimon raised his eyes and locked gazes with Solamar, recognition clear. Every other time Rimon had become aware of Solamar's presence in a vision, the Farris had returned skittish and unstrung, obviously remembering it.

Not daring to consider further, Solamar reached out with hands, tentacles and spirit, twisted Rimon's shining tether around his hands and sought his own body, diving through time, space and otherwhere, dragging his disoriented and terrified passenger with him, tumbling, whirling, spinning down and down until he let go and....

"Solamar! Solamar!"

Gasping in a huge lungful of icy air, Solamar pushed himself off Rimon's limp body. Selyn once again pulsed through both the channel's systems. The heart beat.

Bruce skidded along the catwalk shouting, "Solamar!"

Solamar called, "He's all right! Be careful!"

The two renSime guards, approaching from either direction along the catwalk, halted at Solamar's command, and Bruce slid to a stop, breathed, focused and approached with his fields in better order. "What happened?"

"He's coming around. You have to help me get him inside. He's taken a bad chill."

That would not do for an answer, Solamar knew.

At last Rimon gasped and began to struggle upright, projecting panic, terror and a bone shattering cold into the ambient. Solamar waved the renSime guards back and covered with his own showfield as best he could.

Had Rimon not been in Need, he could never have overridden the nageric chaos the Farris was producing.

It only lasted a few moments as Bruce offered a steady field, as if working to offset a psychospatial disorientation, inserting Rimon back to the here and now.

Solamar let himself ride on Bruce's wonderful field too, his head still whirling from the fall into his body.

"What happened?" asked Rimon.

"Let's get you warm first," said Solamar, "then we'll compare notes." They got Rimon to his feet. He was shaking so hard he could barely stand.

They took Rimon to the room they shared in shifts, having BanSha build up the fire and fetch trin tea from the dining hall. They wrapped Rimon in the quilt off the bed, sat him on the edge of the bed and put his feet in a basin of warm water. Solamar was struck by the size of this man. The baby quilt center of the design barely covered both shoulder blades, but with the extension all around the original quilt, it wrapped all the way around him.

All the while the channel shivered and shook, teeth chattering too hard for him to talk. Bruce sat on the floor beside Rimon, massaging his legs. Nobody said the word *frostbite* but Rimon's hands and feet were white, the paleness extending to elbows and knees. The tepid water felt searingly hot to him.

Rimon finished a glass of tea, sighed and stopped shaking. His eyes locked with Solamar's seeking answers to the questions he couldn't ask.

Solamar nodded. "I left the party to bring you some of the luscious cake Dayyel made. When I came out the door of the infirmary I zlinned something wrong with your fields. So I ran up the stairs. I think I dropped the cake somewhere. You were unconscious on the catwalk."

Bruce was doing his best to be part of the furniture, his massive field oozing his own fears for Rimon. "I don't know why I came out too. It was just that I suddenly had to see that you were all right."

"I wasn't," said Rimon hoarsely.

Bruce asked, "I felt...I must have done something wrong. I felt I had to be with you, that maybe you Needed transfer right away. I couldn't sit still. What happened?"

Though he was zlinning his Companion, Rimon's eyes were still locked to Solamar's. "I don't know, but something is wrong with me."

Solamar said into Bruce's sense of horror, "Not wrong but new, a change. Rimon, I've seen things like this before. It can be dangerous, but there are ways to deal with it."

"What is *it*?" demanded Bruce.

Rimon accused, "You are doing *it* to me!"

Solamar dropped his showfield so Rimon could zlin his primary field clearly. "No, I'm not doing it to you. But I did do something to you that started this happening, and I think I know how to help you get control of it."

"And what exactly is *it*?" Bruce demanded again.

"You haven't told him?" asked Solamar.

"Not yet," admitted Rimon. "I meant to."

"Told me what?" fretted Bruce, his staid pose of being a piece of the wall deteriorating. Even the smallest deviation affected both channels harshly because the Gen was replete with selyn, ready for Rimon's transfer.

Solamar kept his attention away from Bruce. "I apologize. I'm very sorry this is happening and I should have said something a lot sooner, but I was hoping it would just subside on its own. Usually it does."

"What is *it*?" insisted Bruce, and this time the insistence was in his nager, filling the room with demand.

Rimon turned his own attention inward, his showfield hardening to impenetrability.

"Rimon has been losing touch with his body."

"What?" asked Bruce.

"That's a good description of what just happened," allowed Rimon, "but it doesn't cover it all. Bruce, I've been seeing ghosts. Like my father did. I saw Aipensha with my father at the funeral. She was out among the trees, standing there with hordes of our dead around her, trying to tell me her death wasn't my fault. Only it was. I led her up out of the underground shelter."

"Ghosts...." repeated Bruce, worried.

"I saw them too," said Solamar. "I didn't know who they were, but I saw and heard just what Rimon did. He was not hallucinating. He is not insane. He is not losing his mind. What happened to him is real. It has happened to other channels who went on to live long healthy lives." *Such as my father. How will I ever be able to tell him what I've done to Rimon Farris?*

Rimon shook his head. "When we were forcing a transfer into Tuzhel in the shelter, I felt my father standing over me, teaching me how to do it. When I was healing Sian, well that was different. You were there too, only you weren't. You said you were asleep, so I must have wakened you by what I did to Sian. But how?

"Then today when Wade was born, it was different. Solamar, I was a Gen doing something with metal, some kind of magic but I understood it! Then my father rebuked me, and I was someone else inventing a healing functional, and then you were there scolding me. I became a ghost, some *time* else! It happened again on the wall only worse, in some far future where there are no juncts at all and you were there too, watching me. What happened!"

He's rambling around in time, the future, our future. He could ruin everything because he remembers more than any untrained wanderer would.

"Rimon, things like this started happening to me during First Year. I was just lucky. I was taught to control it. I can teach you. It doesn't have to be something that happens to you. It can become something you do or not do as you choose."

"How could you have made this happen to me?"

"I don't know. I've never heard of such a thing. On the other hand, I've never done anything like what you and I did on the wall during the battle. Maybe that started it, but when we worked on Tuzhel together in the shelter...."

"My father was there, showing me how to do it. Solamar, my father is dead. But he was there. A ghost. And you were a ghost!"

"I'm alive," protested Solamar.

"I'd have thought so," said Rimon.

Bruce blew the fields. "Rimon, your father...."

Solamar damped the fields. "Bruce, Rimon's not crazy. He's

wrestling with a new perception of the world, like he's learning to zlin."

"I wish I could believe that," Rimon, hugged his quilt around him.

Solamar realized the quilt was a heavy ward. Inside it, Rimon felt safe from his new perception, and that could make him way too bold with it. *What have I done?*

"If it were true, why would you be so afraid of me?"

Solamar's laugh exploded out of him, blowing off the tension. The Farris had misread his nager. "No, Rimon, not afraid of you, afraid for you. And guilty. I've never felt so guilty before. I've got to make things right with you."

At last, Bruce relaxed back into his imitation of the furniture. At the relief, both channels sighed, and Rimon said, "So I am going crazy and you want to save my sanity."

"Not crazy," insisted Solamar. "But exploring this new ability randomly, could be fatal." *Not just for Rimon!*

"I'm not doing it on purpose."

"I can show you how to stay in your body." Usually people worked hard to learn how to step out of their bodies, even for an instant, to prove that the Self isn't the Body. He'd have to reverse the training, re-arrange the sequence in which skills were mastered to turn a wanderer into a wayfarer. He, himself, had never been such a great student, and certainly never a teacher.

"But you don't want to."

Wrong again? "No, I do want to, but Rimon you're so strong, different from other channels, and I'm no expert at what I want to teach you. I can only hope that a clue or two may help you devise your own way of doing this."

Bruce's nager fairly screamed, *doing what??!!*

Solamar elaborated to Bruce, "Staying in his body. During transfer, he could go out there and not know how to get back. A body with no occupant is a corpse."

I shouldn't have said that! thought Solamar, bracing and feeling Rimon bracing a half second before Bruce's reaction filled the room.

Rimon said to Bruce, "I think he's right. This last time, on the wall. I think he's saying it the way it felt, out of my body, and no way to get back. He came after me and brought me back." He shifted to Solamar. "Didn't you?"

"Yes," admitted Solamar, not mentioning that he hadn't done an elegant job of it.

"See, Bruce? He's not going to harm me."

Bruce accepted it into his soul. He had to be feeling the burden of the selyn his body was carrying. His selyn production was locked into step with Rimon's selyn consumption, letting the Farris relax in the confidence that life would be there for him when he had to have it or die.

With Bruce settled again, Rimon asked, "So what do I do to keep it from happening again?"

In a burst of unexpected inspiration, Solamar remembered the belt he'd seen curled up in Rimon's top drawer the first time he'd gone through it looking for socks.

He went to the drawer and rummaged behind the stacks of thick wool socks. The drawer now supplied socks for three large men and a woman who occasionally slept here. He had to unload the drawer before he could extract the belt from where it had drifted to the back corner.

It was a wide strip of polished black leather with a buckle in the form of a Starred Cross expertly carved of dark, satin finished rowan wood. The buckle was set with tiny chips of gemstones and there was a fine line of silver wire embedded inside the folded leather forming the belt.

When he'd found it, that first time he'd slept in this room, he had been astonished. You couldn't see that silver wire, and would barely notice it when zlinning, but Solamar's other senses registered nascent power there. The belt had faded from Solamar's mind among all the other exquisite treasures of Fort Rimon.

Now, as he ran the supple leather through his hands and tentacles, he wondered how he could have dismissed such an article so easily. "This should do the job once you learn how to use it. Where did you get it?"

Rimon shrugged. "I inherited it from my father."

Bruce added, "He always said he had run across a gypsy whose cart horse had died leaving the man stranded with a load of trade goods. He offered the man his pack horse, and was repaid with this belt. Remember Rimon?"

"Yes, and he said that when he objected that the belt was worth far more than a horse, the gypsy just said he should wear it all the time. My father never did. As you can see, it's like new."

Gypsy? Well. Solamar ran the belt through his hands again, twining his fingers through the weave of the belt's design, the five pointed star, fifth point upwards for the human body and spirit welded onto the equal armed cross of Nature. His handling tentacles throbbed with the charge in the jewels kept alive by the pattern of the symbol.

Mentally, he filled in the pattern between the jeweled points. With touch and sight, he traced the symbols and visualized them brightly glowing against the wood.

He couldn't see that glow with his eyes, but he felt it with his handling tentacles, a localized sizzle of power. He smiled, "This should do very nicely, then. Here put it on."

Rimon shucked the quilt spreading it so the odd symbol was squarely in the middle of the bed. Then he pulled on dry clothes and looped the belt around his waist.

Solamar adjusted the buckle to align with Rimon's navel. "There, that should do it. Always wear it like that. Now let me show you how this works. Try the same functional you were doing when feeding the baby selyn this morning. Here, I'll be the unborn fetus."

Warily, Rimon held out his hands to cup the other channel's hands and tentacles and supply a diffuse field gradient as he had with the fetus.

Solamar soaked up the ambient selyn, as a fetus would, and selyn began to move through that protected space. Solamar noted Rimon start to separate from his body, then meet the barrier of the charged Starred Cross bouncing back to align with his physical body.

"I felt something," said Solamar, dismantling the contact. "Didn't you?"

"Yes, but nothing happened."

Solamar grinned. "Exactly what I'd hoped for. Here, now take the belt off and we'll test it this way."

Rimon slipped the belt off, set it on the bed, then repeated the functional. This time, as Rimon got deeply into the functional, his form separated from his physical body and started to move. Solamar stopped soaking up the excess selyn, and grabbed Rimon before he could fall sideways.

Bruce's alarm abated when Rimon's eyes opened and focused on his Companion. Rimon gasped, "That was just like this morning, only you stopped it."

"Now put the belt on and we'll do it again."

Predictably, Rimon wasn't able to leave his body through the charged barrier of the patterned gemstones.

With only a very few repetitions, Rimon gained confidence and Solamar prayed he had done the right thing. Surely, the mere presence of that belt in Rimon's drawer was enough of a hint for anyone with a brain.

By the time Solamar had finished explaining, Rimon had edged back from the conviction that he was losing his mind and regained confidence in his ability to work.

Then they split up, Solamar to meet Kahleen and work as senior channel on duty for the rest of the night. Rimon and Bruce would try for what rest they could get.

No doubt, thought Solamar, *they'll talk all night, and Rimon will grill me on issues I don't want to discuss.*

Sure enough, just before sunrise Rimon showed up, wearing the belt. Bruce followed struggling to stay awake.

Before Rimon could send Solamar and Kahleen to rest, Oberin stuck her head in the door, holding it against a frigid morning wind and yelled, "Solamar! Fort Hope! The first of them almost here. Delri! Get ready."

The first Fort Hope refugees to arrive were the most seriously injured, then came the ill and an assortment of transfer related problems caused by the inadequate channeling staff. Rimon worked tirelessly right up to his scheduled transfer with Bruce.

Then the two of them spent a few hours secluded in one of the best insulated rooms in the infirmary building.

Solamar's only clue that the transfer had gone well, but the Postsyndrome had been devastating was when he saw Rimon in the dining hall afterwards. The Farris's fields were a glory to behold, but his face looked ten years older. Though he'd just had a great transfer, he was shoving his food around on his plate without interest, barely containing the pall of his bereavement.

As more Fort Hope people arrived, Solamar worked the shift opposite Rimon's, crossing paths with him just long enough to brief him on patients. At every opportunity, he asked, "Is the belt still working?"

Rimon always brushed him off with, "Seems to be. Haven't had a problem yet."

"We have to talk," Solamar would insist. "I have more to teach you." And Rimon would shrug that off.

Then Solamar's transfer drew near and Solamar's attention inexorably focused on his own Need and on the unfamiliar Gen who would serve that Need this month.

Kahleen stuck to his side day and night. As he had come to know her better, he trusted her more and more, leaned on her steady field during channeling functions, and came to see the world through her eyes.

Her personality was not like Bruce's. She couldn't play at being a piece of the furniture. She would interject a comment, lose focus on the fields, grin fetchingly and resume. Her field work rarely drifted far enough to affect the job. She was just always interacting with everyone.

She had the same enormous selyn production and deft, sensitive field interaction that Bruce had. When she meshed fields with Solamar, he felt laved in soothing balm. Bruce's touch never did that to him. Kahleen had been Clire's Companion since Clire had arrived from Fort Intalace. Before that she'd been trained by the Farris sisters.

Though Kahleen hadn't known Clire all her life, they had become friends. More, Kahleen had always believed no Farris could ever go junct. Then she'd witnessed Clire's Kill and the death of Aipensha.

Kahleen had been as busy as Solamar, working beyond exhaustion, and even when they had a short respite before Fort Hope had arrived, Kahleen had kept her attention away from her own grief. Solamar knew they both had to face it.

As their first transfer together approached, Solamar began talking to Kahleen about Losa.

He'd known Losa only since he'd arrived in Fort Tanhara, bereft and alone, and more than a little desperate. She had saved his life. She'd had a great husband, three children, and two dogs and a cat. They had welcomed Solamar into their family.

He warned Kahleen, "I'll be inconsolable after transfer."

"Me too. There's no future, only the present."

He nodded. "That's about how I'm looking at things. It's just that I know that's not true. My Companion in Tanhara had two children who have survived. They've been adopted by a Tanhara neighbor. I visited them briefly yesterday. They had children from five Forts crammed into their tiny half room of one small house, playing *Zeor*, a ring toss game someone had carved for them. I relearned a valuable lesson.

"Every time one of them missed a toss, the others would chant, 'Do it again. You'll do better this time.'

"Kahleen, I've been searching for the future for quite a while and missing my target just like."

He plastered a grin onto his face. "Let's 'do it again' and 'do better this time.' Let's find the future together."

She answered with a smile that lit her nager like a beacon. "I'd like that. Clire isn't coming back. This transfer will prove that to me. Then there'll be a future."

"You're such a young, beautiful woman. I've zlinned the

hopeful interest of so many of Fort Rimon's men, but I don't know if you have a steady Postsyndrome partner."

"I doubt I'll be in the mood for sex this time, no matter how good a transfer you take from me."

"I don't have the draw speed or capacity of a Farris."

"I know, and I'm used to the Farrises. Even Clire couldn't Kill me in her current state, if she's even still alive. I'll have more than enough selyn for you."

"You already do," agreed Solamar, wanting that selyn with a proprietary greed. "I understand that in Fort Rimon, transfer partners don't usually form sexual liaisons."

"Oh, but it does happen." She considered him critically. "You're asking me, aren't you?"

"I'm asking if you'd consider it."

"It seemed to me you were becoming more interested in Lexy before she left."

"I had noticed her. She hadn't noticed me."

"She noticed you. Told me so flat out. She'll be back before our next transfer, but you two aren't in phase for your transfers. She wouldn't be interested when you are."

"Is it...." He just didn't know enough of the customs in this Fort. "Would she find it um, awkward if you and I spent a few days together?"

"Oh, I doubt that. And neither would I." She laughed at his relief. "I take it where you come from, people consider sex a matter for exclusivity?"

"Usually," he agreed with some relief, though that had not been the custom in Fort Faraway nor Fort Tanhara.

Her delight with him surfaced. "So let's spend this Postsyndrome together, even if we only cry on each others' shoulders and talk about the lovers we've buried. Maybe next time you can be with Lexy. She'll give you a chance, I'm pretty sure. If not, well, I just might be available next month too." The sadness in that was palpable.

The transfer was better than Solamar had thought it could be. Because she was used to serving channels with such exaggerated speed and sensitivity, he knew he couldn't hurt her, so he just relaxed and let his body do what it would, and was astonished at the increase in his own speed and capacity.

Kahleen was left with a warm glow of satisfaction just as solid as his own. With time, they could become a match.

He knew that come Turnover, he would begin to fear something would happen to snatch this gorgeous new future away from him, but during the first few days post transfer, he was just happy to have found such a Gen. They spent the time together, talking and crying for all those lost.

Solamar had to restrain himself from telling her the whole truth about himself. One day he might, even if she were the only one in Fort Rimon to know it all.

CHAPTER NINE
WINTER INITIATIVES

The day they finished the new wall, Lexy and Garen returned with Jhiti's guards and wagons laden with more than enough food to see them through spring harvest.

Oberin had a detail of guards set up winches and ropes to bring the heavy food wagons over the pass. With all the practice bringing in the rest of Fort Hope, they had wagon hoisting down to a routine.

The rest of the work on the wall had gone just as well. All that remained was to mount the old gates into the new wall. So, as Lexy approached, Rimon stood in the gaping hole where the gates would go waiting to welcome her.

By the time Lexy rode up leading the rest of the contingent, the first of the wagons behind her had reached the valley floor on this side.

Rimon's attention was riveted on his daughter as she approached him, glowing, grinning, and making no effort to mask her condition from anyone who could zlin it.

She fairly bounced out of the saddle and ran to Rimon where he stood in the gateless hole in their wall.

He hugged her tight as they zlinned each other and estimated a little more than two weeks pregnant. "So who's the father?" he asked.

"He's dead, Daddy." She hugged him tighter and trembled as he engulfed them both in a controlled field.

"Cry sweetheart, let it out. I'd have loved him."

She sobbed. Finally, she added, "It was an avalanche. He zlinned it coming and tried to gallop clear, but the horse stumbled, and when he jumped he was swept away. I was too late getting a rope out to him."

"RenSime?"

"Yes. Taller than you. He had a sister who was a Companion. I want this baby so much."

By this time Garen had dismounted and taken up position as Lexy's Companion, watching Rimon absorb this news. Garen noted the growing crowd. "Where's Bruce?"

"In his office trying to catch up. We expect BanSha's change-over soon, though he's showing no signs I can zlin. Bruce is helping Val and Benart make sure all the possible Companions for him have the necessary training."

To Lexy he added, "The Fort Hope people are grand." He gestured at the walls, "They have carpenters, artisans, and foresters, and metal tools we've sorely lacked. Four new houses have already been started. Bekka, Tuzhel and BanSha have organized a *Zeor* tournament among the younger children and it's introduced the Hope families to everyone very quickly. You were right how short they were of channels. We're managing, but we'd looked forward to adding you to the schedule."

"I should have sent a message about the baby, but I just couldn't. It might not...I know the odds, but I loved him and I'm not sorry I'm having his child."

Rimon met Garen's eyes again. "We'll manage that too. Meanwhile, your mission was a great success. The kiln has been working overtime since your message. We should have enough vermin proof jugs for the grain. The Fort Hope people are still camped in tents, but in a few days we'll have more sleeping space. They even have stonemasons. Their craftspeople have survived, and they're doing things we didn't have the skilled people for. We're going to be all right, Lexy, and so is my grand-child."

In that first greeting, he didn't mention the internal strife that had been tearing Fort Rimon to shreds, nor any of the bad news coming back from the scouts watching Shifron.

Lexy's triumph was well celebrated by all of Fort Hope and Fort Rimon's original people plus most of Fort Unity and Fort Veritt. There were enough people at the party that evening that Rimon could reasonably hope Lexy wouldn't notice it was only "most" not "all."

The party had been planned to celebrate hanging the gates, but now it was also in Lexy's honor, both for her bringing in the food and for the hope of her pregnancy.

A large troop of young Church of the Unity children under the direction of Bekka, BanSha and Tuzhel, put on a play depicting the cooperative effort to deconstruct the old wall, move it, and reconstruct it around the larger circumference. Someone had taken detailed notes about every mistake that had been made during the procedure and the children were merciless in recounting every painfully embarrassing moment the adults had suffered.

The older children played the workers while Tuzhel, just four days past his transfer, was in fine form. As the oldest among them, he played Benart, standing to one side with a tablet and calculating how many logs would be required for the larger circumference, conspicuously counting on his fingers and tentacles, schooling his nager to resemble Benart's ponderous solemnity.

The younger children standing together at one side of the stage, shouted at his mistakes, chanted the mathematical formulae, and criticized him for counting on his tentacles because Benart was Gen and didn't have any tentacles. The chorus was taken from the game, *Zeor*. "Do it again. You'll do better this time." The children twirled the tossing rings from the game around their fingers while they sang.

Everyone who had ever played *Zeor* broke up laughing, those not in Need howling hysterically. Rimon found out later that BanSha had written the script and Bekka had done the mathematics under Benart's tutelage.

The celebration was marred for the Fort Hope people by the

news of the death of the father of Lexy's child, but she was welcomed among them like family, receiving tributes to his heroism and hopes for her child.

Sian brought the shiltpron he had been playing obsessively to rehabilitate his left arm for work at his loom. His grim determination to regain full use of that arm and leg had worked, for his playing tonight was flawless and inspired. As he played, his wife sang dirges, remembrances, and uplifting tributes followed by rollicking advice to Lexy on how to care for an infant and still put in a day's work.

Meanwhile, people came and went, nobody staying longer than to warm up and grab a bite to eat. With the full moon two days ago had come a shift in the weather pattern that had held since the first storm. Their experts predicted more storms, and the race was on to get shelters built. The Tanhara and Hope stonemasons worked non-stop, making foundations, hearths and chimneys using unskilled laborers.

Logging crews were ranging far, and even saddle horses were being used to drag logs back for buildings. The draft animals returning with Lexy would be a big help.

Most of the logistics of deploying this labor force was being done by Benart and the few assistants he'd trained working with Val, Dakin and Rimon, to keep the renSimes from using too much selyn at heavy labor. Nobody consulted the argumentative new Council over any decision.

Surrounded by warm, welcoming commiseration, celebration, cheer and the aromas of home, his daughter didn't yet know about the new Council or the strife it had continued to create, nor did he want her to know tonight. Rimon couldn't recall a single constructive accomplishment of the duly elected group. Strife seemed to be their primary product, and that would not do Lexy any good tonight.

Eventually, Benart turned up and circled the room hugging and congratulating, thanking those who had worked so hard to get the new wall up only hours after the old one had come down. Then Jhiti blew in on a gust of icy wind, followed by two women and a man who had to wrestle the outer door shut against rising wind. The man's riding boot was missing a heel. The four of them came in searching for Rimon. That caught Lexy's attention.

A child came out of the kitchen carrying a jug of tea, stopped at the stage to pour for the performers and spoke to Sian. Sian handed his precious shiltpron to one of the Fort Hope channels and headed for Benart.

Jhiti, Benart and Val converged on Rimon. Before they made it across the crowded dining hall, Bruce came in via the kitchen door followed by Kahleen and BanSha. From the front door came Zedros dressed in the coveralls he wore when working in the laundry and still limping from his injury, followed by Tuzhel.

Noting this parade, Dakin the Tanhara scheduler, and then Maigrey excused themselves from their conversations around the room and drifted toward Rimon while all the newcomers sped through their greetings, grabbed some food and made for Rimon's position. Xanon was conspicuously absent from Maigrey's side.

Lexy detached herself from her well wishers and wound through the crowd, working the fields with Rimon in the long practiced manner. Aipensha's absence hung in the pattern they wove. Then from the kitchen door came Solamar, sliding neatly into the third position Aipensha had usually occupied as if he'd trained with them all his life.

The room flowed with warm, ever brightening glee as Solamar felt Lexy working the fields with him.

Everything in Rimon wanted to flee out the front door and climb to the new catwalk. *This will spoil her homecoming. I don't want her stressed like this.*

He shifted a few steps to his right, wrapped his grip around Bruce's fields and took charge of Lexy and Solamar's fields as Rushi, the Tanhara Companion trainee, mounted the stage beside the Fort Hope channel who had the shiltpron. The channel struck up a strange tune but Rushi seemed to know it and began to sing. Within the first three bars of the tune, half the room was up and dancing.

The shiltpron, when played by any Sime created music that could be both heard and felt nagerically. When played by a channel, working with a Companion, the instrument was a powerful nageric amplifier that could damp the Sime's awareness of Need, or sharpen it to an irresistible pitch. In a large group like this it was potentially either therapeutic enjoyment or a major disaster.

This Fort Hope channel had musical skill, and worked smoothly with Rimon and the two other dominant channels in the room to raise the mood. *Maybe that's what Fort Hope is about,* thought Rimon, *hope.*

Jhiti reached Rimon first and stood tapping his toe in time with the dance music, enjoying the ambient. "I called a meeting, Rimon. We all have to talk." The guards who had followed Jhiti in converged through the crowd.

"Lexy hasn't had a minute to rest since she rode in."

"She'd be more upset if she didn't hear this first hand. And I don't think any of those new Councilors will be here. We have to craft a decision."

Now Rimon understood the channel taking the shiltpron, using the artistic field work of the instrument and the mass of dancers to obscure any nageric hint of the secret meeting taking place in the middle of the party.

"New Councilors?" asked Lexy, and by turn as they arrived everyone else filled her in on the growing factionalism threatening to paralyze the Fort building efforts before shelters were completed for the winter.

Tuzhel, joining them last, finished the story with, "And just this morning, Alind told Val not to let me have transfer from Rimon because it would be a waste of Rimon's channeling talent."

"Alind said that?" asked Rimon astonished. *Val won't pay any attention.* He locked eyes with Val and shook his head. She grinned back.

Lexy drew Tuzhel close to her side with one arm, reaching across him to embrace BanSha too while Garen put his arm around her shoulders from the other. She zlinned BanSha no doubt looking for any trace of changeover as she said, "Alind thinks that's what he was elected to do?"

"Lexy," interrupted Rimon. "We'll talk about this Council problem another time. Tuzhel, don't you worry about your transfers. Lexy, Solamar and I will take care of you. You are not a waste of our resources." Privately, Rimon was worried about Tuzhel. If he was skittish about his next transfer now, only four days after his second disjunction transfer, he was headed for trouble.

Jhiti said, "It's this whole Fort's wellbeing that I wanted to talk to you all about." He looked around at the senior management of Fort Rimon, the group of people from which the Council was usually drawn. "I've been talking to Oberin all day, getting updates on what the scouts have been seeing over at Shifron. Then tonight, came this report." He flicked a tentacle at his scouts. "Go on, Kreg, tell them."

Rimon recognized Kreg as one of the first three Fort Hope scouts to arrive, a frostbite case. Now he was walking around in a boot without a heel.

"Tuib Farris," said Kreg, "the Freebanders are raiding out-Territory, have been we think since they took Shifron. As you predicted, they're stockpiling Gens for the winter. We followed a group of them, all in Need, to the border, and waited. They returned not in Need, hauling unconscious Gens slung over horses, with a dozen more Gens walking behind a wagon loaded with grain. Some of the bags leaked leaving a trail we followed. In the bushes near a latrine pit, we found this." He pointed to a folded paper Jhiti held.

Jhiti handed it to Rimon. "Looks like Genlan to me."

"It is," said Rimon, whose training had included the Gen language, but he couldn't decipher the handwriting that appeared to have been written clumsily in blood not ink. *Probably pricked a finger to get the blood, and if so the author is long dead. The selyn disturbance, even from a tiny prick, could trigger Killmode in a Raider.* Rimon handed it to Tuzhel. "Can you read that?"

Tuzhel took the paper and held it up to the light shed by the overhead chandelier. It held smoky tallow candles among the usual beeswax ones. They could be short of candles before spring, too.

A drop of wax fell on the paper like a tear. Tuzhel stepped back from Lexy's shadow. Reading, the young renSime paled, his nager spiraling in on itself. "They're taking us to a town called Thiprin, it says. It's got to mean Shifron. It says their leader is named, I don't know. It's spelled out like it sounds. I think it's the Simelan word Stonedragon like in the working song the stonemasons sing."

That puzzled everyone. Tuzhel continued reading, "Something blurry, and then it says they seem to worship her. Don't try to save us. Burn the woods on the sides of this valley and in spring the floods will drive them out. Be sure to get their outpost too. It's on a hill with a wall, so it could survive a flood." He looked up. "It's signed by my best friend's mother. She was a kind woman who made the best roast goose ever. Was. She's dead, isn't she?"

For several seconds, Solamar, Lexy and Rimon were very busy containing the nageric pulse that statement produced in all of them. The shiltpron and whirling dancers masked it from everyone else in the room.

Rimon agreed, "I'm very sorry, Tuzhel. I wish there were something we could do to save them all."

"I know. Everyone's told me all the stories of what happens to Forts that interfere with the juncts. I guess I know why they hate you so much, don't I?"

"I'd guess you do," agreed Lexy gathering him up against her again. "But if we can survive, one day there won't be any more Kill. No Gen will ever even think to fear a Sime. No Sime will ever crave Gen pain."

Her words echoed the vision Rimon had almost forgotten, of

standing in an amphitheater and reading to more people than anyone could ever imagine gathering all in one place. It was a vision that would one day come true.

Unconsciously, he put one hand on his belt buckle, took a deep breath and focused again on the matter at hand. "But who's this Stonedragon?"

"I don't know," said Tuzhel. "There's always new people, and they give everyone a new name when they join." He looked shyly up at Rimon. "Tuzhel isn't my name, you know, it's just what they called me."

Rimon was mortified. "I'm so sorry I never thought to ask your real name." Tuzhel simply meant Shorty.

"I've kind of gotten used to being just Tuzhel."

Emotional adjustments to the unthinkable were nearly instantaneous during the first few weeks after changeover. "You may choose any name you wish here. You don't have to accept what the Raiders decreed."

"Let's just keep it Tuzhel, unless I get taller. When I rode with them, I never heard of anyone called Stonedragon, and I wouldn't expect anyone to just show up and suddenly become leader of the band. They had a sort of order among them and fought to be leader."

Rimon noted how Tuzhel thought of the Raiders as "them." Psychologically, he was disjuncting already, though his body might be giving him a fight.

BanSha said, "I know who Stonedragon is!"

They had all forgotten the child among them. A child's nager was so faint, even Rimon couldn't clearly zlin him in this ambient. "Who could it possibly be?"

"Clire of course," answered BanSha. "Remember she always wore that little stone dragon around her neck? She always ended up bossing everyone." He amended with swift embarrassment, "Except you, Lexy and Aipensha."

It was pure supposition, but it fit. Rimon nodded and then said, "Kreg, you intercepted this message, and that may buy us some time before someone in that Gen village decides to wipe us out. Were there any Gens following the Raiders back in-Territory?"

"Not that we could zlin," answered Kaires, a renSime Rimon knew as Tanhara's best tracker who often partnered with Kreg on scouting missions. "I climbed a tall tree and zlinned their backtrail, but there was nobody as far as I could make out." She ran tentacles through her short graying hair. "If you'd like, I can run their backtrail and zlin what the Gens are up to."

"No," said Rimon and Tuzhel together. "Don't worry, Tuzhel," said Rimon. "Kaires is not junct. She wouldn't hurt anyone."

"I'm sorry," said Tuzhel.

BanSha moved a little closer to Tuzhel.

Rimon looked around at the people who had grown into their positions in Fort Rimon, and noted how the Fort Hope and Fort Tanhara people blended smoothly into them. He zlinned the room and noted the absence of Fort Butte.

Rimon gave his decision. "The only thing we should be doing right now is racing to get shelter built before the really bad storms. That, and stockpiling firewood and storing the food dry and safe from vermin. Jhiti, you and Oberin should bring in your scouts to help with the building, as Benart recommends. I want to spread the augmentation work evenly among our renSimes and give the Gens as much physical labor as they can manage side by side with the Simes to stimulate their selyn production. If Clire survives the winter among the raiders, we'll deal with her then."

He didn't think she would survive. If she lost the baby, she'd probably die of complications. If she kept Killing often enough to survive the baby's prenatal selyn drain, she'd probably die of complications. If she gave birth prematurely, she'd no doubt die of complications. Meanwhile, she was using that supremely well educated brain of hers to engineer raids on Gen Territory, Raids more successful than any Freebanders had managed before.

The Gens would retaliate because the out-Territory Gens didn't differentiate between Freebanders, Licensed Raiders, town juncts, and Fort holders.

The small meeting broke up before any of the new Council's followers came in to warm up, and they went their separate ways to carry out Rimon's decision.

After the party, he had a long talk with Lexy and Garen in one of the infirmary rooms while Solamar worked an extended shift in the Dispensary. Bruce fell asleep the moment he sat down, though every once in a while would wake up to interject, "He's right you know, Lexy."

Eventually she agreed. After that, they all worked to keep things moving without involving the new Council.

By noon the next day the weather watchers predicted a big storm within three days. Foundations for fifteen large houses were finished, and the logs for their walls had been split, and piled beside the foundations. The hearths were in, though the chimneys were not yet complete.

Walls went up at a panicked rate, and by the time the storm hit full force, most of the fifteen new buildings had three families huddled together in unfurnished open space trying to keep warm despite the partially functioning hearths. They calked chinks with bits of flax, felt, tenting fabric, anything handy. They had people sleeping in the infirmary, the Collectorium, and the dining hall, as well as taking turns in the underground shelter.

Since Fort Tanhara arrived, the only way they'd had enough blankets was by sleeping in shifts. Now with Fort Hope people unequipped for a mountain winter, and with everyone indoors and inactive, clothing was inadequate and blankets went to the Gens so the Simes wouldn't have to endure a frigid ambient too. But nobody was left in a tent.

The winter had finally closed in.

* * * * * * *

The day before Tuzhel's third disjunction transfer, a few hours before dawn the Fort battened down under the assault of another in a series of major snowstorms. Going off-shift,

Solamar cornered Rimon in his office.

Solamar was supposed to be sleeping as were all those on his shift. Lexy, on light duty now that she was more than a month into her pregnancy, was supervising and working Collectorium. Solamar's shifts had been getting longer as hers got shorter, but he didn't mind as long as she lingered to talk before heading off to rest.

Solamar strode into Rimon's office the instant Rimon's nager signalled that he'd noticed a visitor. He spoke before he reached Rimon's desk. "Rimon, you've been having nightmares again."

Rimon set aside the slate he'd been reading. "You should stay out of my nightmares. Surely you have enough of your own."

"Tomorrow's your Turnover day."

Rimon met his eyes. "Yes."

"If the belt has failed you, I have to know about it."

"I was hoping whatever had gone wrong with me had cured itself when you stopped the incidents. So I slept without the belt on, only twice. Right after my transfer."

Solamar was sure he could name the day and time when Rimon had set the belt aside. "Eskalie would appreciate the consideration, I'm sure, but I'll bet you woke her with your thrashing later." The nightmares had been shattered, confused images centered on one figure.

Rimon propped his elbows on his desk, rippled his tentacles through his arched fingers and zlinned Solamar. "It'd be ridiculously easy to get to dislike you," the Farris said deadpan, but his showfield danced with embarrassment.

"Rimon, I did tell you, several times, you have more to learn. A simple Starred Cross on a belt buckle is not going to change anything. Only work can do that."

"I've been working."

"Not channeling. Exercises designed to teach you how to leave your body on purpose, but not by accident."

Rimon suppressed a shudder and leaned back in his chair. "Sit down, Solamar." Solamar settled into the guest chair before the desk and waited.

"Here's how I understand it," said Rimon at length. "Something went wrong with me when you and I put on that little performance on the wall during the battle. Something else happened to me when you and I joined to get a transfer into Tuzhel. Whatever happened left me unsteady somehow...." He waved a tentacle, searching for a word, then made one up, "disattached to my body in some strange way. As I figure it, that injury will heal itself with time, if I can just keep from stretching and straining the wound."

"I knew we should have talked about this sooner. That isn't the right model for this problem."

"Talk? When?" asked Rimon. "I'll probably hit Turnover tomorrow, and in all that time it hasn't happened again. It probably won't."

Rimon was right. There really hadn't been time to talk. Before Lexy returned, they were shorthanded and scrambling to get all the Fort Hope people back on their feet expecting Lexy to pick up the slack as soon as she returned.

After she returned pregnant, Rimon began reducing her working time in noticeable increments, saying she had to get used to a reduced workload before the baby's draw became a serious impairment.

During the storms that hit them every few days, they had worked hard to get everyone in shape to work non-stop the moment the storm let up.

The work crews were still building, which meant strained tendons and burn wounds from the fires to soften the ground. They were laying un-mortared stone because the mortar froze before it could dry, but the precious metal tools would freeze and shatter, which meant slice wounds, punctures and even a couple of concussions from falls.

Still, with all that, they had five more buildings habitable, and the school building cleared of residents so the children were back to learning again. The firewood consumption increased so they had to keep foraging teams out and they returned with more injuries to heal.

Between injuries, frostbite and renSimes over-augmenting using too much selyn and requiring early transfers, the channeling staff was overloaded whether there was a storm or not.

"I concede the point," said Solamar. "There hasn't been time to breathe, let alone talk. But now we've got until Bruce's Companion Staff meeting lets out to settle this. So let me teach you one of these exercises."

Rimon shook his head. "I don't think so. Look, Solamar, this last time it happened just wasn't the same."

"Nightmares right *after* transfer?" asked Solamar. "Wouldn't you say that's a bad sign?"

"It was different. It wasn't that I was *out* of my body, not like before."

Solamar sat up and provided his full attention.

Rimon slumped. "It's a ghost. I'm sure of it. I'm haunted by a ghost. It wasn't a nightmare, it was a visitation." He looked up. "It was Clire." The guilt resonated off the walls. "Solamar, she must be dead. How else could she torment me like that?"

"Clire?" Solamar remembered the nightmares he'd stumbled into thinking the figure was merely another dream symbol among the many whirling through Rimon's unconscious. "Very tall woman, taller than Lexy, bushy black eyebrows, wide set black eyes, long fingered hands, a dimple in her chin? Looked a lot like Lexy but not as beautiful?" *Beautiful? Why did I say that?* "Wearing dark brown coveralls and a white shirt? Come to think of it, there was some kind of pendant around her neck."

Rimon leaped out of his seat and began pacing. "Yes. That's what they wore in Intalace, what she was wearing when she arrived here. That little stone dragon of hers. I know you were there, in my dream. I saw you. Solamar, I'm so guilty over what I did to Clire, I could have just made her ghost up out of sheer Postsyndrome. Or maybe Clire's dead and really haunting me. I'd deserve it."

He hasn't discussed this even with Bruce. "Rimon, you didn't make it up, and she's not haunting you, even if she's dead. This has happened to other channels I've known, and the cure is more not less."

Rimon stopped and gazed at him, zlinning warily. "Where did you know such channels? Fort Faraway?"

Solamar didn't want to add more layers of deception and misdirection to his biography. "And other places," he temporized dropping his showfield to invite Rimon to zlin him deeply for the truth of that.

Rimon declined the deeper examination. "It's not that I don't trust you, Solamar. I just simply don't believe it. Who could know such things? Where? How?"

"High in the mountains beyond Fort Faraway, where there are so few people there are no Territory borders between Sime and Gen, there's a community where Ancient books have been preserved by copying. They've trained some people from such books, and a few have developed odd talents. One of those people taught me a few things, but I never learned it all. I never expected anything I'd learned to touch off some such explosion in another person. All I can do is tell you what I know and what I suspect, and hope we can experiment until something works." It was true as far as it went, but didn't mention he hadn't grown up in Fort Faraway.

Now Rimon was zlinning him more deeply. Solamar opened himself, looked up into the tall channel's eyes and waited for the verdict.

"This lore you picked up secondhand suggests that people who wander away from their bodies by accident have to go wandering on purpose to be cured?"

"You have to gain control of it, like any new channel's functional you discover. It's a capacity you've developed, not an injury. It takes practice to control it. If you practice, you won't keep pulling me into your dreams."

"I'm doing that?"

"Well I didn't resist because I feel so guilty about this mess. Still, I'm glad I saw Clire. Rimon, I don't think she's a ghost. I don't think she's dead. I saw her so clearly because she's wandering out of her body as you've been."

"What we did on the wall affected Clire too?"

He shrugged. "Here she is invading your dreams."

"Could it have affected Lexy too then?"

"I haven't seen any sign of that. Have you?" *I haven't searched for any.*

Rimon leaped up and paced, tugged his ear with two tentacles. "Maybe I should ask Garen."

"He'll probably tell you to talk to her." Companions rarely discussed their channel's affairs with others.

Rimon laughed. "You're right. I'll talk to her. It's still odd to think of her as an adult."

We're the same age. He sat up straighter. "So, since there's no benefit for us to sit here and lace the ambient with our various guilts as if we were both in hard Need, why don't we just do a little exerci...."

"Rimon!" called Garen pelting down the hall. He flung the door open. "BanSha's in changeover!" He was gone on some urgent errand. Running was not allowed inside the buildings.

CHAPTER TEN
OPINIONS

The building rang with reaction to Garen's nageric shout more than the word that BanSha was in changeover. Solamar felt the happiness, the relief there would be another channel overwhelming other responses from the Fort Rimon natives. BanSha was one of them.

Solamar fell into step with Rimon. They raced along the hall, down the stairs, around to the changeover room. It was still littered with items owned by a family that had camped there until they moved to their new house yesterday.

As they slid into the room, Lexy was arguing with BanSha. He stood clutching a basin, digging the toe of one worn shoe into the carpet. Sweat beaded his forehead, and he zlinned nauseated but happy.

As always when entering Lexy's presence, Solamar discovered her anew and it threw him into fantasies where he could spend long evenings and whole nights alone with her. *"Beautiful" is such an inadequate word.*

"No, BanSha, you will *not* be able to work as a channel tomorrow," said Lexy in her most patient voice. Then she switched to teasing. "Why have we spent five years teaching you if you've forgotten everything you've learned!" She felt Solamar's regard and tossed him a nageric grin that warmed his soul. "You still have all of your First Year training, and that means a lot of study."

"But this is an emergency like in the stories of Fort Freedom...."

Rimon declared, "Not *that* much of an emergency. We'll find useful but boring chores for you."

BanSha spun and saw Rimon and Solamar, drew himself to his full height, and smirked. "I know, holding the fields and all that. I can be a big help."

"In a little while," added Rimon, "you'll know what a field is, but not how to hold one, nevermind a lot together."

"I can't wait!" squeaked BanSha. "Solamar, don't forget you promised to teach me too."

Solamar had nearly forgotten his first encounter with this short, spunky and helpful child. If he could retain his spirit into adulthood, he could be a cornerstone of the Fort. "Yes, BanSha, I will do for you whatever Rimon and Lexy want me to." He raised his eyebrows at Lexy, zlinning her as he asked, "And who has been chosen to be the lucky Companion for this young channel?"

While Solamar inspected her fields for signs she had experienced what Rimon was going through, Bruce stumbled into the room. The sole of one shoe had flapped loose.

The Gen gracefully wrapped his burgeoning fields around himself, sidling carefully up to Rimon. "Sorry," he apologized. "BanSha, you should have told someone!"

"I did. Lexy. She was on duty. It was fun trying to get her alone without Xanon noticing!"

Fun? "Xanon's here?" asked Solamar who had volunteered to work with him. "He should be sleeping."

Rimon laughed, filling the room with his admiration for Solamar's coping with Xanon. "Well, *you* aren't."

Everyone stared at Rimon, but it was such pure *Del Rimon Farris* there was nothing to say. BanSha was aware of all the silent subtext he was missing.

Solamar returned the admiration, interpreting for BanSha, "Guilty! I'm overworking, doing exactly what I told Xanon not to do, exactly what you do." He changed the subject back again, "So which of our trainees gets the honor of being BanSha's Companion?"

"It's BanSha's honor," countered Bruce. "And you, young man, will have to work hard to earn the full attention of," he glanced at Solamar, "Rushi."

Rimon's approval filled the room.

Solamar grinned at BanSha. "Oh, and I do think she likes you already."

"Rushi," whispered BanSha with reverence. "Wow, I'm going to work with Rushi? I'm getting a Tanhara Companion? And she already knows everything!"

"Well she's ready to give your First Transfer. She just went with Fengal to the Glasil's to deliver Melina's baby. She'll be here as soon as the baby comes which shouldn't be long now. We'll see how your First Transfer goes with her before deciding the future."

"I know, I heard about Melina. I'll be good with Rushi," promised BanSha. Then his face fell. "How will I explain this to all the others who wanted me?"

Rimon said, "Until you're out of First Year, it won't be your choice and all your friends know that. Meanwhile, Bruce or I'll do any explaining necessary."

"And now," announced Bruce, "we should clear this room and let BanSha get ready for a very long night."

Zlinning, Rimon judged, "Maybe not so very long. Zlin that, Lexy?"

BanSha's knees collapsed and he bent double panting.

Lexy and Rimon caught him and deposited him and his basin on the bed. Extra blankets were piled at the bottom of the bed, for though the first stages of changeover brought on an elevated temperature, preparing the body for the Sime's higher body temperature, the third stage often produced teeth chattering chills.

Usually the transitions between stages seized the victim with unpredictable symptoms. As BanSha recovered from the weakness of the stage two transition, he adjusted rapidly to the changes in his body. Now tentacles and the nerves to serve them were developing. He was still sweating and panting, but somehow enjoying his miseries.

Watching the child, Solamar fell in love with Fort Rimon all over again. Any place that could nurture such a spirit had *home* written all over it.

Bruce said, "Out now. BanSha has to change clothes before he ruins what he's wearing."

Solamar, Rimon and Lexy retreated so they could dress BanSha in the now traditional yawal, the simple white smock usually worn by Gens bred and raised in Pens and sold for the Kill. The garment had come to symbolize the child's dedication to a life without Killing.

As they left, BanSha shouted, "My yawal! Mine!"

Solamar, muttered. "He really hates being a child!"

"That about sums it up," replied Lexy.

Rimon said, "Bruce, I'll be back and bring you another pair of shoes." He started to shut the door.

While all of them were observing Bruce's careful non-reaction to that, out of nowhere, a form running under high augmentation, bent double, scooted under Rimon's extended arm and into the changeover room spreading a roiling black cloud of Need. It was Tuzhel.

Behind Tuzhel ran Xanon arms outstretched. He grabbed for the young renSime junct in the grip of hard Need but missed. Surprise shattered the ambient.

Unable to stop in time, Xanon knocked Rimon into the door. It swung into the room. Xanon spun sideways to avoid falling, and blew the fields. Rimon staggered but held the fields as Lexy caught him. Tuzhel dodged Bruce's grab and dived onto BanSha's bed to kneel zlinning his friend. Maigrey arrived behind Xanon but stopped without hitting anyone. The patchwork of shifting fields finally righted.

"It's true!" screeched Tuzhel. You're changing over! You zlin all crazy." The junct hugged BanSha. "You'll give me transfer tomorrow!"

Xanon plunged across the room, intent on gathering the junct away from the channel in changeover. Bruce stopped him with a solid nageric wall of denial.

Rimon said, "Xanon, wait! BanSha, what have you told Tuzhel?"

"I didn't.... Not...um, well I did say when I learned *how*, I'd give him the best transfers, and I will. I'm going to study so hard...."

Xanon decreed, "BanSha, you will be a non-junct channel. You will not be giving transfer to...."

Rimon joined his nager to Bruce's creating a wall that startled Xanon to silence. Solamar marveled, then was dazzled when Lexy and Maigrey joined to protect both BanSha and Tuzhel from Xanon's ire. From his vantage at the side of the effect, he zlinned BanSha and Tuzhel on the bed as well as Xanon transfixed in the center of the room.

"Xanon, we'll explain the facts of channeling assignments to BanSha once he can zlin what happens during a transfer."

"Tuzhel can zlin already," said BanSha. "Can he stay and watch me change over? He wants to zlin a non-junct First Transfer and I told him he could watch me. Well, that is if Rushi agrees."

"Rushi?" asked Tuzhel suddenly very alert.

BanSha sat up grinning. "My Companion!"

"Who is as much a trainee as you are, BanSha. It's not her decision to make," said Rimon firmly.

"Good, now that that's clear," started Xanon.

Rimon said, "*I* will decide on BanSha's behalf."

Xanon froze his field. "Come on Tuzhel, you belong in your room until after your transfer tomorrow. You must learn discipline if you are ever to disjunct."

"Val said you aren't in charge of me today. Fengal is." The air congealed with Tuzhel's distrust heavily laced with fear and all of it carried on the throbbing darkness of Need. The ex-Raider had no intention of going with Xanon.

The Farrises had Xanon nagerically walled away from Tuzhel so Xanon couldn't zlin Tuzhel's Need grow from his burst of augmentation. Xanon started, "Fengal went...."

"Xanon," warned Rimon underscored nagerically, "There's no point arguing with a renSime in hard Need."

"He's not in hard Need yet. His transfer is still more than a day away. He's just...."

In unison, Rimon and Lexy dropped their showfields, shunting Bruce's and Maigrey's fields aside. Like parting a curtain, they let Xanon zlin.

To his credit, Xanon flipped his showfield to neutral to protect the disjuncting renSime. But Solamar didn't zlin the reaction he expected to Tuzhel's condition. A channel should feel sympathy for any Sime in that condition.

Tuzhel scrambled over BanSha and plastered himself against the wall. BanSha rose on his knees to shelter his friend. Solamar felt the junct's effort to deny his Need, as if it were merely rising intil. Tuzhel's fear of Xanon made every cell in Solamar's body yearn to serve that Need. And such intense Need so close to a channel in changeover could produce complications.

Rimon and Lexy blocked Xanon off again, while Rimon stepped to the bedside. So smoothly Solamar barely understood what was happening, Rimon touched his belt buckle with one hand and shifted his showfield to become a ripe, glowing, bright Gen with a warm, welcoming, attitude. He offered the abundance of selyn to the Sime in Need.

Solamar helped Lexy block Xanon. *Rimon is becoming dependent on that belt.* Bruce grasped Rimon's intent and focused on his channel. Maigrey shifted to full focus on Xanon. Lexy adjusted the fields to give Rimon a small null-field zone to work in.

Solamar watched Rimon avidly. He had never mastered the knack of giving a disjunct channel the surge of Gen pain and fear they craved at the end of a transfer so he was always eager to observe non-junct channels doing it.

Rimon held his hands out, tentacles extended toward the junct, inviting with his fields. The instant Tuzhel started toward Rimon, the channel inserted a flash of terror into his Gen projection. Tuzhel attacked in helpless reflex and Rimon let feigned terror become a scream of panic.

Tuzhel's handling tentacles lashed about Rimon's, and Rimon twined his laterals around Tuzhel's lateral tentacles in a standard channel's grip. A flicker of nageric brilliance carrying a searing crescendo of Gen pain and it was over.

Then Tuzhel's junct nervous system discovered the fear had been phony, the "Gen" was not dead, and his own body just not satisfied. *It would have been satisfying enough for a disjunct,* thought Solamar.

With BanSha looking on awestruck, Tuzhel donned his bravest demeanor and smirked proudly at BanSha. "See? That's how it's done. That's all there is to it. You'll be able to do that. Maybe not next month, but soon."

Solamar zlinned Tuzhel's deep sob of anguished loss, and the slamming headache of Kill deprivation that had the youngster frowning. His back muscles were spasming and nerve impulses weren't getting through to his knees.

Rimon lifted the junct from the bed to the floor, using the interpenetration of body fields to soothe the backlash for the renSime. "Now that you're not in Need, you may stay with BanSha, if that's what you both would like. You've certainly earned it, Tuzhel, by giving BanSha a valuable lesson in the channel's art."

"He can stay?" whispered BanSha. "Really?"

"If he still wants to."

Solamar zlinned the junct's anticipation of staying with his friend override his personal misery.

Behind the nageric wall Lexy had built in the ambient, Xanon seethed with astonished outrage and a dozen other emotions blurred behind the nageric shroud Maigrey created.

Both Farrises moved as one to sweep Xanon out of the room before his ire disturbed BanSha.

Bruce shooed Solamar after them, and the door closed leaving him in the hall with Lexy, Maigrey, Xanon and Rimon. Down the hall, the late night shift was all astir preparing for the changeover party they would hold in the dining hall after

BanSha's First Transfer.

Solamar and Lexy positioned themselves with Maigrey and Rimon to contain Xanon's irate nager.

Xanon regarded Rimon silently.

Rimon said, "Would you expect the Council to decide when to give Tuzhel transfer?"

"He wasn't due until tomorrow. How can you expect him to disjunct if he doesn't learn to defer gratification?"

"He's learning. His disjunction won't be impaired."

The opposite, thought Solamar. Rimon's decision won the love and loyalty of both the young people.

"That is a judgment for the channeling staff to make," conceded Xanon. "But the Council is debating the trustworthiness of all the disjuncts within these walls as well as the place an ex-Raider might have. What to do about the disjunct population will be a Council decision."

Solamar and Rimon exchanged astonished stares with Lexy and Bruce. Their hesitation disconcerted Xanon.

Solamar asked, "Do you suppose news of this Council debate had reached Tuzhel when he was in Need?"

Understanding dawned in Rimon's nager. "Oh, I'm certain it did. If there's one thing a disjunction candidate is vulnerable to its fear of rejection after disjunction."

Though Rimon was opaque to Solamar, he could read Xanon's nager to the core. Xanon had no idea what Rimon felt and no intention of delivering anything Rimon wanted.

Rimon's ventral tentacles drummed on the belt buckle. He locked eyes with Xanon. Solamar watched the tentacles but eyed Rimon's expression. *Could Rimon be so afraid of sliding out of his body during a channel's functional that it might impair his judgment?*

Xanon spun on his heel and headed for the latrine exit at the end of the hall. Maigrey was caught flat-footed. Holding the door, Xanon glanced over his shoulder at her. She looked to Rimon who nodded. She followed her assigned channel. Xanon noticed her reluctance though.

Solamar hoped that would unsettle Xanon enough that he'd reassess his position. "Rimon, I'd like to talk to Val about finding someone else for Xanon."

Rimon nodded. "Me, too. But if Val assigns someone who agrees with Xanon, we won't know what he's up to."

"I hadn't thought of that. I'm not cut out to stand in your shoes."

He felt Lexy assessing him. "Don't be too sure of that, Solamar. It's amazing how fast some people learn."

Her attention slid over his shoulder. Solamar zlinned a ripe Gen field speeding toward them and turned to find Rushi, cloak covered by snow and ice, tracking slush down the hall. "Melina's fine. They've named the baby Mhairin! Isn't that a beautiful name for a little girl? Fengal says she had practically no selyn draw at birth."

Rimon said, "I wish we knew if that meant anything!"

Nobody could know if a child was going to become Sime or Gen at maturity, but about a third of the children of two Gens changed over into Simes and about a third of the children of two Simes established as Gens. In the Forts though, Simes and Gens married and all bets were off. Only the severe and deadly selyn draw of the channel gave any clue. And that was not always a reliable indicator.

"Dad," said Lexy, "I'll go talk to Val about Maigrey. You should brief Rushi and stay with Bruce to manage Tuzhel. Solamar, why don't you come with me. If you're not sleeping, Kahleen is likely waiting for you to show up in the dining hall and I should eat."

Rushi shot Solamar an inquiring look. He had been working to blend Tanhara's authority structure into Fort Rimon's so he just said, "Rushi, congratulations on getting a First Transfer assignment. You'll enjoy it. Rimon has a lot to tell you before you go in."

Lexy hooked an elbow around Solamar's biceps and scooped him down the hall toward Val's office. Solamar looked back at Rimon. There would be plenty of time to talk him into doing exercises after BanSha's changeover.

Rimon turned to Rushi.

Solamar marched off at Lexy's side, matching her long stride, conscious of how much taller she was, how very pregnant she was, and how Post he himself was. Still it felt good to move beside this formidable woman, nagers twined.

* * * * * * *

Rimon sat at the head table in the dining hall with most of the channeling staff. The place was jammed as everyone associated with Melina and her new baby crammed in with everyone who had known BanSha all his life.

On the stage, Sian played shiltpron, one long tone at a time in a simple tune for BanSha who sat on the edge of the stage and zlinned the chiaroscuro of fields rippled by shiltpron modulation, oblivious to the party behind him.

Gradually, Sian moved into playing a new song. They had heard parts of it during the last few celebrations, but this was the first time Sian had played the whole thing.

"My wife wrote this song so we can remember our dead and include them all in our times of joy."

It started as a beautiful, slow dirge that lightened verse after verse until it became a paean of joy blunted by gentle sadness. She had written it as a tribute to all who had died this last, terrible year as Fort after Fort had failed and sought refuge here. Sian called it *Pasts and Futures*.

Rimon had been told the song had already become the new traditional opening for all the Fort's festivities.

Tentacles playing over his belt buckle, Rimon watched Lexy dancing with Solamar to the simple melody. As they whirled across the floor, they volleyed the field management between them, keeping the room's ambient steady even as they moved. *Their fields dance.*

Rimon noted they had re-phased their transfers so that they would be in Postsyndrome simultaneously. That wouldn't last with Lexy pregnant. Visually they made a stunning couple exploring each other with tender but unspoken questions. *Now when* ever *did all this happen?*

Rimon resolved to pay more attention to what was going on around him. The party had barely started when Oberin announced, "Storm's over! First crews head on out!"

That day, Rimon hit Turnover but was too busy to notice. Then it seemed no time at all passed before his transfer was upon him. Just measuring by Bruce's field, it really had been two weeks since his Turnover.

Now the shortest day of the year was approaching, the most brutal part of the winter ahead with the season of infectious illness. As Rimon reduced Lexy's working shifts and increased his own, his days consisted of Collectorium, Dispensary and patients with barely time to clear his desk of assorted skirmishes with the Council.

Lexy's pregnancy was going very well, too well. He had begun to suspect this child would be Gen or maybe the rarest of the rare, a Farris renSime. The ferocious prenatal draw of the Farris channel just hadn't materialized.

Only one incident stood out in his memory of the days leading up to the shortest day of the year. The building crews had roofed and sealed the last of the new houses and were finally finishing the wall's catwalk and defenses. What had been a couple of crude boards laid across sparsely placed supports was now a solid walk wide enough for two men to pass on sentry duty. The inner railing was almost finished, complete with handy racks for storing weapons.

On the night of the full moon, Jhiti and Oberin found him in Bruce's office discussing BanSha's lessons. The young channel had made considerable if chaotic progress with all the willing tutors he'd enlisted.

Jhiti said, "Rimon, you've got to come settle this now before they start digging."

"Settle what? Digging what?"

"The latrine pit. Where to put it."

"I thought that was settled."

"Just get your cloak. Everyone's standing around in the cold wind waiting for you."

Rimon said to Bruce, "Stay here and finish up. We have to restrain BanSha's enthusiasm and focus his learning pattern starting tomorrow with his second transfer."

Jhiti and Oberin both laughed. Bruce commented archly, "I'm sure it wouldn't be so funny if it was your job!" The guard captains laughed harder. They'd both known BanSha all his life, and his father Garen too. After a moment, Bruce joined them. "He'll never grow up."

Rimon led the way out of the building, tromping carefully along the icy walk. "I always knew BanSha's First Year would be a trial. The problem is that he's decided to learn everything brought in by the channels from other Forts, and all within the next three weeks!"

"I can well imagine," said Oberin. "Garen was saying something similar last night. There, zlin that crowd? That's where they want to dig."

"But that's not where...." As they drew closer, the full moon high in a clear sky, Rimon zlinned this was Xanon's Council, led by Alind.

Jhiti said, "So you see the problem. We can't have an outhouse there. If we have to defend this section against a concerted attack, it would make it impossible to maneuver."

Rimon ploughed into the group's nageric chaos and sorted the fields into a reasonable order. That quieted all the Simes and the Gens finally noticed him.

"What's the problem?" asked Rimon. He remembered discussions when they'd first chosen this hill for Fort Rimon. The new houses had been placed according to their original expansion plans for a reason.

"This is where *we* planned to put latrines," said Alind. "The Council decided before those houses went up."

Rimon zlinned the now completed houses with their shutters tight against the weather, chimneys smoking, and many people asleep inside. It was a convenient spot for a latrine. But the symmetric spot on the other side of this row of houses was where it had to go. Had he missed something?

One hand on his belt buckle, he zlinned the ground beneath their feet. "Stand back, please," he said motioning the crowd away from the target area. Nobody could zlin through solid ground, especially when there was no Gen on the other side of the packed earth. When ground was not solid, it didn't zlin evenly.

The hill they had built the Fort on had been built upon before. Underground, there was an occasional collapsed pile of old rotting logs and other detritus. He found traces of what might be such a pile here, and far beneath that, barely perceptible, was a not quite solid area. *Water.* It just wasn't enough water for a well. Seepage. They couldn't build here. There could be a collapse.

He stood back and surveyed the position again and remembered the discussion in his office a few days ago. Some of the Fort Hope builders had brought in plans for new wells. Benart had pulled their original survey of the hill. "If we put a latrine here," said Rimon "it will pollute the groundwater. It runs from here into the river, then on downriver to Shifron. We can't put a latrine here."

A voice exclaimed, "He can't zlin that!"

Someone argued, "Maybe not, but it's what the builder calculated just from the slant of the land."

Another Councilor objected, "Ground water under this hill is not going to be polluted. It's way too far down to matter or we'd put a well here. We discussed all that when we voted to put the latrine here, and it took three days to negotiate that compromise."

Rimon said, "Where to put a latrine can't be negotiated to a compromise. You can't vote the water flow out of existence. If we put it here we risk making the folks living in Shifron sick."

"Raiders! They won't be there long. That town will be dead by spring. Juncts won't return to a ruin."

"Some juncts may come back," insisted Rimon.

"If they get sick, they'll leave."

"If they get sick," countered Rimon, "the illness may spread to us. We're not putting a latrine where it can pollute water anyone might someday want to use."

"But...." started Alind.

"The channeling staff is in charge of the health of this Fort, and we won't permit a latrine to be dug here."

Rimon turned to the work crew where they stood leaning on their shovels. They were mostly Fort Rimon natives. "You know where we originally decided this latrine had to go. If you have it dug out by morning, the carpenters may get the outhouse built before the next storm. People will appreciate that." It was indeed a long walk to the closest working outhouse.

The diggers walked off pulling the sledge piled with firewood for softening the ground. The ambient nager around them was decidedly mixed. Not all of them thought Rimon was right. The onlookers dispersed, most emitting a satisfied air, and the Council was left to talk to themselves.

Some people who had voted for these Councilors just to get the Council working again were now not so interested in their opinions. Rimon knew he had created more trouble in the last ten minutes than he could deal with in the next ten months. He turned to trudge back to the offices. *Where do people get these ideas? Imagine voting on where to put an outhouse! Next thing you know, they'll want to vote on where to dig a well!*

He had thought the Council was still debating the matter of disjuncts. The Fort Hope representative on the Council had told Rimon there was a proposal to send all the disjuncts off to form their own Fort and the majority felt that an ex-Raider would be even more untrustworthy than the other disjuncts. *Maybe Tuzhel won't hear about that until it's defeated,* thought Rimon. He'd seen Bekka and BanSha taking Tuzhel into Church of the Unity meetings several times now and it seemed to be helping Tuzhel come to terms with changeover. But with no Church of the Unity members on the Council, who would defend the disjuncts?

At the celebration of the shortest day of the year, the Council usually handed out achievement awards to the children before the report on the year's progress and plans for next year. This year, however, the Council set aside Fort Rimon's customs and substituted with a communal sing.

Not knowing any of the songs that were chosen, Rimon found himself in the back of the crowd watching and talking to Lexy as they managed the ambient nager for the crowd. Those who knew the songs were having a good time.

"You and Solamar are getting along pretty well."

"I like working with him. And...well, we want to step our transfers so we can spend Postsyndrome together."

"Let me know if I can help that project out."

She almost dropped the fields. "I thought you didn't like him, you've been avoiding him so much lately."

"I like him a lot, Lexy. He's a great channel and a fine man. He could make a good father for your baby." She was already almost three months along and hadn't chosen a man to help raise this child. As far as Rimon could zlin, it seemed Solamar had chosen himself.

"Let's not get too far ahead of things, like BanSha always does."

Rimon laughed. He was a day past Turnover, but BanSha's antics could make him laugh even when he was in hard Need. "All right, just be sure to let me know when you've chosen the lucky man."

"The way things are going lately, I'll bet the Council will expect to be the first to know!"

There was more bitterness behind that remark than Rimon thought there should be though she didn't let it show in her field work. "What have they done now?"

"Oh, nothing. Well, I really don't know. I think those people govern by rumor and sly hints."

Privately, Rimon doubted they governed at all.

"Dad, it's probably nothing, but it seems the main dividing

line is how people think about you and me."

"That started while you were away rescuing Fort Hope. They think I'm a tyrant dictating by whim."

"I think they think that about me, too."

"What makes you say that?"

"I heard some people from Fort Rimon and Fort Hope, people who've never said anything against us, saying you took out that old jeweled belt to wear just after Alind put you in your place. They said it was a conspicuous display of wealth designed to remind everyone that Fort Rimon is the direct heir of Fort Freedom, and filled with ancient wisdom and authority regardless of how incompetent or dishonest the current holders of that authority are.

"They said wearing the belt is your statement that you don't have to listen to the Council. I only heard one person argue for you, Shaddyr Esren. She says since you gave up our house to the new families and are sharing your room with a stranger, you have no place to keep such a valuable object, so you have to wear it. Her husband made a big speech to his Church of the Unity people about how you're just like your grandfather, guided by God's Will."

"It's just a Starred Cross. Lots of people in the Forts wear them." He could zlin several dozen here without even trying. None were jeweled though. "Lexy, I inherited it from my father. He got it from a gypsy, and nobody has a clue where the gypsy got it. It's just a belt."

His daughter was too busy holding the fields in the room steady as people sang a particularly nostalgic song to zlin his utterly truthful misdirection.

But about two weeks later, after Rimon's transfer, he remembered her remark and set the belt back in its drawer when he went to visit with Eskalie for a little sex and relaxation. To his delight, he slept afterwards with no visitations from Clire.

Upon waking though, he decided that meant Clire was dead, beyond even being a ghost now. He knew if she were a ghost, she'd be doing her best to haunt him.

On the other hand, it might also mean that whatever was sending him out of his body might have finally ceased. Maybe he'd healed. Solamar was the first to admit he didn't know everything about such phenomena.

So Rimon left the belt off when he went to work that day. For most of the day, he had no trouble at all staying in his body during his channeling functions. Then, late in his shift when he was beginning to tire, it happened again.

He was healing a strained tendon and torn muscle in a renSime logger's leg. The injury had been caused by a boot heel that came off, taking the whole boot sole with it while the woman had been climbing a tree to saw the top off. She had lost purchase, throwing her weight against a safety belt, which broke, and she had fallen.

Both boots had thinning leather uppers with a few cracks. Rimon had noticed an increasing number of people in worn footgear lately. There were at least four master cobblers in the Fort now so this shouldn't be happening. He made a mental note to inquire after the problem then fell to the job of healing the renSime's injury.

For the first time since he healed Sian's paralysis he saw his patient's second body hazily floating outside her physical body.

Without even thinking about it, he seized the image of the ruined tendon and muscle, molded it into healthy tissue and put it back into the woman's leg hastily before Solamar could turn up in the vision world.

He fell back into his body with a jarring, frightening jolt, but managed to mask his terror until he'd caught his breath. Even Bruce didn't notice.

Rimon excused himself to go to the latrine while Bruce finished wrapping a pressure bandage around the renSime's ankle. He raced to his room where he slung the belt around his hips as fast as he could and sobbed with relief when the buckle was in place.

Except for swelling and tenderness, the leg returned to normal in a matter of hours instead of the week or two Rimon would have expected. No one was amazed because Rimon was the only channel who knew the extent of the injury and everyone expected his Healings to work faster.

Later, he considered asking Solamar for that training. As Lexy had said, people would notice how he was avoiding Solamar, and people were already noticing the belt.

Rimon thought about how much more effective he could become at Healing and how vital that skill might be come spring when the Raiders attacked again, or the Gens did. Either way, they'd have to defend this Fort again.

Yet everything in him shied away from that offered training. *I'm getting too old and weak to face the rigors of learning something like this.*

Watching BanSha race through the sequence of skills that had become the traditional fare for second and third month old channels convinced Rimon he was right about himself. The vitality of youth was long gone. He had tried to shed the belt too soon. Older people took longer to heal.

If they were going to defend this Fort again, people must have solid footgear. He saw Sian coming in for his transfer and brought him into his office. Sian was wearing shoes with holes over his little toes. The cobblers worked next to the looms and Sian talked to them every day but he had no idea why shoes were in short supply. "Find out what's going on," finished Rimon seriously.

For the next three days, Rimon avoided Solamar as he had been all winter. Since Lexy and Solamar were the only people other than Bruce he could really talk to, that made life lonely. *But it's only temporary,* he told himself. *With time, I'll be stable again unless I let Solamar start pulling me out of my body on a regular basis.*

CHAPTER ELEVEN
EXPEDITION

Solamar knew the best time to find Rimon on the wall seeking solitude was when Bruce was ensconced in his own office hearing the problems of the Companion staff. If Rimon had finished his own work, he'd walk the walls, no matter how cold it was.

This first month of the year, it was cold. The snow came driven on high winds, tiny hard flakes that no sooner hit the ground than flew into the air again. In addition to the guards, Jhiti posted sweepers to clear the catwalks and cut paths through the snow even as it was drifting.

Jhiti did not put it past the Raiders to hit the Fort in the middle of a blizzard, so he welcomed Rimon's nightly patrol. Lexy too would take a turn during the day, and Solamar gravitated toward the dinner hour, though Kahleen would haul him in to eat before he was through meditating.

So he went out late at night, too. From time to time he'd catch Rimon alone. At first, Rimon was skittish, apparently expecting Solamar to demand an explanation, insist on teaching him tricks, try to talk him into learning. But after zlinning the belt Rimon still wore, Solamar kept silent. If he spoke at all, it was on some bit of business, or some artistic addition to the Fort's new buildings.

After a while, they'd lean on the wall and zlin the distance or observe the Fort's interior, just letting their senses roam to the horizon, reveling in how good it felt, sometimes without talking at all.

Once, they discussed Jhiti's new defense drills that involved every able bodied Sime except the channels. Jhiti was well aware of the factionalism tearing at the Fort. His cure for this was mixing people who stood on opposite sides into combat drill teams who had to learn to work together.

Another time they discussed plans to build Rimon a new house since he'd given his away and taken to living in his on-duty room instead. He didn't want a whole house with Aipensha gone and Lexy about to start her own family.

In time, Rimon began to relax, believing Solamar would not press about teaching him. They discussed everything from Shiltpron techniques to Genlan invective, anything and everything but channeling.

Searching for another topic, Solamar said, "Oh, and someone left new blankets on the bed, so I took the liberty of hanging your quilt back on the wall."

"You did? Thank you. That's a very old quilt and I really didn't want to see it more worn from regular use."

"It has a story behind it, I'll bet." Solamar remembered the first time he'd slept under it and felt the passionate hope glowing from every stitch. It was packed with love, hope, triumph. He'd never felt such a complex warding spell either. Someone with untrained but major power had made both the baby quilt and the enlargement.

"Many stories. I think I told you, the center piece was made for me when I was a baby. Since then it's been involved in births, deaths, and even one wedding."

Solamar kept his nager to himself, avoiding anything such as the penetrating nageric interlocks that had triggered Rimon's problem. Still, he felt Rimon's love of that quilt. He'd just have to wait to be told the whole story.

The third night, just a few days before Lexy would be three months pregnant, under a cloudless sky, with the air so still they could hear the river, Solamar was standing beside Rimon, leaning on the railing wondering how to open the topic of Lexy and her child. He had to find a way to convince her to marry him. He wanted more than to simply stand as father to her child. He wanted it all. If anyone knew how to convince her, it would be Rimon.

Eventually, Rimon gave him an opening. "I examined Lexy again today. She isn't exhibiting the signs of a woman pregnant with a channel. This child will be Gen or renSime, and I'm betting on Gen."

"I'd love to be the father to raise that Gen. She said the renSime father had a sister who was a Companion." He paused judging Rimon's nager. But he didn't get to say, *Rimon, I'm in love with your daughter* out loud.

Behind them, BanSha stormed up the stairs, leaping them three at a time with youthful confidence in his zlinning ability to spot ice before he stepped on it.

Oberin tromped over to lecture the young channel before letting him on the catwalk. Rimon met Solamar's eyes and they shared a private chuckle. "I suppose where you grew up, they had an Oberin too?"

"Oh, yes," agreed Solamar, remembering a number of scoldings all too keenly and being very glad his father wasn't here now to comment on how he was failing.

"Tell me about it sometime," said Rimon zlinning Solamar quickly. Then he pushed himself away from the wall and moved toward BanSha but not to rescue him.

Maybe he'll trust me if I tell him how my grandfather thought the Farris channel mutation would ultimately be the key to uniting humanity, Sime and Gen together without fear. But then I'd have to tell him, and Lexy, about how my father could talk for hours presenting philosophical proof that the whole concept of channeling was wrong headed, a dead end that would be the source of more misery than salvation.

Solamar followed the Farris channel over to BanSha. He added his nageric support as Rimon reinforced Oberin's lesson in how a channel should behave.

Here I am helping ram home a hard lesson just as my father taught me. I wonder if he loved me the way I love BanSha. I wonder if BanSha knows how we delight in him?

Finally, Oberin left Rimon and Solamar to escort the young channel down the slippery stair. On the ground, Rimon asked, "So what is this about?"

"Sian and Jhiti want you at a meeting. You too, Solamar. I'm supposed to go find Kahleen and Bruce too."

"Who else?" asked Solamar. "And where?"

"Everyone important," answered BanSha. "By the looms. There's nobody sleeping in there anymore." The youngster was off at a dead run over the slippery snow as if he hadn't been scolded. *Of course I never paid any attention to my father either.*

Solamar followed Rimon across the Fort at a more reasonable pace aware Rimon was zlinning him curiously.

The factory building was a long, slender edifice next to the old front gate where so many of Fort Tanhara had died that a monument had been erected. With the wall moved out, the monument now stood alone where the gate had been.

The wainwright, cabinet maker and the potter had the end of the building nearest the gate, and the looms were on the other end with the wicker workers. Between were the tailors, the cobbler, and other crafts. The candle makers, though, worked in the school building next to the laundry where there was always a well stoked hearth to keep the children warm. Now that they'd expanded the walls, they were planning additions to the crafts building to give everyone the space to supply the whole Fort's requirements.

Solamar had seen the kitchen staff petitioning Rimon for space for a cannery that could double as a dye processor, tripling the value of their trade goods. He'd heard summer here produced riots of berries and grapes. Some of the timber they were using came from clear cutting the area they would use to expand the fields. That should have been a Council decision, but apparently they'd been too busy.

They arrived at the factory door as Lexy and Garen came from the stables. Lexy said, wiping her hands on a rag, "We're going to have a lovely new colt born in a few weeks, several in fact, and then it'll be lambing time. I don't know where we'll pasture these flocks."

Kahleen joined them as Lexy and Rimon led the way into the building discussing pasturage.

Val, Bruce, Jhiti and Benart straggled in, and Zedros smelling like fresh laundry brought up the rear with Rinda.

Solamar had taken a donation from Rinda, a Gen woman who had come out of retirement to accept Fort Hope's seat on the Fort Rimon Council. She was a level headed woman with experience at juggling conflicting demands on a Fort's economy. She liked Tuzhel and that endeared her to his heart. She reminded him of his mother.

Everyone talking at once made a growing uproar. BanSha tucked himself into a corner, sucking on some dried fruit. He watched the fields with the absorption only a First Year channel could bring to bear.

Sian built up the fire in the hearth as the door closed for the last time. There were five others there, one the Fort Tanhara cobbler, Eric, who made superb saddles too. He'd been born out-Territory and raised in leatherworking trades.

Sian introduced everyone and then said, "Frevven here has news. He's the Fort Hope cobbler."

Frevven stood, respect suffusing his nager. "I'm a Fort Rimon cobbler now, and very glad of it, but sorry to report this Fort has problems. We didn't invite the two Fort Butte cobblers to this meeting because we feel Rimon has to decide."

Everyone nodded. There were very few from Fort Butte who would ask Rimon anything.

"Eric, Endra and I have been discussing this boot problem that Rimon brought to Sian's attention. For the last two months, we've been repairing shoes, not making any. The two cobblers from Butte told us to make the leather go as far as possible, and that the Council would tell us when to make new boots and shoes, but meanwhile only two people would make new boots, the Butte cobblers.

"Well, you all know the record of this new Council, so when Sian told us Rimon was concerned about the boot problem I got Endra and we went to the store room to check the leather supply. Endra says there was plenty last summer before Tanhara and Hope arrived. Only now the leather store is empty. We can't make any new boots."

Solamar felt Rimon's and Lexy's shock as well as his own. Rimon said to Sian and Endra, "This wasn't reported to me. Have we used all the leather we had in stock just repairing boots and making the new ones for Fort Hope?"

Endra stood up, an older Gen woman with rough hands and thick muscular forearms. "Rimon, I let the Fort Butte people manage the store room. I didn't keep the records, so I don't know if we've used all the leather stock you traded for last summer. My sense of things is that no, we haven't. That leather went somewhere other than through our hands and into shoes, tack, hinges, vests, and so on. It wouldn't have been adequate to make new boots for everyone here this winter, but we haven't even tried."

Rimon said thoughtfully, "Lately, it has seemed to me that the people originally from Fort Butte have boots and gear that isn't worn to shreds. Am I right?"

Many thoughtful frowns were exchanged but the consensus was that no one had noticed worn boots on those from Fort Butte, though Fort Unity and Veritt people were also wearing boots thin with use.

Solamar said, "I've been assuming that since some people had new boots, we'd all get some eventually. I didn't notice who did or did not have solid footwear."

"My assumption exactly," said Kahleen. "I never thought about it, and nobody has mentioned it to me."

"Ordinarily," said Bruce, "we'd send to Ardo to trade wool for leather. Or get it from traders in Shifron who got it at Ardo. We can't do that in the middle of winter."

"Wool stock is low, too," put in Sian. "I can account for every strand. We made linen/wool blended blankets, cloaks, underwear, shirts, pants, and knitting yarn for socks, gloves, hats. All we could produce went to the children and Gens first just as you instructed. The un-spun wool and linen left is for taxes, if they even send a collector this spring. Of course we'll have plenty after shearing."

The products of the Forts went mostly to pay the head-taxes on the Gens. Any Sime was entitled to keep one Gen for the Kill that month, but any extra Gens were taxed. Right now they had many extra Gens, but the selyn a channel collected wasn't useful for paying taxes. Companions were ruined for the Kill and had no market value, but they would be confiscated if their taxes weren't paid. The regular donors would be sold for the Kill.

Rimon said, "So we must find a more local source of good, thick strong, well tanned leather. We don't have the skills and means to tan leather. We do have a large supply of horsehide though, from all those animals that died in the attack this fall. And there were some cow hides, a few sheepskins. All of that was saved, wasn't it?"

"Yes. We found them," said Eric, "when we rummaged to the back of the store room. They're well scraped, but raw, and have been pretty much frozen solid for months now. No vermin have been at them, so they're whole. A few were used to make rawhide to braid into rope, but most of the hides are there."

"They're tradable. Benart, didn't you say we have a surplus of grain?"

"A wagon load or so of extra wheat."

"But with Shifron gone," said Frevven, "there's no place to buy tanned leather."

"The leather we traded for in Shifron, or Ardo for that matter, had been stolen out-Territory," said Rimon. "We're very close to the border here. Somewhere over that mountain at the south end of this valley is a Gen community that has a tanner. We have to set up a trade."

"I know who you can trade with!" said BanSha jumping up. "Tuzhel's uncle."

Solamar had forgotten the young channel was in the room. "BanSha we can't trade right over the border in the town where Tuzhel grew up. The Freeband Raiders have been raiding there. There's no way we could convince those Gens we're not Raiders."

Eric said, "People would never agree! Fort Hope has told everyone how they tried trading out-Territory and it destroyed them. Some of the Fort Unity and Fort Veritt people, at least the ones willing to do anything you say, might go for it, but the fight will tear this Fort apart."

Rimon's eyes met Solamar's and then Lexy's.

Solamar had left home, traveled far, escaped death repeatedly, and buried many friends, all because he believed Rimon Farris and the Forts were the hope of humanity. Even with the Forts failing, his mission was to make that hope survive. Instead, he'd found a woman and a home. He let Rimon zlin that in him.

Rimon studied BanSha. "Go get Tuzhel. And do not even think a word about any of this outside this room."

When the young man had left, Rimon again looked around at his lifelong friends and current allies. "I have seen too many injuries due to flimsy boots. The situation is a critical health issue. RenSimes augmenting must have reliable footgear and gloves. Come spring, they'll have to work like that again, clearing stumps from the new fields, planting, shearing sheep, all the rest."

Jhiti said, "We can't defend this Fort with boots that are falling off our feet. My scouts are all right now because we're not keeping a watch on Shifron while the weather has the Raiders confined. The truth is, we don't have the boots and gear to mount that watch again."

Rimon said, one hand on his belt buckle, "So, I won't put this decision to a debate of the whole Fort, or a vote."

If his staunchest supporters deserted him over this, Rimon would have lost Fort Rimon.

Rinda said, "The Council will be angry when they find out what you're up to, but they won't find out from me. Just don't make the mistakes we made trading with Gens. Fort Hope is gone. This is our last refuge." The Gen Councilor's nager trembled with apprehension not age.

"And it's my home," said Lexy. "We could send an all Gen team of traders. Fort Hope sent Simes, didn't they?"

"Yes," said Rinda nodding at Frevven.

"Do any of our Gens know Genlan?" asked Frevven.

It was a reasonable question especially for a renSime raised in-Territory to ask. The only people who came over the border from Gen Territory to live here were Simes who had changed over among the Gens. If they made it over the border, usually they had Killed someone they loved who had tried to care for them or who tried to murder them.

Either way, they arrived in Sime Territory ignorant of the language and customs and with no means of getting a Kill. Most died very quickly at the hands of the civilized juncts or joined Freeband Raiders where they died within a couple of years of the dissipating lifestyle. Few ever wanted to speak the Gen language again.

A Gen born and raised out-Territory, stayed snug in Gen Territory never knowing Simes even had their own language to portray the reality of their Sime senses. A few Gens though, in border towns were children of Gens who established in-Territory and escaped to live free as Wild Gens. Some of those taught their children a little Simelan.

In the Forts, channels learned as much Genlan as they could. Some Simes from Gen Territory spoke Genlan to their children, to give them the option of going there if they should establish instead of changing over.

Bruce suggested a few Gens who knew Genlan, Kahleen came up with more, Rimon added some, and several people contributed names. Benart and Val made lists.

Frevven said, "At least one of the people we send has to be familiar with grades of leather. And Endra is too old to be making this kind of a trip in winter."

Eric and Endra suggested one Gen who tooled leather as a

hobby, and another Gen who prepared sheepskin for documents. Neither spoke a word of Genlan or could grade boot leather. Other than the master cobblers, the most expert judge of leather grades was Bekka Esren.

Rimon brightened. He filled them in on Bekka's qualifications. He had an encyclopedic knowledge of every individual born in Fort Rimon. Bekka was a child who might change over soon.

Bekka's parents were the leaders of the Church of the Unity in Fort Rimon. The Church counted learning a little Genlan as a religious duty, though their only daughter had little interest in the Church or its social status in the Fort.

"I didn't know," confessed Rimon, "that she was studying leather craft."

Endra added, "She wants to be an artist in leather, and we've found a good market for well tooled items. Bekka is level headed, responsible, old enough to control herself. She's tall enough to pass for adult among the Gens, even if she is still flat chested. If I can't go, Bekka's my choice."

There was heated discussion of the ethics of risking a child too young to understand the dangers, but then Rimon said, "I'll check her for signs of changeover before mentioning this idea to her parents. They might decide on the basis of who would be her guardians on this trek. If they decide against it, we'll try your second suggestion. Just remember, Frevven is right that to justify the risk, we have to bring back the right sorts of leathers."

Solamar thought Bekka's parents would agree. They were both renSimes he had come to know when giving them transfer. They both proudly traced their lineage to the original Fort Freedom, before Rimon Farris, Delri's grandfather, arrived there. They had even tried to recruit him to their Unity worship services and he intended to go at least once to see how they worshipped.

As few Unity families as there were, they wielded a great deal of influence on matters of ethics even among those not of their religion. Their support of Rimon against this new Council was unwavering. Bekka, a close friend of BanSha, had already befriended Tuzhel and was trying to teach him about the Church of the Unity.

Before BanSha returned, they had a list of Gens who could handle pack horses, rough camping, and speak Genlan.

Solamar said, "I'd be worried that a group of Gens would get lost in the trackless hills. If they stick to the trails our scouts have seen the Raiders using, they'd surely be caught by the Raiders."

BanSha opened the outer door, letting cold air in.

Jhiti said, "I can send scouts with them all the way to the border, not by the known trails, but over toward the southwest. The pass there is worse than Fremir, but we can get them through. My scouts can set up a beacon and when they zlin the Gens returning up the next valley, light a fire to guide them right to the correct pass. It's a very rough approach from the Gen side. Even Simes could find themselves trapped in a box canyon."

Solamar said, "I volunteer to be waiting at that pass when they get back. I'll take down their fields so we'll be less of a target, and do any healing necessary."

The whole room rang with Kahleen's silent determination to be at his side during this venture.

Even the Gens who just donated selyn to the channels produced many times the amount of selyn that a Gen from out-Territory would. Now their production was greatly exaggerated, thanks to Rimon's schedule that exposed them to Simes working under augmentation. Even just a few days after donating selyn, they would be easy for the Raiders to spot from a distance.

Rimon said, "Val will find a volunteer channel for that duty then. You're right, Solamar, it'll be necessary to have a channel waiting for them. I'd choose myself."

Lexy looked from one to the other wanting to elbow Solamar out of that job. Solamar was oddly gratified that his welfare had become important to her as hers was to him.

Tuzhel followed BanSha in just in time to hear Jhiti's

comment and couldn't hold his tongue any longer.

"What pass?" asked Tuzhel. "What Companions? Who's in trouble? Can I help?"

Rimon explained what they wanted to do, and Tuzhel rounded on BanSha jabbing a tentacle at the young channel. "You fooled me! I never suspected a thing!"

Solamar edged forward prepared to augment to keep the youngsters from tearing each other apart, but a moment later they were both laughing hysterically at BanSha's marvelous nageric achievement of fooling a renSime.

BanSha demonstrated how he'd lied to Tuzhel under orders from Rimon and had everyone laughing. It took Rimon, Lexy and Solamar nearly a minute to reform the ambient and get their attention.

"Of course I'll go," Tuzhel told Rimon. "My uncle always has stocks of tanned leather by this time of winter. Even if my uncle has been taken by the Raiders other people know where his stock is hidden. They'll trade."

"Tuzhel, you can't go," announced Rimon.

Tuzhel objected nagerically and BanSha grabbed the fields. Rimon showed BanSha how to handle the nageric spike and left him to it. "Tuzhel, all our traders will be Gens. We want you to help in two ways. Make us a map to the town, and where to find the tannery. Then we'll want you to help concoct reasonable lies to tell the Gens."

Solamar had forgotten that Gens could lie among themselves undetected.

Crestfallen, then stubborn, then disappointed, Tuzhel finally accepted Rimon's verdict. BanSha handled Tuzhel's riotous fields better than Xanon would have after only one lesson.

Solamar asked, "How long will the trip take?"

Tuzhel said, "On foot, from High Crossing to the border southeast of here, it's about six days. In this weather though, with loaded horses in tow and staying off any useful trails, it could take twice that. More if it's only Gens."

Discussion raged again, but a real plan emerged that Solamar thought could actually work.

Rimon raised his voice and delivered his decision. "Benart will enlist three or four Gen volunteers to take pack horses loaded with trade goods and return with leather stock. Jhiti will prepare and secure a trail to the border and have his experts search for a weather window. Also Jhiti's scouts will equip the expedition. Tuzhel will work with the volunteers to develop a plausible lie about where they're from and why they're making this emergency trade in the middle of winter. It has to be something that won't be discovered come spring and bring them down on us."

Rimon zlinned Solamar's cracked boots. "I'd like to see them ready to ride during the next break in the weather. With such a long trip, they must expect to endure two or more storms on the trail."

He paused, then suggested quietly, one hand unconsciously straying back to his belt. "It might be best if the new Council and their supporters don't hear about this until the group has departed."

Rinda's nager proclaimed adamant agreement with that. "I'll do my best to keep them busy and distracted."

* * * * * * *

I knew it wouldn't work, thought Solamar.

It had taken six days to ready the expedition and in all that time, Rinda kept the new Council from noticing the conferences and meetings as volunteers were enlisted.

Jhiti's scouts cut a new trail southwest and cached supplies, preparing to support the group that would wait for the Gens to return to the border. Rinda told the Council Jhiti was supporting a logging expedition that would also forage for pine nuts. That elicited total disinterest from the busy Councilors and it was also true since the firewood consumption had stripped out local supplies.

Val juggled the schedule so that all the Gens who were going donated selyn the last evening before they left.

The day Lexy celebrated the first three months of her pregnancy, everything was ready for the trading expedition to High Crossing. The Gens assembled with Jhiti's scouts and the loggers outside the stables just before dawn.

The laden horses were brought out, stamping and huffing steam into the chill air. It was a much larger group of Gens than Solamar had anticipated, but Jhiti had insisted the traders had to have people along who could build a camp that would survive the worst mountain storm.

Lexy brought Bekka out of the Collectorium door, followed by Bekka's parents. Apparently, Bekka was now cleared to leave with the expedition.

Solamar watched Lexy walk with one hand on the child's shoulder, bending over to talk to her quietly. *She'll make a fabulous mother.*

Then Lexy was beside him. Rimon lifted Bekka into the saddle, her parents, Jor and Shaddyr Esren, watching.

At that very moment, Alind and Xanon slammed out of the dining hall doors and tromped across the open yard followed helplessly by Rinda. Xanon didn't even bother to control the fields around the two, and ignored the presence of the elderly Gen woman. Before they reached the stables, others had noted the disturbance came out to see.

Alind went right up to Rimon. "Where do you think you're going? You can't leave the Fort. Everyone here depends on you. No Council member would authorize this, so don't bother to lie."

Lie? thought Solamar. *Lie!* Rimon's stony nager had made these understandably insecure people paranoid.

Rimon faced Alind, a hand on his belt. "I'm not leaving."

"Well you're certainly not sending your daughter. She's pregnant! We're not sending anyone near Shifron!"

Rimon made no signal either physical or nageric, but Jhiti swung into his saddle, gestured the gatekeeper to open the big central gate, and moved his party on out. Alind ran after the horses shouting, "Wait. We haven't cleared you yet. Close that gate!" His voice was drowned by the noise.

The opening appeared as Jhiti's horse's nose reached it and the party kicked to a trot on the well shoveled area in front of the gate. The hooves tossed up bits of muck before Jhiti slowed for the descent to the valley floor. Alind retreated, mud spattered, as the gates shut in his face.

When Xanon rounded on Lexy's father aghast, Solamar edged closer to shield her.

Xanon spat, "What have you done, Rimon?"

Alind picked his way back over the churned snow watching his supporters rush out of nearby buildings. Xanon and Alind both wore new boots, as did many of those coming to support him. Those supporters had not been out logging and augmenting to get houses built.

Rimon's right hand gravitated to his belt buckle. "I've sent a well equipped expedition of volunteers on a well planned mission that may save this Fort. And I've done it without any orders, authorizations or votes." He cocked his head and asked brightly, "What have you done today?"

Alind halted beside Xanon and addressed his crowd. "I'm calling an emergency Council meeting in the school building right now. Go wake up the other Councilors!" He pivoted, pointed one tentacle, "Oberin! Send guards out to stop them and bring them back!"

Oberin glanced at her people spread around the wall's catwalk. "Anybody want to go for a ride?" she shouted. There were no takers. She had chosen the guards on duty this morning from Rimon's supporters. She shrugged at Alind. "Why don't you try again tomorrow?"

Alind snapped, "Rimon, Lexy, Solamar, five minutes and I will see you in front of the full Council."

"Not now," countered Rimon. "Val has us scheduled for Dispensary, and Lexy has to rest. See me in the dining hall at sundown and I'll tell you all about the plan. Come on Solamar, we have work to do." Rimon led his group to the Dispensary building, an easy swing to his stride despite boots worn beyond safe use.

But when they were inside, he tossed his cape onto the hook by the door and leaned his back against the wall. "I made a mistake asking Alind to run the election. People are using him, and he's bewildered. These are emotionally shattered people growing more fearful by the day that this Fort will be overrun too. This Council can't handle it."

Solamar knelt to clean Lexy's shoes.

Kahleen said, "Soon, everyone will have heard about the trading mission. They'll be even more afraid especially if rumors get the facts all backwards."

"True. Lexy, do you have the notes I asked for yet?" She nodded, and Rimon scraped muck off his shoes. "I have to tell Val to clear the schedule for sundown. Kahleen's right, we have to nail every fact in this announcement. Be sure Benart goes over every figure you give me."

Solamar should have expected this. Rimon knew he couldn't deal rationally with the Council, so he had to get the facts to the whole Fort, not let the new Council hide the truth to prevent panic. Facts countered fear.

"Yes," agreed Lexy, as Solamar peeled off her cloak. "I just have to add that Jhiti decided to lead the scouts himself, but I have the notes from Benart and the others."

"Good, leave them in my office and go get some sleep. Where's Garen?"

"Sleeping. We're on duty at noon, remember? You cut me another two hours a day."

"In a few days you won't be objecting so much."

"Probably not," admitted Lexy, which was a big concession. She flicked Solamar a warm smile that raced through her nager too, then took off down the hall in her long legged stride. Her hips swung just so, and Solamar thought they seemed a little broader.

"Come on Solamar, let's get these transfers done. Kahleen could you find Bruce for me? He's in the infirmary probably checking on yesterday's frostbite victims."

Solamar followed Rimon into the Dispensary corridor. "Do you think Maigrey is going to regret volunteering to stay with Xanon after this? Or will she be changing sides?"

"I told her what to expect for today," said Rimon. "She says she'll stick with him, but expects consideration when we get this Fort united. She's got her eye on one of the youngsters who'll change over soon. I told her she can have her pick of any channel I can match her to when we get a real Council elected."

"That's more than fair. But then what of Xanon?"

"Maybe he'll come to his senses by then."

With that, they arrived at the Dispensary check in desk, picked up renSimes who were fidgeting, and took them into transfer rooms.

Solamar worked steadily for hours, using Rimon's technique of spending extra time with each person, both before and after giving transfer. He enjoyed talking about their families, their housing situation, and now about boots and other essentials, making the Fort seem more like home.

Today, conversation quickly centered on the departing expedition, but all Solamar could say was, "Rimon's scheduled a talk in the dining hall later. I understand from Lexy that it'll be very informative."

And it was informative.

Near sundown, the dining hall filled with Council supporters plus some who hadn't decided yet. Since everyone could not fit into the hall, Rimon had asked those who agreed with him to come to a second, shorter meeting later that night. Here he intended to give a detailed account of what he'd done and why.

Privately, Rimon had told Solamar, "This'll be for those who don't believe I can take advice, form an opinion and decide, so you'll be bored, but could you please come work the fields for the audience?" Rimon had recruited Fengal and five other channels for the job, and Solamar agreed to manage them just to watch Rimon in action.

The new Council had swept in early, set up tables and chairs just for themselves on the stage the musicians used, leaving Rimon to stand below them. He took Lexy's notes in hand but faced the hall full of people, not the Council.

Channels and Companions positioned themselves among the standing crowd muting the thread of hostility.

Lexy was in the infirmary with the few patients who weren't mobile. Her notes, though, were complete, and Rimon ticked off the points one by one as he explained.

Solamar watched Rimon's free hand hover at the belt buckle as he spoke. Despite the distrust in the audience, Rimon was confident, his voice relaxed and vibrant.

He detailed how he'd noticed injuries from worn footgear mounting, went through some graphic cases, and explained why bad footgear could be a threat come spring, how the store room was empty of tanned leather, and how their normal supply line through Shifron was gone.

He avoided mention of the uneven distribution of new footwear, and focused only on what the deficiency would cost them in injuries in both defending the Fort and in planting the crops they'd be depending on next winter.

He illustrated with inexorable logic, how trading out-Territory was the only way to avoid certain doom.

Rimon said, "Such a trading venture destroyed Fort Hope. Our situation is different, though. We are so remote that the tax collector doesn't even come every year to count our Gens. There are no laws against trading out-Territory. Our danger is from the Freeband Raiders in Shifron, and from the Gens themselves."

He proceeded to present their plan one bit at a time, and listed objections Solamar hadn't even thought of. Then he explained how their plan countered each objection.

Tuzhel's suggestions for a plausible lie gave the Gens a story that would not arouse suspicion in High Crossing. They even had Gen Territory wardrobes and the horses bore brands recognizable as Gen owned stock.

The Fort Gens were to pretend to be part of a group trying to settle on the Gen border and hold back the Simes. Come spring, Jhiti's guards would deposit evidence on the Gen side of the border that would appear to be the remains of a settlement Simes had destroyed. Some of the tanned leather would be found there, and that would end the matter if the Gens ever searched for the fictitious settlement.

Rimon emphasized how each and every trail disaster they could anticipate had been prepared for. He told them about each Gen who had volunteered to go, what their qualifications were, feats they had pulled off in the past, bartering skills, rough camping skills, combat skills, and how they knew local Gen customs.

He detailed the trade goods they were offering, and gave them Benart's facts and figures.

He presented the immense challenges spring would bring, and countered each with a plan created by his senior management team. He produced facts and figures from Jhiti's defense plans showing they would win any battle if all their equipment were in top condition, which it would be once this expedition returned.

He cited the remarkable job they had done expanding the Fort, and did not mention latrines and wells. He ended with plans for the future. He listed births, changeovers and Establishments, and weddings in the offing, painting a vivid picture of a vital, united community that clearly exemplified the dream of Fort Freedom made real.

By the end, Solamar, who was managing fields at the western edge of the room, saw Rimon's glowing vision wrought upon the ambient. Almost everyone in the room was contributing, as if Rimon's vision were their own.

The tremendous Farris nager commanded the ambient, replete with confidence, optimism and voracious eagerness.

The doubters were swayed toward Rimon's side, and the Council supporters became doubters of their position.

When the Council began to ask questions, mostly questions Rimon had already systematically answered, people began unobtrusively leaving, hugging that intangible vision to themselves. The spell that couldn't last.

Solamar had to pay more attention to the fields and the work of the other channels and Companions sprinkled around the room compensating for the exodus.

Solamar once again concluded that he'd done the right thing in coming here, dedicating the rest of his life to the building of the Forts. This, right here in this room, was humanity's future. Here is where all would be decided. And this was the right man for the job. *If he can survive the erupting of this talent.*

CHAPTER TWELVE
CHANCE

"Oh, come on, it's just luck the expedition got back at all! We have to stop gambling our lives on the sheer dumb luck of a man we can't even zlin properly! He actually likes the disjuncts. They like him enough to request him for their transfers. Who knows what really goes on there!"

Rimon overheard this whispered remark as he and Bruce, wrapped in a null field, approached the rear of the crowd at the main gate. The trading expedition was returning only eighteen days after they had left.

The two whispering renSimes, both wearing good boots, spooked as Rimon dropped the masking field. Rimon smiled at them cordially and waded in to manage the fields.

As usual the greeters had lined up in rows on either side of the gate, facing each other, leaving a path for the arriving group. He was plowing through a miasma of hostility on this side, toward welcome on the other side.

Tuzhel emerged from the crowd behind Rimon, tucked himself inside Rimon's influence and followed them to the front of the crowd. *Oh, no. He heard those two talking about disjuncts.*

Rimon gathered the disjuncting renSime under his arm letting Bruce get ahead of them. "You'll have to go into seclusion tonight, Tuzhel," said Rimon. "You'll hit Turnover before morning."

"But it's so nice out. I hate that room."

"I know. I've been confined on occasion too and I truly hate it. Especially in spring. Just think, next year will be marvelous for you."

"I've got this year to get through first. I sometimes wonder if there's any point." He exuded an inappropriate grimness, maybe from the poison spread by whisperers.

"They won't split this Fort," assured Rimon. "We traditionally welcome those determined to disjunct."

Bruce had cleared them a path to the front row, so now even Tuzhel could zlin the crowd across from them.

"There's BanSha!" exclaimed Tuzhel. His grimness dissipated with the capriciousness of a First Year renSime.

When Rimon zlinned BanSha joining the other channels smoothing the ambient, he flashed Bruce a grin.

Bruce smirked back. "BanSha hasn't much talent, but he tackles every exercise with the determination to do it better next time. He'll be one of our best."

Rimon's optimism soared even higher as the gates finally began to swing open. Jhiti had sent his fast riders ahead of him with word of the success of the expedition. The Gens had brought two extra horses laden with a fine pottery clay, an item in very short supply, plus all the leather they had gone after.

Rimon and Bruce had just taken transfer which left Rimon's nerves sizzling with Postsyndrome, but it didn't seem that his optimism was just physiological.

This early spring day hinted that the unusual series of pounding winter storms was over. The expedition had enjoyed perfect traveling weather, clear with calm for eighteen days. *Just good luck, as they said.*

Oberin however was not pleased with the early break in the weather. Freebanders would be stirring out of Shifron and the Council had not yet authorized her to restore surveillance of the town. As Jhiti led his Sime escort through the gate ahead of the Gens, Oberin advanced on him with a situation report in hand.

Bekka, the bravest and now most famous child in the Fort, was leading one of the horses laden with tanned leather. She came through the gate behind Jhiti, sitting erect, chin high, hair flowing straight and shining, cheeks rosy, grinning for all she was worth. Rimon was delighted to zlin that she was indeed still a child. *It won't be long, though,* he thought privately, hugging Tuzhel to his side.

Tuzhel wanted to break and run for Bekka. They would be a couple, if Tuzhel didn't hurry her.

The rest of the party streamed in, dismounting, walking their horses toward the stable, handing them over to the waiting grooms. The families of the returning Gens swooped in to hug, kiss and celebrate their triumph.

When the last horse had cleared the gate, Rimon led the charge across the open space bringing the two lines of greeters together. Outside the closing gates, he saw the rear guard of Jhiti's scouting unit strung across the valley obliterating the expedition's backtrail. Jhiti reported he had used the break in the weather to plant the remains of an encampment to support the story told in High Crossing.

Rimon turned Tuzhel over to BanSha with instructions to see him to his confinement room immediately and without contact with Bekka. "BanSha, stay with Tuzhel all night. I'll clear it with Val and send Rushi and a few others along. You all can have your own party. Tuzhel isn't stable enough to attend the big party, but it's not fair that he shouldn't get to celebrate too."

"Now?" wailed Tuzhel.

Rimon hugged him again, using his handling tentacles to investigate. On his forearms at the roots of the tentacles, the ronaplin glands were swelling. No wonder he was peevish and grim. "We're going to see you through this, Tuzhel. It's very hard. We admire every Sime who's faced this ordeal. Now go with BanSha and I'll bet you'll have quite a few visitors during the party tonight. I'll see you have plenty of hosting supplies."

Rimon went to spread word among the more stable disjuncts to visit Tuzhel tonight. Isolation was particularly bad when everyone else was enjoying company, and BanSha was good enough with the fields to protect Tuzhel.

BanSha proudly took his charge off across the churned mud of the yard, Tuzhel brightening with every step.

In the end, Tuzhel's party lasted longer than the one in the main dining hall. While Bruce and Rimon were there, it even included shiltpron music. Kimra and Kreg and other scouts from Fort Hope brought garlands of pine cones gaily painted to spell out "Congratulations" in large Genlan letters and repeating it in Simelan.

About half the channeling staff filtered through escorting various disjuncted renSimes who owed their status to Aipensha, Lexy or Rimon. They brought dishes of pine nuts, and trin tea laced with pine needles giving it a wintry flavor and additional nutritional value.

As word of Tuzhel's private party spread, Endra, Frevven and Eric stopped in. Though they had to start work on new boots immediately, they wanted to thank Tuzhel again for his help getting the leather.

Fengal, Maigrey, Lexy, Iriela, Dayyel, Melina and her new baby, Kahleen, Eskalie, Solamar, Oberin and Jhiti made an even bigger point of congratulating Tuzhel on helping the expedition succeed.

Sian, however, made a different point. He brought a white, bleached linen yawal, and presented it with a flourish. "You should have this at hand for the moment you disjunct. It'll be the day of your real Changeover, the start of a whole new life. Wear it for your transfers until then."

Tuzhel clutched the simple tunic to his chest, winding all his tentacles through it and flung himself into BanSha's arms. "It's just like the one you wore at changeover!"

Rimon was gratified by the quick adjustments BanSha and Rushi made to the fields, protecting Tuzhel perfectly.

As the night progressed, the rest of Rimon's friends paraded through Tuzhel's isolation room, dropping off presents to ease his confinement, offering encouragement, reporting on the official party in the dining hall with hilarious parodies of Xanon's officious speeches.

They included Tuzhel in adult conversation about the wonderful sex he could expect once he disjuncted and could experience a real Postsyndrome for the first time.

Talk drifted toward the Fort's current prospects, now considerably improved thanks to Tuzhel, and his opinions were sought on a number of issues. It wasn't flattery. They wanted his perspective on what the Raiders might do next.

Rimon used the opportunity to drill BanSha and Rushi in managing the ambient in tight quarters to teach BanSha to monitor for Turnover despite nageric noise around him.

The room brimmed with absolute confidence and joyful anticipation for Tuzhel's disjunction.

When Tuzhel hit Turnover, the party broke up amid predictions it would be legendary before morning.

Though his control was shaky, Tuzhel's body was adjusting to a disjunct's transfer intervals. Still, he'd have to spend the two weeks before his sixth channel's transfer locked into the isolation room, visited only by those who could keep the fields from stimulating a Raider's hair-trigger Kill reflex.

The next day, a monumental ice storm hit the valley. Rimon treated a number of Gens for injuries from falls despite the lines rigged between buildings, and the renSimes didn't fare much better largely due to inadequate footgear.

Jhiti retired his wall guards for the duration. Even Freebanders in hard Need couldn't mount an attack.

During the storm, most worked on equipment for the spring tilling, but the Council spent the time talking, and fomenting trouble. Later, Rimon heard that Tuzhel's party was viewed as Rimon's deliberate affront to their authority.

Rimon was certain they would not be elected again, maybe not even serving out their year. They were just not doing the project management work of a Fort's Council. When they did attempt something, it never came out well because they hadn't consulted the channeling staff.

This Council's failures would be more evident if the seniors who would normally be on the Council weren't doing the management work, ignoring the Council's advice.

So, in spite of the Council, new boots began to appear on the hardest working renSimes and Gens, and the mood in the Fort brightened. New dishes and bowls appeared in the dining hall made from the fine clay that was the bonus negotiated by their Gens. Then work gloves appeared neatly stitched by the Fort Unity craftsmen.

After the paralyzing ice storm, the world turned to mud again, and Tuzhel plunged so deep into the miseries of disjunction he was not allowed visitors. BanSha dashed up to Rimon and Bruce in the dining hall and whispered in Rimon's ear, "I think Bekka Established selyn production."

"Where is she?" asked Bruce rising.

"Mucking the stables. I'm supposed to be learning to zlin pregnant animals. It's hard. They haven't got any selyn. Bekka does, I think."

Rimon swallowed the last of his pine needle laced trin tea and motioned BanSha on. "Show us."

BanSha had called it correctly. Rimon was inordinately pleased with his student channel.

That evening, Bekka was accepted into the ranks of the adult Gens with a celebration in the dining hall. It took a new Gen a month to produce enough selyn for a renSime's transfer, and about four months to reach real maturity. It was usually a smooth development, barely perceptible to the Gen, not at all like the wrenching shifts in the physical body that a Sime underwent at changeover. Still the changes in a Gen were emphatic and marked the onset of adulthood.

Bekka's party was attended by all her closest friends and relatives along with almost all Fort Rimon natives who came to congratulate her parents. She gave a lovely speech about the values of Fort Rimon and declared her intention to become a master leatherworker.

"Tuzhel told me that out-Territory women aren't allowed to learn such trades. Here, Simes get nervous around Gens handling sharp instruments. So if we can find out how tanning's done, maybe that's what I'll do."

Her parents, Shaddyr and Jor Esren stepped up beside Rimon and Bekka to accept the congratulations of the Church of the Unity community that looked to them for spiritual leadership. The Esrens were descended from the old Fort Freedom Young family with Bron family ties.

Rimon kept the medical histories of all the families of the Fort, but had yet to start with all the new people. He was wary of too much intermarriage among the small a group surrounding the Esrens and wondered who they might accept for Bekka from among the refugees if Tuzhel's attraction didn't work out.

His father had said his grandfather insisted they had to learn to predict how a renSime would respond to different channeling techniques, and how to teach it to channels. The clue must be in heritage and medical histories.

Most of what Rimon did, he could not teach. He just zlinned, did something and it worked even if he didn't know what he'd done. Lexy had picked up a lot from him, as had Aipensha, and Clire, but nobody else had, not even Solamar.

If their lifestyle was to spread through the junct communities, it had to be made teachable. That meant keeping clean records so someone in the future could look back over generations and find the rules that governed channeling and healing.

Bekka's father Jor spoke of his great grandfather's day in Fort Freedom, when a child who Established as a Gen would be escorted to the border, given a horse and valuables and sent to a new life in the nearest Gen town, a life among other Gens who had come out of Fort Freedom.

He recounted how that very fact had saved Fort Freedom in Zeth Farris's day, and had actually saved Zeth Farris's life during his changeover. "My daughter Bekka has continued the finest tradition of this family in concluding an equitable trade with our own Gen neighbors. We expect to make a splendid match for her with the son of one of the best scholars of the Church."

This, Rimon noted, was bad news to Bekka who knew who

they meant. Her parents could not zlin Bekka's objection in her barely perceptible nager.

Finally, Rimon gave his traditional speech, thanked Bekka for bringing fine leathers, completed his social duties and went in search of Bruce.

The good weather lasted only three days, and then a blizzard was followed by a series of heavy snowstorms.

Jhiti was glad Oberin hadn't sent scouting parties north toward Shifron and south toward the Gen border. Instead the scouts had helped build two new wings on the stable and clear the courtyard of picketed horses.

Four days after one blizzard, Rimon was in his office with Jhiti, peering at Jhiti's plan for expanding the underground shelter for the Companions and channels' combat infirmary. Lexy and Solamar came in as Rimon asked, "Jhiti, how deep you intend to dig this?"

"Not deep. We can layer sod and stone over the top, make it look like a natural hump."

"I'd rather build it off this way, digging it deeper and running under these three houses. It'll be easier get from the shelter into the infirmary building. We could also put another entry into the channels' on-duty sleeping rooms."

"My main concern is the huge channeling staff we have to hide during the next attack. Our wall is so much better now, we may not have as many casualties."

Lexy said, "Dad, you've been discussing that for days. Set the teams to work on it. We may not have much time."

Jhiti said, "We'll surely be attacked before the thaw."

"That's why you didn't plan to dig it as deep?"

"Partly, yes, but I like the idea of another door."

Rimon asked Solamar and Lexy. "Is it worth it?"

Lexy said, "If it can be done in time. Solamar?"

Solamar nodded. "Can you do it Rimon's way in time?"

"I don't know. I'll go talk to Benart."

"Whatever you do," said Rimon, "don't talk to the Council about it or we'll still be debating years from now."

"If anyone survives!" said Jhiti rolling up the sheepskin the plan had been inked into. "I'll see you later."

Rimon settled into his chair wondering where Bruce was. "Is there a problem?" Lexy zlinned healthy. Though she was taking extra selyn for the baby, it was definitely not a channel's heavy demand, and she insisted she could work longer hours than he was allowing. She probably could, but Rimon saw no reason she should.

Solamar looked around, zlinned the hallway, and said to Lexy, "I don't believe it. We've got him alone."

She grinned. "We came to discuss Tuzhel's disjunction but since we've trapped you alone...."

Solamar said, "I've been trying to tell you for a couple of months that I think I'm in love with your daughter."

Rimon sat up straighter. "You only think?" Her unconditional love for this man was obvious, but only Aipensha could have made Lexy see herself clearly.

Lexy said, "Well, since I'm not sure, how could he be? I just thought I ought to warn you. It wouldn't do to shock an old man to death, would it?"

"Shock?" He played into their mood. "Like this?" He produced a showfield riddled with horrified amazement, dimming into a faint, then stared at them eyes wide, one brow raised, innocent and attentive.

They both laughed. Their voices harmonized perfectly, and Rimon didn't miss the two handling tentacles twined between their bodies, or how closely they stood.

"Well, you let me know when you're sure, all right?"

"All right," they chorused then laughed at themselves.

"So what about Tuzhel's disjunction?"

Solamar said, "From what he says, he's about seven months old now and Killed several times in his first month. Day after tomorrow will be his sixth disjunction transfer. I might expect disjunction crisis at his eighth disjunction transfer, but it could happen this time, or next."

"I'd guess sooner rather than later," Lexy shrugged. "As

we've discovered, you really can't ever tell."

"I'd guess sooner rather than later, too," agreed Rimon. It was what he'd been thinking since Bekka's Establishment party. They could only guess. "I've noted he's stressed, vacillating between eager acceptance of a place here and morose rejection of all our rules. He's made some friends though. That may be the deciding factor."

"According to the Council," said Lexy, "we should keep him locked away from his friends until he disjuncts."

Solamar added, "The Council will not accept that a disjunct Freeband Raider can earn a place in a Fort, and they're not sure about the other disjuncts we already have. It's just that Tuzhel was a Freebander for a very short while."

Rimon said, "The most crucial short while of any Sime's life."

"Exactly, and now his upbringing is asserting itself."

Rimon wondered why they were repeating what they all knew so well. "Tuzhel must have had a loving family," agreed Rimon and repeated his prescription. "Let him roam within the limits we've set before Turnover, but be sure he's always boxed in by channels because you can't predict when he'll spike intil or hit a premature Turnover. Don't let him zlin the surveillance."

Solamar took the game to a new level. "Disjunction crisis is like First Need. We've all seen it. Soaring, spiking intil, that ravenous, desperate and terrified Need, driven, instinctive. Only death by Attrition comes any worse than that. At least in Disjunction there's some cognitive ability left and that's the crucial element because there has to be a deliberate choice to accept satisfaction from a channel...."

"...forever leaving the Kill behind," finished Rimon, nodding. What were they trying to say that they couldn't just say? "Without that conscious choice, the decision doesn't have the strength to withstand future temptations."

Solamar said, "The sooner Tuzhel makes his choice the better chance he has of choosing channel's transfer, setting a new pattern for the rest of his life. I want to be that channel for him."

Surprised, Rimon buried his reaction behind a tranquil showfield. Lexy wasn't buying it though Solamar deduced Rimon's real reaction from Lexy's skepticism.

Solamar, guilt politely buried behind a bland showfield he knew was transparent to both Lexy and Rimon, confessed, "I told her why you're wearing that belt, Rimon. I had to because everyone who's been on your side has been pressuring her to get you to put that belt away again. The opposition keeps pointing to it as clear evidence that you think you're above the Council's authority. Lexy was upset over it because she started to believe it too."

She discussed this with you but not me? That explained the roundabout approach to claiming Tuzhel's disjunction transfer, which Rimon had planned to handle.

Solamar added, "Besides, I wanted to make sure she hadn't been hiding any similar experiences. I know you hadn't zlinned anything amiss with her, but I can't zlin an inch into her showfield most of the time."

Lexy countered, "More like two or three inches. He's too modest."

"So the belt buckle has become a major issue tangled into this whole disaster of a Council," said Solamar. "Lexy had to know what was really going on. So I told her."

"Executive decision," sympathized Rimon. "A hard call, but not at all a bad one."

"I didn't know what to do," explained Lexy. "That belt was your father's. With Aipensha gone, and no time for any of us to grieve properly, I thought it was just your way of being close to Grandfather, and I couldn't bring myself to suggest you should give that up when so many of us are depending on you. I knew you had to have a good reason to ignore what people were saying. You should have told me."

"I should have," agreed Rimon. He zlinned his daughter, four months pregnant and still carrying it lightly. Gen or renSime for sure. Still, family lore said Farris women tended to die in childbirth.

At least she hadn't been affected by whatever he and Solamar had done on the wall during the battle. He and Clire were the only ones wandering around outside their bodies. "So" he prompted Solamar, "you judged it was less stress for her if she knew than if she didn't?"

"I should have talked to you first, asked you to tell her, but...." Solamar shrugged with an eloquent ripple of handling tentacles.

Rimon had been studiously avoiding Solamar, and when he couldn't, he'd refused to talk about curing his sliding out of his body by sliding out of his body on purpose. Besides, the problem was gone.

Rimon took his right ventral handling tentacles away from clutching the belt buckle and unfolded the hands that lay over the innocuous bit of artwork, a symbol of Unity. He placed his hands on the desk and sat up.

Lexy continued, "So since the origin of this problem is either the stunt you two pulled on the walls during the battle or that First Transfer you forced into Tuzhel, I don't recommend you doing his disjunction."

Solamar added, "She wanted to do it, but I figured it'd be better if I did."

"And I figured," countered Lexy, "it would be far better for Tuzhel if I did. I'm in much better shape than you give me credit for, and I'd be glad of the work."

"So we decided," ended Solamar, "to ask you to decide before we talk to Dakin or Val about the schedule."

Having delivered themselves of all these guilty burdens, they both pulled chairs up before Rimon's desk and sat down. They behaved as if they'd been married for ten years already.

Which, Rimon felt deep inside, was a very good thing. Despite pestering about the out of body thing, Solamar was an ethical, reliable, skilled channel with a generous heart and steady, kind disposition who was totally besotted with Lexy. He couldn't imagine a better son-in-law. Rimon just hoped he didn't get Lexy pregnant. Such a child would be a channel with a truly deadly pre-natal selyn draw.

He made a mental note to make family record updating a top priority. He might be able to find a father for Lexy's next child among the new people who would not be so likely to produce death rather than an heir.

"So?" asked Lexy.

"Quiet," admonished Solamar. "He's thinking and I want him to get the right answer."

The only answer Rimon had right then was that Kahleen would make a much better candidate for mother of Solamar's children than Lexy would. From all signs, he thought Kahleen might well agree.

"Oh!" Rimon thought, "I'll do Tuzhel's transfer this time, and then I think I'll be doing his disjunction."

"You're sure that's wise?" asked Solamar. "He might be a major source of your problem."

"I've been doing his transfers without incident, and in fact haven't had any incident in a long while now. I think what's best for Tuzhel is the more crucial consideration."

Tuzhel favored Rimon but would have gladly accepted Lexy or Solamar. If he had a free choice though, he'd have chosen BanSha, and Rimon was not about to allow that.

Lexy said, "That's your decision?"

"Yes."

"Sure?"

"Yes." *I'm old enough it doesn't really matter what happens to me, only I do so want to live to see this grandchild grow up.*

She sighed. "I'll go tell Val, Dakin's on duty in scheduling. Then Ill find Garen and get some sleep."

They rose in unison, in totally unconscious coordination. "I'm on duty," said Solamar. "I told Kahleen to meet me...there she is now."

They all turned as Kahleen and Bruce entered with Garen trailing behind calling, "Wondered where you three had gotten to. Imagine hiding in Delri's office! I'd never have thought to look here if Jhiti hadn't suggested it,"

Solamar enjoyed the way Garen molded Lexy's fields. Rimon thought it zlinned comforting, too.

Rimon dropped the fields and watched the two channels and their Companions weave complex patterns as they bade Rimon both hello and goodbye and whirled out of his office. Bruce edged behind Rimon's chair and put both hands on his shoulders. Warm selyn fields shafted down into Rimon's tense muscles. "Benart says you'll get your underground shelter just the way you want it."

"Good. Once that's built, we'll be asking the families in the houses nearest the entries to the new shelter to switch with any channel or Companion families we have scattered about. We'll want to arrange things so that during an alert, the channeling staff won't have to move into the on-duty building just because it's the only entry into the shelter."

"Jhiti will be ecstatic."

"Oberin will dance for joy."

"That might be fun to see."

"What? Are you still Post? My Turnover's in two days!" He relaxed into his Companion's therapy.

"Two whole days to Turnover, so I wouldn't have expected this much tension. What's going on, Delri?" He paused, feeling Rimon cooperating. "That's much better."

"Let me enjoy what you're doing, then I'll tell you."

"Sometimes I wonder why I ever got involved being your Companion. Don't you realize how hard it is? There are so many new channels here now, maybe I can...."

"All right," surrendered Rimon, as if unaware the Gen was teasing. "I'll tell you now. Then you'll owe me a good hour of this."

"Deal."

Rimon told him everything, saving his speculation on who should father Lexy's children and who should bear Solamar's for last. He knew Bruce would have a number of opinions on that, some of them very good, too.

CHAPTER THIRTEEN
REVERSALS

Rimon knew that Tuzhel been told to expect ever deteriorating satisfaction from channel's transfer until after the crisis, and then his Need would be adequately met. He was an intelligent lad who had taken it all in, asked endless questions, and did a little better with each try.

Rimon had great hopes. So the day of Tuzhel's sixth transfer, Rimon decided to let Tuzhel ride through Rimon's own Turnover with him instead of scheduling Tuzhel's transfer before or after his own Turnover.

The experience should convince the non-logical part of Tuzhel that Simes live through it. Raiders, unlike the juncts who lived on Pen Gens, typically took a Kill at or before Turnover, believing Turnover was death. Fort lore said dispelling that notion was the key to disjuncting a Raider.

Bruce and Rimon had spent nearly two hours with the junct, and Tuzhel was now nearly berserk with what felt to him like hard Need, but was actually just an edge on his intil. Fear of Need magnified it monstrously.

Rimon explained his offer to Tuzhel fifteen minutes before his scheduled transfer time, ending, "This might let you wait a few more minutes before your transfer."

"If I do it, I'll have more control around Gens after I disjunct?" Clearly that had become important to him.

"That's the theory," agreed Rimon. Bruce was being part of the walls and doing a good job of it too. Rimon felt his

Companion had something to add but couldn't disturb the working ambient to insert his comment. Rimon made a mental note to ask him later.

Tuzhel paced the room, body rippling with the oily grace of full hunting mode, though he was duoconscious, seeing and zlinning. "You won't let me die?"

"No, there's no danger to you. It's just difficult."

Tuzhel paced again. "I can't zlin you all the way through. How do I know you're telling me the truth! Why would you want me to live?"

This was the problem all the new people from other Forts had with Rimon. They hadn't known him all their lives. They had no reason to trust him, and the one way they had of determining trustworthiness didn't work. Even when he dropped his show-field, they couldn't tell if he really had dropped it or just altered it to make it seem so.

Rimon's hands strayed to his waist where he'd been accustomed to resting them on his belt buckle. It wasn't there. Yesterday, since it had become so important to people, he'd put it in its drawer, sure he didn't require it.

Solamar had been horrified, Bruce worried, and Lexy didn't know yet. Others were beginning to notice. So far nothing had happened, even when he was working, except he no longer knew what to do with his hands.

"Tuzhel," said Bruce as Rimon's hands searched, "we want you to live because too many people died in the battle that brought you to us. You survived against all odds. So you have become the symbol of our hope for the future."

"And more than a symbol," added Rimon. "Already you've saved us by helping with the leather trade. You've worked in the stables when you could, and helped with that play the children put on. You've earned your place here."

Bruce's flat, honest sincerity impressed Tuzhel. Bruce was capable of lying to a renSime, but Tuzhel believed him.

"All right, I'll wait and watch your Turnover. Just don't blame me if I die on you. Or worse, take your Gen." He zlinned Bruce and slid hyperconscious, zlinning without being able to see, hunting mode.

Rimon flashed Bruce a smile and went to Tuzhel, pulling him back to duoconsciousness. "Don't worry, I won't blame you," answered Rimon. "And I'm not worried about my Gen. He can take care of himself."

That stopped the junct in his tracks. "You've never, ever, referred to Bruce as your Gen!"

"Not to his face, no," said Rimon giving Tuzhel a Sime-to-Sime nageric twinkle.

Bruce let his own comment on that seep into the ambient, then sat down in the only chair and disappeared back into the furniture. Tuzhel blinked at him.

"If I didn't feel so bad, I'd be laughing my head off."

"Bruce does have a sense of humor, for a Gen."

Prepared for Rimon's ploy this time, Bruce didn't react, at least not where Rimon could zlin it. *No doubt I'll pay for this later.*

"Gens don't have a sense of humor?"

"Not where their selyn is concerned, anyway."

Tuzhel circled the seated Gen who never let a quiver disturb his attention even as Tuzhel deliberately went into hunting mode as a Raider approaching a Kill, then struggled to suppress it again, horrified when Rimon had to help him.

"I guess they really are unKillable. What's it like to have a Gen of your own to supply your selyn."

"He serves my Need as I serve yours. I pass my experience with him on to you. Right now he's working to me. It's a little rude to try to disturb his concentration."

Rimon shifted his attention to Bruce, then slowly dropped his showfield, letting Tuzhel zlin his primary field, letting the creeping tension of approaching Turnover fill the room. Bruce's body adjusted to the shift in the fields. The insulated room filled with the incessant thrum of the Gen selyn production pacing Rimon's selyn consumption. "Zlin that, Tuzhel? If he weren't working to me, he wouldn't adjust so smoothly. Then you and

I would be tripping all over each other unless I managed the fields with my secondary system. So it's rude to him and to me to disrupt his concentration." Bruce didn't react.

"Rude? You should have heard what Solamar said when I was teasing Kahleen while he was trying to zlin me for disjunction crisis."

"Solamar's a little hard on the discipline, huh?"

"Only when I'm...what's that word?"

"Incorrigible?"

"I think that's the one he used."

"I'll just bet he did." Rimon had heard him use that word to describe BanSha, usually while laughing.

Then suddenly Rimon drew a long, deep breath and put his hand out to stop Tuzhel in mid-stride. The junct turned, attention pulled away from his own internal misery as the bottom fell out of Rimon's stomach.

When caught in public by Turnover, Rimon masked this plummet into the Need half of his cycle with his showfield. For him, the shift was a longer, scarier fall than for most Simes, even channels. But he let Tuzhel ride this out with him, making no effort to protect the renSime from his spiking intil.

As they had planned, Bruce let him fall free, plunging past that halfway point in his Need cycle, all security gone, suddenly ignored by his Companion. Every Sime cell in his body yearned to reach out to the Gen and clutch at the selyn he had to have to survive. He didn't. He just let Tuzhel zlin a channel at Turnover, reduced to being just an ordinary Sime without any of the comforts a Companion provided.

Rimon's internal time sense clocked about five seconds before his brain made the adjustment from relative security to the thrumming beat of ever increasing Need. The shock passed, but Tuzhel reflected it back as an echo, junct Need shrieking into the ambient.

Rimon reconstructed his showfield, and signalled Bruce to go back to work as he gathered the renSime in a transfer grip. "Now you see. A channel is just a Sime. We all share that experience, Tuzhel. That was easy for me this month. I had a great transfer last month, and I expect another great one in a couple weeks. Bruce is right here for me as I am here for you."

"Now? Do it now!"

"A few moments. Remember you can always come to the channels for your Turnovers, though eventually you'll gain confidence, knowing Turnover is a much longer way from death by Attrition than it seems now. We all feel that panic at Turnover, and we all feel Need and routinely survive them both."

Tuzhel begged, "Is that enough lesson now?"

Rimon closed the contact and poured selyn into the renSime, letting Tuzhel draw as much as a junct renSime could. He portrayed the Gen terror he had so studiously learned, infused with his fresh memory of Turnover and its savage impulse to rip selyn from any nearby Gen.

Right in the middle of Tuzhel's frantic selyn draw, suddenly the ambient in the room shifted and Clire stood behind him, wrapped around him like a cold vapor, oozing over his hands on Tuzhel's arms.

"Watch what your baby is learning to do before he's even born!" She paused at his shock. "Oh, yes, Del Rimon Farris, I'm carrying your son!" With a laugh of cold hatred, she whipped her lateral tentacles over Rimon's and around Tuzhel's, surrounding the junct's laterals with insubstantial shadows fraught with twisted, distorted streams of selyn.

Gen pain, terror, and insane despairing surrender to death exploded between them.

Tuzhel came alive with the unfettered release of the junct fulfillment, Killbliss, then relaxed into the aftermath, basking in unutterable relief. And Clire was gone, had never been there, couldn't possibly have been there.

Rimon wrapped himself in his most impenetrable shell, and focused on his patient. "Yes, Tuzhel, that's enough lesson for now," said Rimon dismantling his grip.

"I'm glad I did your lesson! That was amazing," said Tuzhel, hypoconscious, gazing about the room that he sensed only with the ordinary five senses. "There's no dead Gen here. Even Bruce is still alive. You made me imagine that, and it worked! It was so real!" He spun about in a little dance step. "I feel incredible! I'm disjunct, aren't I?"

"No," answered Rimon. "No I'm sorry Tuzhel, but that's not it yet." It might have set him back too many months to let him disjunct before he was too old.

Bruce had come to his side at some point, and Rimon hadn't even noticed. The Gen was worried.

"Tuzhel, you're free to go now. See Val to pick up your escort and whatever assignment she has for you. You did sign up for the work crews, didn't you?"

"Yeah. They're planning to dig a big ditch and wanted a lot of hands. I think Val said I'd haul firewood to soften the ground, but I was in such Need when she came by I don't remember."

"Go check that out then, and don't leave the building without an escort."

As Tuzhel gathered his things and opened the door, BanSha, Rushi and Bekka were waiting in the hall. "Oh, you zlin fabulous!" exclaimed BanSha, dragging Tuzhel toward Val's office.

Tuzhel resisted BanSha's guidance and stopped to zlin Bekka. "They told me you'd Established, but you're absolutely beautiful."

Young love was such a delight to behold.

Bekka, though, as an untrained Gen, shouldn't have been in this part of the building. BanSha was not certified to protect an Establishing Gen from a disjuncting renSime, even right after his transfer.

BanSha and Tuzhel sensed Rimon studying them, though Bekka was oblivious.

"Tuzhel, step back in here a moment. I'd like a word with you. BanSha you and Bekka wait a moment."

When the door closed behind Tuzhel, he said, "You're locking me up again?"

"No, I just wanted to remind you, privately, that Bekka Established barely ten days ago, and you're at least six months past changeover. She's way too young to be interested in what you're interested in." While he spoke, he brought Tuzhel to duoconsciousness, to mute the shout of his ordinary senses so he could think straight.

"I'm Post? I thought that wouldn't happen until after disjunction."

"Oh, you'll notice a difference after disjunction," assured Rimon. "Remember this. If you ever want a real chance to get close to Bekka, you have to stand back for at least another four months, maybe five or six. Let her grow up naturally, or she could end up hating you forever."

Rimon knew that along with all the rest of the lessons the channeling staff had put this youngster through had come the basics of sex education, Fort style. "You've been warned you would begin to feel this way."

Tuzhel took a deep breath and nodded. Clearly he was disappointed and Rimon could see why. After a great transfer which he'd been told would be a disastrous ordeal because he was nearing disjunction crisis, he was feeling wonderful but not allowed to pursue that feeling any more than he'd been allowed to assuage his Need at impulse.

"I think you and Bekka would make a fine couple, if she's willing. Right now, concentrate on being her friend."

"I got that part of the lesson. She just seems so...."

"Oh, yes, she does definitely just seem 'so.'"

"Do you think she could become a Companion?"

"She hasn't asked. It's hard, hard work. It has to be her choice. That's something else we'll just have to wait for. She hasn't even given her first donation yet. Tuzhel, let her grow up, then let her decide what she wants."

"But could she if she wanted to? Become a Companion?"

"We'll know that after she's done a few donations."

"Wait-wait-wait! Is that all life is ever going to be?"

"Well, if you start waiting soon enough and wait for enough things all at once, something you're waiting for happens almost every day. It's just a question of having enough things developing."

Tuzhel frowned at him, then burst out laughing. "I don't believe you said that."

Rimon listened to what he'd just said again in his mind. "Neither do I. It may have some merit, though."

"So now I'm waiting for Turnover, waiting for disjunction, and waiting for Bekka. I have to add more things to wait for so things will always be happening?"

"Try it and let me know if it works."

"May I go now?" asked Tuzhel with impeccable grammar and a very clean accent.

"Yes, as long as you go directly to Val or whoever's on duty now and get your assignments straightened. And tell her I said you should be eating a solid meal before going to work. You still have a little growing to do."

"I'm not a child anymore."

"Your body is still developing. The better you eat, the longer you'll live."

"That's what Rushi keeps saying to BanSha."

Rimon opened the door, glancing at Bruce as the Gen let him know exactly how hungry he was at that moment.

Rimon dismissed them with a wave of two tentacles. "BanSha, you and Rushi stick with Tuzhel until Val assigns someone else. Take Tuzhel right to Val's office, and that's an order. Good job, Rushi. Bekka, don't forget you have lessons and Tuzhel has work."

They swarmed off down the hall, chattering about some new project of BanSha's. Tuzhel stuck to Bekka's side as he grinned back at Rimon exuding a sense of being accepted that was another brick in the foundation of his disjunction. Rimon sent back his approval on the ambient.

BanSha started to intercept, protecting Tuzhel, but then relaxed his showfield and let Tuzhel zlin Rimon. Tuzhel's joy lit up the corridor to Sime senses, but though Rushi grinned too, Bekka did not. *Not yet,* Rimon thought hopefully. *She's oblivious, still in a child's world.*

Bruce closed the door and leaned against the handle as if sealing Rimon in and skewered him with one of those soul chilling Companion's looks with eyes and nager together.

"What happened during that transfer?" Bruce's eyes were wide, but he didn't let his alarm show in his nager. Or he tried not to. Rimon's nerves were raw enough that he couldn't help recognizing that *his Gen* had indeed felt something. *Who says Gens can't zlin? Some of them, you can't keep a secret from to save your life.*

"I'm not sure, Bruce. Maybe Solamar will know. He apparently knows things he hasn't told me yet."

"He's been trying to."

"I know," answered Rimon, grim beyond what a Turnover day called for. *I should never have taken that belt off. I have to get my lessons done, just like the children.*

Rimon and Solamar were still sleeping in shifts, sharing the on-duty sleeping room that had always been Rimon's temporary quarters. During the Need half of their cycles, their Companions bunked in the room with them, making it very crowded. Rimon had given priority to building the underground shelter, rather than new houses for the channels, so he had nobody to blame but himself.

Solamar opened the door just as Rimon was about to reach for the handle. Solamar, aching with Need, ushered them into the room.

"It happened again. Clire. You weren't there this time. This was different."

"He wasn't where?" asked Kahleen, wrapping a blanket around her. "What was different?" The fire had burned to embers and the room was chilly. Solamar lit a brace of candles so Bruce and Kahleen could see.

"You haven't told her?"

"No."

"Told me what?" asked Kahleen grabbing a heavy leather glove off the mantle to shove wood into the fire.

Bruce explained, "Solamar has been working on some fancy

nageric tricks with Rimon, but they don't have a good handle on controlling it yet, so odd things keep happening."

"Oh. Solamar told me something about that."

Rimon ran tentacles around the nape of his neck. He was barely at Turnover and Solamar was due for transfer in less than a day. It wasn't fair to burden the man with his miseries. He rearranged the fields, and Solamar helped. In a few moments, the strain in the room had leveled out.

"Bruce, fetch yourself and Kahleen something to eat, and some trin tea for us," suggested Rimon. "We'll fill Kahleen in on the details. After all that time as Clire's Companion, Kahleen might be able to supply some insights. Solamar, I think Clire's still alive."

"Alive!" said Kahleen. "How could you know...?"

"Bruce?"

"Save the Clire's alive part until I get back."

"Don't worry," said Solamar pulling Kahleen down to sit on the bed next to him. They wrapped the blanket around the two of them. "This is a long story, so take your time."

By the time Bruce returned followed by two kitchen staffers with trays, they had Kahleen well briefed on why Rimon had been wearing the jeweled Starred Cross belt.

Rimon cleared the small table and the dresser top by heaping all the personal items on the bed. The repast was laid out and the kitchen staff left. Bruce had brought enough for six Gens, probably hoping Rimon would eat something, and maybe Solamar would nibble.

As they ate, Rimon cradled a glass of tea in his icy cold hands and tentacles. He gave them every detail of what had just happened during Tuzhel's transfer, finishing, "So Clire's still alive. Or I hallucinated. Or maybe she's dead and haunting me."

Kahleen was having trouble taking all this in at once. "Delri, am I understanding this right? All the other times you wandered out of your body, Solamar was drawn into it too, if he was asleep at the time?"

"Yes, just about."

"You were asleep this time. And weren't drawn in?"

"Maybe I wasn't asleep just then. All I can manage this close to transfer is a short nap here and there."

"No nightmares, though?" asked Kahleen.

"You do good work, Kahleen. I've been able to sleep without unpleasantness. It could be significant that I wasn't drawn into it this time. Rimon, if she's alive and was affected by what we did during the battle as you were, then maybe she was out of her body and came to you."

"You know how to just go outside your body at will?" Kahleen asked Solamar.

Solamar, seated beside her on the bed nibbling off her plate, nodded silently. He pulled back to watch her as if he expected her to run screaming from the room leaving him without a Companion to give him transfer.

Kahleen hitched a little closer to Solamar, blending her ripening Gen nager into his dimming center. "Relax, Solamar. I'm not going anywhere. I shouldn't have asked about what you weren't telling me."

Bruce said, "No, he should've told you a long time ago. You have to know these things to do your job. I'm used to it. Delri's spent his adult life coming up with new things he doesn't tell me about until I mess him up by not knowing. Maybe this one's not what we think it is. After what he did for Sian, though, I do halfway believe it ."

Solamar said, "Think of it this way. Rimon can imagine something, shape and hone it, create it in this other space where people don't have solid bodies. He can take what he's imagined and make it real. He healed Sian's nerves not in Sian's body itself but in the part of Sian that can move out of his physical body. And then he put Sian's healed image back into his body and the body did heal."

Is that what I did?

"Maybe," continued Solamar, "he imagined Clire as a way to give Tuzhel the kind of transfer he Needed. And that became real to Tuzhel."

"There's more," said Rimon heavily. He told them what Clire had said about the baby she carried, his baby, learning to give selyn in a scream of death and hatred.

Kahleen said, "Delri, that's just insane. It's the kind of nightmarish thing you'd expect when you're in Need, and you gave that transfer right after your Turnover. I still can't believe you let Tuzhel ride your Turnover with you! Clire would never have done anything that generous."

Solamar said, "He's still guilty over what happened to Clire."

"Me, too. I was her Companion. I was supposed to get her down into the shelter! My conscience never lets up yammering about that. Your conscience is tormenting you, too. As Solamar said, you gave Tuzhel a great transfer using just your imagination."

Bruce nodded, "You can't control what you imagine?"

Rimon asked Kahleen, "Could Clire really hate me?"

"I doubt it. I don't think she could possibly be alive."

She was lying and Solamar zlinned that too.

"Rimon," said Solamar, putting his arm around his Companion's shoulders and holding her tight to his body. "Even if Clire's alive, it isn't the Clire you knew. Having the Council turn on her when she was guilty of nothing worse than an error in judgment, then feeling that you had betrayed her and your own child, she broke. Pregnant and in Need, I can't imagine how I'd feel."

"You'd hate me?"

"No."

And that, strangely enough, was the whole truth. Here was a man who couldn't hate if he tried. It just wasn't in him. Rimon knew he himself wasn't made so fine as that. He'd made worse mistakes than Clire had, and things had worked out well but only by sheer luck.

"Rimon, put the belt on again and keep it on. After my transfer, I'll show you some of those exercises I keep promising you. Lexy's on shift all by herself. You'd better get back out there before she tries something she shouldn't."

Since the boot problem had been solved, and most of the building had been completed, the channeling staff had been dealing with far fewer cases of frostbite and injuries. That reduced the workload to where they had a surplus capacity again, with the majority of a duty shift spent collecting and dispensing selyn. But there were always problem births, unexpected changeovers, and now in the depths of winter with the first harbingers of spring, illness.

Rimon got to his feet, piled the detritus from the meal back onto the trays. "You're right, I want her to take it easy. She's tiring quickly already."

Rimon rummaged in the back of his drawer for the belt and put it on. "Let's go see what Lexy's up to and make sure Tuzhel talked to Dakin about his schedule."

* * * * * * *

"Delri! Come quickly! The Council is hammering on Tuzhel and he's about to break to pieces!" It was BanSha's voice outside the door, the young channel's nager identifiable through the insulation.

Rimon released Bruce's arms from his transfer grip. The vast abundance of radiant selyn coursing through his whole body, warming his soul and bringing a wondrous peace, had barely had a minute to work its way into him. The anxiety and gloom that had gripped him during Need had just started to dissipate and already some dire emergency hammered at the door of the transfer room.

"I'll get it," said Bruce.

They both had had other plans for the next few hours.

Bruce opened the door and BanSha raced into the room, finally zlinned the state of the ambient. "Oh, sorry!"

Rimon began to protest but Bruce forestalled him. "No use telling a First Year channel not to overreact."

"I overreacted?"

"Not by much." Rimon injected approval into the ambient. "I

was preoccupied. So what's the problem?"

"Does preoccupied mean transfer?"

"No. Just not paying attention," translated Bruce.

Enlightened, BanSha pulled wisdom over him like a cloak. "Oh. It's Tuzhel! The Council! He's almost at Turnover and they won't listen to me. You have to come now! I'm supposed to be his escort until Solamar's on duty, but I had to leave him with Rushi and Xanon is there. Maigrey is in despair over Xanon. He's backing everything Alind gets the Council to say. You have to come."

"The Council has Tuzhel? Why?" Rimon hauled his body into gear, gathering his warm vest and cloak. He was wearing the belt. *Tuzhel is near Turnover! Surely Xanon is not that irresponsible?* "Where are they?"

Once, after he'd objected to them trying to reclaim the old Council room from two families caring for orphans, he'd heard they stopped the looms to meet in the weaving area.

"I left when they started to move the meeting from the school to the dining hall because the crowd got too big."

Of course. They couldn't seem to do anything without an audience. "Let's go," said Rimon.

The dining hall was full. There were still a number of people trying to eat and get back to their work, ignoring the crowd filling three quarters of the space. The Councilors, with Alind in the middle, sat behind a row of tables facing their audience which included an inordinate number of Church of the Unity members.

At one end of the Council sat Xanon, attempting to manage the fields from that awkward location. His skills hadn't progressed much beyond what Rimon had taught him while managing that meeting planning the election.

In a nagerically awkward array in front of the Council stood Tuzhel, with Maigrey behind Tuzhel on one end of the table, Bekka Esren and her parents, Jor and Shaddyr, in the middle, and a cluster of Church of the Unity members at the far end. Tuzhel was indeed too near Turnover to be here.

A few off-duty channels who were supposed to be eating had drifted over to manage the fields for the group but they were too few for the size of the disturbed crowd.

BanSha and Rimon joined their effort, countering Xanon's clumsiness. People felt Rimon's touch on the ambient and opened a gap in the crowd. Silence spread.

Bruce, conspicuously low field, followed in Rimon's wake. That focused all the attention in the room on them.

Rimon walked to Tuzhel's side, noticing the youth had grown since he'd first arrived. He had probably reached his full adult height now. Rimon wrapped Tuzhel in a nageric shield, agreeing with BanSha that the renSime had been about to crack. The youth was bewildered, and scared, and probably dwelling on his dread of Turnover.

With one tentacle, Rimon signalled Bruce that he didn't have to work. Now, he couldn't influence the ambient much, so Rimon wanted him to absorb as much of the sense of things as he could.

Alind, seated in the middle of the long Council table, said, "I suppose you expect us to stop and explain this proceeding to you."

Rimon zlinned Xanon who was striving to level the field gradient around the Council from his awkward position at the end of the table. He was making a hash of the complex fields. "I admit I'm curious about why the Council would call on one of my patients, especially when he's so close to Turnover. I can just ask someone else, later."

Xanon started to reply but Alind cut him off. "According to our witnesses," Alind said gesturing to the Church group at the far right, "you've sanctioned this Raider's unpardonable behavior despite the ruling we handed down last month. Your complicity makes you as guilty as he is."

Raider? Rimon felt Tuzhel react, nerves raw, as if expecting a death sentence. "What unpardonable behavior?" *Ruling?* Tuzhel hadn't Killed, that was clear from his fields. *What could he possibly have done?*

"It isn't his fault!" cried Bekka Esren, her voice husky from crying or screaming. She lunged forward. Her parents grabbed her shoulders and drew her back against them. Rimon felt the bruising tentacle grip the two renSimes had on their Gen daughter.

Bekka had begun to develop an adult Gen's selyn production and she was as upset as Tuzhel, her adolescent rage fracturing the ambient. Since her field was still so pale, her Sime parents, though non-junct, were too embroiled in their own anger to notice what they were doing to their daughter or she to the room full of people

Rimon pulled BanSha forward. He had Bruce step in closer to Tuzhel on one side and Maigrey on the other, then said to BanSha, "With me now."

He walked toward Bekka but spoke to the Council, "Whatever is, or perhaps is not, Tuzhel's fault we're not going to resolve the matter while embedded in a nageric stew so thick nobody can think straight."

He reached the Esrens and said, "Bekka, come here. Jor and Shaddyr, you should stand back a little." Her parents noticed what they'd been doing. They moved with alacrity, their chagrin evident.

Rimon placed Bekka in BanSha's nageric care with a brief instruction, then positioned them near Tuzhel. Since he couldn't move the Council members he moved a few Church members to balance things out.

Zlinning what he was up to, the other channels in the crowd repositioned themselves and reworked the crowd's fields into a coherent ambient nager. Soon the renSimes grasped the pattern Rimon was creating and shifted to help smooth it out. The Gens reshuffled themselves.

Even Xanon's work smoothed out when Rimon motioned him to stand behind Alind. Rimon was certain the Fort Butte channel had no idea what had just happened, but now the few channels available could manage the ambient. The tension abated especially among those trying to eat a meal without getting involved.

Rimon zlinned his handiwork. The anger was still there. "So Bekka, tell me what is not Tuzhel's fault?"

"He was kissing me. I didn't like it. I knew he'd have stopped if I'd asked him to. I told him to kiss me. There's nobody else I'd ever let do that, and I wanted to see what it felt like! Then they," she gestured to the witnesses, "they saw us and said, well terrible things!"

He flicked Tuzhel an I-told-you-so look, then asked Bekka, "So what did Tuzhel do wrong?"

"You see!" crowed Alind. "He actually urges people to ignore the rulings of this Council!"

"What ruling?" asked Rimon.

"What ruling!" said Alind. "Is there anyone else here who does not know what ruling has been blatantly ignored?"

Zlinning behind him while watching Alind, Rimon noted that most of the channeling staffers were bewildered while the rest of the people had varying opinions.

Jor eyed his daughter and answered, "The only ruling this Council has come up with that shouldn't be ignored, the prohibition against unions between ex-Raiders and non-juncts or Gens."

What?

Rimon locked eyes with Bruce who was likewise bewildered. Jor was head of the Church of the Unity that had been founded by an ex-Raider. How could he think that way? And what business was it of the Fort Council anyway? What marriages would be safe and stable was a matter for channels to judge, not the Council.

Jor moved up to the Council table and challenged Alind, "So are you going to take that vote or not?"

"Of course we are. We're not going to allow Rimon or any other *Farris* to disrupt these deliberations."

Rimon expected Jor to object to Alind's language. Jor said nothing. His wife said nothing. The other Church supporters expected no objection.

Alind went on, "According to the resolution passed by this Fort Council, though existing unions will not be disrupted, no future unions between disjuncts and non-juncts or Gens will be permitted. Now we must vote to prohibit sexual liaisons between juncts and non-juncts or Gens, with specific application to the Raider known as Tuzhel who hasn't seen fit to confess his actual out-Territory name."

The Church of the Unity members were of mixed opinion but Jor and Shaddyr watched with great satisfaction as the Council members each voted to pass the new ruling.

Tuzhel zlinned the reactions near him with a cold horror. Rimon remembered Bekka's Establishment party. Her parents had already chosen her husband, probably for social position. If Rimon supported Bekka's preference, Rimon no longer had Church support.

The vote progressed with only Rinda, the Fort Hope representative, dissenting. Tuzhel turned to Rimon with a silent plea to stop it. The desperate intensity reminded him of Clire's last plea to him.

Those who had come to eat had gathered to watch, some aghast and some faintly approving, most bewildered.

Rimon stepped up to the Council table, "Before you finish voting, you should know one thing. If you attempt to enforce any ruling treating the juncts or disjuncts in my care differently from everyone else here, I will leave this Fort and never return."

Bruce's shock would have knocked the renSimes unconscious if he hadn't just given Rimon transfer.

Shaddyr Esren said, "That would be a great loss, but we would survive."

"It's not my preference either," said her husband, "but Rimon, you and Lexy have done nothing but cause trouble by ignoring the duly elected authority in this Fort. You seem to have lost the call to follow God's Will."

The Church members' shock filled the room.

Jor explained, "The other Forts have failed and returned to us, so we must lead the way forward. We must become a non-junct community, leaving the Kill behind." To Rimon he said, "The Council is right. There's no place in a Fort for the disjunct. They must prove themselves elsewhere. Their children may join us if they can."

The Church was a small but powerful minority throughout the Fort, a solid group that acted of one accord. The Church had members among all the Fort factions except Butte. All acknowledged Jor Esren as their leader. He no longer supported Rimon Farris. He supported this Council.

Rimon would not abandon Tuzhel as he had Clire.

"I will not live in a Fort where the Council builds walls between the people. Our disjuncts have paid the most dearly to uphold our principles, and they are the most honored among the exalted of this Fort. Abel Veritt who founded the Church of the Unity and nurtured the discovery of channeling had been a Freeband Raider. He died trying to disjunct before it was known to be impossible after First Year. Anyone who has succeeded in doing what Veritt yearned to accomplish will be accepted wherever I live."

Rimon gathered Tuzhel and headed for the door, wrapping them in a nageric bubble. The stunned silence, audible and nageric, paralyzed everyone else.

CHAPTER FOURTEEN
DISILLUSIONMENT

Rimon and Tuzhel had passed through the dining hall's outer door having rudely left the inner door open when movement shattered the crowd's paralysis.

Bruce then BanSha came out of the door behind Rimon, then a slow trickle of individuals, and finally a small stream. Not a majority, but he didn't stand alone.

Tuzhel whispered, "The Unity people'll let that Council take over the *whole* Fort."

Even the innate optimism of Postsyndrome couldn't deter a muttered, "They might."

Rimon instantly regretted it because the junct still lurking in Tuzhel was terrified. "You said you'd keep me safe, but you can't," Tuzhel accused. He twisted out of Rimon's grasp and ran for the infirmary, augmenting. The infirmary had been his home in Fort Rimon, his refuge. Rimon let him go measuring the junct's condition. *Turnover before dawn. A little after midnight, maybe.*

BanSha started after Tuzhel, floundering toward the path through the snow. He stopped at Rimon's nageric flicker. "Later, BanSha."

Rimon turned to the supporters gathered around him under the dark gray sky. "Fengal, would you go tell Val or Dakin that you and Aislinn should keep Turnover vigil with Tuzhel? Turnover will be a few hours before dawn. This one will be very hard."

"Disjunction?" asked Fengal gathering his Companion with a glance and starting to move.

BanSha flared anticipation. He headed for Rushi who had stayed on the path, treasuring her new boots.

"Not disjunction," said Rimon, "but...I could be wrong. BanSha, Tuzhel is more volatile than I want you handling right now."

Grimly, Aislinn muttered, "Let's go Fengal. Last I saw Val's schedule board, she'd have to assign Xanon to Tuzhel if he's run away from BanSha."

BanSha did an amazing job of hiding his hurt. Rimon reassured him nagerically. Fengal loped off leaving his Companion to skid through the muck after him. The snow banked beside the path was waist high on the Gen woman.

Rimon remembered how Tuzhel and BanSha had taken a turn shoveling around the infirmary after the last storm, working side by side with Rushi, Bekka and other young Gens, all of them laughing and teasing Tuzhel who teased right back. Rimon remembered noting how the youth felt completely accepted in the Fort. Now that feeling had been ripped away at his most vulnerable time. *What will he do?*

"Fengal will take care of him," Bruce offered. "Now tell me, when are we leaving and where are we going? Dayyel will want to know what to pack and there's the baby to consider. Iriela's fine, but that baby is a lot of work."

The group around them now included Benart and the guards Lhazron, Kreg, Kimra and Jokim and a group of scouts led by Kaires. They were people Jhiti had come to rely on. They hung on Rimon's answer. If they were going to leave and rebuild elsewhere, spring was the time to do it so there was not much time left to plan.

Rimon looked at the people who believed he would not mislead them. His mind went blank. Words flew out of his mouth. "We won't have to leave because they will."

Even these staunch supporters couldn't quite accept that absurd prophecy.

Rimon projected the optimism that should be his in the grip of Postsyndrome. "I'll look in on Tuzhel as soon as Val lets me back on duty. Let's not decide anything until the Council tries to enforce that new rule of theirs."

Bruce said, "Very little of what they've voted for has ever happened, so I'd say that's a good strategy."

Then Tuzhel took the decision out of their hands.

Just after midnight, BanSha pounded up to the door of the room where Rimon was sleeping, young nager slamming through the walls in a jangling alarm. Every channel snoozing in the on duty wing leaped out of bed.

Breathless from the shock, Rimon found himself standing over the bed where Eskalie had been sleeping. "What's the matter?" she asked groping for the blankets Rimon had flung aside.

Rimon grabbed his pants. "BanSha, damp your nager!" Rimon was not sure if he was having one of those horrid nightmares. He grabbed the Starred Cross belt off the floor and slung it around his hips then reached for his shirt.

"BanSha's overexcited," he told Eskalie. "Go back to sleep. I'll quiet him down." He untangled his sweater from the last of the blankets. BanSha had run down the hall apologizing loudly to the channels he'd rousted. Rimon flipped the blanket over Eskalie, and headed for the hall still buttoning his shirt.

"Rimon!" called BanSha racing back to Rimon's door. "Tuzhel's gone! Fengal's hurt. Aislinn's hysterical. Rushi's gone to the stable searching for Tuzhel. Lexy said to get you because she shouldn't do this, but I don't know what this is. I can't find Bruce. Solamar and Kahleen are on duty and trying to treat Fengal."

"We're Post, BanSha. Bruce is home! Go get him and don't wake the whole family." Rimon took off down the hall toward the end of the building near the infirmary and galloped up the stairs three at a time.

The upper hall of the infirmary was frigid. Rimon followed the cold breeze to the end room, Tuzhel's residence. Aislinn stood in the open doorway, so distraught she was useless as a Companion to Fengal. Rushi, hair and boots soaked, face rosy from the cold, gripped Aislinn's shoulders with one arm. Both stared into the room, Rushi's calm creating an interference pattern with Aislinn's anguish over Fengal's condition.

Rimon edged between them zlinning Fengal. Rushi panted out her report, "Nobody's seen or zlinned Tuzhel. Oberin mounted search parties in and outside the Fort."

The window shutters flapped open, icy rain sheeting off the roof and spraying into the room. Solamar and Kahleen knelt over Fengal, dim streaks rippling his nager.

Head injury, diagnosed Rimon. He picked his way to the window and zlinned the darkness. Oberin's searchers were saddling horses. A foot party dispersed around the yard. A Gen rounded the corner of the dining hall carrying a smoking torch, lending enough nageric glow for Rimon to zlin the snow heaped against the building below the window.

The pile almost reached the sill of the window below him. Rain had gathered in a deep hollow on top of the snow, draining where the lip of the hollow was depressed. He zlinned a trail of what might be footsteps along the wall of the building opposite, the Collectorium.

Someone about Tuzhel's size had jumped from the window into the snow heap, slid to the ground, crept along the wall of the building opposite them toward the cemetery gate in the new wall. He'd either gone over the wall or through the gate and down the hill.

Tuzhel's gone to Shifron! No! No!

Just then a great cry went up from the cemetery gate. *He's taken out the guard at the gate, or maybe on the wall.*

Rimon, stiff with dread, wrapped himself in a granite hard showfield, pulled the shutters tight, then built up the remains of the fire in the hearth. He kept his attention on what Solamar was doing, nagerically assisting his effort.

When Rimon approached, Solamar looked up, attention on Fengal. "Concussion. Skull fracture, not depressed."

Rimon admired the high precision work Solamar and Kahleen were doing. He couldn't have done better.

With one tentacle, Solamar indicated the blood on the corner of a counter. "Aislinn says she went to get them something to eat and returned to find this. Maybe it was an accident Fengal fell, then Tuzhel panicked when he thought Fengal was dead. He nearly was when I got here."

Kahleen's concentration was rock steady, even when Rimon strode to the door. "Don't send Bruce after me. He hasn't enough selyn to cope with a disjuncting renSime."

He raced down the stairs, grabbed two wool cloaks and oiled cloth slickers. He raced out the infirmary door, rounded the dining hall and headed for the stables.

Scouts and guards were still organizing. Some horses were saddled. Rimon vaulted aboard a saddled horse with a big blanket roll and galloped toward the now opening gate. Augmenting wouldn't help Tuzhel much slogging calf deep snow. Rimon could catch up with him before it was too late.

Behind him the Fort lit up with spreading ripples of alarm. Guiding the horse down the familiar path to the level valley floor, Rimon turned left, rounded the hill eastward, then angled north northeast, calculating where he'd cut Tuzhel's trail if the youth was really heading for Shifron.

As he moved away from the Fort, the ambient dimmed. Soon both Rimon and his horse were nearly blind in the night. He kept going by dead reckoning and his innate sense of location, straining to zlin the ground through the snow and rain to guide the horse's feet.

Behind him, a nageric disturbance signalled BanSha chased by Jhiti and several of his guards. Jhiti scolded BanSha, and the young channel blew the fields sky high, totally forgetting to use his showfield to shield others.

Surely BanSha zlinned Rimon though Jhiti probably couldn't. The youth wasn't slowing down for any adult's order. Rimon's horse stumbled. He snapped attention back to his horse's footing. He had to stop Tuzhel before he hurled himself back into the

Freeband Raider existence.

A pre-crisis disjunction candidate typically plunged into suicidal depression followed by an eruption of violence. No candidate had ever had a better reason to give up. From Tuzhel's current point of view, after that Council vote, he had nothing to gain by disjuncting.

Just before dawn, Rimon finally zlinned Tuzhel up ahead, floundering through the hip deep slush. The rain had abated and the clouds were parting. Five days past the full moon, there was still enough light to see the melting landscape clearly, but this close to dawn the moon was setting, casting long, dense shadows from the nearby peaks. The moon would be gone long before pre-dawn but sunrise was two hours away.

Tuzhel was heading east across Rimon's course, approaching the trail from Shifron that led south along the east wall of the valley. He was circling the east end of the range of hills that separated Shifron from Fort Rimon.

The renSime hadn't spotted him yet. Rimon angled east toward the Shifron road. The rain had long since soaked through his clothes, the chill numbing him and his horse, but if he could keep going, he'd intercept Tuzhel a good hour's ride south of Shifron.

Far behind him, BanSha, and Jhiti's group were strung out across the flat valley floor. None of the horses had fallen, nobody injured. If that happened, BanSha couldn't handle a bad injury yet.

I'm too old for this, thought Rimon not for the first time that night. He rose in the stirrups, stretching and flexing his legs, careful of the horse's balance. He augmented a little to raise his body's temperature and increase circulation to his extremities, worried about the numbness in his feet and hands. His tentacles were retracted far up his tentacle sheaths, tensed against the cold.

The youth he chased would be in far better shape despite having made this trek on foot and no doubt in Need by now. His joints and tendons wouldn't stiffen and his muscles would still flex even after such exertion. Rimon had never appreciated youth when he had it.

An hour before dawn, the moon had gone, the clearing sky barely glowing, when Tuzhel finally spotted Rimon.

Rimon had kept his showfield muted and seeming renSime for the last few hours so Tuzhel probably thought he was one of Jhiti's guards. Still, he fled with renewed desperation north on the trail into Shifron from Fremir pass.

Rimon hit the trail too, his horse steaming and huffing. This was a horse of Fort Freedom breeding, conditioned by Jhiti for his hard riding scouts. The animal had made it through the night in better shape than Rimon.

On the trail, footing evened out drainage was better, and in spots, the horse's hooves landed on mud, slippery and more treacherous than the ice.

But Rimon zlinned Tuzhel now, in much more detail. He hadn't Killed on his way out of the Fort.

It was the one thought Rimon hadn't dared think through the long, horrible night. Tuzhel sped into a fast jog. Recklessly, Rimon pushed his horse into a canter. The youth was tired. His throat was raw, his feet blistered but numb with cold.

Rimon was so intent on Tuzhel that he almost missed it when a large group of renSimes emerged from the distant haze that represented Shifron. Mounted renSimes, dim with Need, picking their way down the dark trail toward them.

Raiding Party!

He noticed the warm breeze and clearing sky. A break in the weather would send the Raiders out-Territory. This trail connected directly to the trail south from Fremir pass to the easy wagon pass into Gen Territory not the steep pass toward Nivet Territory. They could raid, and bring back Gens in the Gens' own wagons.

Sure that Tuzhel did not yet zlin the approaching Raiders, or the Raiders him, Rimon hunkered down along his horse's neck and urged the tired animal faster.

There was enough light now that the horse was willing to go

faster while Tuzhel was pushing himself through his last wind. They hit a stretch of trail that was clearer and Rimon burst from a fast walk to a trot and into a canter, closing on Tuzhel. The youth put on a burst of augmentation, desperate to get away.

Rimon knew it was a suicidal chance with the footing of the trail so bad, but he pushed his mount into a gallop. Seeing the running person as the goal of the race, the horse gave the extra effort.

Rimon was not sure how his aging body would perform, but his young self had executed the maneuver he planned so often that brain and nerves remembered.

Then he was beside the running Sime, following him off the trail into the drifts. Hanging off the side of his mount, Rimon scooped the running figure up with one arm, then righted himself as the animal circled to rejoin the trail but going back the way they'd come. He swung the squirming body astride the horse in front of him.

"Come on, Tuzhel, we're going home. You made me a promise and you're going to keep it. You are not going to Kill again."

He held onto the wet, cold body until Tuzhel finally capitulated. "Why did you come after me?"

"Because you don't want to be a Raider and Kill and Kill until you die young and in misery."

Carrying the extra weight, the tired animal wheezed and dropped to a walk, sides heaving, sweat foaming. Rimon guided the horse off the trail, into the snow but diagonally across the valley, directly toward BanSha and Jhiti's party.

With the sun rising behind them to the left, Rimon told the renSime what was coming down the trail behind them. "They'll zlin us soon, but all they'll zlin is an old tired renSime on an old tired horse. By then they may zlin or even see BanSha and Jhiti's party up ahead, but there they'll zlin only Simes. They're after Gens for an immediate Kill. We aren't interesting."

Tuzhel sat up straight, "BanSha came after me?"

"I suspect he just leapt onto a horse and took off. Jhiti's guards were saddling up to fetch you back. Jhiti chased BanSha for hours before he caught up. You had everyone in the Fort awake and running around."

"Rimon, I murdered Fengal."

"He was alive when I left. Solamar and Kahleen were working on him. Listen, I would have come to get you even if Fengal had died. Disjunction makes people strike out at what they hold dear." Rimon hugged the slender body to him, trying to infuse the youth's spirit with confidence.

"I don't think I want to go back. I don't want to talk to BanSha or anyone. I can't. I don't belong there."

"You're past Turnover. The world is seeming dark, dreary and hopeless. No one blames you for despair."

Rimon was so intent on arguing Tuzhel out of his determination to fling himself into death, and so focused getting to Jhiti's group that he missed the moment when the Freebanders zlinned him. He realized the advance riders in the group must have been aware of him since they came around the ridge of hills. When five Raiders split off and arrowed directly toward them, he knew.

Clire!

She was riding with the five Raiders, still pregnant, and his casually erected showfield had not fooled her as hers had fooled him. Now he knew she was giving the orders.

He spurred his horse to a trot, urging the exhausted animal on. The fresh mounts of the Raiders gained too fast.

Ahead of Rimon, Jhiti finally spotted the Freebanders and sent his guards faster toward Rimon. Jhiti wisely dropped back, protecting BanSha.

Rimon recognized Filo, Jokim, Lhazron and Kreg coming toward them. As they closed, Jokim held out his arms for Tuzhel. "Let me take him. I'm much smaller than you, so my horse isn't as tired."

Tuzhel held back, undecided.

BanSha broke away from Jhiti, shrieking, "He's all right! Tuzhel! Tuzhel!"

The young channel had still not remembered to use his showfield, and Tuzhel zlinned something from BanSha's primary field that changed his mind. He slid over to Jokim's horse while Rimon zlinned with true horror that Rushi and Bruce were behind Jhiti's party and closing fast.

BanSha studied Rimon's tight showfield, and suddenly remembered his skills. He wrapped a field around Tuzhel and Jokim, displaying a renSime showfield, a credible imitation of what Rimon had been doing, but nothing that would fool Clire.

As they all circled to head back toward the Fort, Rimon yelled to Jhiti, "Clire is leading that band and she's still pregnant! They'll zlin Rushi and Bruce!" Kaires was with the group of renSimes approaching from the Fort with remounts. "Go, go! Get everyone back to the Fort!"

Rimon whacked the rumps of the horses, shooing them into fleeing the approaching Raiders who already had their whips out. The animals began to move, a race in slow motion as the freshly mounted Raiders bore down on them.

Kreg and Lhazron dropped back behind Rimon prepared to defend him. That positioned them so he couldn't deploy his only weapon, his nager.

Three of us to five of them, good odds, thought Rimon zlinning to assess the Raiders as Lhazron unlimbered her whip and Kreg got between Rimon and the Raiders.

Then Rimon's horse foundered.

One instant he was struggling through the raw, mushy drifts and the next the animal went to its knees, pitching forward with momentum, neck to one side, hindquarters to the other in a twisting roll. Rimon's body flew into the air, and he knew the animal's heart had burst. His body flipped in mid-air, twisting. He felt his brain instructing his body on how to rotate for the landing.

Pitching off a horse was a familiar maneuver. His brain knew exactly how to come out of this into a neat roll and nail the landing.

His ancient sinews, frozen and strained muscles, and arthritic joints simply could not do it.

He saw the ground coming at his face.

CHAPTER FIFTEEN
GRAVE DIGGING

"Where's Rimon!" demanded Solamar. He worked his way across the chaos in the gate area.

Arriving horses and riders, shouting grooms trying to capture the exhausted animals peevishly heading for their barn stalls, and staff receiving the party with comforts created nageric soup. "Where's Rimon!"

The noon sun on the dripping ice dazzled the eyes when he searched for what he couldn't zlin. There was no body draped over any of the horses, no grief in the ambient.

Then he noticed Kreg and Lhazron were missing. The two Fort Hope scouts had ridden out with Jhiti. *They're with Rimon. He's all right.*

BanSha slid off his horse, inner thighs bleeding from sores, hands blistered by the icy reins, every joint in his body screaming pain into the ambient.

BanSha staggered into Solamar's arms, showfield in tatters. "He's not dead! I zlinned it. It was too far for Jhiti to zlin, and he thinks Rimon's dead, but he wasn't when the Raiders got him, and they didn't murder him. They didn't! Jhiti wouldn't let me go back and rescue him. He grabbed the reins of my horse, and Jhiti had his guards box me in, and when I tried to jump off, they threatened to tie me on. Solamar, we've got to go save Delri!"

Bruce dismounted handing his reins to a groom. The Companion's shock was wearing off. "BanSha, I hope that's not wishful thinking." To Solamar he said, "Delri's horse went down and then the Raiders were on top of him."

On the other side of the churning chaos, Jhiti announced, "Rimon is dead. Freeband Raiders caught up with us and attacked. Lhazron and Kreg fought bravely and died protecting Rimon. I zlinned their deathshocks. They weren't juncted. They died bravely!"

BanSha croaked, "He's not dead! He's not!"

Tuzhel scrambled down off Jokim's horse as the renSime guard slid down and staggered. Tuzhel was frostbitten, his clothing torn and filthy, his skin scratched and bleeding, and he was soaking wet standing in the icy wind. Still, with the resilience of youth, Tuzhel ran to BanSha and seized him. "It would be better if he were dead. They'll torture him! Why, *why* did he come after me!"

He's not dead. In the next breath, Solamar thought aloud, "Lexy!"

Tuzhel heard him and said, "What's wrong with her? She's not dead is she?"

"No. She's pregnant, and this will be a bad shock. BanSha take care of Tuzhel," ordered Solamar knowing the two would take care of each other.

Solamar made for the infirmary where Lexy was preparing to receive the returning party, certain her father would bring Tuzhel back. Her father had never failed her.

He found Lexy in the middle of the receiving hall directing traffic, the most badly frostbitten and exposed to one side and the lesser problems to the other, high fields here, low fields there, this channel to this problem, that to the other with Val to one side taking notes.

In all, five parties had gone out in the rain after Tuzhel and Rimon, and Jhiti's had been the last to return.

Lexy spotted Solamar. "End of the hall. Hypothermia and possible lung infection that started before they went out. Nobody checked these people before they rode!"

His feet started to obey the call of duty, but he stiffened

against the impulse. "Lexy, I have to talk to you."

She zlinned him then, and her eyes widened. "What's wrong? What's happened?"

Three minutes later another channel had taken over directing traffic and they were alone in Rimon's office. He gathered her into his arms and whispered what he knew she already suspected.

"Your father didn't return with them. Kreg and Lhazron died protecting your father. BanSha was close enough to zlin and said Rimon survived when his horse foundered. Then Raiders got to him. Jhiti is saying Rimon is dead, but Jhiti wasn't close enough to zlin. BanSha says there was no deathshock that could have been Rimon, but BanSha hasn't zlinned much of such things yet. Still I think he'd have known the difference between Rimon's deathshock and Kreg and Lhazron."

She stood still, not breathing, selyn consumption shocked into nearly nothing, showfield collapsed, primary field paralyzed. He zlinned her four month old fetus clearly, and that had never happened before. It lasted more than a minute. He'd never zlinned anything like it.

If she had been affected as Rimon and maybe Clire had been by what he and Rimon had done during the battle with the Freebanders, then in this moment she'd have flown so far out of her body he'd have lost her forever.

She drew a long, shaky breath and began talking in a husky but efficient tone, her fields swirling back to normal.

"BanSha and Tuzhel. Solamar, I have to talk to them, plan a rescue with Jhiti and Oberin, mobilize the guards. The Council won't do it, so we have to."

She started for the door still talking. "I'm glad you got me away from everyone to tell me this. Now I have to handle it. Aipensha isn't here to do it. I have to do it. There's no one else. It has to be me. I owe it to Aipensha. I owe it to my father, to Grandfather, to Fort Rimon."

"You've got to think of the baby, Lexy. Let me...."

"Yes, I am," she said striding down the hall. "Solamar, help me. Find Garen. He was here just before people started arriving. Kahleen and Bruce. Rushi. Aislinn. Get everyone. I have to talk to BanSha and Tuzhel before memory gets muddled. Tuzhel doesn't know Shifron because we caught him before the Freebanders moved into town, but he knows the band. We'll figure something out."

So he peeled off to hunt up the people she kept listing as she marched down the hall. He spread the word for a meeting in Sian's weaving area, then rejoined Lexy as she alternately healed and grilled BanSha and Tuzhel.

They set up a double channel watch on Tuzhel, though he seemed to have recovered his ambition to disjunct. Still, he was deep into the process and could be swept away at any moment by irrational convictions based on Need.

Then Lexy insisted on visiting Fengal and Aislinn. Dayyel, Bruce's wife, opened the door. Bruce's daughter Iriela was there with the new baby, Wade. Bruce was sitting on the edge of Fengal's bed with Aislinn, talking about Rimon as a child. It was Delri this and Zeth that, a story of mischief and mishap during Rimon's First Year making him sound very much like BanSha.

Lexy stormed past Dayyel, fields flying. "What are you doing! This is no time for a wake! My father is not dead yet, not unless we abandon him to the Raiders."

Quietly Bruce stood, pulling himself to his full height, his craggy, weathered features sagging in grief. His nager began to recover its discipline when Fengal said, "I'd gladly ride with any rescue party, but I think I'd fall off my horse."

"Make that a definite," said Solamar, having worked on the concussion, though the fracture was healing well.

"Look," said Fengal, "Tuzhel sent a message with Bruce about how sorry he was and he didn't mean to hurt me, but only to get away. I believe him. It was stupid to be caught off guard by a disjunction candidate."

Lexy nodded, zlinning the other channel. "I think Tuzhel will make it, but now we have to rescue my father. Aislinn, you take care of Fengal. Dayyel, Iriela, stay here as much as you can. Val just told me the Council is having a session right now. Bruce, you should come with us and talk to them about Dad."

* * * * * * *

When they arrived at the dining hall Council meeting, Jhiti, still mud spattered, was reporting, standing before the Council's line of tables, facing a throng of desperately curious, alarmed and horrified residents of the Fort. He stopped speaking.

Bruce, Kahleen and Garen plowed a wedge into the crowd for Lexy, Solamar, BanSha and Rushi to follow. People made way, some grudgingly and others with respect, but most simply wanting to see what would happen when Lexy tackled Alind and the Council.

Jhiti resumed, "Delri was trailing behind us. I signalled Kreg and Lhazron to fall back and escort Delri. His last order was for us to get BanSha and Tuzhel back to the Fort, and protect the Companions who were on their way out to us, so I only detailed those two to stay with Delri while Jokim, carrying Tuzhel, and I rode ahead.

"I will remember his last words until the end of my days. As he swatted our horses into motion from behind, he yelled, "Clire is leading that band and she's still pregnant!"

One of the Councilors asked with shrewd skepticism, "How far did you say he was from the Freebanders when he collected Tuzhel and turned back toward you?"

Jhiti gave them his best professional estimate. The guards and scouts in the audience all knew every bush and tree across the valley and had given many of the groves names. Jhiti told them where he was and where Rimon was and where the Freebanders were just as Rimon turned back toward them and the Freebanders sent a party after him.

Xanon, who had positioned himself behind Alind at the center of the Council table, bent over the speaker's shoulder and told him something. The man shook his head stubbornly. Xanon insisted.

Silence fell as everyone tried to hear the quiet exchange. Solamar heard the Councilor concede that Rimon could have zlinned Clire with the Freebanders if she had in fact been there.

So why would Rimon have lied? These people just made no sense to him.

Jhiti reported on the shifting of Tuzhel to Jokim's horse and his worry about Rimon's horse. Jhiti had figured they could reach the Companions who had brought remounts for them all and then they'd make it home fine.

Jhiti, his renSime nager trembling, choked out, "Then Delri's horse foundered. Delri catapulted over its head. He didn't make the tuck. I saw Delri hit head first."

BanSha lunged forward, drawing breath to contradict that, but Solamar and Lexy pulled him back between them. Rushi edged closer, chewing her lip to keep from crying.

Jhiti glanced at them, then said into the thick pall of gloom, "I was too far away to feel any deathshock. Kreg and Lhazron were closer when Delri started to go down. They didn't react as if Delri died when he hit the ground. I saw the Raiders whips get Kreg, one around the neck and the other around one forearm, lashing his tentacles. They rode their horses in opposite directions. Pulled him apart.

"I saw Lhazron un-horse a Raider. They went down in a heap and rolled and I think the Raider must have died. Another Raider reared his horse and the hooves and full weight of the horse came down on Lhazron's chest and the Raider's too. I felt neither deathshock. Delri's would have split the ambient like a thunderbolt. I was too far, I wouldn't have felt it. I don't think I would have.

"The Raiders did react as if Delri's deathshock had reached them. They didn't come on after us. They dismounted and crouched down around the dead. Then they picked Delri up, slung his body over the horse of the dead Raider, and set off for the Raider band. Trees and then the hills cut us off and I never saw them again. If the band had continued south toward Gen

Territory to raid, we'd have seen them along the road before we reached the Fort. I'm sure they turned back to Shifron.

"If Delri didn't die when he hit the ground, he must have been dead when the Raiders took him. After all, who would move a living Sime who was unconscious?"

Who indeed? Solamar glanced at Lexy and knew they were both thinking of poor Tuzhel who had been shoved around while he was unconscious and just barely alive. It was relatively easy to bring a renSime back to psychospatial orientation. A channel was another matter, and a channel like Rimon, maybe Bruce could manage it, but few others would dare try with a head injury. Maybe Clire would.

Why would Raiders take Rimon's dead body? That made no sense to Solamar. Raiders didn't even stop to collect their own dead.

He whispered as much to Lexy, offering her hope, but she replied, "If Clire sent them to capture my father, they'd bring his body as proof they'd done what she ordered."

If Clire is alive? She'd be, Solamar calculated quickly, *twenty-four weeks pregnant now.* Would she still be capable of the intricate nageric control necessary to offset another channel's psychospatial disorientation? *If not, we might go out there to rescue a raving lunatic.*

Lexy squeezed his hand as she worked through the same thoughts, then she strode into the clear space before the table. "If he's that badly injured, we have to get him back into Bruce's care. We have to go, now."

Suddenly everyone was talking at once. Alind consulted the other Councilors and Xanon, but Solamar couldn't hear.

Alind called for attention. "If Rimon did survive that fall, and was moved while alive after a head injury, he'll have used up a great deal of selyn, and even more fighting through disorientation. We've all noticed how unstable Farrises are. Clire went junct at the slightest provocation. If Rimon has survived, even for a short while, he will be junct by now too. Clire will see to it in revenge."

BanSha lunged forward shouting, "He was alive! When they took him, he was alive. I zlinned it clearly. The Raiders didn't murder him. I would have zlinned the deathshock. I zlinned the guards dying, like it seemed to take a thousand years. The whole ambient went stark white! That was the first deathshock I'd ever zlinned but I knew what it was. Solamar and Lexy taught me. I know what I zlinned and he's not dead!"

The crowd broke into murmurs and Alind called them to silence. "He's just a First Year channel," explained Alind dismissively. "We forgive that outburst, young man, but it was not appropriate. When you finish your year, you'll be allowed to testify officially, but not now."

Alind then moved the discussion on to setting a time for Rimon's funeral and assigning someone to dig the grave. Solamar drew BanSha back between him and Lexy where they could shelter him from the room's ambient.

As the Council began to debate which to discuss first, where to put a monument to Rimon or who to appoint as the new head for the channeling staff, Solamar met Lexy's glassy eyes. He had to get her out of there.

They worked their way back through the crowd as people expressed condolences to Lexy. Even supporters of the Council were listening to these new plans with dismay.

They emerged into bright daylight, the sun shafting between two black clouds. Ahead of them to their left, the sheep shearing was in progress, a portable pen filled with shorn sheep set up before the stables.

Solamar always thought that shorn sheep looked like the world's most pathetic creatures, but today the ridiculous sight didn't move him even to a smile. He just thought it was much too cold still to be denuding the animals.

Behind them people emerged from the dining hall, gathering in tightly clustered groups and talking earnestly.

Some of the runners Solamar had sent to gather the group he thought of as the real Fort Council found them marching across the yard toward Sian's looms at the west end of the factory building.

BanSha and Bekka, not being children anymore, were no longer among the messengers. The leader was now Cody, a very young boy whose family had arrived with the Fort Unity people. A serious, earnest youngster, he was suitably impressed with being successor to BanSha. His parents were, as far as Solamar knew, staunch supporters of Rimon.

"It's all set. Half an hour at Sian's," panted Cody. "We found everyone but Jhiti."

Lexy looked at Solamar who returned her gaze gravely. "Jhiti has just finished his report," she told Cody, "and he has to rest. We'll talk to him later about the meeting, so you children can go on back to your schooling. Cody, aren't you scheduled for cabinetmaking lessons?"

"Yes, and I'm getting good at it. I'm putting the finish on a table for Rimon's new house. My last one was too rough, but this time I'm doing much better."

Solamar stepped in front of Lexy who suddenly couldn't breathe. "That's great. I'll come by to look later. Right now, you can all get back to what you were doing. I'll certainly call on you the next time I have a confidential message to send around."

All the children beamed, then ran in every direction. A few even headed directly for the school building.

Lexy began to breathe again. "Thank you."

"Welcome," he said, overcome with a tender love.

She injected a sad smile into the ambient that wasn't on her face. "Not now, Solamar. I have to get through the real Council meeting. Let's go talk to Sian."

But the meeting didn't get all the way to planning a rescue mission. They arrived while Sian was supervising the stowage of bales of raw wool near the dyeing vats. The place was almost empty, no one working in the carding room, nobody at the spinning wheels, and the looms were all empty. Some of them had parts missing.

Before they'd finished briefing Sian, people started arriving, each group with their own agenda for this meeting.

Last to arrive was Rinda, the Gen who represented Fort Hope on the new Council. Her nager was marbled with joy backed by grief and fear. She whirled right up to Lexy who was standing in the middle of the circle and said, "That Council has dug its own grave!"

She proceeded to tell everyone about the schism throbbing through the Fort.

The Council and a few supporters insisted they had to bury Rimon in absentia and put up an impressive monument to him, then forget him and go on to make the Fort into their own Fort. They were split, though. Many of those who had supported the new Council, because of Rimon's disregard of the voice of the community, now remembered how his plans, schemes and preferences always worked out well. They had shoes, clean water, and good health because of Rimon's choices. So some wanted to send a rescue party.

"They're still arguing it among themselves," the old woman reported. "If we send out a rescue party before they've convinced themselves, we'll lose them all."

Being young, BanSha was against waiting and here in this Council, his young voice mattered. "This is the second time the Raiders have gotten one of our channels." In the sing-song chant of the *Zeor* game, he pointed out, "*This* time we'll do better!"

Without Jhiti and Oberin, though, there wasn't much they could do. They brainstormed four plans but all depended on the scouts and guards volunteering to go. It would take time, and much talking especially while Jhiti still believed Rimon to be dead.

They broke up to go their separate ways. Each had a list of people to talk to privately while BanSha exhorted them to remind everyone that this time they will do better. "We'll rescue both of them!"

Solamar watched the meeting dissolve without Lexy's objectives being met. They had respected her leadership, but the talk had erupted again and again with reports of key people wavering in their support of the Council.

Val motioned her Companion, Merie, on ahead and stopped by Lexy and Solamar. "You're both off-schedule until noon tomorrow. Alind called a shutdown of the schedule tomorrow afternoon for Delri's funeral."

She choked up, took a deep breath, and adjusted her showfield. "I told him he couldn't have a shutdown until sunset and he threatened to have me replaced. Frankly, that's fine with me. I'm only doing this because Benart is way overloaded with the expansion for all these people. If we're going to shut down for a couple of hours for the funeral, then I've got to double-schedule both of you between noon and shutdown to clear all the transfers. I can't ask people to go to Delri's funeral in Need. His ghost would haunt me forever!"

Lexy said, "He surely would! If he were dead!"

"But," added Solamar, "don't over-schedule Lexy. I'll make up the slack."

"Don't worry, Dakin and I will manage. You two are exhausted. Go rest." She hurried off after her Companion.

Lexy sighed. "She should take her own advice."

Benart had lingered, talking to Sian, and had overheard Val's admonition. "Is Val as tired as I think she is? She's been both channeling and covering the scheduling board for weeks. I don't know where we'd get someone else as good at juggling details as she is."

"She's fraying around the edges. We all are, and we won't rest until we get my father back."

"I agree, Lexy," said Benart. "We'll do it. Just remember the scouts and guards will follow Jhiti. I talked to Oberin. She says she can't ask anyone to risk their lives on such a mission without better information. I don't know how to convince Jhiti to rely on BanSha's zlinning ability. So somehow we have to change Jhiti's mind."

Lexy nodded to the Gen. "I'll think of something. If you can keep tight control over our material resources so the Council doesn't pull another shoe affair on us, I'll handle the rest. My father will be back within a few days. I expect his new house to be ready for him. Is that practical?"

"Yes, I think so, and the new underground retreat is almost finished just the way he wanted it. I think everything will be finished before we have to pull all the labor for work on clearing the new fields." He went to the rear door, threw his cloak's hood over his head, tucked his notes under his cloak and dashed out.

Outside, it had started to rain again, and the temperature was rising, the white world turning brown.

Lexy said, "Let's go talk to Jhiti. I expect he's feeling he hasn't a friend left in the world because he wasn't able to save my father."

Solamar followed Lexy out into the rain, and together they both zlinned Jhiti up on the walls talking to Oberin. She was pointing him toward the stairs, obviously arguing he was way too tired to be commanding a watch. They met him at the bottom of the stair next to the stables.

The new stable construction had added two wings onto that building, and the sheep shearing was still going on under a broad canopy between the two wings.

Jhiti tried to avoid them by veering off toward the laundry, but Lexy lengthened stride and cut him off.

Her showfield enfolded the renSime gently, supporting his fatigue. "It wasn't your fault," she said.

He stopped, head down, enduring.

"It really wasn't your fault. My father had no business riding out like that. It was just something he felt he had to do, and it would have been all right if the Raiders hadn't chosen that particular moment to ride."

"I should have brought remounts with me. I've thought of a hundred things I should have done and didn't."

"And I've thought of a hundred things my father should have done and didn't. You haven't failed us. You rode out as fast as you could and left others to bring the remounts and supplies. They'd have been faster if the Companions hadn't insisted on riding too, but if I were Bruce, I'd have insisted."

He looked up, as unable to zlin through the Farris nager as

anyone else. "You believe he's alive."

"I think there's reason to doubt he's dead."

"I expect," said Jhiti to Lexy while looking at Solamar, "you'd have gone in his place if you could have."

"Of course. Tuzhel trusted us, and we let him down. He's very near his crisis. Don't take this as any kind of reflection on who he really is underneath it all. He's going to be one of the finest people in this Fort. Next time he breaks, I'll be there for him and he'll find out what a channel really is."

"I...I wish...I really wish I could have been there for Delri. Lexy, we have to face it square on and move ahead. He's gone."

She met this with silence both audible and nageric.

"You're going to ask me to send my people out?"

"No. Just when you're ready to do that, let me know."

"You think I'll change my mind."

"I know you will." The ambient rang with certainty.

"If you weren't pregnant, you'd be at Shifron now."

"There'd be nothing I could do once I got there."

Privately, Solamar thought that a good contingent of the guard would follow her. They could do plenty.

"We can't live with Freebanders for neighbors."

"The new Council seems to think they can ignore the Raiders until they just leave." Solamar watched Lexy work the fields, giving Jhiti a quiet space for thinking.

Jhiti said, "They will attack us again, and this time we'll do a lot better at thinning their ranks. Our strength is Delri's doing. Nobody's forgotten that. We'll destroy those who have destroyed Clire and Delri."

"I don't want revenge. I want my father back."

"So do I." They were in total accord until Jhiti added, "He might have been alive when they took him, but he's dead by now. I can't order my people into a battle they would likely lose in order to rescue a corpse."

"Will you prevent them from going on their own?"

That stopped Jhiti cold.

Solamar said, "Lexy would never subvert your authority with

your people. The security of this Fort is in your hands. You're trusted."

"Until now. I've lost one of our most valuable channels, and I know Aipensha's death and Clire's juncting were my fault too. That's three of our most valuable channels lost because of me."

Lexy said, "What matters is how well you do next time. Do you believe that?"

"Yes. I always have held my guards to that standard. Why not myself too?"

"Right. So we start our next attempt now. When you're ready to send out a rescue party for my father, let me know. I promise, I won't ride with them."

She hugged Jhiti, wrapping her showfield around him like a warm blanket, supporting the renSime's exhaustion and not letting him zlin her own. "Ask for me when you come in for transfer."

She took off across the yard, picking her way between sheep turds and mud puddles. Solamar followed, his whole heart and soul caught up in pure revelation. Though he couldn't zlin through that Farris mask, he knew in his bones that she was being perfectly honest with Jhiti. She couldn't find it in herself to blame him for what he truly believed.

Solamar could barely contain the fountain of joyous love that had erupted within him during that conversation.

He followed her through gathering dusk to the door to the channels' on-duty dormitory. She turned to scrutinize him with her eyes and her Sime senses as she kicked at the boot scraper by the door. "Yes, I know he's not dead. And I know Jhiti will realize it soon. It'll be soon enough. It will be!" She pulled the door open.

He held the door open for her as he kicked mud off his own boots. "Think about this. Clire is still pregnant. She wants Rimon alive, to deliver her baby. She may not care if he goes junct to survive, but she wants him alive."

She ducked under his arm and entered the building. "I have to find Garen, look in on Tuzhel, and talk to Bruce."

"The minute Garen lays eyes on you, he'll sweep you off to the dining hall to eat then make sure you lie down."

"I couldn't sleep now."

"Garen is one stubborn Gen."

"And Kahleen isn't?"

"Kahleen's a tyrant, but so far she's never been wrong. I've never had a better Companion."

"Hmmm. I couldn't imagine anyone better than Garen. All right, let's go see Tuzhel before they catch up to us. If Val zlins us in the building, we're cooked."

Tuzhel was sleeping in the shallow napping pattern of the pre-crisis candidate. Both channels and Companions in the room were vigilant. Lexy zlinned the youth carefully, not waking him, and left instructions with his guardians.

Then the Gens caught up with them.

Bruce tried to insist that he would provide Lexy with her extra transfer to support the pregnancy, but she finally lost all control, screamed at him in the middle of the infirmary hallway, "He's not dead!" then turned to run.

Solamar stopped her and the Gens closed around with Companion nagers, firm, insistent, irresistible. Lexy muttered, "I'm not hysterical," and to prove it marched herself to her on-duty sleeping quarters. She started to close the door, then reached back and pulled Solamar in, leaving Garen outside. "So bring dinner up. I'm not going into that dining hall today."

As she closed the door, Bruce said, "I don't want him to be dead either, but he'd want you to take whatever you Need from me."

"Later, Bruce," gritted Lexy. She collapsed into Solamar's arms and he felt her love of him spill out of the cracks in her showfield. He was irrationally certain it was her genuine feeling, not just another Farris perceptual trick.

"I love you," he confessed aloud for the first time in just that special, unequivocal and matter of fact way. "I've known I was falling in love with you, but I hadn't realized how much I already loved you before I fell in love."

"I know. I felt it. It's so insane. I think I'm falling in love with you, but there's just so much grief in me, I can't be sure. I'm numb with it all. I don't know who I am anymore. I just have to rescue my father. I should have started that hours ago but I've failed."

She pulled restlessly at him, but he hung on. "They'll be back with food soon. Some hot soup with crusty hot bread. Things will look better after we eat."

The thought sent her stomach roiling. He altered that, "Well, maybe some tea and flatbread." He went to build up the fire so they could reheat whatever the Gens brought. "Want Garen in here instead of me?"

"No. I'm not in Need or sick. I'm just tired. Scared. Miserable. I'd rather Garen didn't see me like this. You still love me if I'm incompetent, confused, scared?"

"Oh, yes. No doubt about that." He set his showfield to project Gen, multi-layered like a Companion's complex and deep fields and absurdly cheerful the way Gens usually seemed when a Sime was in Need.

She laughed. His pride surged at his success and his heart melted. Her laugh didn't last long though before it transmuted to tears. She flung herself onto the bed, prone, bunched the pillow up and sobbed.

The room was well enough insulated that she could let go of her fields and just wash the place in her anguish. He pulled in on himself and let her ride it out while he put the wash pitcher on the hearth to warm and arrange the table for the food their Companions would bring.

When the ambient shifted slightly to the arrival of the Gens, she held her breath and he slipped outside to accept the trays and explain. As he spoke, a renSime came by to light the hall sconces. It was getting very late.

Garen said, "Take good care of her. I'll be in the recovery room if she wants me later." He started away then turned back. "And I mean *good* care!"

"I will. I think you should go home and get some sleep

though." He related what Val had said.

He nodded. "I'd just rather not participate in this farce funeral the Council is putting on. If that's what Lexy wants, though, then that's what we'll do."

"Maybe she'll change her mind tomorrow," said Solamar. "Right now she's too exhausted to think straight and too keyed up to sleep." The heat of the dishes was soaking through the heavily wrapped trays stacked in his arms. "Whatever happens, she'll be depending on you to be rested. Take care of yourself."

Kahleen opened the door for him and Bruce closed it behind him. The insulation was so good that even the three Companions nageric disturbance barely registered. He put the trays on the hearth. Lexy had dozed off, her body tense but her mind ceasing its whirling fury.

Even sleeping, she was Farris opaque. He was just minutes before Turnover himself, and knew his wan appetite would vanish after that point. So he set his wet boots by the fire, and propped his feet up to bask in the heat while he nibbled at the enormous repast on one of the trays.

As Lexy's sleep deepened, he pulled her boots off, dried her feet and wrapped her in wool blankets, letting his nager sing her body a lullaby of Gen steadiness. He knew, even asleep, she was zlinning right through his showfield, but whatever she found inside him, it didn't disturb her.

Then she was crying in her sleep. Her nager clearly indicated she was deeply asleep, beneath the level of out of body wandering or dreams. Her breath came in little gasps and her eyes overflowed with tears and she shivered uncontrollably.

He built up the fire again, but seeing and zlinning no pathology but the impossible weight of emotion, he didn't know what to do. So he followed his heart. He stripped off his own clothes, wriggled under the covers with her and freed her icy body of her own damp clothing.

Skin to skin, in the now familiar embrace they'd shared right after transfer, she stopped shivering but it took longer for the hiccupping sobs to abate. Then he realized she was awake. His time sense told him it had been nearly three hours since she'd cried herself to sleep.

Her head was nestled on his shoulder, fitted right beneath his collarbone. Unbelievably, he was responding to the wondrous feel of her in his arms, of his tentacles caressing her back, of her legs bent around his. His response cultivated a welcoming reaction in her.

They'd had sex before. It had been wonderful, but really just sex. This was something else. This was coming to them both from above the body's yearning. Solamar decided his soul was aroused.

He surrendered, opening and relaxing into it, letting it take him to some place he'd never been before. Senses he'd never known existed came alive and drove him into a reality where he saw himself as one soul in two bodies, one heart with two minds.

Release came to them both as a long, sweet, gentle wave of warmth culminating in little aching spasms of completion. Physical awareness emerged when he felt Lexy's uterine spasms working out against his abdomen.

It hadn't been anything like the hard, driving passion and flaring bodily orgasm normal to Postsyndrome. When it was over, he held her close and whispered, "I don't think I ever had sex while totally hyperconscious before."

"Me neither. Solamar?" She struggled free and leaned up on one elbow to look down at him. "Solamar! That was Turnover for you! You had sex with me when you were in Turnover! I don't believe it!"

A quick inventory of his own condition told him Need now ate at his vitals, thrumming that muted panic through mind, body and soul.

She flopped down, sprawled over his chest and ran her fingers through his hair, then laid her face against his chest again. "Let's try to do that again sometime. I'd like to know how it feels from the other side."

"Any time you like," he said fighting an overwhelming desire to sleep.

"You should move in here. It'd be handier."

"It would. I will." Feeling like the most special man in the universe, he fell asleep twining her thick hair around his tentacles while cradling the back of her head in the palm of his hand. She drifted away with him.

He woke late the next morning having slept nearly six hours straight through. He sat bolt upright alone in Lexy's bed, jolted awake with a gasp, or maybe a voiceless scream.

He knew that falling sensation. He'd returned to his body. He remembered grayness swirling around the fiery gemstone pattern of Rimon's belt. The belt was curled tightly in on itself, buckle inwards, and surrounded with a haze that might have been cloth. The image, however, carried an unmistakable vibrancy.

He's alive! The stones would not produce that searing glow if Rimon were dead. They would glow like that even if he weren't wearing the belt. So if he wasn't wearing the belt, why wasn't he wandering around out of his body and easily findable? *I'll never understand Rimon Farris.*

Against odds, Rimon Farris had survived what would have buried any other channel. Against all reason, Solamar had experienced Turnover while in orgasm with a pregnant Farris channel and something truly odd had happened to him. Against everything Solamar knew about the ability to leave the body, Rimon Farris had acquired the ability just from joining nagerically with him to create an illusion strong enough to stop Freeband Raiders in mid-battle. Then, without any tutelage, Rimon had spontaneously summoned other entities, maybe ghosts, manipulated the fabric of the non-material body to heal the physical body, and had even traversed the infinite.

The two Farris channels he knew functioned in ways no other channel he'd ever heard of did. Everyone else who could do any of these things had acquired the skills only after decades of concerted effort. They were so rare, many people were skeptical that such things ever did or could happen, though Solamar had personally witnessed all this.

With that realization, all that he'd observed of Rimon and Lexy came together for him into a new pattern. *The Farrises aren't just a family of outstanding channels. The Farris is a totally different kind of person, as different from channels as Simes are from Gens.*

CHAPTER SIXTEEN
GRAVE ROBBING

Rimon's funeral was a disaster.

The rain was frigid and incessant, the ground was soft mud, the grave hole collapsed on itself taking the grave monument with it, the clouds were so thick the sun seemed to have set a good half hour early, and the Council could barely read their speeches in the dark to a soggy crowd of less than a third of the Fort's residents.

Alind was halfway through his speech when the people at the lower end of the area noticed they were suddenly ankle deep in water and fled uphill to the Fort's cemetery gate, quickly followed by everyone else.

At that time, Solamar was ensconced in the channels' recovery room letting Kahleen eat dinner from the buffet while he expounded his new theory about Farris channels. Val, BanSha, Fengal who still wasn't back for duty, a couple of channels from Fort Unity and one from Fort Veritt and their Companions all listened with rapt attention.

During his impassioned explanation, Xanon and Maigrey arrived, drenched, muddy to the ankles and walking in their socks. Kahleen handed them glasses of hot trin tea, without even asking what had happened at the funeral. Oddly, Xanon listened as Solamar paced and embroidered on his theme. Maigrey nursed her tea and nodded.

Others came in to dry out by the fire and fell silent to listen. Solamar realized he'd found the explanation for the observations that irked people. Pleased, he fell silent. People started talking at once. Then they took turns dredging up incidents that confirmed his theory that there were Gens, Simes, channels and Farrises.

The Companions debated whether that meant Companions would then be recognizably different.

Consensus grew that if you didn't count the Farris channels as just channels, then things began to make sense; the killingly intense pre-natal selyn draw that set the Farris channels apart, the incredible sensitivity to selyn fields, the precision control of any ambient around them, the vast Need that could be handled only by a few Companions, but most especially that totally impenetrable Farris nager.

BanSha said to the Council supporters who'd clustered by the fire, "If it's not a trick to keep people from zlinning the truth, if they can't help being impenetrable, then maybe they aren't always hiding something. How would you feel if people who can't zlin you always thought you were lying?"

Argument erupted all over the now full room. Everyone was explaining Solamar's theory to newcomers, and not exactly getting it the way Solamar had explained.

They were, however, talking to each other, and for the first time he could remember, certain of these channels were not dismissing Rimon and Lexy as merely fearful of losing the power grip they'd always had on Fort Rimon. They were actually thinking like channeling staffers, and so distracted by it that they forgot how wet and muddy they were.

Solamar sat and propped his feet up to the fire, marveling at how Xanon listened to those who had agreed with him now questioning the core of his premise.

Eventually though the cleared time in the schedule was over and Val shooed people off to get cleaned up and get to work. The story of what had happened at the staged funeral was told and retold and grew in the telling.

Solamar, worked to a frazzle, retreated to Rimon's favorite spot on the walls at sunrise and found that the flood that had cut

Rimon's funeral short had grown. Water now surrounded the Fort's hill, knee to hip deep, and still poured over the banks of the river. Rimon had chosen the right place for his Fort.

The flood lasted six days. The first few hours, while Solamar had been working, others had gathered the livestock into the Fort in makeshift corrals. Then they sat around the dining hall telling stories of previous floods.

Solamar talked with the renSimes who came to him for transfer, and was informed that this happened every year for two or three days. However, as days passed with no way to send rescuers after Rimon, even Fort Rimon natives began to worry.

Kaires, the tracker who'd found the Gen captive's note, commented, after her transfer, "Just imagine how bad this flood would be if the Gens had burned off the hills around us! That could happen naturally some year. Be glad we're up this high."

Solamar reported every development to Tuzhel, visiting him with Lexy and on his own three or four times a day. They had moved him to a room with three little slits for windows, up high near the ceiling. Pacing, fretting and miserable with approaching crisis, Tuzhel's only distraction seemed to be tales of the Council's doings. So Solamar always brought plenty of news to report or discuss.

One afternoon, when Tuzhel was glum, Solamar offered, "Now I see why Rimon fought the Council so hard to keep the yard free of houses! He wasn't being unreasonable or meddling outside his area of authority."

He sketched on a slate to show Tuzhel how deep the water was around the Fort and how cramped the animal pens were even with the yard area expanded. Now the yard was filled with split log fences, penning the animals that had wintered on the flat below. The chickens, geese, and rabbits had makeshift huts. The noise and smell was bothersome, especially to the pregnant women, but the wealth of the Fort was preserved without hazard to their health.

Not only that, but the animal waste was used to fertilize the two garden plots, one next to the dining hall and the other nestled in the L made by the Dispensary and Collectorium buildings. They even created a new garden plot on the side of the Dispensary facing the Fort's wall to give those windows and the infirmary windows a nice view and help feed their increased Gen population.

The adventures of those caring for the animals almost brought a smile to the Need-crazed ex-Raider's lips.

Rimon had wanted fruit trees planted inside the Fort, for food and shade. Sketching where the trees should go kept Tuzhel occupied for nearly an hour. Turned out he especially liked watching wild deer eating windfall pears because of the silly, blissful expressions the animals wore. Seeing that again was something to live for.

Lexy and Solamar brought Tuzhel a sketch by Bekka of what the Fort would look like with fruit trees in bloom. They hung it on the wall of his bleak little room.

During the flood, sheep shearing continued, buildings were finished, carding and dyeing of the wool began though most of the idle labor force gathered in groups to talk politics. Usually, they flew apart in disagreement when there wasn't a channel to manage the fields. As Sime tempers heated, many Gens began avoiding public places when they were high field.

Jhiti held three alert drills to drain off some of that nervous energy. Solamar and Lexy had the duty of escorting Tuzhel to the underground shelter and controlling him.

Lexy followed her father's routine during the flood days of stepping up the Collectorium schedule to take down the fields of the Gens before they became a serious irritant, thus spurring their selyn production for next month but providing all the renSimes some relief from Gen nerves.

So all the channels were working hard and holding too much selyn in their secondary systems, causing fatigue. And that meant they spent more time than usual sitting around just talking.

At one of their visits to Tuzhel, Lexy and Solamar described the ebb and flow of discontent in the Fort. More and more were chafing at the Council's edict to abandon Rimon while some plotted rescue. Jhiti still had not agreed to send the Fort Guard to Shifron.

For those six days of flood, Tuzhel's room often became the site of a bull session between the channels and Companions about Solamar's Farris theory. Tuzhel inserted comments about BanSha's awesome zlinning ability.

The fourth day of the flood when observers reported the waters had begun to subside, Val and her Companion Merie were on duty with Tuzhel along with Fengal and Aislinn. Lexy and Solamar made one of their frequent short stops. Solamar used these visits as an excuse to get her off her feet and to send Kahleen and Garen to eat.

Often Bruce accompanied them but not on this visit. He was working with Benart and Sian to engineer a new Council election without telling the current Council about it until the very last moment.

Lexy pointed out to Val that as soon as the ground firmed, teams would be plowing the existing fields and pulling stumps in the expansion zone, tending the vines and trin bushes on the terraces, burning selyn profligately day and night and taking extra transfers.

Tuzhel loved the idea of augmenting and getting extra transfers. Lexy informed him that it would be years before Rimon could safely let him do that.

"Rimon doesn't rule here anymore," he replied sullenly. "And neither do you!"

"We're going to get him back," insisted Lexy, with an untoward edge in her voice and nager. Solamar, Fengal and Val reinforced her conviction nagerically.

Tuzhel shook his head. "Everything you promised. Everything he promised! None of it is ever going to happen! Not for me. Not ever! The Council will throw me out and I'll end up Raiding again. Why didn't he just let me go! I'll never have Bekka, I'll never have anyone!"

Tuzhel leaped up and began stalking the room again, panting

with the effort to wail out his inner cry of despair.

The four channels wafted serenity into the ambient of the heavily insulated room weaving Gen nager into a peaceful zephyr breeze. It was an artistic masterpiece.

The moment Tuzhel subsided, Solamar and Lexy zlinned for signs of crisis. He screamed, "Don't do *that!*"

"Not yet," said Lexy to the other channels. They all shifted their attention elsewhere, relieving Tuzhel of the feeling of being transparent to a hostile force. Solamar perched on the edge of the little square table.

Lexy tilted the rocking chair that had been brought in for her, propped her feet up on Tuzhel's bed and said, "You're at the hardest part of the process, Tuzhel. No one can do this for you. No one can even help. You have to maintain your resolve on your own. You must convince your body to accept channel's transfer instead of the Kill. That's what's hard about disjunction, Tuzhel, deciding on it all alone. In the end, you will get one chance, one moment, to choose. That choice will rule the rest of your life."

Stalking in a circle, Tuzhel whirled and pointed at her, "And why should I choose channels! It's all going to be for nothing! They won't let me have Bekka. Or anyone! They control things here, not you. Nothing you say counts!"

Solamar said, "We are going to rescue Rimon."

As if driving a point home to an idiot, Tuzhel bent at the waist and hammered his fist wrapped tentacles at Solamar. "They won't let you!"

Solamar rose and assumed the same posture and tone. "We won't let them stop us!"

Tuzhel subsided, rage quenched by the humor of the situation. He paced another circle. His mind understood. His body refused.

Lexy explained, "From what people have been saying, my father's plan is working. Even some of the Council's staunchest supporters have had enough of them."

"What plan?" asked Tuzhel curiously, stopping between the

four chairs his vigil monitors occupied.

"He's letting them prove their inability to manage the Fort. He's only opposed them where decisions endangered everyone's health and safety."

"Like the shoes," said Tuzhel thoughtfully. "So Bekka and I weren't important enough to fight about?"

"No, no, you are!" said Lexy. "I didn't get a chance to talk to him after he decided we wouldn't leave, but I'm sure he was thinking his plan was working perfectly. So many people were furious over what the Esrens and the Council did that I think my father expected that single issue would end it if they stewed long enough."

Val said, "Rimon is good at predicting how people will react emotionally. He zlins deeper...." She flashed a glance at Solamar.

"No," answered Lexy, "Farrises can't read minds." Nervous laughter greeted that. "He's just a good judge of character and has a lot to teach me yet. Tuzhel, you know we were ready to leave the Fort and take you and Bekka with us if my father's plan failed."

Tuzhel stopped. "And I ruined his plan?"

"Well, no," allowed Lexy, "a foundering horse ruined the plan. You can't blame the animal. It gave its all."

Fengal added, "You could blame me for letting you get away."

Val nodded, "Or me for assigning Fengal when he was too tired to stay vigilant."

Merie said, "Or me for going to get something to eat."

"Or Oberin for not intercepting you at the gate," added Aislinn looking at Fengal ruefully.

"You see," said Solamar, "blaming detracts from your own sense of responsibility and thus of personal strength. The Council tries to arrange things so nobody can be blamed for anything. They live in fear of blame. I think that's what Rimon zlinned in them, but everyone else has to have time to figure that out from the mistakes they make."

Tuzhel sagged onto the bed. "They think Rimon's dead so they can do what they want. He's not, is he?"

"I don't think so," said Lexy.

"Neither do I," offered Solamar.

The others all chimed in with their own conviction. By the time they left, Tuzhel had slumped into the daze that substituted for sleep during this difficult time.

All winter, Solamar had watched as the logging crews had clear cut an area of the valley floor three times the size of the existing fields leaving only a hedge or stand of trees here and there. The lumber had gone to building the new wall and houses and they'd still had to range far and wide up the hills for the right kinds of logs. The clear cutting made the flooding last longer than the usual day or two.

The experienced farmers had taken to the walls, watching the calendar and the weather, measuring the depth of the flood, and muttering incessantly about the growing season and which crops to put where. Finally, on the fifth day, the water had subsided visibly.

And finally, someone told Solamar that Fort Rimon had long ago dug out an exit channel for the river at the end of the valley. The project, undertaken when they'd first arrived, had brought them much unwanted attention from the junct town of Shifron.

Solamar's transfer clients were happy to fill in the background for him and he listened avidly because each tidbit was ammunition for calming Tuzhel. Shifron had always lost a couple of buildings to the annual flood before Fort Rimon arrived, and the first year the Fort people had cleared the valley floor, Shifron lost their Pen building.

After the Fort's diggers went to work, and Shifron's streets remained high and dry a couple of springs in a row, the juncts grudgingly forgot their weird neighbors personal habits. "Not that they'd ever help dig every year," finished Zedros, "even though now the river can be forded even before the mud dries."

Ha! Before the mud dries!

The young renSime had requested Solamar for his transfer because the channel didn't scold him for the chapping of his tentacles by all the laundry soap he made and handled. In return,

Zedros was a bottomless source of Fort gossip.

Everyone went to the laundry to drop off and pick up clothing, and most worked there a few hours a month. Everyone talked. Zedros knew everything. He felt opinion in the Fort was now balanced on a knife-edge.

Late on the sixth day, the first mud began to appear. It would be a week before they could begin working the ground. The scouts didn't expect to ride out for at least three more days, but only two days later, a single rider leading two remounts pounded across the muck toward the main gate at suicidal speed.

Jhiti's guards sounded the alarm and his teams took to the walls, manned their positions in the stables, saddled horses, escorted the channels and Companions. As drilled, Solamar and Lexy escorted Tuzhel into the underground shelter, now capacious enough for everyone. The rest of the Gens were inside buildings with slate roofs. Jhiti's Guard assembled sortie parties by all the gates.

Solamar heard later that the drill had gone perfectly, but the rider was all alone. His horse went down in the muck and he leaped aside and then just left the horse with a broken leg, mounted one of his other horses, galloped up to the gate. He hurled a single object up onto the trail leading to the gate, turned and galloped away toward the river ford leading his last remount.

He was beyond a renSime's zlinning range before Jhiti let the channels come up to survey the situation.

Solamar and Lexy took Tuzhel, protesting vigorously, back to his room, and waited until his vigil duty channels arrived with their Companions. As they were turning to go, one of Jhiti's runners came with a summons for both of them to the wall.

Solamar called over his shoulder, "We'll be back and let you know what happened."

At the top of the wall, Lexy declared, "There's nothing out there. They didn't deliver my father's body!" She had taken longer than usual to climb the ladder even with Solamar's help, worrying aloud all the way. She was almost five months pregnant now, and slowing down physically though the baby's selyn drain was within her abilities to handle.

Solamar walked around the catwalk to the larger platform over the main gates zlinning the package. The smaller door beside the gate was open and Kaires had gone out to pick it up.

She was understandably cautious. She wore heavy gloves and arm protectors and a mask, circled, kicked the package to roll it over, peered and zlinned before picking it up and scraping mud off the wrapping.

Solamar watched her, unable to think of a motive for Raiders to send the Fort a package of infectious material, certainly not in such a dramatic delivery. All he could zlin from a distance was some kind of cloth around something dense and it just didn't make sense.

Raiders wanted to Kill the Gens, not murder them with disease. So far the spring respiratory infections had been mild in the Fort. Though the work kept the channeling staff busy, nobody had yet died of lung fever. It was possible Clire had more fever than she could cope with among the malnourished Raiders but why send infection to the Fort? No, this was something else. Had to be.

When Kaires turned with the package in her hands, her renSime nager was behind the package. Solamar zlinned the contents clearly and hid his shock and horror.

It was Rimon's belt, curled around the buckle, facing inward, stones glowing to his senses. It was packaged in Rimon's shirt, wrapped in several layers of oiled cloth, exactly the way he'd found it when he was out of his body.

I wandered into this future moment the same way Rimon wandered far away in time.

He'd hardly absorbed that idea when Xanon grabbed the belt and shirt out of Kaires' tentacles. Before the small gate had closed, Alind had snatched the items from Xanon who was left holding a piece of paper. Solamar shelved his worry about what effect working fields with Rimon had had on his control and worried about Xanon and the Council.

Jhiti was busy sending Gens to put the horse out of its misery and salvage what they could from the carcass. Then he dismissed everyone, demanding they stand down in an orderly fashion, clean and stow their weapons, and not all crowd around to find out what was in the package.

Oberin's Guard detail released the Gens from confinement, and they gathered to see what was in the package. Looking down on the crowd, Solamar saw Bruce at the back of the press, Lexy and Garen beside him and Kahleen moving toward them looking up at Solamar.

Xanon read the message to Alind who immediately moved back toward the dining hall, shouting as he went. Obviously an emergency session had been called.

It seemed that Alind deliberately chose a path that would keep Lexy from catching up with him. Many of his supporters were between him and Rimon's daughter.

Solamar headed down the stairs and plunged into the crowd, working the fields with the other nearby channels but heading directly for Lexy.

He caught up to her outside the hall. It was full, but even more curious people massed outside the doors. As he approached, people with children in tow gave up and went home. The rest stood outside, hearing only garbled word passed back by the throng.

Solamar felt a channel zlin him. He and Lexy turned to find Val glaring meaningfully. True they weren't deep enough into the crowd to manage the fields, and they weren't hearing anything useful, and they were not working.

"I'm not leaving," growled Bruce. "I have to know what that was!"

"My father's Starred Cross belt," said Lexy. "And I think it was his shirt."

"I saw it from above," said Solamar. "It was the shirt he was wearing that day."

"There was a note!" Bruce's concentration was scattered, his fields bursting with frustration that he was spraying across the yard. Rimon would now be close to Turnover. Bruce's field was dominating the area.

Lexy frowned at him. He reined in his reaction. "I'm going in there, Lexy. Don't try to stop me."

Lexy looked forlornly at Garen and Val. "I'm going with you."

Solamar exchanged silent messages with Val who shrugged, waved a tentacle, and stalked off to round up some other channels to do the work.

Solamar took point, not wanting renSimes exposed to a raging Bruce. Kahleen and Garen flanked him leaving Bruce to take care of Lexy. Solamar waded into the press, flicking his showfield in a polite request for passage.

Most people made way willingly but others flashed resentment until they realized Lexy was the passenger in this flying wedge. If she reached the Council, things would get even more interesting.

The interior of the dining hall was lit more by the last rays of the sun slanting through the partially open shutters than by the candles. Smoke from the hearths and candles and several oil lamps billowed in the sunlight overhead.

People, this time, were not here to agree with the Council but to monitor them. Xanon had taken a stance behind Alind at the middle of the table, but the ambient was so skewed, he was in the wrong position and didn't know it.

Solamar and Lexy worked with other channels scattered through the crowd, but without Rimon's sure touch, they weren't balancing it.

Rinda, the Fort Hope representative, stood and shouted, pointing at Bruce, "There's his Companion! I say it's for Bruce to decide if he'll go!" She grabbed Rimon's belt from the table in front of Alind and tossed it to Bruce. "Is that really Rimon's belt?"

Solamar intercepted the weighty object and handed it to the Gen. Bruce's hands closed over the buckle as if it were Rimon himself. "Yes," he told them.

Lexy demanded, "What was in that note?"

Rinda read it to them before Alind could say anything. "'I'm still alive but I won't be long unless you send Bruce. If Clire zlins anyone but Bruce coming, she'll take the Fort apart one log at a time. Send him now!' Just signed with his initials. Xanon says it's Rimon's writing, and it looks like it to me, but I don't think it sounds like him."

Bruce said, "I'm sure Clire dictated it."

Bruce broke away from Solamar's field management and took the note from Rinda. He nodded, his nager drawn to a tight solidity nobody but Lexy could zlin through.

"It's his writing. Delri isn't dead. Solamar, get Jhiti to outfit a horse for me. Lexy, I'll bring him home." He turned toward the door holding the note.

Alind leaped up onto his chair and shouted, "Stop him! The Council has voted! We will not allow this unconscionable risk to the Fort for nothing!"

Several men captured Bruce in a box, the renSimes wary of his nageric strength, and the Gens wary of what Bruce could do to the Simes. Bruce subsided but looked wildly back at Lexy and Solamar.

Alind sat down again, gestured the other Councilors to sit, shouted for silence and flicked his nager repeatedly until he had everyone's attention.

Solamar and Lexy led the other channels in calming the ambient.

Alind said, "We can't risk one of our best Companions. We'd just be turning over a prime Kill to the Raiders!"

Another Councilor said, "If Rimon's still alive, which none of this proves, he's junct like her by now and she wants him to Kill his own Companion. Her revenge on us."

There was a buzz of agreement. Solamar zlinned distrust aimed at the Council and disillusionment coming from Shaddyr Esren holding onto her daughter Bekka's shoulders, Jor Esren beside them.

"Nothing has changed," insisted Alind. "Rimon died in that

fall. Clire could be capable of Killing Bruce, probably dreams of it by now. She worked with Rimon long enough to learn to forge his writing and long enough to become jealous of his Companion."

Kahleen bristled at that but most of the renSimes thought it made sense.

"This is a trick," Alind insisted, "just to get herself a Choice Kill. Or Rimon wants a Kill that could satisfy him."

Chillingly logical, thought Solamar. He was gratified that so much of the audience didn't believe it.

Yet most of the Council did believe it. Alind called another vote, and the Council voted, not unanimously but solidly, to lock Bruce up so he couldn't ride out on his own.

Amazingly, the renSimes on the Council somehow missed the sea change in opinion among their supporters. It didn't escape Lexy's notice. She worked her way back to Bruce and managed to mutter something to him before his guards took him away.

The hall began to empty, and Solamar caught up to Lexy just as Sian moved up to her from the other side.

"We've won!" said Sian. The noise was still so loud that Solamar had to repeat what he'd said for Kahleen and Garen standing behind him.

"It seems so," said Lexy, "but maybe too late to get Bruce to my father."

"We're ready. We can do it tomorrow and...."

"Do what tomorrow?" asked Solamar.

Kahleen and Garen chorused, "Hold the new election."

Sian continued, "...then we'll take Bruce there and get Delri back. The note in Delri's own writing will change Jhiti's mind about what could be gained by taking the risk."

"Yes, though I could wish we could do it tonight," said Lexy. She turned to Solamar, "Locking Bruce up seems to have done the trick, wouldn't you say?"

Sian said, "This Council'll never know what hit them."

Lexy added to Solamar, "I didn't get a chance to tell you that

Sian's going to head the new Council. He's got people lined up to sit on it, and if this changes only a few minds, they'll all win. Did you zlin Jor and Shaddyr Esren when the Council voted to lock Bruce up? That's the whole Church of the Unity vote."

Through the ambient chaos, Solamar had read them as disillusioned. He wondered if Lexy's sensitivity had spiked up because of the pregnancy. That could become a worry. "Is there anything I should be doing?"

"No," said Sian. "The channeling staff can't be involved in this election. Go back to your regular schedule and whatever you do, don't let Bruce go before we get this settled. It's too slippery to ride hard out there now. A broken-necked Gen won't help our cause. For this election, he has to appear to be the level headed, methodical Companion we've always thought him to be."

Kahleen and Garen chuckled, and Kahleen said, "Nothing will stop Bruce, trust me. The only reason I didn't go with Clire is that she had Killed. I'd have let her try to Kill me any time, but she wouldn't have wanted me because it wouldn't work."

That silenced everyone for a moment. Lexy nodded, and ran her tentacles over the note Bruce had given her. "Clire hates my father, too. This isn't her hatred driving her. This is love for my half-sibling. This will probably be my father's last child. My father will Need Bruce to get that baby born alive. Tomorrow or the next day it'll be possible to ride in this muck, and if my father is still alive now, he'll still be alive when we get to him with all Jhiti's Guard."

Solamar said, "Let's go talk to Jhiti then." He plucked the note from her tentacles. It had been handled by so many now that any residue of Rimon's presence had been obliterated. Still, he had to believe that without the belt, Rimon would surely be out of his body tonight.

When Solamar handed Jhiti the note, the renSime stared at it. "Then he's alive?" He dropped to his knees before Lexy, imploring her, "Forgive me! I should have gone after him that very day! If he dies, it's my fault."

"It's what you honestly believed," said Lexy.

Jhiti buried his face in his hands struggling against sobs. "No! I began to believe the lies that Council kept spreading. Delri never lied to us. When he made a mistake, he just did it over again until he got it right."

"Jhiti, you're still Post. Take a deep breath. Zlin me," said Lexy, and gave him nageric support as she put out a hand and levered the man to his feet. "Get ready to have your men moving the moment Sian gives you the word."

"I'll send out scouts tonight. I know a few who'll volunteer. Oberin will be very happy."

Lexy took the note back. "I have more people to show this to." They parted company then, Lexy to go check on Tuzhel and talk to the staff and Solamar to talk to Bruce who was being kept under guard in Rimon's room.

There were two of Jhiti's guards, a renSime and a Gen, on the door and another pair beneath the window. The Council had sent one of their own to watch each set of guards from a distance.

When Solamar arrived, the two guards on the door were the Fort Hope scout, Kimra who had been badly gored by a bobcat while trying to find Fort Rimon, and Eirelle, a young Gen woman from Fort Tanhara who had been a farmer but became a hardened fighter on the trail.

Bruce's wife Dayyel and his daughter Iriela holding her infant son were arguing with Kimra about a food basket Dayyel held. The family of course wanted to take it in themselves, right now. The guards had orders that the door opened only at shift-change when there were four guards. Bruce was not to have visitors.

Eirelle stepped forward when Solamar appeared at the end of the hall, but darted a glance at the Council's monitor. "Solamar, what should we do?"

Solamar said, loudly enough for the Council's monitor to hear, "Dayyel, I'll take the basket in to Bruce. I'm sure the Council didn't mean he's to be kept in isolation, but only that people he could overpower are kept away."

With that, he opened the door and went right on in carrying the basket, adjusting his showfield so that his advanced state of Need wasn't so obvious.

Bruce looked around from where he'd been staring out the window, saw his wife and daughter outside and threw his hands in the air. "Go on home! They aren't going to hurt me. They're just trying to protect me."

"Don't do anything we'll regret," called Dayyel as the guards moved her away from the door.

Solamar closed the door, saying to Bruce's family, "They aren't going to starve him either, but I'm sure he'll be happy to have a good meal now."

Farther down the hall, the Council representative looked wary but resigned. Solamar's unauthorized visit would surely be reported. *Why do these things always happen when you're in Need?* he asked the universe.

The insulated door made from two layers of hardwood laminated around a layer of selyn refractive sand closed off the protests as effectively as it masked the nageric static. Solamar put the basket on the table. The Gen stared at it without appetite. "When do I get out of here?"

"Earliest would be tomorrow afternoon." He lowered his voice. "Sian and Lexy are planning to oust that Council tomorrow morning."

Bruce's attention finally came to focus on Solamar. "Shen!" he swore. "You're in Need."

"And happily fixed on Kahleen." *So much for showfield work around Bruce.* It confirmed his new opinion that Farrises were different from other channels, so Farrises required very different Companions, or created that difference in their Companions. "Don't worry about me. There are more urgent issues."

Bruce nodded and turned back to the window, focusing the shaft of attention outward. Unconsciously, his hand rested on the Starred Cross buckle of Rimon's belt that now circled his waist. The belt was let out fully and still bit into the Gen's flesh. "I should be on my way now."

"Bruce, if you just break out of here and run, you'll be hurling yourself into Clire's power."

"Clire can't Kill me. Delri has taken her measure. We discussed it when he discovered she was pregnant."

"Lexy doubts Clire plans to Kill you. Clire wants you to serve Rimon so he can deliver her baby in about three months. After that, she'll see you two murdered or worse."

"I wish I could say Delri and I can take care of ourselves, but it's not true anymore. We're too old. If he weren't badly hurt, he'd be here by now, Raiders or no Raiders. I should just go and let Jhiti rescue us later."

Solamar sat on the bed he'd so often occupied when Rimon was on duty. "You should just wait."

Bruce whirled from the window and paced hands on the belt buckle. "He's lost the belt, Solamar. He goes crazy without it! Clire doesn't know that. She didn't take it to destroy his sanity, but it will. I have to be there! I should have ridden out through the flood!"

"Jhiti worked all winter thinking up strategies to oust the Raiders from Shifron. He's ready to move. Tomorrow."

"How can you be sure Rimon'll be all right that long? Did you see him out of his body or something?"

"No. I haven't seen him...yet. It might happen tonight, or maybe he's learned how to control his wandering for himself. Bruce, he's alive now, and Clire wants his Companion there. She'll keep him alive until you get there because she wants her baby to live."

"I can't wait!"

He changed the subject. "Garen has his hands full with Lexy too."

That stopped Bruce in his tracks. "How is she?"

"None of this is good for a pregnant woman, nevermind a pregnant Farris woman."

"She has to have Delri to deliver her child too. If Delri told Clire that Lexy's pregnant...Clire was good friends with Lexy...."

"You can't count Clire as sane at this point."

Bruce sat down on the bed next to Solamar and his fields softened. "Solamar, what would it take to get you to help me go now?"

Bribery!?

Stunned, Solamar shook his head. "A complete change in the situation."

Bruce scrubbed his face. "I thought you liked Delri!"

"I do. And I think he's our main hope for rescuing the non-junct way of life from extinction. If this Fort is destroyed, well...I doubt if any of the others survived. We can't afford to make any mistakes. That's why we have to wait. It isn't enough to rescue Rimon. We have to unify these people behind him and they have to rescue him."

That's what I came here for, thought Solamar bleakly, *and maybe tomorrow it will start to happen.*

One of their plans did work. The election went overwhelmingly for Sian's new Council, people accepting the argument that Alind's Council had not been properly elected by Fort Rimon's customs. That made this the first election after all but three of the previous Council had died. Sian ordered Jhiti to move, but cautiously.

Sian's slate of Councilors included Rinda from Fort Hope plus leaders of all the other Forts, even a few who distrusted Rimon's style. Benart put up as the opposition both Alind's elected Council and all those who had run in that election and lost. There were plenty of choices.

Xanon told Lexy publicly that he had been wrong about Rimon's motives and was voting for Sian's Council. With that and the Church of Unity voting block on their side, they won by a huge majority, all clamoring to rescue Rimon and Clire too if they could manage it.

Tuzhel, heartened immensely by Sian's win, especially with the Esrens turning against Alind's Council, breezed through his disjunction crisis, easily choosing Lexy over the Gen Lexy offered him for a Kill, Bekka.

The post election furor died instantly when Jhiti's first scouts returned from Shifron and the Gen border at an insane gallop and reported, "The Gens are coming through the pass in force!" and "The juncts' Border Patrol is heading for Shifron to retake it. I've never seen so many Patrol all at once! Their scouts have spotted the Gens."

CHAPTER SEVENTEEN
ZEOR

When Clire had yanked the belt from around his supine body, she had unknowingly released him.

For a long time he had known he was unconscious but had been aware in bright flashes embedded in gray murk.

He had no idea how he'd come to be in Clire's power, held captive near some out-Territory Gens worn to sick exhaustion by sustained terror. He had no idea why he couldn't move, why he couldn't seem to get a grip on his body and on reality, or why though he was aware of the passage of time as his body consumed selyn, he couldn't remember how much time had passed.

He remembered suddenly finding himself disconnected from time and space, whirling insanely, groping for the world. He had been riding through a cold dark, desperate to catch up to Tuzhel, to recoup his error with the youngster. Then he had been...nowhere he could identify.

Clire had been in nowhere with him, holding a steady field around him, grabbing his consciousness and nailing it in the Pen building in Shifron with ruthless Farris precision, her hatred of him infused with cold junct passion.

He lay suspended, unable to care if he ever connected with his body again. He heard people talking, felt nageric interactions, understood the ambient around him, knew when he swallowed something warm or cold, felt cloth washing his body, felt Kills done in his presence in an attempt to wake him, understood Wild Gens were placed in his cage to stimulate him, knew that Clire knew this wouldn't work.

She wanted him to wake up to save her child which she insisted now must be his own child too. She wanted to punish him for what he'd done to her. She wanted him junct and awake to watch her destroy Fort Rimon. He heard her spell out her scheme, so sure he couldn't understand.

When her Raiders had discovered he had traded out-Territory for leather, Clire had ordered Freebander raids on that one town to plant clues to lead the Gens to Fort Rimon. Clire wanted him to watch, helplessly junct, while Gens destroyed all he treasured. Then, after her child was born, she would watch him die slowly, by Attrition of selyn.

She had defeated herself when she had yanked the belt from around his waist. He had flown free, floated high looking down on his cell, on his supine body, Clire standing over him whipping the belt through the air. He couldn't feel his impending Turnover, his helpless paralysis. *Am I dead? Am I a ghost?*

The out-Territory Gens in his cell had cringed as Clire whipped the belt near their faces. He didn't feel their alarm or fear that was intended to wake him. That was the last he knew of Shifron before the fog took him elsewhere.

Del Rimon Farris knew he was in trouble, even if he was dead because an old dream swept him into the amphitheater where he stood reading out the story of Rimon Farris founding the House of Zeor.

He knew it was himself reading about himself.

The audience was unbelievably huge. Circular rows were ranked one above the other to an impossible height. A visible mist, and a nageric fog, shrouded the upper ranks. The faces came in every skin tone, and in colors he couldn't believe were human. The people lacking any perceptible nager were not human, and this didn't surprise him.

But what did shock him was the sight of his long dead and much beloved wife, Ehren, in the front row center, looking up at him tenderly. She sat with her arm around one of those nagerically null non-human beings. She was young, and looked very different than when they'd been married, but she was beautiful, and most important, happy.

He knew that everyone in that amphitheater, everyone who had ever pledged their lives *Unto Zeor, Forever*, had to be reminded that they might ultimately have failed. They had to understand that they had succeeded because every single time they failed, they had started again and excelled their previous mark. When they had failed again, they had renewed their efforts, doing a little better which had moved the world one step closer to this moment.

Each of them had died and been born anew to live all over again, and again, just a little better each time. Now they sat and listened to the story, hearing how it had seemed to Rimon Farris but remembering it from their own memories, remembering Rimon as they had known him, remembering Fort Rimon in that awful year when the other Forts had failed and returned beaten.

They remembered the founding of the House of Zeor from the ashes of Fort Rimon's destruction.

From the podium, standing before the members of his Householding as Klairon Farris ambrov Zeor, Rimon looked up at the ranks of seats banked impossibly high in front of him, and soaked up their non-junct, never junct ambient throbbing with the joy of total fulfillment of the dream.

Rimon knew that dream. He had dreamed it thousands of times before he'd changed over. It always began with the beautifully colored, glowing, shining image Slina had woven into his baby quilt. He had learned to walk clutching that quilt. He had slept with it so stubbornly that eventually they had stitched the little quilt into the center of a larger one that he could sleep under until he was full grown.

That beautiful image, the sweeping, graceful abstract outline of Slina's dagger, became his heart in later dreams, his vriamic node where his two selyn systems joined to make him the powerful channel he was. Crazy dream.

This moment, in a weirdly insane distant future, the dream was real. If he turned he would see Slina's dagger projecting outward, an image made only of selyn fields. He didn't want to zlin that image. It was too impossible. Such a thing could not exist. Oddly, though, in reality beyond death, it did.

He knew the way to get to this moment of unification of Sime and Gen was to understand failure and even death as part of a repeating cycle. *Just do a little better this time.* Excellence was all you had to know to get here.

This was the second time he'd been here. So this time he'd take a piece of it with him to remember what it felt like to be here, to remember that excellence was the way to success not perfection.

He made himself turn and confront that looming symbol above him, the image Slina had made for his quilt.

Solamar had said, "Rimon can imagine something, shape and hone it, create it in this other space where people don't have solid bodies. He can take what he's imagined and make it real. He healed Sian's nerves not in Sian's body itself but in the part of Sian that can move out of his physical body. Then he put Sian's healed image back into his body and the body did heal."

So in his mind, Rimon made an image of that huge selyn-rich symbol so vivid he could see it, then gathered up the tone and tenor of the non-junct ambient nager. He packed all that textured emotion into the image, just the way he'd put Sian back into his body.

To keep the vibrantly glowing image safe, he built a small coffer around it, polished so smooth he could see his reflection in it. The top he inlaid with an image of the Starred Cross belt buckle with all its colored gems sparkling.

He worked on every detail until he could open that box, breathe this supreme ambient any time he wished, and remember how to get here.

Finally, he turned around to face the huge crowd of people arrayed in endless ranks above him.

There was nothing but blank gray mist. He whirled about and

the huge, selyn-glowing symbol was gone. He was once again nowhere. Tucked under one arm was the small coffer he had made and sealed with the Starred Cross.

If I'm dead, then I'm a ghost. Maybe I can appear to Lexy? No, it would frighten her and now is no time to be frightening her. I could appear to Solamar and give him the box. He can give it to Lexy and they'll know we'll all do better next time. Where is Solamar? He always turns up.

* * * * * * *

"They're all just sitting out there watching each other," complained BanSha.

Tuzhel, Solamar, and BanSha were on the wall watching developments in the valley around them. Solamar was teaching BanSha how to hold their fields neutral and transparent to any watching renSimes while interpreting faintly zlinned information.

Tuzhel was supposed to be learning to stand a guard watch but was fascinated by BanSha manipulating fields. Solamar sighed and used Tuzhel as BanSha's study subject.

Solamar was in hard Need just a day and a half from transfer, zlinning keenly. Being away from Kahleen set his nerves on edge, but he couldn't let the newly disjuncted Tuzhel zlin it. BanSha on the other hand was all too aware of it because he checked the channel's duty board often.

Solamar compared the nageric haze of juncts camped in the hills between the Fort and Shifron with the bright blaze of selyn from the massed Gen militia that had moved in from the border. So far, the Freebanders hadn't stirred from Shifron. "I'd say the Patrol is making the town juncts wait because they're professional militia and figure the Gens are professionals too. They're not Raiders. They're not going to gallop into battle, each one for himself, just for the fun of it. The town juncts want Shifron back not a war with the local Gen militia or us."

BanSha complained, "They've been sitting there looking at

each other for a whole day."

"The juncts are wondering when the Freebanders will attack them," said Tuzhel astutely. "If the Patrol and the town juncts attack the Gens, the Freebanders will attack the juncts from behind. But if the juncts attack the town, then the Gens will attack the juncts from behind. Who knows what they're thinking we'll be doing during all this."

Solamar noted that *we'll be doing.* He said, "They're both doing what we're doing; trying to figure out what everyone else is going to do."

"We have to rescue Rimon, now!" said Tuzhel. "The juncts will take Shifron. The Raiders will escape, run south into the Gens, snatch a supply to Kill later, and head for the pass taking Rimon with them into Gen Territory. Maybe they'll raid High Crossing while all the Crossing Gens are here, then they'll ride around back across Molland Pass into Sime Territory and we'll never get Rimon back."

As Tuzhel spoke, Jhiti had come to lean on the railing beside them. "A very astute analysis, accurately repeated from Oberin's lecture. Tuzhel, hanging out with the channels won't teach you much about being a guard."

"I thought you were in favor of rescuing Rimon!" accused Tuzhel.

"I am. I will. I just know that Rimon would throw me out of the Fort if I led our people out there now."

"I'd go," offered Tuzhel. "So would Bruce. It's my fault Rimon got captured. I don't understand what I was thinking! This is all my fault for being such a complete...oh, it doesn't translate!...horse's ass!"

Solamar noted to Jhiti, "Well, he's old enough to know what sex is all about!"

"Sex?" asked Tuzhel.

"'Ass'—what the stallion looks at when checking out a mare," offered BanSha wisely. The young channel's maturity was coming along nicely, observed Solamar.

"Don't zlin me like that," complained BanSha, hardening his

showfield and forgetting to project the right appearance to the juncts. Solamar picked up the fields. BanSha put his mind back on his training.

Dizzy, Jhiti went hypoconscious. "Solamar, is Lexy up to attending another planning meeting tonight if we can't move out until then?"

Their last planning session had ended at noon. "She's in Need too, you know, and Garen's being a tyrant. I'll come and then report to her. There's time. It zlins as if a storm might be gathering off to the west there."

"I don't...oh," said Jhiti. The western rim of the valley had started to boil with black clouds. "Tuzhel go alert the duty scouts. A dark, rainy night is a good chance to scout the Gen camp. They can't zlin."

Stubborn Lexy dragged Garen, Kahleen and Bruce to Jhiti's planning session.

The new Council had intended to meet in their usual space near Sian's big looms, but with the juncts gathered on their perimeter, all the Gens had to stay behind insulation. So they met in the underground shelter. Gens who had to move outside had to be escorted by a channel muting the fields to mask their presence.

The big question Sian put to them tonight was, "Can we assume those juncts are from Shifron come to take their homes back and not the Patrol bringing other juncts to take the town? If they're our old neighbors, maybe some would talk to us?"

Jhiti said, "From what my scouts report, the juncts are mostly uniformed Border Patrol, mixed with civilians. I've sent three teams out tonight each with someone who's done business in Shifron to see if they can recognize anyone."

Oberin asked, "If they find Shifron folk who know us, what do we do? Offer an alliance against the Raiders?"

The Councilors who were from Forts that had been overrun shattered the ambient with alarm, horror, and real fear. Lexy cut into the miasma nagerically and Solamar helped her. She said, "True, an alliance with the juncts could easily lead to our own destruction. We don't want them to learn to fear us because we fight more effectively than they do."

Solamar watched BanSha think that over. Of all the channels, this youth was the most gregarious. He'd heard every detail of how each Fort had failed.

Jhiti summarized, "So if we can make contact with someone we know from Shifron, we should tell them our objective is to rescue Rimon, not to interfere with them?"

Sian listened to the Council debating whether they could rescue Rimon without alliance with juncts, and what the juncts might assume if they succeeded.

It took less than an hour to list the Fort's priorities: rescue Rimon, then Clire. They'd tell the juncts the Gen Militia was here because the Raiders had captured too many people from High Crossing that winter. Let the Patrol figure out that the neatest way to get rid of the Gen Militia was to give the Wild Gens in Shifron's Pen back to the Gens. Of course, the juncts might not see that. Each of those Wild Gens could be worth a year's salary at a Choice Auction.

Without taking any votes, the Council and the channeling staff agreed on what Jhiti had to do, and what everyone had to do to support him. They even agreed that if the scouts found anyone they knew, the Fort's mission to Shifron's juncts would be headed by Pearl, the woman who traded with Shifron for kitchen supplies.

As the meeting broke up, Kahleen said, "Solamar, you are out on your feet. You haven't slept in two days."

"Neither has Lexy. Need does that to channels." They had been giving transfers and tending ills to prepare the labor force to pull stumps and plow, but those were same people Jhiti relied on. "We've been too busy to sleep."

Kahleen dutifully produced a laughing sound but it didn't reach her nager. "Then get Lexy and Garen and we'll see if we can give you two some rest. Benart designed some nice shielded cubicles down here, and this is a good time to test them. Maybe you'll find Delri."

Both sides of the tunnel were rigged with drop-down cots, like the original underground shelter. The aisle was wider, though, and at the north end of this new branch of the tunnel, another tunnel set off at a right angle. It was lined with insulated cubicles for critical patients. At the end it connected to a stair to the channels' on duty sleeping rooms.

The contagious patients had been moved to these little rooms, most of them suffering from coughs with fever.

Kahleen led him to a room where Garen had Lexy trapped in one of the two bunks inside. She was saying, "I admit it's good to put my feet up. My back is strained."

Alarm vanquished fatigue. "Let me zlin you."

"Oh, you fuss too much," Lexy fretted.

"No he doesn't," said Kahleen. "If you don't want Solamar, I'll see if I can find BanSha and Rushi."

"I don't require a midwife yet!" Lexy sat up.

Solamar pushed her back down, altogether too easily. Sitting beside her, he offered his laterals. She twined her lateral tentacles around his allowing him to zlin her as best he could, which they both knew wasn't clearly enough.

"You're fine, but your back muscles are spasming. You want Garen to work that out for you?"

She whispered, "If I fall asleep now, you'll regret it. I dream loudly, remember?"

He brushed his lips over her hair. "Oh, yes I remember. I'll be asleep too. Kahleen's a bully."

"Isn't that sweet?" asked Kahleen from the open door. "He knows the real me."

Solamar straightened and flipped a blanket over Lexy, tempted to tuck the sides in so she'd be warmer, but they might have to leap and run at any moment. He favored the Companions with a weary smile. "Close the door and get to work. Don't let us sleep more than three hours."

The Companions took places in the two crude chairs made from what looked like kindling. The seats and the backs had nice thick cushions though.

There was a ventilation shaft near the ceiling and a slot under the door for air. At the moment there was a fire in the hearth and the chimney was drawing nicely. Solamar wrapped himself in a blanket and stretched out on the other cot, Kahleen in the chair near him.

Sleep billowed up around him within a few minutes of Garen's starting to work on Lexy's back muscles.

He set himself to go out of his body, though he'd been taught it was inadvisable when having such a difficult time with Need. And he was having a more difficult time than usual. He shouldn't be feeling quite so desperate. His father would seriously disapprove. *Don't think about him,* he admonished himself. The last thing he wanted was an encounter with his father during this foray.

It came to him why he was so tense. Fort Faraway had been destroyed during a very similar situation, surrounded by juncts, Raiders and Wild Gens. Then he had lost his Companion to the Raiders only three days before his scheduled transfer. By the time he'd reached Fort Tanhara, he could only throw himself on their mercy.

From Fort Rimon, though, there was no place to go.

Acknowledging his fear didn't help as much as his teachers said it should. Eventually, he felt sleep take him and surrendered to it, focused tightly on Kahleen's vigilant nager. She was his security now.

Slowly, he became aware of himself outside defined reality, in the familiar realm that was always strange. He built his anchor to himself as he'd been taught, visualizing his body, identifying his psychospatial position and running selyn up and down the chord that connected him to his body even as he separated himself from his flesh.

He built an image of Rimon Farris, tall, lanky, weathered old skin, long face, huge narrow nose, black eyebrows and piercing black eyes, but hair streaked with gray. He added the man's graceful tentacle gestures. Even adding details of shirt, pants and boots didn't summon Rimon. He added the impenetrable

Farris nager, uniquely Rimon, not a bit like Lexy, though the quality was similar.

Rimon's nager could grip Solamar's own systems, soak into and through him and draw him out beyond reality. He remembered the blending they'd accomplished on the wall during battle, and again driving a transfer into Tuzhel.

It didn't help. He was still lost in a strangely thick grayness.

Then he was standing in the rain, though the drops fell through him leaving odd little cold streaks but no wetness. Around a fire before him sat five male Gens, wrapped in oiled cloth coats against the rain. Broad brimmed hats with narrow crowns shaded their bearded faces.

They watched Rimon pace in the shadows at the edge of the fire, explaining in labored Genlan pointing with one hand and tentacles. Under his other arm he cradled a small coffer that sparkled in the firelight.

"...I know this is true because they had me prisoner and I heard them talking. Then I died, but I couldn't let you people go to your deaths too. You have to turn around and go home tonight. You're in more danger than you know.

"The people who raided High Crossing also raided that town up there behind the hill. They stole the town and stayed there all winter. They're the ones who have been Raiding High Crossing and tricking you into thinking it was the people on that little hill over there. They spoke Genlan and let you overhear comments about a raid on that new Gen settlement you traded leather to. You found the ruins of that settlement, but there never was such a settlement. It was a trick. Nobody ever lived there. Nobody was Killed or captured there, certainly not by the people on that little hill.

"It was the Raider Simes in the town behind that ridge of hills over there! They took that town and threw the owners out. Now the real owners have come to take it back. As soon as the owners attack the town, the Raiders will run in this direction, heading for the pass you just came through. They'll Kill any of you they can catch, then raid your town again since you're not there to defended it now.

"You have to go home. Leave the people on the little hill over there alone. They'll never harm you." He stopped pacing. "Can you hear me? I'm trying to explain this."

Clearly the Gens saw the frantic ghost limned against the shadows by flickering firelight. Solamar thought two of them actually heard him, too, which was surely a marvel to behold. *Farrises are definitely a breed apart.*

Rimon resumed pacing. "I know I'm repeating myself, but you have to understand this. That other Sime army up there is the Border Patrol. They're trained fighters and they have the town's owners with them. They don't care where the Raiders go as long as they leave this valley. You have to go home now, rain or no rain."

He stopped again and glared at his audience in pure Farris exasperation. "Listen to me!" he shouted. "Go!" He charged at them waving his arm and tentacles yelling, "Go! Go home you stupid Gens! You've got to defend your families!" He ran right through the fire and kept yelling.

The Gens around the campfire scattered in every direction screaming. Satisfied, Rimon stopped, turned and paced back to the fire. He passed his hand through it, shook his head at the lack of heat, and walked back through it.

Then he spotted Solamar. "You found me! I'm so sorry I'm dead! I really didn't mean to die. Here," he held out the coffer, sparkling in the firelight, "I've made something for Lexy. Here, take this!" He held the coffer out to Solamar. Its top was decorated with a replica of the Starred Cross belt buckle that Bruce now wore.

Solamar propelled himself toward Rimon, numb with the shock of the Farris's death. When he got a little closer, he saw with that odd sense native to this realm that a very thin pale thread stretched from Rimon's navel, twisted around him several times in tangled knots, and disappeared into the granular grayness behind Rimon.

"You're not dead! Rimon, return to your body!"

"I would if I knew how."

"You're almost there. You're in Shifron. Just turn and head back up the trail and you'll find it."

"I'll try. Here, take this to Lexy. She's got to have it. Here!" He held the coffer out, striving to reach Solamar but somehow unable to approach.

Rimon was lost, and of course it was Solamar's fault for not having been able to get him to learn how to navigate the formless levels. If he was wandering in time, that would explain how his cord got so tangled.

Solamar reached for the coffer that Rimon held out to him, planning to grasp Rimon's arms and tentacles and take him back to his body which must still be in Shifron.

Rimon pushed the coffer at Solamar and pulled his hands back. The coffer stuck to Rimon, and suddenly he was spinning away into the gummy quicksand beyond him, not up the trail toward Shifron.

Solamar felt contact with Farris nager, and with a charge of nageric power like nothing he'd ever felt before. Then the contact slid away from him. "Rimon!"

And he was sitting bolt upright in the narrow cot he'd gone to sleep on a few minutes, no over three hours ago. His stomach insisted he'd just fallen from a great height.

"...quickly! Tuzhel's missing."

Heart hammering, Solamar was on his feet and moving before he knew which reality was he was in.

At the doorway, Bruce stepped aside to let Lexy and Garen out. Kahleen was untangling herself from the blanket she'd wrapped up in. Her chair tipped. Solamar righted it, and straightened without breaking stride. He reached Bruce, took his arm as he urged the Gen along the underground hall, noting he still wore Rimon's belt.

Loudly enough for Lexy, Garen and Kahleen to hear, he told the Gen, "I found Rimon. I think he must be in a coma. He thinks he's dead. I didn't have time to convince him otherwise." Lexy clamped down on the fields.

Bruce stopped. "He thinks he's dead?"

"He's not dead!" insisted Solamar.

"He's in Attrition?"

"He's not at the verge of death for lack of selyn. His selyn consumption rate flattened when he slipped out of his body when Clire took the belt. We can still get him back alive if nobody does anything stupid." He told them what Rimon was saying to the Gens. "If he spooked the Gens enough that they move out tonight, Jhiti will be able to make a deal with the Border Patrol more easily."

Garen said, "If the Patrol moves to capture Tuzhel, the Gens may attack thinking the Patrol is moving to attack them."

Lexy's alarm shuddered through her fields leaving Bruce's upset clear for all to zlin.

Sometimes, thought Solamar, *a Companion's brilliance isn't helpful.* "Where was Tuzhel last seen? Are you sure he's out of the Fort?"

Kahleen said, "Don't put anything past Tuzhel. BanSha is his best friend, and everyone loves BanSha."

...and would do anything for him. "Yes. Let's check with Jhiti and see if we can get above to search."

"From the middle of the yard, I could zlin Tuzhel if he's in any non-insulated room in the Fort," said Lexy.

"You," Garen decreed, "are not going out there until the combat situation is fully resolved."

Kahleen just tapped her foot and distributed her weight evenly. Her nager never even flickered. Gen menace could be truly unnerving.

"Only if Jhiti says it's clear," assured Solamar. He led the way back to the new shelter's stair up into the on duty sleeping rooms. The channels masked the Gen fields, then started up the stairs.

They ran into Cody, the chief messenger, near the insulated room where Tuzhel had been quartered before his disjunction. "You're not supposed to be up here."

"You're looking for Tuzhel?" asked Lexy. The children

could move freely about the Fort because they barely registered nagerically. They had their safe retreats assigned in case of attack, though.

"Tuzhel's not in either of the rooms he used here," putting two checkmarks on the slate he carried. "He was supposed to be moved to BanSha's family's house, but he's not there either. We've looked almost everywhere."

Solamar just knew Tuzhel was not in the Fort. Lexy told Cody to find Jhiti or Oberin and deliver the message she scribbled on Cody's slate. The boy ran off.

In an hour, they found how Tuzhel had gotten out using a rope tied to the top of the wall. "He's after Rimon."

At dawn Lexy trudged up the stairs to the top of the wall. Bruce, Garen and Kahleen had been abandoned in the shelter, garnering vast sympathy from the other Companions trapped down there.

Freed of high-field Gens, Solamar and Lexy circled the walls, zlinning for Tuzhel. It didn't take long. Lexy spotted the renSime nager heading northeast around the hill to approach Shifron from the west, where there were no trails. "It's him," she asserted. "How many disjuncts are out there?"

She also spotted Jhiti's emissary to the Patrol approaching the juncts openly by riding due east from the Fort to join the north-south road into Shifron, incidentally providing a diversion for Tuzhel's insane rescue attempt.

Lexy stared into the distance where Solamar could zlin Tuzhel once the renSime was pointed out to him. He couldn't see the youth though. "Solamar, if I'd come up here directly after Bruce woke us, I might have found Tuzhel when it wasn't too late to stop him leaving."

For no reason he could figure, Solamar found his whole body and soul awash in love for this woman. She went hypoconscious and just looked at him, loving back.

Tuzhel slipped behind the hill and was gone.

Lexy sighed, turned her back to the wall, leaned against it facing south and zlinned down into the Fort. New buildings were everywhere. There was no sign of the new underground shelter, not even a plume of smoke from the hearth fires Solamar knew were burning.

The kitchen chimneys were smoking though. There was activity by the stables, and a few renSimes accompanied by guards were out tending the animals housed outside the Fort. The next guard shift was forming in the yard.

"Solamar, do you zlin that?"

"Where?" Most of his attention was on the wisp of Kahleen's nager he thought he zlinned from the underground shelter. Desperate Need returned, vaporizing that moment of pure love.

She pointed and he followed the gesture. Then he stood tall, extending his whole Need sharpened sensitivity. "The Gens are leaving! Rimon succeeded!"

* * * * * * *

At noon Jhiti's emissaries returned. Pearl had found three Shifron merchants she knew who introduced them to the Patrol Captain. "They say," reported Pearl, "we can block the Raiders from the trail south into Gen Territory, but we have to stay away from Shifron. Also if we chase the Raiders back into Shifron and make this fight harder for the Patrol, we'll be cleaned out of this valley as soon as they can get around to it. The Captain advised us to stay in the Fort and let the Patrol deal with the Raiders and the Gens."

Consensus was that the Patrol didn't want to oust the Raiders only to find the town occupied by the local perverts who'd try to save Gen lives. The Patrol was here to return the town to its rightful owners with the least expense, which meant taking possession of any Wild Gens left in the Pen.

"What about my father?" asked Lexy, showfield null.

"The Patrol has no interest in him. So I talked to my contacts, and they said if Delri survives they'll return him to us, but getting their homes back is their goal."

Solamar repeated Tuzhel's assessment of what the Raiders

would do when the Patrol moved on Shifron.

Jhiti looked at Sian and Lexy flanked by Garen and Solamar with Kahleen staying close. Lexy decided, "Ride out in force and block the road. Build a trap. Get my father back, Clire too if possible, but get my father back alive. And Tuzhel. Don't lose Tuzhel."

Solamar felt her desire to ride with the Guard, but this Fort had learned its lesson. No channels or Companions would get near combat. Individually and collectively, they were all determined never to make the same mistake twice. He'd even heard some of the adults humming the children's tune to *Zeor* as they worked. This time they'd do better.

Jhiti turned to issuing orders. Oberin took a small force composed of people known to Shifron's merchants into position to enter the town with the Patrol. Jhiti took his main fighting force to block the road south to the pass, and left a contingent of his best to defend the Fort.

His reserve unit took remounts, wagons and medical supplies out across the fields, positioned where either returning force could reach them without their horses foundering. There wasn't a channel or Companion in the Fort who wasn't contemplating ignoring the rules and just going with them anyway. Many of them, Bruce included, had well reasoned arguments to back up their desires.

Solamar didn't dare say, "You stay here and I'll take a quick transfer and go with the remounts to do the work." Lexy would follow, and that wasn't going to happen.

He found Bruce fidgeting by the stable doors as they were leading the horses out for Jhiti's foray. Oberin and her group had already mounted and filed out the main gate.

Bruce's nager focused briefly on Solamar then politely away from the channel in Need. "I've got to go with them," he muttered. "Rimon could die by the time they can get him here. You said he thinks he's already dead. He could die just from giving up." The Companion had been working with every low field channel he could get close to, bringing his field up because

Rimon's Need would be peaking sooner than usual due to the head injury.

"I don't think so," said Solamar. "He's lost his way back to his body, but that's typical of the coma state. If we can get him back, we should be able to bring him around."

"Can you get him back into his body now?"

"No. And I doubt it would be a good idea. He'll be in pain. Disoriented, or worse. It'd be better if he wakes up here, in his own bed with you right beside him."

"You really believe that?" asked Lexy coming up behind them as handlers brought more horses. Kahleen and Garen flanked Lexy and listened for Solamar's answer.

"Yes, actually I do. Let's go make a secure place for Rimon and prepare to receive the injured."

CHAPTER EIGHTEEN
WAYFARER

Jhiti had left strict orders with his watch commanders to keep the channels and Companions in the shelter, and that is exactly where they sat out the whole long ordeal.

Solamar counted the toll on Lexy from this strain and wondered if she'd have been better off riding out with the reserve force. An hour after they were sent below, she suffered a severe attack of sneezing. Three hours after that, she broke out in a rash of raised welts typical of her pregnancy induced reaction to wool next to her skin.

They treated her with teas and tinctures and washes while she snapped at them irritably.

Even knowing he should be searching for Rimon, Solamar couldn't close his eyes. Every noise, every nageric twang brought him to his feet heart hammering. His Need was a strident screech that just wouldn't quit.

So he called another channeling staff meeting to review preparations. They were patient with him because he was in Need but Solamar couldn't stop himself from hammering away at every detail.

He even double-checked the readiness of Marliss, the man who had been Aipensha's Companion during her First Year and occasionally served Rimon or Lexy though he preferred to work with his wife, Shani. Val had scheduled Marliss to be free to deal with Clire if necessary.

Finally, dawn brought the time for his transfer. He retired

with Kahleen to the most insulated room below. Transfer took his mind off Rimon, battle, loss of this Fort, and the inevitable flood of wounded even if they won.

Kahleen released selyn into his system with a much anticipated, smooth abundance that laved him in ecstatic satisfaction followed by a plunge into the sensory world that should have had every nerve tingling.

Instead, the true horror of their circumstance penetrated all the way. He had come here to help Rimon Farris bring a new day for humanity. Now Rimon was lost far away from his body, and there was nothing he could do.

He emerged from the brief seclusion, one arm around Kahleen's shoulders in apology, and found that Garen had barely managed to get Lexy to sleep when the first report came down. "Battle with the Raiders on the trail. Lots of riders headed this way."

Everything had been prepared three times over. There was no possible reaction but white-knuckled fear. Every channel strove to keep the Companion's reaction from ballooning into the ambient, but couldn't contain their own.

There ensued nearly twelve hours of tension. Then injured Fort Guards trickled into the shelter, brimming with fragmentary reports Solamar pieced together as he worked.

Raiders pursued the Fort Guard retreating from Shifron toward the Fort. The Fort's advance riders returned across the muddy valley at a mad gallop. They picked up their remounts before crossing the river at the only possible ford. The tired horses had been cut loose to be rounded up later. Half Jhiti's rear guard hung back to fend off the pursuing Raiders and the other half protected the Fort riders returning from Shifron at a more sedate canter.

Rimon wasn't in Shifron, concluded Solamar. *Tuzhel was right. He's alive. He's got to be.*

Then came a shouted report, "Twenty horses carrying bodies!" The runner disappeared back up the stair. If Lexy or Solamar had been up on the wall, they'd know if the bodies were dead. Nothing would make Lexy sit down. She paced and paced, her showfield controlled into a ludicrously unconvincing calm. None of her inner turmoil reached Solamar, but he had plenty of his own to contain. So he paced with her, one arm around her waist, one hand holding hers. He could barely feel the Postsyndrome sizzling through his nerves.

They all went over and over the plan for receiving the wounded, for bringing Rimon, and maybe Clire in. Every contingency had been planned for.

Another report: the Fort's own Guard had opened the small door beside the main wagon gate. The first returning riders were squeezing in. The Guard reserve deployed out.

Solamar heard the advance riders pounding across the yard, halting by the entry to the underground shelter. Then wounded poured down the stairs and all the rehearsals paid off. Channels with the right skills picked up the injuries they were most familiar with and went to work.

Lexy, Solamar, Kahleen, Garen and Bruce gathered at the bottom of the stair, the Gens placed so their presence wouldn't zlin as a plume of nageric brightness. The staff spread out down the corridor waiting for assignments.

One of the renSime guards with a broken leg clutched his stretcher as bearers passed it down the stairs and gasped out a report. "Raiders in the worst shape I've ever seen. Weak. Sick. Skin and bones, but there's a lot of them and they're terrified of the Patrol. Followed us in. Attacking."

Solamar and Lexy waited by the stair directing traffic and searching for Rimon. Another renSime was carried down the stair, reporting to someone who followed with a slate ignoring the blood pumping through the bandage wrapping the guard's torso. "Tuzhel's dead!"

Solamar felt BanSha's reaction, shock, guilt, horror quickly throttled with the beginnings of a channel's discipline. "What happened?" BanSha demanded.

The renSime guard, raising his head whispered to BanSha, "I think Tuzhel went junct to make Clire trust him with Rimon.

He was riding with the Raiders, leading the horse Rimon was tied over. Then he cut out of the Raider's line and rode toward us, bringing Rimon.

"Clire rode out after him. Tuzhel whipped Rimon's horse toward us then turned and blocked her way screaming at her, 'Out of death was I born, unto Zeor, forever!' She blasted the ambient to knock Tuzhel off his horse. I felt it when Tuzhel's neck broke. She almost got Rimon. Jhiti's whip lashed around her neck, yanked her off her horse. Raider's knife got me. It's not so bad...," and he fainted.

Xanon picked up that renSime, then three renSime women went by, two on stretchers and one hobbling. Lexy consigned them to channels. Finally they zlinned the shift in the ambient they'd been hoping for.

"It's Rimon!" said Solamar.

"He's alive!" Barely two seconds later, she said, "And Clire, too!"

Clire is six months pregnant.

"BanSha, Rushi, Marliss, with me," barked Solamar while Lexy was still holding her breath against a flood of tears. "Lexy, you, Garen and Bruce go with your father and I'll be with you as soon as possible, just as we discussed."

From above howling erupted, screaming horses, snapping whips. The Raider attack.

Rimon's stretcher came down the stairs. Bruce followed it along, ran his hands over Rimon, poking, prodding, working fields, shouting for medications. They had to work before Solamar could do anything for Rimon. Lexy shouldn't be exposed to Clire if she miscarried, so she was Solamar's problem. Why was he so apprehensive?

Others replaced them by the stair. As Solamar raced beside Clire's stretcher, he zlinned, almost penetrating her opaque Farris veil. He assessed the damage a choking and a bad fall had done now overlaid with massive disorientation.

Kahleen's attention focused on their patient, not on himself. Her field was weak from having just given him transfer.

"Kahleen, this isn't the Clire you knew, not the channel you served so ably. Let Marliss handle her."

Kahleen drew herself in, doing a fair imitation of Bruce's fade into the furniture. She swallowed hard and closed her eyes. "I will. She's skin and bones. Her baby's bound to be underweight, premature. Clire died during that first battle. I don't know this woman."

"We might save the baby if we can save Rimon. Just delay the birth until Rimon can deal with it."

She looked him in the eye. "Rimon's not junct?"

"No!" he said positively, though even the comatose Farris nager had not been so clear. "So let's get to work."

"All right, I'm with you," she said and planted her attention firmly on Solamar.

By the time they got to Clire's room, the stretcher bearers had moved her onto the bed and left. Rushi was seated on the bed probing the distended uterus gingerly, no doubt hyperaware that Clire was junct as well as Farris.

"What have we got?" asked Solamar of the Gen midwife as he positioned BanSha and set him holding fields.

The young woman reported, "No contractions. No vaginal bleeding. The baby is low, and moving. She's six months at least. Not in labor. Yet."

Solamar gestured Marliss away from Clire, giving himself room to study the Farris. "BanSha?"

"Me?" BanSha reported what he zlinned. "No broken bones, but plenty of tissue damage and I think concussion but who could zlin her that well except Rimon, or Lexy? I don't know why she's still unconscious. I can't even assess her state of Need except that her ronaplin glands seem swollen, but maybe it's just she's so thin."

"Good. Hold the fields tight," coached Solamar. He moved in to take over from Rushi. BanSha swept the fields into a steady, coherent beat. "She's in Need, but then Raiders always are and no Kill could ever satisfy her. The injuries are voiding selyn, zlin that, BanSha?"

"Yes, but I've zlinned much worse. That baby is voracious, too. Lexy's baby isn't like that."

"True, but a Farris channel should be voiding more profusely than this. Not enough selyn in her secondary system. She's severely unbalanced. It'll be bad if she comes to." She wouldn't. Her Self had wandered far away. "Get the restraints on her. Marliss, don't try a transfer yet."

The room had extra strong padded restraints anchored to the bed, fitted to the upper arms, torso and thighs, and the bed frames had been anchored to the floor for disoriented patients waking suddenly. They cleaned and healed the wounds to stop bleeding, repaired the swelling and the strain in the neck. The skin burn from the whip didn't fade much though, and she didn't regain consciousness.

Solamar let Marliss near the bed and coached BanSha and Rushi until they could hold the fields even when Marliss moved. "Good, now Marliss is in charge here. You two do what he says. Kahleen and I will help Lexy with Rimon."

Solamar noted how BanSha restrained himself from asking if Rimon would be all right. *I'm going to hold that kid tight all through Tuzhel's funeral.*

He waited until BanSha fell into the rhythm of maintaining the ambient for Marliss, then Solamar excised himself and Kahleen from the selyn field matrix.

They crossed the hall to Rimon's door, a solid hardwood laminated around a selyn diffractive sand core. The air was damp, the ambient nager equally blunted.

Solamar noticed the sounds of battle drifting down with the smell of blood and death. Kahleen distracted him. "Lexy is probably tiring by now," she said. "Despite that, she expects to be able to work non-stop all night."

Solamar focused his attention through the door. "Every once in a while she remembers she's pregnant."

Insulation or no, Lexy noticed him. A moment later, Garen opened the door. "He's alive," he whispered.

Lexy and Bruce bent over Rimon, visibly thinner, nagerically haggard, and again with the Self absent.

Solamar closed the door behind Kahleen. "He's not dying," said Solamar in a normal voice. "He's simply not in his body and hasn't been for way too long...." It struck him. *Clire! They're both out of their bodies!*

Rimon had confessed he'd dreamed of Clire.

Solamar waded through the ambient to Rimon's side. "Lexy, let me. Bruce, stand back."

Bruce had been trying to coax Rimon's flaccid tentacles into a transfer grip. He paused, searching Solamar's face. "He hasn't responded at all."

"I think I may know why. Clire's still unconscious and shouldn't be. If Clire has found him, she may be trying to prevent him from returning to his body."

"Is that possible?" blurted Lexy over Bruce's shock.

Without looking at her, he said, "Yes. And you should sit down. Garen, don't let her back muscles go into spasm or I'll have to ask her to leave."

Garen scooped her into the second chair in the room.

"Kahleen?" She had been staring at Rimon. Now she took a deep breath, closed her eyes and with a ragged sigh shifted her nager back to a working stance. "Good."

Solamar hadn't had time to teach her how to guard him when he was out of his body, so he said, "I'm going to lie beside Rimon and I may seem to be asleep. Hold the fields as tightly as you can. Lexy, if you can't stay clear of me go on over to the recovery room. Bruce, stay focused on Rimon. He may be able to find his body by finding you."

He gestured the Companion to the end of the bed. Bruce moved without rippling the fields even as he wrapped himself in a quilt, settled at the end of the bed, leaned against the wall, and rested his hand on Rimon's foot. His massive nager filled the room with confidence.

Solamar stretched out beside Rimon. Kahleen flipped a quilt over them both. It took him much too long to slide out of his body and search for Rimon again.

* * * * * * *

Everything whirled around and around. He felt queasy. Cold panic shot through him like psychospatial disorientation. Since he had no body, that was impossible.

Sick and dizzy, Rimon clutched the small, sparkling coffer to himself, tucked his head down and shrieked into the mists, "Solamar!"

I'm not dead. Solamar said I'm not dead. The dead can't experience psychospatial disorientation so maybe he's right. I have to get back, get oriented again. I'm not dead. "Solamar! Help! Help me! Here I am, Solamar. Here!"

Without transition, he was in a Fort. He was sprawled in the yard of the Fort, clutching the coffer. He sat up. It was a strange Fort. The walls were some kind of mud brick. The buildings were dull tan mud brick. Funny looking roofs were made of some kind of half-tubes that glinted in the sun. It was hotter than he could ever remember feeling.

A woman said behind him, "It was you!"

He turned. "Clire! What're you doing here? Where is here!"

"Someone called for help! It was you."

Clire's sharp features were contorted into malice. Streaks of searing hatred shattered her nager. Rimon had never thought a nager could zlin like that, but then there was no zlinning in this place. Or there hadn't been until now. He zlinned her emaciated body six months pregnant, the baby draining selyn. *Does a woman stay pregnant after she dies? Are we both dead?*

"Clire, where are we?"

"You want help? I'll help you like you helped me!"

Her tentacles snared his hair. She yanked him around. He fell prone to a hard-packed dirt floor, cold against his cheek, the coffer hard under his chest.

The door slammed before he knew there was a door. Clire's spite filled the ambient. "Stay there until you die of Attrition or Kill!"

There was a narrow vertical slit for a window, and he sensed

Clire lurking outside, zlinning him avidly.

Then he became aware of a Gen nager in the small, unfurnished room. A moment before it hadn't been there. Now, another person was huddled in the corner, Gen arms wrapped around a brown haired head. Her sobs ripped into him and a Need he'd never known erupted. Attrition.

The person looked up, stifling sobs. It was Bekka Esren, but an odd Bekka Esren. She was still a child in appearance though her nager crackled and pulsed with selyn.

This isn't real, he told himself. Clire never saw Bekka mature. *This is Clire's imagination. Somehow I'm trapped in Clire's imagination.*

Solamar had hinted at the skills that could let him traverse this realm safely, sanely. He'd accepted a few lessons but hadn't practiced what Solamar tried to teach him. If he were still alive, if his body lived somewhere, then his only way out was to get back to his body just like Solamar had taught him. *But I've lost my body!*

Without volition, his mouth opened and a cry of sheer unadulterated terror ripped from his lips. "Solamar!"

"Shen you, who is Solamar!" demanded Clire. She was standing in the room, screaming at him. "Whoever it is, he's not going to help you! You're dependent on me and you will get the help you gave me! Kill your precious little Bekka Esren and then we'll see how the Fort worships you."

I am not dead. So Clire's not dead. We can get out of this. "Solamar!"

"I said stop that!"

Suddenly Rimon was inside a white box. His cries echoed deafeningly. He was sealed in with his desperation.

Tucking the coffer under his left arm, he circled the featureless box, running his right hand, tentacles and fingers spread, over the surface. It felt as smooth as it looked, but there seemed to be an effulgent nageric haze.

The Gen was in the box with him. She hadn't been there before. She curled on her side in one corner, crying softly. It was

Bekka Esren.

A peculiar, empty echo of Need verging on Attrition seized his body. He staggered into the opposite corner from the Gen and slid down to sit with knees bent, the coffer braced between stomach and thighs. He clutched it with his left arm. With his right hand, he shielded his eyes.

She isn't there. This isn't real. It's only two weeks since that fabulous transfer with Bruce.

He knew it but that didn't matter. He felt it as real. And Clire somehow watched from outside the white box.

He set himself to endure this torment as he had so many others in his long life. *I'm too old for this.*

Or maybe he'd never yet been old enough, mature enough, to face the consequences of his own mistakes.

Unbidden, the endless list of mistakes flowed through his mind, each accompanied by an ugly image.

One ill considered moment, and he had fathered a child on a Farris woman. There was a good chance Clire was a descendent of his grandfather, making it worse. In irrational weakness, he'd let a popular opinion overrule his good sense and let them vote to delay Clire's transfer. Then because he knew he'd done wrong, he'd been so furious with himself that he couldn't sit still in the underground shelter and let Jhiti's Guard deal with the Raiders and rescue the Fort Tanhara refugees.

The result of his childish fury was Clire's Kill and Aipensha's death and the loss of the Council that had held the Fort together even though the refugees far outnumbered the Fort Rimon natives.

He had tried to help with the combat by grabbing the strange channel who had just arrived, and using him in a moronic scheme for chasing the Raiders away. The results of that, admittedly awesome, field work on the battle's ambient were a series of disasters.

If he had let Jhiti's guards slaughter the Freebanders, perhaps Shifron's citizens could have fought off the rest of the Band. Instead, they had overrun Shifron and Clire was using the

Freebanders to destroy Fort Rimon.

Meanwhile, his crazy stunt with Solamar on the wall and his even crazier attempt to save Tuzhel had dislodged him from his body, and he had begun seeing ghosts, even perhaps traveling with them while he slept. Maybe both he and Clire were dead. And his new baby.

He'd learned to Heal the part of another person that could leave the body, then put that person back into their body, Healing the body as well. He could imagine things and they would become real. The potential was staggering, but when Solamar had given him the chance to learn to control it, Rimon had nodded, and accepted, learned the bare minimum and then neglected to practice.

He pulled his knees up, letting his thighs and chest be dented by the edges of the coffer so near his vriamic node.

He folded his forearms on top of the coffer, his left outer lateral cruelly pressed against the jewels in the Starred Cross image, his right arm resting on top of his left. His forehead sank to rest on his right forearm's inner lateral.

The dizzying pain of that position cut off most of his awareness of the Gen and distracted him from the immediate do-something, do-something, pounding of escalating Need.

He had sat like this often when he was a child, knees braced up, arms folded against himself, his quilt wrapped around and folded over his head. In those days, the position hadn't hurt, hadn't spun his senses into nauseating loops.

Now, he could only imagine his quilt wrapped around him, folding him in his parents' love. The coffer was solid against his body, against his lateral, against his vriamic node where his primary and secondary selyn circulatory systems joined. He focused his attention on the coffer as if he were doing a complex channeling functional.

Inside the coffer was the knowledge that, no matter how many dire mistakes he had made, if he didn't give up the striving toward that moment he'd sealed into the coffer, if he always excelled his previous mark, Sime and Gen would be united.

Humanity would survive. Non-junct.

I will not Kill Bekka. No matter how or when I die, I will be born again. I will make mistakes, some worse than misplacing my body because I lost the respect of some frightened people who didn't believe me when I told them a woman was pregnant before anyone else could possibly know. I will do better next time. Solamar!

* * * * * * *

"Father!" blurted Solamar with a humiliating lack of maturity. "What are you doing here!" He had usually taken care to avoid his father when venturing out of his body, but in his haste to get to Rimon he'd forgotten caution.

The older man turned from surveying the thick mist around them and eyed Solamar with disapproval. "If you don't hear *that*, then what are you doing here?"

The ambient throbbed like rhythmic rocking of a child worn by terror. The shape of the nageric noise vaguely resembled his own name. "Some Wayfarer's calling me."

His father's eyebrows went up as he gestured lazily with one tentacle, just the posture he always displayed when teaching. "Wayfarer?" he prompted.

His father vanished.

Solamar identified the call as Rimon. What could possibly make the dynamic leader of Fort Rimon whimper like a baby? He followed the call to a tiny adobe room with a vertical slit for a window. On the wall was a weaving that spelled out, *Fort Intalace, Where Borders Don't Separate.*

In the center of the room was a white box with a transparent top. It was about waist high and cubical.

Clire stood over the box gazing into it. As Solamar arrived, his father yanked her away.

Twisting out of the older man's grip, Clire kicked at him. When that didn't work, she grabbed the edge of the white box and blasted Rhodilan Grant with a nageric shockwave. The elder Grant ignored the channel's tricks with his usual contempt for such untrained talents.

Rhodilan spun Clire around, breaking her grip on the white box. He grabbed her by the cord that connected her to her body. Solamar noted the care taken to avoid harming the tiny thread that anchored her fetus. Rhodilan drove a shaft of glittering selyn into the mother's cord.

The cord contracted in a series of spasms, whipping her around the room until she was drawn out through a wall, screaming terror and rage.

"She's insane," commented his father in that low, calm, instructive, totally maddening voice. "You'll have to deal with that. What will you do with your Farris...oh! She was holding the box!"

The white box expanded until its walls melted into the adobe walls around them revealing a miniaturized Rimon Farris huddled inside whimpering. Rimon's figure expanded to normal size as the adobe walls began to dissipate. That left them surrounded by the formless mist again.

Before them sat Del Rimon Farris, curled in on himself, his baby quilt folded about him, positioned so the dagger image was a shield on his back. He clutched something to his stomach protecting it behind raised knees. He rested his forehead on his forearms. *I think I'd vomit if I tried that position!*

Solamar knelt beside the huddled figure and reached out one hand, tentacles spread feeling the Farris showfield hardened into a crumbling granite wall. Waves of throbbing Need escaped through cracks. Rimon's attention fixed on a spot not far away. Only, there was no Gen there.

Behind him, his father said, "That woman's talent is projecting illusion. Solamar, she was torturing this poor soul with his greatest weakness, and taking real satisfaction from it. I'm not surprised. Trafficking in selyn!"

He glanced back at his father who waited for him to handle Rimon. He was not saying *Are you sure the fate of humanity should rest on the channels' ability to traffic in selyn? Are you really sure you want to risk doing that to yourself?* Nevertheless, the oft-spoken words reverberated around them.

Solamar moved closer to Rimon, blocking out awareness of his father, reaching toward his friend. "Rimon, she's gone. Let's get you back to your body...."

Before Solamar could untangle the cord that was crisscrossed around Rimon's torso and send him back to his body, Rimon's form turned to wisps of smeared color, whirled around and poured through an invisible hole into nothing. A single word hung over them *Solamar!*

Solamar tried to follow, but suddenly he and his father were floating free, suspended in formless mist without even a solid floor.

Feeling as if he were back in First Year again, having bollixed up some simple exercise, Solamar stood before his father, struggling to hold his feet oriented in the same direction as his father's feet. He created a floor.

"So where did he go?" his father quizzed just as if Solamar were a First Year student flunking a basic lesson.

Solamar didn't want to say, *I don't know.* "I guess he's wandering Time." He told his father everything that had happened since he'd left home in such a cloud of acrimony that it had summoned his grandfather's ghost to scold Rhodilan Grant on his child rearing skills.

Solamar finished the tale with, "Every moment through all of this I've been wishing I had paid more attention to your lessons and practiced them harder."

"But you still think the Farris mutation is the key because they're better at selyn trafficking than the others?"

"They're different, father. They're not just channels. I told you how Rimon became jarred loose from his body. There's a lot more going on here than the obvious."

His father digested that. Solamar gave himself points for having found something his father thought significant.

At length, his father nodded. "Well then you'll have to find him and put him back into his body."

"How?"

"If he keeps screaming like that, it shouldn't be very hard." Rhodilan Grant paused, then added with puzzlement, "Clearly he holds you in high regard,"

All right, there is no avoiding it. Rimon's life is at stake here. "Father, what would you do?"

"Well, since we haven't been able to hold him from out here, I'd suggest working from his body's side."

We?! We haven't been able to hold him? That admission alone was worth everything Solamar had gone through since he left home. "What procedure would you suggest?" Solamar congratulated himself on making it seem like a consultation not a plea for help.

"I'd find something meaningful to him, set up resonances of similarities, connect with him through that which he reveres. Then pull him back into his body. If that can't be done, then cut the cord and let him go."

And with him all the hope that humanity will survive?

"I can get him back into his body," said Solamar. He was fully adult, standing before his father eye to eye as an equal, a unique experience.

"You may have to Heal him, or better, get him to Heal himself. Psychically, he's taken a terrible beating from that woman. Before you insert him into his body, be sure he doesn't bring back more memory of all this than he can bear or you'll have another Farris like that woman." He turned to go, hesitated and said over his shoulder, "I *think* I got them both back into her body and locked them there long enough for the fetus to mature."

My father admitting uncertainty?

For the first time, he noticed how gray the man's hair was. He was no longer just slender for a Sime. He was too slender. Older than Rimon, he was still healthier, yet he wouldn't always be there to fix what Solamar broke.

"I'll monitor the baby carefully until Rimon can take over," promised Solamar.

"It's his child, you know. If anyone can give that kid life, Rimon can."

"I understand."

"I just wish you did. I have to go write this up in my journal before I forget any details. You just be sure Rimon forgets enough of it to protect his mind. These Farrises you want to stake the fate of humanity on are a hopeless failure of a mutation. There is no way they can carry this burden and succeed. They have power but no strength, endurance but more to endure than anyone else." With that oft repeated opinion, his father misted away.

Solamar was convinced the right Companion could supply the strength to govern the channel's power and heal the ravages of what had to be endured.

Solamar closed his eyes and followed his own cord back into his body. As always, it was like jumping off a cliff, but this time he didn't get smashed to a bloody pulp on jagged rocks. This time it was like diving into deep water, slicing cleanly into cold black depths and coming back to the surface, erupting in a burst of selyn. He'd never done such a neatly controlled return before.

He jackknifed to a sitting position next to Rimon's limp body, gasping and panting, sweat standing out on his face but not the least bit disoriented.

"Are you going to try to find him now?" asked Bruce.

Only a few minutes had passed, though it had seemed like half a day. "I know how to get him back. I'll use both the quilt and the belt, with only Bruce here with me. Even you, Kahleen, should leave, I'm sorry. So go see what you can do to help with Clire. She could be awake by now."

"Clire?"

"Go!" Solamar rolled off the bed and stood to stretch.

"I'll go get the quilt," said Lexy starting for the door.

"No!" chorused Bruce, Garen, Solamar and Kahleen.

She was out the door before anyone could stop her. It was true though that of them all, she could best mask her nageric presence to remain unnoticed by any attackers. They had to hold Garen back. His Gen nager would surely attract danger to her and the fight was still going on.

When the door opened, Solamar zlinned distant combat, not inside the walls.

He detached the buckle from the belt and wrapped Rimon's hands around the jeweled Starred Cross while he planned. But it was hard to think under Garen's frozen stare and Kahleen's held breath. Bruce was furniture. He'd have been a better student of Rhodilan Grant than Solamar had ever been. Which gave Solamar an idea.

Lexy flew into the room with the quilt over one shoulder. She was tall enough that it cleared the ground by a handspan front and back.

"Bruce, help me sit him up. Get cushions to hold him. Let's put this quilt around him so the dagger goes straight down his spine." They struggled with the lanky body, dropping the belt buckle, getting the quilt caught, folding and refolding it, and then propping the lax knees up. Lexy balked at the cross-armed position Solamar was trying to achieve, but he just said, "I have my reasons."

Finally, with rolled blankets, pillows from other rooms, and even one horsehair mattress rolled up, they had Rimon propped into the position, the belt buckle against his chest resting on a box about the size of the coffer.

Then Solamar sent everyone out of the room except Bruce. "Be ready to serve him transfer. He's in hard Need, has been for days."

The Gen's nageric answer left no doubt of his readiness.

Solamar eased onto the bed and knelt behind Rimon, leaning his chest against the stylized dagger symbol in the center of the quilt. He extended his two right hand lateral tentacles and reached around to touch the center between Rimon's eyebrows. With his left lateral tentacles, he probed at the center of Rimon's chest, at the vriamic node, where the channel's dual selyn transport systems joined. With both contacts secured, he prepared to ram selyn into the flaccid body in the emergency revival technique he had been taught but never actually executed before.

I've zlinned it being done. I can do this.

He found the cord that led toward Rimon's true self, stretched tight and dissipating.

We're losing him.

CHAPTER NINETEEN
HEALING

Solamar! screamed Rimon, knowing he was dying.

And Solamar was there, reaching selyn rich tentacles toward him, offering strength and life.

Though he'd been stationary in formless mist, Rimon was dizzy from images whirling around him. All the scenes had been the same, but different. There was always an audience of ghosts, flickering around a space where a young Farris channel stood before an older Farris channel.

Sometimes they were dressed in colorful robes, sometimes strangely tight fitted garments, sometimes plain and sometimes richly embroidered but always with the same flowing blue capes. Always there was a question, an answer and the coffer with the jeweled Starred Cross on the lid opened before the younger one. It contained the dagger Rimon had charged with the essence of that final moment of total triumph of the nonjunct lifestyle.

The younger Farris would gaze into the coffer, seeming to understand what it would be like in those days when nobody Killed. Usually the young Farris learned that the practice of excellence would lead to that moment. There was so much more in that little coffer that few could absorb.

Every time he found himself among such a group, he strove to give the whole of the experience to the young person, but he couldn't. The coffer he clutched had grown attached to his arm. Nothing he could do would let him give it away.

Now, once again alone, aware that he was dying, he lowered

his knees and stretched out his left arm with the coffer growing out of it where his ventral tentacles and left outside laterals should be and tried to give it to Solamar.

Solamar backed away. "Solamar, take it. Please. This is for Lexy. Take it! Help me."

Solamar reached with both hands, tentacles spread to take the coffer. But his hands closed on Rimon's upper arms. "I can't. It won't let me touch it. Rimon, you must come back with me. You must give this to Lexy yourself."

"How! It's attached to me." He tried to keep the dismay out of his nager, but failed. Panic twisted his guts.

Solamar knelt back on his heels and nodded. "I zlin the problem. You must finish creating this object and separate yourself from it, then heal yourself. I will help you, but I can't do this for you."

"How? How can I do that?"

Solamar's grip slid back toward the coffer, fingers and tentacles rippling over the blurry joint between Rimon's flesh and the coffer. "Put more memories into the coffer, everything that's happened here in the mists. Look closely at this side of the box here."

"It doesn't have a side."

"It does. Look closely. See the side, see and zlin all the detail work where your experiences are recorded. It's a beautiful box. See the exquisite artwork. Hold it away so your eyes can focus on it."

"I almost had it!" exclaimed Rimon as the coffer nearly separated from his arm. He had glimpsed the writing on the side, a list of all the ghosts he had encountered, all of them gazing raptly into the coffer.

"Again. You'll do better this time. Go on."

It took four tries, but at last Rimon detached the coffer and held it in his hands, glowing, sparkling, and somehow throbbing with selyn as if it were a living thing.

"Good! Now, let's stand up."

Rimon was suddenly standing, the blanket cascading off his

shoulders into a pile on the oddly solid ground. Solamar's hands came onto his shoulders urging him to turn.

"No! I'll get dizzy and lost again." As panic rose, the coffer glued itself to his arm again.

"Relax. Let's get you ready to go back to your body."

Solamar's hands and tentacles did something near his waist and Rimon recoiled at the invasive touch, turning away and turning again, dizzy. Solamar's hands were there again, stopping him before he fell through another hole.

"Good, all untangled. Doesn't that feel better?"

Oddly enough, it did. As he relaxed, the coffer became again a separate object he could relinquish.

"So let's put the coffer on a shelf."

"What shelf?" asked Rimon.

"Here I'll make one. Watch carefully." He stepped up to the mist wall and raised his hands.

A shelf slowly etched itself out of the mist wall. It was of dark red gleaming wood, supported by three ornately carved wedges. On one end stood a glass candelabra and on the other, two crystal bookends between which were three large books with blank spines. Above the shelf was a round picture frame of the same wood but it had no picture in it.

"Do you like the shelf?" Solamar glanced at Rimon.

"It's beautiful, but shouldn't there be a painting?"

"You create the picture. Here, put the coffer right here in the middle. And put a picture of Lexy over it. She'll know it's for her when she finds it here."

"It'll just stay here?" asked Rimon reaching up to lay the coffer on the shelf. He put it down and stepped back. Then he decided the shelf would be better if it were the mantle of a fireplace. With that, a brick hearth appeared under the shelf. With some fumbling, he added a pile of logs and flames licking up, emitting warmth and light.

"Do you remember what Lexy looks like?"

Rimon blinked and his daughter's pregnant image appeared in the frame.

"Beautiful!"

There was a fervent warmth in Solamar's admiration not for the image but for the woman herself.

While Rimon contemplated that, Solamar had moved up behind him. "Let's sit down before the fire here, together." Rimon let Solamar guide him into the position he'd retreated into out of unreasoning terror. His knees came up almost to his nose, one arm rested atop his knees, and the other curled against his abdomen, though it no longer held the coffer. Solamar knelt behind him and made lateral contact on his forehead and his chest.

"Now what does Bruce zlin like? You remember?"

* * * * * * *

The impenetrable Farris nager collapsed into the void of Hard Need but they remained in the mists. With his laterals touching Rimon's forehead, Solamar zlinned the swelling in Rimon's brain and the image of disrupted selyn flows in the image of Rimon that he held in his arms.

"Rimon, when you fell from your horse, you hit your head and damaged your neck. You can't go back to Bruce like this. First Heal yourself, then you can return to your body and take transfer. Just do what you did when you Healed Sian of his paralysis."

"A channel can't Heal himself!"

"Well...but I'll help. We can reform the damaged tissues in your brain *here*, and then your body will reform healthy *there* just as Sian's did."

His sense of Need meant that Rimon was receiving some feedback from his body. Untangling his cord had restored contact.

Solamar brought up his showfield in his strongest Gen projection. "Come on, use my field, lean on me, just pretend I'm really Gen, and zlin yourself."

"Solamar, nobody can zlin themselves. You can zlin your

own hand, but not...not like that!"

"Just imagine. Come on, now, watch me zlin myself."

Solamar zlinned himself. He held his showfield Gen, then stood outside himself and regarding himself critically, noting how replete his primary selyn transport system was, and how strong that made his control of his secondary system which also carried a good amount of selyn.

"Now you try it. Here the impossible is routine. Just forget about the limitations you normally live with."

He held on as Rimon fumbled to detach his awareness and look back on himself from outside.

It took five repetitions before Rimon got the hang of it, but when he did, it became something far different from the simple training exercise Solamar had demonstrated.

Rimon actually produced a whole separate image of himself, reached out tentacles and made a Healing contact.

The tangled knots that represented Rimon's injuries melted. Rimon's uncharacteristic fear evaporated. The second Rimon image melted back into the original making it sharper, more vivid, more detailed. Right after that, Rimon's fields went deep, complex and opaque, then back to his normal impenetrability.

Solamar was sure his father wouldn't believe it no matter how he reported it. "Good, now watch what I'm doing here. This is how to get back to your body." Solamar took Rimon's left hand and slid it around the cord that bound him to his body. "Feel that?"

"Yes! What is it?"

"It's your connection to your body. All you have to do is follow it. Close your eyes. Focus on what you feel in your hand, push off and slide right down that line. Just think of Bruce."

Solamar narrowed his focus to his own cord which stretched up into the nothingness around them. They rose leaving the mantle and its precious coffer behind.

Together they slid back into their bodies. There was none of the horrifying sensation of falling infinitely, none of the gasping shock.

There was no time to think. Rimon was up and out of his grip, going for Bruce like a rampaging berserker.

The disconnection sent shock up his exposed laterals.

Bruce yelled, "Kahleen!" Selyn movement slammed through the room.

Solamar's body curled up fighting hot lateral spasms crawling up his arms and down into his chest to his vriamic node. Seconds later, Kahleen's marvelous Gen hands came to his arms, Gen fields locked onto his, and purely Gen concern penetrated his awareness.

Her body's selyn creation pulses synchronized divinely with his body's selyn consumption rhythm. The whiplash shock melted away. "Gen magic," he gasped. "What a marvel!" He struggled to sit up.

Rimon and Bruce were sitting on the floor off the end of the bed grinning at each other as the residual field pulses of their transfer dissipated. Bruce had filled Rimon's primary system and had enough selyn left to partially fill his secondary system, and now the channel burst with joy.

Rimon dismantled the contact. "Bruce, I thought I'd died without even being able to zlin you again!"

"When did you have time to think that?"

A puzzled expression flitted across Rimon's face as he nager rippled with effort. "I don't know."

"I would have come for you, but it seemed the best way to be sure I could give you transfer was to wait. It was terrible, but I've seen you do harder vigils, so I waited. Solamar said you weren't dead but he couldn't find you."

Rimon said, "The last thing I remember was riding with Tuzhel in front of me and then shoving him onto Jokim's horse. Then...nothing, until now. How did I get...where is here? We can't be here...the new underground shelter! They finished it!"

Solamar heaved a sigh of blissful relief. Rimon had a head-ache which was only marginally worse than the ache in his whole body. He was madly hungry, and throbbing with Postsyndrome, but he wasn't disoriented and had no memory of his adventures in time. His health and his sanity were safe. *I did it!* He thought with glee. *I did it!*

Then Rimon's nager reassembled itself into a new mysterious Farris presentation. This time it was like a deep, translucent marble fraught with dark crimson veins. The impenetrable Rimon Farris was back.

Solamar suddenly remembered, "The battle!"

"What battle?" asked Rimon.

Kahleen, Bruce and Solamar gathered themselves to their feet all talking at once. Solamar untangled his feet from Rimon's quilt and bent to retrieve Rimon's belt buckle.

Rimon began to draw his knees under himself to rise, and suddenly collapsed, shaking and totally astonished at his weakness. He tried again, and finally Kahleen and Bruce helped him up. He sagged between them, his legs unable to support him. Solamar was certain it was just the weakness. The head injury had cleared up.

Thus supported and half carried, Rimon was first out the door. Solamar grabbed the leather belt and followed, attaching the buckle as he moved. Already people were shouting in the hall.

Suddenly Lexy was there in front of them with Garen.

Rimon stopped dead just outside the doorway and Bruce almost kept going as Rimon stared at Lexy and said to Bruce and Kahleen, "I've been, what? Unconscious? For a month? It really has been a month! Lexy, let me zlin you! The baby has grown so much!"

Solamar felt Rimon adjusting to the impossible as people yelled up and down the corridor.

"Rimon's alive!"

"Rimon's all right!"

"Solamar did it!"

Although the ambient was total chaos around them with wounded and fast moving staffers intent on critical cases, Solamar couldn't hear any more battle noise coming down the stairs at the end of the hall.

The upper door to the outside stood wide open.

* * * * * * *

Rimon leaned on a cane, still very shaky on his feet, tiring easily. But he was once again standing on the flat topped rock at the cemetery. He squinted into the setting sun to survey the gathering crowd. He had to conduct yet another funeral, the third that day.

First, in the morning, they had buried the Raiders who had come against the Fort. Mixed in with them there might have been some of Shifron's people or the Border Patrol who had come to oust the Freebanders.

As the Freebanders had attacked the Fort, the Patrol had attacked their rear. Patrol scouts reported that Raiders who had escaped into Gen Territory had been taken by the Gens on the other side of the pass. All the Freeband Raiders, except Clire, were dead.

At noon, the Fort had buried those few of the Fort who had given their lives in that battle.

Now, separately because Rimon requested it, they would bury Tuzhel. The gathering crowd was just as thick as it had been at noon. This time, at his feet lay the painting of Fort Freedom that had always hung in his office, over his head, symbolizing his father's mandate not to let the Forts die.

Since the moment he'd wakened in Bruce's transfer grip, he had known without knowing how he knew, that Fort Rimon had died the day he'd denied Clire transfer.

For Rimon, the day had been full of shocks, horrifying news as people had told him of events while he'd been captive in Shifron, but with a few bright spots.

Their old neighbors were back in charge of Shifron and had accepted the Fort's offer of help rebuilding the town since the Fort had spent the winter training builders.

Clire and her baby had survived, though she was still unconscious. Solamar had described her vicious hatred of him and the

Fort in graphic detail.

Lexy was fine. His grandchild was thriving. Definitely not a channel, and he was fairly sure not a renSime. She was more besotted with Solamar than ever. *She couldn't make a better choice.*

Bruce was a marvel beyond all belief. He had not done anything too stupid during this ordeal. Had their roles been reversed, he wouldn't have performed as well.

His Companion stood behind him now, supporting him as if he were about to perform some difficult functional. Bruce was wisely prepared to catch him if he fell over again. They had barely had time to talk about Rimon's plans for the Fort, but his best friend was ready to follow him into anything.

Rimon extended handling tentacles and hung both hands on his belt buckle, fingering the jeweled Starred Cross as he watched Solamar helping Lexy climb onto the rock followed by Garen and Kahleen. *There is the next generation. They are the ones I'm doing this for.*

Jhiti and Oberin both followed them. Their winter-long regimen of drills, plans, construction of defenses, and more drills had paid off. Only a few had died in this battle. Jhiti was absolutely triumphant.

Rimon saw the Esren family reach the bottom of the path and motioned them up onto the stone. He had asked Jor Esren to give Tuzhel's eulogy, Church of the Unity style. That Jor had accepted was heartening.

The new Council Sian headed was managing the daily tasks of the Fort. As Sian descended from the new Fort gate, Rimon motioned him and some of the Councilors to come up onto the rock. He had spent half the evening with them sketching his plan, and they were already enthusiastic.

Fort Freedom had been founded by Abel Veritt to harbor juncts who regretted the necessity to Kill but accepted that the Kill didn't make them Evil. They had embraced Rimon Farris and his gift of transfer.

Despite all that good, the Fort concept had not been designed to harbor the channel-centered life. The new Council, most of whom had been involved in the mistakes he'd made with Clire, understood what he meant when he said it was time to put aside the concept of the Forts, to create a new way of living.

Finally, with the sun lowering in the spring sky and the moon not yet risen, he called them to order to lay to rest a young disjunct who had deserved so much more from them than they had been able to give him.

When Benart had settled with his slates to record everything, Rimon grabbed attention with a nageric pulse. "The Forts have failed. Tuzhel's death has taught us that.

"We must recognize and acknowledge our failure."

The ambient congealed with shock. The Companions and channels scattered through the crowd worked the fields. Not everyone had been warned of the changes he proposed.

"When I saw my own grave there on the hill, I saw that the time had come to admit that I have failed my grandfather's mandate handed to me by my father.

"When I first saw the gravestone, they were breaking it up to use in a hearth. But I could read the inscription.

"Refusing to acknowledge failure will never lead to success. And we must succeed. Clire Farris lies junct, unconscious, beyond retrieval because this Fort failed. Tuzhel gave his life and much more, his disjunction, to save my life and this Fort. This last winter, each of you has sacrificed to unify this Fort community, and the result was my gravestone over an empty grave.

"Tonight, we will fill that grave and mark it with a new stone. Tonight, Tuzhel will lie in that grave, the last martyr to Fort Rimon and the first martyr to a new way of life. For we must succeed in establishing the nonjunct lifestyle, even if it means admitting the Forts are a failure.

"Tuzhel taught us that. Raised out-Territory, he had never played *Zeor*, never even heard of it. He came here as an adult, but took to the game as if it were life itself. He understood the principle in a way none of us ever has.

"I've been told how Tuzhel came through disjunction with a whole new view of life, and how that view led him to give himself just to rescue me. He held himself responsible for my capture, even for the fall that nearly took my life. He had missed that toss, but wanted to do better.

"This time, he held nothing back. This time, to convince Clire he meant to rejoin the Raiders, that he too had rejected the Fort, he Killed again, renouncing his disjunction knowing he could not disjunct again.

"Some Gen, possibly someone Tuzhel knew, died so that he could rescue me."

He let the horror of that sink in, then reached behind him and brought up BanSha and his Companion, Rushi. He stood between them, leaning on them instead of Kahleen and Bruce. He put one hand on each of their shoulders watching the people think over what he was saying while he demanded his legs to keep holding him up.

"BanSha has told me that when Tuzhel went out to rescue me from Clire, he had decided that he'd Kill if he had to, but not twice. He felt that his disjunction was his moment of birth, and that he'd been granted life out of death, the deaths of others that he had caused and the death he had faced in disjunction.

"From all reports, this young man was a philosopher, a poet, a spirit buoyed by the highest ideals my father taught me. These are out-Territory ideals as much as they are ours. These are the ideals that bind us together as one people.

"I've been told Tuzhel died shouting, as he had at his disjunction, 'Out of Death Was I Born, Unto Zeor, Forever.' He was irrevocably committed to living the principles of this simple child's game, *Zeor*. No matter how disastrously he failed, he would *do better this time!* Even if it cost him everything he had, he would excel his previous score.

"He understood us better than we ever understood ourselves because of the loving Gen family that raised him to exceed limitations. He understood what we are, how far that is from what we want to be, and that we must not let others define what we can do to get there. He voiced the pledge that will become the foundation of our new way of life. I give you that pledge now, from my own lips, as I too have been born from Tuzhel's death and the death of those he Killed."

Rimon reached down and hefted the painting of Fort Freedom. "Now, this evening, I bury Fort Rimon with the body of Tuzhel, and I pledge to you to do better this time. *Out of Death Was I Born, Unto Zeor Forever!*"

Firmly hypoconscious, aware only of sight, sound, touch, taste and smell, he summoned augmented strength to steady his legs and stepped down off the boulder relinquishing his spot to Jor Esren.

With the painting in his left hand, he shoveled dirt into the grave that had been dug for him but now held Tuzhel. Shorty. Once known as Harve Zamir, according to BanSha.

He couldn't bear to listen to Jor Esren's speech. They had discussed what he would say about his daughter Bekka, and Tuzhel, about hope for the future. Rimon knew that if he listened, he would simply blow the fields to smithereens. Even Lexy wasn't strong enough to protect people from that, and Bekka herself deserved better of him.

So Rimon placed the painting in the grave atop the shroud wrapped body and kept shoveling dirt over it. Two women came to help. The three shovels hit a cadenced rhythm. They had barely begun when Xanon came with another shovel and silently joined the effort.

CHAPTER TWENTY
FORTY-NINE DAYS

It took forty-nine days to create the House of Zeor.

Rimon was on fire with ideas. As people discussed what the Forts would become, Rimon would overhear a comment and blurt out ideas. People grabbed his ideas and gleefully generated unrecognizable new ones, concepts erupting out of nowhere as people worked together.

While the stump pulling, tilling, planting and pruning was going on at breakneck pace, the laundry ran at full capacity. The spring trading expedition was mounted, and lambing, calving, and foaling kept pulling the channels out of the Collectorium and Dispensary into large groups where people were working and brainstorming.

All agreed, the Forts had failed. The reason they had failed though was hotly debated because each Fort had failed for a different reason, and Fort Rimon appeared to be strong and successful now.

Many, however, saw Rimon's point, that even Fort Rimon would eventually succumb to the divisiveness that was generated within. They had to become united in such a way that no external issue could divide them.

Others disagreed, seeing the continual debate as a source of new ideas that would be lost if they were too united. Rimon contended that debate and even disagreement could thrive in a unified community. So what could unify this community? Into what could it be unified?

So Rimon strove to communicate his vision of what had happened among them over this last winter and why. Benart, Lexy, Bruce, Garen, Kahleen and even BanSha and Rushi spread out to repeat his explanation, which continued to evolve with the telling. Rimon hardly recognized his own words when they came back to him.

Oddly silent though was Solamar.

Near midnight, four days after Tuzhel's funeral, Rimon finally felt strong enough to climb to the top of the wall to his favorite spot. He paced the guards' catwalk, mulling over the source of his irrational certainty that the zeor concept was their key. He should remember why.

With that odd timing Rimon had come to expect, Solamar arrived just when Rimon was so frustrated with the gap in his memory that it had to be obvious in his showfield.

Solamar leaned beside him and together they zlinned the darkness, noting the animals sleeping, the renSimes working the fields accompanied by Gens who provided a selyn field to zlin by. Inside the Fort, a group of Gens was moving Rimon's personal possessions into his new house. Next to his house, some renSimes were building Lexy and Solamar a new house to share with their baby while yet another new family moved into Rimon's old house.

As had become their custom, they just stood together and watched the Fort working. It made him relax to have this young, strong channel beside him. Sometimes that made him neglect to ask the questions burning holes in his mind. Just not tonight. Tonight was for answers.

Rimon and Solamar had spent the afternoon forcing selyn into Clire, keeping her and Rimon's baby alive as her body wasted selyn in the typical Raider burnout syndrome. Nothing odd had happened to Rimon during these now routine sessions, as it had when they'd forced selyn into Tuzhel, no visitations or visions.

"Solamar, you said Clire isn't out of her body. But...was I?"

Rimon zlinned the hitch of alarm that rippled deep inside

Solamar's nager. Besides himself, only Lexy would have been able to zlin the quickly buried reaction.

"So I was," concluded Rimon. "And you don't want to talk about it. So where did I go and what happened that you don't want to tell me?"

* * * * * * *

I knew it would come to this, but not so soon.

"All right," said Rimon insightfully, "then why don't you want to tell me?"

"Rimon, sometimes it's better not to remember a nightmare, isn't it?"

"I had nightmares? For an entire month?"

"I was searching for you, trying to bring you back to your body."

"I know. Bruce and Lexy told me. They're convinced you rescued me from some kind of horror, but they won't even tell me what you told them."

"And what I told them wasn't the whole story."

"So what is the whole story?"

"I don't know the whole story. I only know that when I connected with you, you were crying, screaming in terror, somewhere beyond sanity. Whatever you experienced, it was more than you could encompass."

"Then maybe I don't want to remember."

They were silent for a while. "I have to remember. Solamar, what I've been doing here, my grandchild will have to live with." He rubbed his left forearm.

"And your new child."

"You think Clire's child is mine?"

"Certain of it. Why aren't you?"

"I don't want it to be."

"That's a useful insight."

"You're no help."

"What can I say, Rimon?"

"Call me Delri and tell me what I have to know about that missing month in my life." Rimon recounted some of the odd ideas that he'd blurted out, ideas others had grabbed as if they were wisdom from beyond the stars.

"Solamar, there's this absolute certainty inside me, and I don't even know what I'm certain of, but *you* know what it is, don't you?"

"Not exactly." He sighed. "You almost lost touch with your body because you got lost in time. I think you may have glimpsed the future. Or maybe just a future."

"The future!" whispered Rimon. *That explains so much!* "So you're saying I'm coming up with ideas from the future? I'm certain they will work, because they have worked. Solamar, that's not possible. That's insane."

"Well, there's no reason to believe that you understood what you witnessed. By the time I found you, you were hysterical. You could have imagined anything. When out of the body there's nothing but imagination. Nothing is real there except what you believe is real, what you make real."

"This is not helping."

"It was you who wanted to discuss it, not me."

Solamar felt Rimon zlin him. He dropped his showfield invitingly. After a moment, the Farris scrutiny abated. Rimon kept rubbing his left forearm.

"All right, I guess I deserved that," allowed Rimon. "What can you tell me that would be helpful?"

"When I found you, there was one task you were attempting to accomplish. Do you remember what it was?"

"No. I told you, I was handing Tuzhel off to Jokim, then Bruce was giving me transfer."

"You had made something you wanted to give to Lexy. Do you remember what that was?"

The swirled granite showfield vanished in a burst of wonder. Solamar zlinned the Farris beneath glowing with relief and joy. A few renSimes below turned to zlin them. Rimon waved at them and reorganized his showfield.

"What do you remember?"

"A box. A beautiful jeweled box with a curved lid. More like a coffer for storing loose coins, only gleaming, carved with inscriptions, as if the value was the box itself and not what was inside it. I made it for Lexy." He turned to peer at Solamar and added, "I made it because I thought I was dead and would never see Lexy again." He nodded. "Yes, out of death was I born."

"You weren't dead. You imagined that."

"But I believed it and it didn't come true."

"Well, there you see? Any future you foresee can be like that, just inspiration, aspiration, wishes, dreams and fantasies, all without substance. No matter how certain you are that something should happen, it might not."

Rimon leaned his back against the outer railing and surveyed the interior of the Fort. "Or it might happen, in a way very different than you expect."

"That's true."

"If it's going to happen at all, it has to be the product of the efforts of many different people each with unique hopes, ambitions, dreams and fantasies."

"That's also true."

"I know I'm right about what's destroying the Forts. We have to organize around a unifying principle or our way of life is doomed."

"People have come to believe you about that."

"Do you?"

"Yes. Definitely."

"Because you saw it in the coffer?"

"No. I couldn't touch it. It's not for me. It's for Lexy."

"So. Then how do I give it to Lexy?"

"You can't. She has to go get it for herself."

"Is it real? Is there really such a thing hidden somewhere around here?"

"No. She has to go out of her body to find it."

"She's never done that."

"Anyone can do it. Doesn't take any special talent. In fact

most people do when they dream at night. They just don't remember. Rimon, your ability to bring what you imagine into reality, is a talent."

"Does Lexy have that talent?"

"I don't know."

Rimon zlinned him again. "Would it be dangerous for the baby?"

"No, even pregnant women dream. Finding what you left for her might be stressful, but the child is not draining her alarmingly. She has enough strength."

"And if she finds it, she'll come back able to see what I'm seeing here, what has to be done if we're to survive?"

"I'd doubt that. I think you left her an understanding of what you saw in the future, but what you see is your interpretation. She will take only what she's able to comprehend and she'll interpret it her own way."

"The way everyone around here is interpreting the things I say in their own ways?"

"Pretty much."

"I have to think about all this. Have you seen Bruce? I don't zlin him."

"In the underground shelter with Clire. He was training BanSha, trying to keep him from dwelling on Tuzhel."

"Val must have changed the schedule."

"Speaking of which, I should go check the board. Let me know what you decide about Lexy. Don't try anything by yourself."

"I will. I won't."

* * * * * * *

With that single image of the little box he had made for Lexy came the peace that Rimon had been seeking. He still didn't remember anything after handing Tuzhel off to Jokim, but the maddening itch to remember abated.

Every time he thought of the sparkling coffer, the irrational certainty returned no matter how dismayed he felt. People presented many opportunities for dismay.

A consensus crystallized that instead of being a Fort defending itself in a hostile land, they had to define themselves as a family with relatives scattered everywhere.

Rimon heard BanSha articulate it when he stopped in the barn to check on BanSha's first solo supervision of a calving. Between calling instructions to the Gen guiding the calf out of the birth canal, BanSha told Rushi, "In Fort Rimon, we've always been a family of people who have chosen each other, like when two people marry. They aren't related, but they become one person by pledge. This new thing we're becoming has to be like a marriage, binding hearts, minds and souls to build a better life for our children. Each generation will have to choose to bind themselves to this lineage, this *House*."

Rimon moved into the birthing stall, grinning. "BanSha, that's it! I just never could put it into words myself! We have to become the House of Zeor."

Everyone in that end of the barn stopped what they were doing and gathered around Rimon, babbling. Rushi announced, "Rimon has named us. We will become the House of Zeor!"

Before nightfall the Fort buzzed with their new name.

Though they suddenly had a name and a new concept defining themselves, debate raged with ever increasing furor over the management procedures a large group had to have.

A little more than twenty days after Tuzhel's funeral, on the first anniversary of the arrival of Fort Butte, they held a celebration in their new, expanded dining hall that could seat almost everyone if the channels worked the ambient fields just right.

Rimon arrived with Bruce, Lexy and Garen. Lexy was more than six months pregnant and suffering through the nearly perpetual Need of her condition, but Garen was not very high field. Bruce on the other hand was soaring. Rimon had another four days before transfer. After a stint in the Collectorium followed by hours in Dispensary, he was still carrying enough selyn to use Bruce to orchestrate the complex ambient here.

He caught the attention of several other channels already working the crowd and signalled them with two tentacles. He and Lexy parted and the others scattered as he directed. That prompted the whole crowd to find places.

In the corner near the kitchen storeroom, Rimon saw Alind, a renSime, huddled close to Xanon who wasn't working with the other channels, just shielding the two of them. Alind stalked out through the storeroom door leaving boiling fury in his wake. Xanon stared after the renSime, but held the fields steady to shield the crowd, then started to work with the other channels. Xanon's skills had improved.

Rimon had heard that Alind blamed Xanon for losing the election. He hadn't heard Xanon berating Maigrey even once, lately, and no complaints from Maigrey either.

Moving on around the dining hall, Rimon encountered Shani at the steaming serving table, discussing Lexy's diet with Garen as only another female channel would. Shani's husband, Marliss, was with Clire in the underground shelter, so she was without her Companion. Rimon wanted both of them at Clire's delivery.

Shani was a medium sized woman with brown hair and eyes, wearing the durable blue smock and trousers the channeling staff worked in, but when she laughed her nager cloaked her in rainbows.

"Come help me get people sorted out so we can all enjoy the play."

Rimon set two channels and Companions on duty near the doors to ease any latecomers into the ambient. Only the guards on watch and those tending the young or ill were missing. There had been much duty shift trading because all the parents and relatives wanted to be there to watch the children put on this much rehearsed play.

The play depicted the arrival of Fort Butte at Fort Rimon, but it lacked Tuzhel's and BanSha's humorous touch.

Sian opened with the now traditional song written by his wife, then accompanied the children on his shiltpron, supplying sound effects for horses and wagons and even the howling wind that had blown that day.

Cody, now famous throughout the community for his leadership of the young messengers, played Rimon making a welcoming speech. One of the children from Fort Butte played Xanon, who had been the ranking channel leading their Fort, accepting Cody's welcome in a shrill soprano voice that carried throughout the large room. "Xanon" then sang a song Sian's wife had written for the play.

None of the words of the speeches or songs resembled anything Rimon remembered of that momentous occasion. Nobody cared. It was art.

After the children finished, Xanon mounted the stage to speak. Rimon had seen him working on the speech with Maigrey in the channels' recovery room. He expected it would be very short, then they would eat.

With his stomach not at all interested in food, he thought he'd prefer a longer speech. Rimon watched his crew playing the ambient and indulged in his vision of this whole mob of people together as one family.

Fort Butte had been the second group to arrive, about two months after Fort Intalace. The Intalace survivors had numbered only five people by the time they arrived. They'd been led by Clire who was now the only survivor.

Fort Butte had brought in hundreds, and instantly outnumbered the Fort Rimon natives. They had arrived desperate because they'd been led by Xanon, a half-trained channel unaware of his shortcomings, and by a channeling staff consisting of eight channels in First Year and only six more barely old enough to train the younger ones.

Since the moment he'd arrived, Xanon had been the trial of Rimon's life. Now, however, Rimon zlinned something different in the channel from Fort Butte.

Rimon speared Maigrey with a glance. She was seated down the table from him among the Fort Butte leaders next to Xanon's empty chair. She looked back with a smug little smile twitching her lips.

Then Xanon's powerful baritone grabbed Rimon's attention. "Fort Butte has failed. We must acknowledge that here today, one year after we reached safety at Fort Rimon. Fort Butte exists no more. Fort Butte is dead, and we will no longer celebrate our arrival here as a group.

"Maigrey, my gracious and generous Companion, has been telling me stories of Fort Freedom and the earliest days of Fort Rimon in Del Rimon's youth." He turned to eye the children arrayed behind him. "In fact, she has told me more about Del Rimon's childhood adventures than you could possibly believe." After a studied pause, he intimated, "Apparently he took after his father."

The children giggled, some of the younger ones pointing at Rimon, whereupon the whole hall full of parents and relatives laughed. The ambient squirmed with embarrassment and even anxiety since everyone knew Xanon's opinion of Rimon, or thought they did.

"Some of the more outlandish tales though," continued Xanon, "I did not believe until Tuzhel's funeral. Del Rimon stood before you all and declared Fort Rimon, and the Forts in general, a total failure. In that moment, I understood what Maigrey and so many others here had been telling me for the past year.

"This last winter, we tried to recreate the conditions that led to our failure. Some of you noticed that and resisted by clinging to Fort Rimon's procedures, which we saw as wrong. And though I now see that you were not wrong, I also see that you were not right. Del Rimon said it. The Forts were created to harbor a junct way of life seeking to Kill without losing touch with the soul that gives life. We can not remain Forts and become a nonjunct community.

"Since Tuzhel's funeral, we've groped for what we can become. Once again Del Rimon has named us. We must become the House of Zeor, the family of excellence.

"Some feel that the Forts, designed as small towns filled with separate families each with different values, are the tradition we started with and are honor bound to keep.

"Yesterday, a delegation asked me to lead a group away to found a new Fort. While explaining why I could not do that, I saw what we must do to make the House of Zeor a reality.

"Fort Freedom was organized around the spiritual leadership of Abel Veritt. He was trusted, and listened to because he was wise and walked in the ways of his god. Under his guidance, the junct population of his Fort came to live Killing occasionally and then mostly not at all.

"Abel Veritt populated Fort Freedom with the changeover victims from out-Territory, the very children who would have become Freeband Raiders just as he had. He gave them a vision of a better life.

"We must find one among us who holds a similar vision, but not a spiritual one, a practical one. We must have a leader who understands how the practice of *Zeor* will lead us to a world where no one ever Kills. We must have a leader who knows that we will succeed, and who knows what we each of us must do to make it happen.

"According to junct law, we are a Genfarm, and all our lands, buildings and Gens are owned by the Tuib. Our leader must be the Tuib all our Gens trust to own them.

"By junct law, of course, that Tuib does not have to be a channel. They don't know what a channel is! I submit that from now until the time when there are no more juncts, the Tuib of our House must be a channel. And not just any channel, but the very best channel in the House.

"That is not me. I had to explain my shortcomings to that delegation yesterday. I am not capable of leading a channeling staff, even where everyone knows what they're doing. In trying to explain what quality it is that I lack, I discovered what we must have in a leader for this House of Zeor, this nonjunct family.

"We must choose an individual we all trust who lives by the principle of *zeor* and who holds our vision of the future. I believe we will always find such an individual to be the one among us who stands at the sec in any room, in any group."

Xanon's gaze went to Rimon, who was at the sec, the point formed by the interference of personal fields to define the shape of the ambient nager.

Rimon was always at the sec in any room, even when Lexy, Aipensha and Clire had been working fields with him. He was the sec. He defined the sec in any ambient, and that was the reason he could orchestrate the field management of so many channels so easily.

"Zlin around you," urged Xanon. "Compare our channels. Is there any question who that is?

"It is Del Rimon Farris, and when she's not pregnant, Lexy Farris is barely distinguishable from Rimon. He has given us this vision of a new way of life. We have all seen, in our day-to-day work, how Rimon takes his failures and does a little better the next time he faces that problem.

"Though Maigrey has had to spell it out for me, I have also seen Rimon do the same with his successes. He never stops. He keeps striving to excel his mark, no matter what.

"At first, I misunderstood what that meant about him. But Maigrey kept explaining Rimon to me until I saw what this man really is. It's hard to see because almost everyone who grew up in Fort Rimon is like that.

"I know, I'm the last person in this Fort you'd expect to hear saying this, but Rimon Farris has become the one person I really trust. I believe he knows what it would be like to live in a completely nonjunct world. I believe he knows what to do to make that world exist.

"Today, I bury Fort Butte as Rimon has buried Fort Rimon. I recognize Rimon Farris as Sectuib of the House of Zeor, and I pledge to you all that I will do better this time as a member of the House of Zeor. *Out of Death Was I Born, Unto Zeor, Forever!*"

The room erupted into a wall of noise. Rimon and the channeling crew worked so hard with the fields over the next two hours that Bruce let him get away with not eating.

Over the next few days, Xanon's naming Rimon Sectuib widened the schisms. Three factions emerged.

There were still those, led by Alind and supported by most of the Church of the Unity members, who were wholly dedicated to the Fort concept.

There were those led by some channels who felt that the House concept was the key to success, but could not see building their unity around a children's game.

There was also a large, exuberant faction developing a new way to govern themselves based on a Sectuib with ultimate authority over everything except his or her Companion.

Rimon's dismay grew as more and more authority and responsibility was heaped on this mythical Sectuib. The Sectuib would select who would be in charge of what areas of the House. The Sectuib would choose the Council to advise him, and they couldn't do anything without his approval. Not only that, but the Sectuib had to approve all marriages and even officiate! The Sectuib would decide everything, and run the channeling staff, too. *Impossible!*

He fled to the top of the wall for some much needed pacing. It was after midnight with the full moon low in the west casting eerie shadows.

The wall sentries had been reduced now that Shifron was inhabited by working folk. These juncts had a growing investment in the land and a well stocked Pen where they could take legal Kills. The two remaining lookouts huddled in the guard kiosk over the main gate while Rimon took his usual place opposite them, overlooking the cemetery.

That afternoon, there had been one last snow squall, the final signal to the farmers to plant. The stumps had been cleared, the fields tilled, beehives prepared, and the pruning completed. In the orchards, a few light green buds were threatening to become leaves.

Tonight, everything was spackled with white, dripping loudly. He paced and worried. He'd touched off this firestorm by declaring Fort Rimon dead. Now what?

By the time Solamar arrived, Rimon was ready to pack up and leave with Alind and the Church of the Unity. If he could beg a place among them, he'd go right this minute.

"What have I done!" shouted Rimon at Solamar. Pacing and gesticulating, Rimon raged, "This is never going to work! It can't work! No one person can do all of that! It's not possible!"

"Sorry I'm late."

Rimon stopped. "We didn't have an appointment."

"Obviously I missed the first half of the discussion."

Rimon laughed. He couldn't help it. He roared with laughter until he had to gesture an all clear to the two guards over the front gate. Then he filled Solamar in on how the concept, Sectuib, had been developing. "It gets worse! This evening, in the laundry, they were discussing inventing some honorifics to set the channels and the Sectuib apart. You know anything they discuss in the laundry really happens! I want to run away and hide!"

"You aren't doing a very good job of hiding."

Rimon drew his showfield down and set himself to keep his histrionics private. "I'm scared, Solamar. What am I going to do?"

"You're going to become the first Sectuib in the House of Zeor. The job will include what you say it includes, and nothing more."

"You've seen that in the future?"

"I can't see the future! I just know your finer traits."

"Lexy is furious with me for igniting this conflagration."

"You think that's news to me? I sleep with her these days and she's finally decided she wants to marry me."

"She figured that out? I knew she'd get it straight in her head eventually."

"So you approve?"

"She'll be the next Sectuib of this House we're building since it seems everyone's decided Xanon's right and it has to have a Sectuib. Are you sure you want to marry her? The Sectuib job is going to be a nightmare!" Rimon realized he'd have to officiate at the wedding.

"Of course I want to marry her! I came up here because she was ranting so much about your conflagration even Garen couldn't get her to sleep. She's on duty again before dawn and even pregnant she's wearing Garen out every day."

"The baby will be Gen. A Farris Gen. Whoever heard of such a thing?"

"You're sure? Well, I still want to marry her. Now she's heard people saying we won't have individual marriages inside the House, that everyone will be married to everyone already."

"That's absurd."

"It's time you told them so, don't you think?"

"You mean...just...decide and say, *this is how it's going to be done?*"

"Seems that's what they expect of a Sectuib."

"I can't do that."

"Look, Rimon...Delri. Listen. Zlin me on this. It's your idea that we are to become a *family*, choosing each other to be one family, a unit connected by mutual obligations, responsibilities and privileges. We are going to become your family, gathered around you by choice, just as I'm joining your family by marrying your daughter. So you have to tell us what your family is, just as you've let me know exactly what you expect of a husband for your daughter. You have to lay down the rules, define this family. That'll stop this creative orgy."

Creative orgy. Rimon swallowed hard, trying to find his voice. "So how would I know any better than they do?"

Solamar shrugged. "Do you have to? Whatever you start with, it'll evolve from there. *Zeor* is the principle, isn't it? Just start anywhere you're comfortable and improve on that.

"That's the lesson of *Zeor*, isn't it? Don't be afraid to fail. Just start. Do it. Study what happened, then do it again a little better. That way you un-define success and with that you un-define failure, and leave only excellence, the process that is the core of life."

Rimon had to agree. He'd played the game obsessively for

years when he was young. That was exactly the lesson it taught. Don't be afraid you're going to fail. Don't be afraid you have failed. Don't get too full of yourself when you succeed. You can always do better. He'd forgotten that lesson, pushing Fort Rimon on through a nightmarish winter even though The Fort concept had died when Fort Tanhara had arrived pursued by Freeband Raiders. "So I have to go tell them what my House is and dare them to join me in it."

"That sounds about right."

"Well, I'm not going to make all the decisions."

"Good. I'll help."

They laughed together, arms around each other's shoulders, and they headed for the stairs. "Just remember," cautioned Rimon. "No titles. Sectuib is bad enough."

In the gathering whirlwind activity surrounding the departure of Alind and his group, there was no time for Rimon to gather everyone and dictate what this House would be. The truth was, he, himself, was almost clueless.

Alind's followers had labored hard building, tilling and fighting for Fort Rimon. They had earned more wealth than the Fort possessed. So everyone who was not leaving turned out to build wagons and tools for them. Weavers and shoemakers worked round the clock to clothe them. Some of the best horses were chosen, tack made, and trail provisions were packed. More seed than they could spare went with them, and as had become a custom among the Forts, skilled workers would go to help, and return the following spring.

Those who went to help the new Fort came mostly from among those who were not sure about the House of Zeor concept, but felt the Fort concept was unworkable.

The vociferous and creative ones already dedicated to Zeor would not think of leaving at such a critical time. They were already planning a pledge ceremony, a formal occasion that got larger and more elaborate every time someone mentioned it to him.

However two groups had been left out. The spring trading

mission had long since left, and would not return until after the fun was all over. And a large number of people who were not going with Alind were also not joining this new House yet. Still there were some five hundred adults who were fervently intent on creating this ceremony to mark the founding of the House of Zeor, and nothing, especially not their Sectuib, was going to stop them.

They weren't even bothering to hold an election. They had simply unanimously declared him Sectuib and started calling him that and referring to him as Sectuib. Worse, someone coined an honorific for all the other channels and in less than a day people were using it in casual conversation. It was, "Hajene Val said...." and "Hajene Xanon wants...." and "Hajene BanSha just learned...." until Rimon wanted to sink into despair.

He wasn't allowed a moment to brood, though. All the bright smiles and nageric delight, so eagerly expectant of his praise, kept him too busy.

So he never had a chance to decree how his House would be run. Between the rash of spring diseases that felled nearly a third of the Gens at once, several critical injuries, and Clire living, just barely into her eight month of pregnancy, he was too busy, and so was everyone else.

Three times he tried to get the Council together, and three times he failed because everyone was too busy. The fourth time, they did assemble, but he couldn't make it.

So the industrious founders of the House of Zeor kept elaborating on their formal pledge ceremony without his input. By his next Turnover, he'd become accustomed to being hailed, "Sectuib!" so a few days later at a Gen's call, he turned to find himself facing a huge mound of blue cloth and a madly chattering, very young Gen.

She was so excited she had no idea she was in a low-field area of the Dispensary with her selyn field climbing. He scooped her and her burden under one arm and into the Dispensary office.

"Now, what was the problem?"

"This is for you to wear. You have to come now! We're almost ready to begin! The ceremony. Remember?"

Ceremony? Now?

She was one of the Glasil brood. *Shali? No, Eshala.* She'd Established as a Gen a few days ago. She'd been working with Cody's messengers, but was now training with Sian as a weaver.

"Eshala, what is this?" He turned the mass of material she pushed at him around trying to understand it's folds and wrinkles. It was the material they had made most of their summer work clothes from ever since Fort Freedom. And there was a white layer of material.

"It's a cloak!"

With that clue he was able to find the collar and turn it so the blue lining hung on the inside. Eshala laughed and grabbed for the material to turn the white side inside. "Here, see the embroidery we did for you!"

All around the edges of the blue material were stitched little images of the stylized dagger from his quilt.

"That's beautiful, Eshala. You did this?"

"I helped. A little. Sian's wife designed it."

Wife? So we still have marriage. Whew!

"We have to hurry. People have work tonight."

He threw the voluminous cloak over his shoulders and let her drag him to the front entry to the dining hall. It was a dark night but the hall was lit to a spectacular blaze both nagerically and with candles and oil lamps. But there was nobody inside. Instead, out behind the building, between the kitchen storage room entrance and the infirmary, a huge excited crowd had gathered.

Bruce was there amidst an ambient that etched the hall in selyn-fire. It was cascading shimmering veils of somber, mellow, reverent joy, marbled with scintillating glee, anticipation and a thousand things he couldn't name but just felt. He'd never zlinned anything like it.

"Come on," said Eshala. "You're supposed to come right in the door and just stand there, just like we rehearsed it, only BanSha played you."

"That could be why I don't remember." *Rehearsing? Ominous word.*

She giggled.

Once inside, he saw decorations everywhere. Skeins of dyed wool had been crocheted into wrappings for the chair backs, sweeping loops on the walls and festoons from the rafters splashing color. White wool draped the tables.

The scents of fragrant herbs, pine, candle wax and scented lamp oil dominated. The floor and tables gleamed. Precious glass glittered on the tables which were set with bright new blue and white crockery.

The tables had been lined up at an angle to a center aisle. On the stage at the end of the aisle, a large wide chair was draped in pristine black with a stand beside it. On the stand was a small wooden water barrel decorated by a knitted drape. He couldn't quite make out what the objects in the barrel were.

It seemed every ordinary piece of furniture had been transformed with material covers.

On one side of the stage, Sian's shiltpron sat next to the plain chair he preferred. Behind the black draped chair was a huge polished wood carving of Slina's dagger, less stylized, more like a real dagger than the embroidery. It seemed to have been created from a single tree trunk.

At the top of the carved dagger, framed by the handle, sat a hollowed stone pot they used to serve hot soup. A wick poked over the side. It had to be filled with lamp oil.

Something about the dagger behind the chair sent shivers rippling down his spine. He had no idea why. Maybe he was just worried about all the material in the room set around open flame. He noted there was plenty of sand in buckets all over the room. He shouldn't be nervous.

As he took his place just inside the front door, leaving the outside door of the entry chamber ajar. Across the room, the door to the kitchen storeroom opened, and Bruce stood there in a cloak very similar to his own. Behind him, channel and Companion pairs stood side by side in a line, though they didn't all have nice new cloaks.

Apparently, Bruce had been to the rehearsal because he didn't hesitate, and was carrying a slate. As soon as the door opened, he came right into the hall, circled the edge, swept Rimon up and muttering quick instructions, marched him straight down the aisle to deposit him in the chair on the stage.

Sian materialized from somewhere, picked up his shiltpron and began playing the tune that usually opened every celebration.

Bruce marched to a spot behind Rimon, to his right, the correct spot, leaving Rimon to sit on the chair which was wide enough for both of them. Whole families with children, streamed in. There wasn't space for everyone to sit at the tables, so two ranks formed at the back. Parents admonished children, children complained, and others asked what they were supposed to do or exclaimed over the decorations. Obviously more had turned up for this than had been planned for.

The channels and their Companions moved through the crowd balancing the ambient. Bruce whispered, "Aren't you glad you didn't have to sit through the rehearsal while they figured out how they wanted this to go?"

"Oh, yes."

"This isn't so bad as some of the ideas. Solamar kept telling them 'no' and they listened."

Solamar?

Turned out it was only a six hour ordeal as each person came up to him and recited the pledge. Sian's music helped, setting a rhythm and a brisk pace, not letting anyone lag as they moved up to the stage and then away.

Right before that march, Bruce handed Rimon a slate with a simple pledge written on it. He read it out in a loud voice, pledging himself to the House of Zeor, as Sectuib Rimon Farris ambrov Zeor. He had read half the final sentence aloud before it hit him that they'd changed his name.

While he swallowed his surprise, Bruce took one of the objects from the water barrel. It was a necklace with a small carved replica of Slina's dagger suspended from it. Bruce draped it around Rimon's neck, grinning, and said, "Sectuib ambrov Zeor, you have founded the House of Zeor." Rimon's rock solid, unmovable, piece-of-the-furniture Companion blew the fields to smithereens.

From somewhere inside Rimon burst an ache of homesickness totally at odds with the occasion.

Embracing each other on the stage, they both struggled with emotion. The entire audience came to their feet and the hall throbbed with a mélange of emotions.

Bruce recovered first saying, "Now they want you to light that lamp they rigged up. There's a little stool. You should be able to reach the wick with the torch they're going to bring."

Rimon turned to the audience to find Xanon marching down the center aisle bringing a smoking torch, flames whipping in the breeze of his passing as if keeping time with Sian's rhythm. Maigrey marched beside him as if lighting his way with her nager.

When they climbed onto the stage, Maigrey told the audience, "We lit this torch by Fort Freedom's memorial stone and by its light we read aloud and in unison the names of those who died that Fort Freedom could survive. Then we carried the flame of their love here.

"Sectuib, first member of the House of Zeor, will light a new lamp. This one burns not just for the martyrs who have and will give their lives that the House of Zeor may live. This lamp burns for the billion or more Gens who died in the Kill before Rimon Farris discovered how to channel."

Rimon took the torch. There was a memory hidden inside him threatening to erupt. He stepped onto the stool, reached as high as he could and touched off the new blaze. When the first curl of smoke dissipated, the stage glowed with light reflected from the high ceiling.

Rimon stepped down and turned, holding the torch high and started to ask Bruce what he was supposed to do with it. Then suddenly he knew. He moved the stool, then flipped the torch upside down and mashed its burning end into the wooden stand that held the huge dagger upright. The flame died leaving a black mark on the wood.

Rimon turned and said, his first words as Sectuib of the House of Zeor, "Fort Freedom, Fort Faraway, Fort Intalace, Fort Butte, Fort Unity, Fort Veritt, Fort Hope, Fort Tanhara, and Fort Rimon, have all died, but all their martyrs are our martyrs. The Forts lived and died so we can live on and become something new."

He handed the torch off to Maigrey and Xanon, and they went down to find places among the tables. It took a good five minutes before the ambient steadied enough to proceed. He didn't know what to do, so he sat down again.

Then Bruce pledged to him as Sectuib in Zeor and he gave Bruce a necklace and welcomed him into the House of Zeor. Then Lexy and Garen and the rest of the channeling staff including Xanon came up to the stage to offer their pledge and change their family name to ambrov Zeor, dedicated to excellence.

Then families came up, and made their pledge, often speaking almost in unison, but rarely repeating the same words except for Tuzhel's proclamation, "Out of Death Was I Born, Unto Zeor, Forever." Some parents held or led their children, who created enough chaos to delay matters. The children weren't allowed to make any kind of pledge, but their parents promised to raise them in the House of Zeor.

Rimon presented each one, adults and children alike, with a carved dagger and a welcome. The carvings had been hastily made, and not uniform, though some were smoother and more gracefully turned. Several people must have worked whole days and nights to create so many of them.

After the first hundred repetitions of, "Out of Death Was I Born, Unto Zeor Forever," Rimon no longer felt the gut stirring awe the phrase had triggered the first time he'd heard it. He didn't let anyone zlin that. They were making history here, and every bone in his body knew it.

As the pledges kept coming, his soul lifted in joy soaring with the shiltpron cadences that penetrated and shaped the ambient as well as the sound in the room. Not everyone who had built this new expanded Fort all through this harsh winter pledged. Many had left. Many others were willing to stay and see what would happen though they weren't comfortable with giving a lifelong pledge.

Still, there were more pledges offered than there had been people in Fort Rimon last year.

After it all, he still had a handful of necklaces left, and Bruce told him they were for the spring trading expedition when they returned in a few weeks. New ones would be made if anyone else wanted to pledge, but they would be different. This set would remain unique, the Founders of the House of Zeor.

CHAPTER TWENTY-ONE
RECEPTION

The day after the pledge ceremony, Rimon ran Solamar down in Val's office when the channel was picking up his schedule. Rimon was supposed to be going off-shift.

Val was giving a changeover class a tour and Bruce had all the Companions in a meeting, sorting out how they would blend the efforts of those who had pledged Zeor with those who had not. They might now be a House, but it seemed they still lived in a Fort. Not much had changed.

Last night, Rimon had officially appointed people to the jobs they were already doing, called a channels' conference for this evening, and asked Benart, who had not yet pledged Zeor, to find out how many had pledged and how many had not, who else planned to leave, and so how many Gens they would owe taxes on if the collector made it this far before winter.

Later, when the party was still roaring, Rimon had gone to sit with Clire in the underground room. His son, a double Farris, might be the first born in the new House. Clire was eight months pregnant, a miracle by itself, but her child could be the future of this new House. Then there was Lexy and her baby to be raised by Solamar. The image that haunted him was of a glittering coffer he had to give to Lexy. So when he found Solamar alone in Val's office, he was full of questions.

"Solamar, it's been a month and a half and Lexy hasn't found that coffer yet."

"Lexy?"

"You said it wouldn't do her any harm. What can I do to make sure she finds it?"

"Is there any real hurry? The coffer won't disappear."

"What if Clire finds it first?"

"She couldn't touch it," he replied without conviction. "Besides, she's not out of her body."

Rimon paced over to the desk and picked up a nubbin of chalk. They were conserving even chalk until the spring traders returned. "Everyone's celebrating, and all I can do is worry. It's just so urgent to give that coffer to Lexy. Isn't there some way to, well, give her directions?"

Solamar thought about that. "Actually, there are a couple things we could try. I thought that her pledging to you last night might have created a connection."

"Connection?"

"She was very involved in creating that ceremony."

"Oh? I'll bet she was the one who put Slina's dagger everywhere?" He'd even found a painting of the image hanging behind his desk in the spot the painting of Fort Freedom had occupied. Apparently, the House of Zeor had acquired a symbol like a shop in a junct town.

"Rimon, you like that image. You know you do. It's very much about what you stand for in life."

"I always felt that was well, private."

"I'd guess a Sectuib doesn't have a private life."

Chilling thought.

"Lexy wanted it for the necklaces based on some family story I didn't quite follow about a Gen Dealer. Suddenly people put it everywhere. My only contribution was simplifying the pledge so you are Rimon Farris ambrov Zeor, and Lexy is Lexy Farris ambrov Zeor and everyone else replaces their family names with ambrov Zeor. People just spoke those pledges from their hearts."

"They did. I wish you hadn't made Lexy and me pledge differently though. That confuses people."

"Oh, but you are different. The Farris is something very, very different. Only time will reveal just how different you are."

Rimon opened his mouth to protest. Lexy was nearing. He ended hastily, "Maybe the answers are in that coffer. I just wish it were *here* so I could give it to Lexy. I won't rest until I've gotten rid of the thing." He laughed. "Not that it's even a real thing."

"Not that *what's* even a real thing?" asked Lexy.

"What are you doing here?" asked Rimon.

"Garen is still in that meeting. Shani and BanSha are sitting with Clire. I came to see what I could do before your first channels' meeting."

So they told her about the present Rimon had made for her while he was unconscious. Rimon finished with, "So though I don't remember making it, I remember that it's for you. It contains everything you have to know about this House to make it succeed."

Solamar said, "From Rimon's way of looking at the coffer image, it is the House of Zeor. It's your legacy for his grand-children."

Rimon added, "I have to give it to you when you're not in your body."

"Can't we just forget about all this out-of-body stuff, a bad nightmare, gone like the Freeband Raiders."

"It seems very important to your father. I have an idea how we can help him give it to you."

"You want to give me the House of Zeor? But it's yours. You're the Sectuib."

Rimon said, "There has to be an heir. There always has to be an heir, even when we only held the ownership of the Gens for the Fort."

"So you want to make me your heir, more than I am already, by giving me this imaginary box?"

Unspoken between them hung the words, *Aipensha should be the heir.*

"Yes," said Rimon.

"So what would I have to do?"

Solamar said, "We'll use the underground shelter. Give me a couple days to gather a few things. Then we'll see if we can get you both out of body at the same time."

It took him three days and several scheduling conferences with Val and Dakin to clear three hours for Solamar, Kahleen, Rimon, Bruce, Lexy and Garen.

Now the six of them stood in the narrow, dim underground hallway. Solamar paused with a hand on the door opposite where Clire still lay.

With Shani, her husband Marliss backed up by BanSha, and Rushi sitting with Clire, that left Fengal in charge of the Dispensary, Xanon in charge of the Collectorium and nobody with appropriate skills on duty in the infirmary. If something happened that Val or Dakin couldn't find someone to handle, their session would be interrupted.

"Let's go, Solamar, I'd rather get this over with before we have to deliver Clire." She was massively malnourished because they could only get her to swallow liquids, and her body was failing in ways they'd never seen happen before. Nobody knew why she was still alive.

"So let's do it," said Lexy, opened the door and stopped dead.

Solamar had removed the furniture from the room and hung one wall with the large black cloth that had been on Rimon's chair during the ceremony. Now the roll of martyrs was embroidered on it in white. In front of the cloth was a table with a big ceramic bowl filled with water.

The bowl held a pile of river stones that supported an oil lamp burning a scented oil. The room was warm, but the fire had burned down to embers. The oil lamp provided the only light reflecting from the dark, still water.

Solamar closed the door behind them and stood a moment, both hands on the door, tentacles spread, as if he wanted to sink into the door and be somewhere else. When he stepped back, he drew his toe across the dirt floor. His nager, deep inside his showfield, blazed.

Rimon asked, "So what do we do?"

"*Out of Death Was I Born, Unto Zeor, Forever.* We are all here because of those who have died. Lexy, call the roll of martyrs." He gestured to the huge black cloth.

It was too dim to read the names even by the oil lamp, but they had been embroidered in high relief. Lexy read them by zlinning. Picking up the old familiar rhythm of this roll call, she pronounced each of the names clearly.

Rimon found himself mouthing the names with her and heard the others whispering them as well. They knew the stories behind the names. Listening, he half remembered and almost saw the people who had lived and died before he was born. It was as if they had gathered here in the shadows around him. These weren't the ghosts who had driven his father mad. This visitation was familiar, warming.

Suddenly, he knew what to say.

* * * * * * *

Solamar had worked hard to create a space that might let both these Farris channels journey together. So many people had helped without knowing why he wanted these things. There was a strong spirit moving through this new family, his own pledge making him part of it.

When Lexy finished the roll call, Solamar had no clue what should come next, and neither did she, but she stood there so proudly pregnant he wanted to hug her.

Apparently Rimon had retrieved a memory from his journey through time. He said, "All of these have died for...for the House of Zeor without even knowing it. Lexy, uhh, Farris ambrov Zeor, step forward if you would become the vessel through which the power of death will brighten and grace the world of the living."

Solamar watched her think about that. He couldn't guess how it must sound to her, but he knew where Rimon had gotten it and she didn't.

Eventually, she stepped toward Rimon, the light illuminating half her face, hair, and one eye.

Rimon asked, "What is Zeor?"

"The acceptance of death as part of the cycle of birth. The acceptance of failure as the necessary condition for success. The knowledge that we exist separate and outside of failure and success, birth and death. That knowledge obliterates fear. Zeor is the fearlessness that protects from the Kill."

There was a long silence while Rimon hid behind his show-field. Solamar wasn't sure even Lexy could zlin his reaction. Lexy was so focused on Rimon that she didn't even look over at him.

That was when he realized they were no longer in the room. *We're out of body together, the three of us, four counting the baby.*

The room he perceived around them was now only a construct formed of imagination and will. He set himself to hold that construct steady.

Rimon nodded and held out his hands to his daughter, handling tentacles and laterals extended. She reciprocated and they made lateral contact, Rimon zlinning her deeply.

Then Rimon said, "Dive deep within yourself and search for Zeor within your own soul so you will recognize it when you find what I have left for you. This is a dangerous journey from which you may never return, and if you do return your soul will be forever changed. You will gain nothing for yourself, but only for others. Are you willing?"

"Yes."

"Go then fearlessly. Reach out, find the gift I have left for you and return."

Forever after, Solamar berated himself for his carelessness in that moment. He should have known then that she had slipped too deep into trance.

Without warning, she streaked for the door and flung it wide open, breaking the protection he had counted on.

Instantly, as if she'd been waiting outside the door, Clire appeared, wispy, translucent, limbs fraying to nothing. She screamed in wordless rage and flew at Lexy.

Rimon hurled himself at Clire and knocked her away from the portal, tumbling as he grappled with the apparition.

Lexy whipped through the open portal and shot off into formless mist. *I warned her illusion is the real danger here. She thinks Clire is a phantom.*

Before he could go after Lexy, Rimon and Clire hurtled at him, spinning end for end. Clire rammed into him, slamming him into the wall. Her image frayed. Rimon, still solid fell through her arms. Astonished, Solamar lost his grip on the image of the safe room.

They were floating in formless mist, and Clire's image was all wrong. "Rimon, she's not pregnant!"

Rimon whirled and stared at her. She flew at him again, streaming the fraying mist of her body behind her while her arms and outstretched tentacles solidified, laterals extended and dripping selyn conducting ronaplin.

"She's dying, Rimon!"

"You murdered me! You murdered my baby! You denied me transfer!"

Rimon opened his arms to receive Clire's transfer grip, "Go! Save the baby!" Tentacles locked to tentacles.

"Solamar!" screamed Lexy. "Solamar!"

The boy is born. Alive or dead, he's born.

Solamar dove through the two Farrises to get to Lexy. Clire's body rammed into Rimon and kept going. Blazing white mist, virtual selyn, flowed Farris to Farris. Rimon's image drained, paled, dissolved and combined into Clire's tattered remnant of a body.

Solamar flowed to a stop in the selyn-filled mist laced with blazing nageric filaments that seized his body, brain, nerves even bones and left him hanging helpless.

It's not really selyn. He can't be giving her transfer. He's not anywhere near her body. Yet Solamar felt caught in the side effects of a real transfer of Farris speed and volume. His nerves would never survive this in reality. He closed his virtual eyes and strove to reform himself so he could help Rimon then get to Lexy.

When he opened his virtual eyes, a last whirling teardrop of mist was draining away through an invisible hole in the mist-walls around them. Otherwise, nothing.

"Solamar!" called Lexy's voice.

"Lexy!" He *reached* for Lexy and he was by her side.

They were on a misty plane, at the mantle and hearth Rimon had built, the painting of Lexy on the wall over the mantle. A sprightly fire burned in the grate and Rimon's white lined blue cloak hung on a rack.

Lexy held the coffer in her left hand, the lid back, her right hand reaching inside it, handling tentacles spread, laterals sheathed. From the knuckles down, her hand had turned to mist that curled around a replica of the Zeor dagger made of some strange, glowing material. Solamar wasn't sure if she was pulling the dagger out or trying to shove it back in and let go.

She whimpered, "Solamar!"

Solamar gathered her up from behind and held the arm that supported the coffer.

"Solamar! Don't panic!"

Ruing Farris sensitivity, he confessed, "This isn't what I'd expected." Oddly, his uncertainty steadied her.

"Help me. I'm stuck! It won't let me go!"

Cradling her back against his chest, he ran his right hand down her right arm, feeling for what was happening.

Suddenly, his father was lounging against the mantle. He had his winter cloak pushed back, hands in the pockets of his formal green robes. He wore the official jeweled Starred Cross emblem on his chest, as if interrupted amidst something important. He exuded an "I told you so" attitude.

Then Lexy looked up and saw him, and forgot about her own plight as she compared him to Solamar. Suddenly Rhodilan Grant was very interested in Lexy.

"Father, I'd like you to meet Lexy Farris uh, ambrov Zeor. Long story there. She's Rimon's daughter, and my intended."

"You're Solamar's father? I mean, I'm very glad to meet you,

Tuib."

Rhodilan Grant ran an appraising eye over Lexy. He knew her baby was not Solamar's. He didn't know that Rimon, Clire and Clire's child might be dead.

"I'm very glad to meet you, Lexy." Then his face transformed into a warm smile filled with gentle affection as he added, "Got your hand caught in the cookie jar, I see." This was the father Solamar had had before First Year, before he'd become Rhodilan's student who could do nothing but make trouble testing wild ideas.

She looked back down at her disappearing hand, and the panic vanished in laughter as her showfield assembled around a clinical detachment. "It seems I do," she chuckled. "I've tried letting go. I can't. Do you have any ideas?"

Rhodilan pushed away from the mantle. Keeping his hands in his pockets, he strolled over to walk all around the two of them, peering at the coffer and the disappearing hand from every angle.

When he came around in front of Lexy, he crouched down and scrutinized the problem from beneath, then rose, muttered, "Excuse me," and pushed his face close to the point where the knuckles evaporated into lighted mist.

Lexy peered at Solamar.

He mouthed, "Shhh."

He had told Rimon and Lexy any number of times that he was no expert to be teaching them these things. He'd rarely mentioned his father, though.

"Ah, I see the problem. Lexy, your only way out of this is through that box. It's a risk, but you'll have to just let it suck you in, then follow along through it until you get back to your body."

"My body's in there?"

"The way back lies through."

His father must have been able to find that Lexy's cord now ran through the box, probably from underneath so he hadn't seen it from the top. "How could that happen?"

"I have no idea." His father straightened and looked him

square in the eye. "It probably has something to do with the unique qualities of the Farris mutation triggered by the exercise of the channeling abilities."

There was no censure in the elder Grant's tone at all. *Something has changed.* Warily, Solamar said, "Lexy has great channeling skills, but no Wayfarer instruction. I had her in a heavily warded room and she broke out of my wards."

His father didn't note that he should have practiced more when he was learning. "I think you'll find the Farrises will always do the unexpected."

"They always surprise me."

"That is no doubt the reason why they will succeed."

They will?

Following his thought, his father merely shifted his gaze to the coffer's contents.

"Excuse me?" said Lexy. When she had their attention, she asked, "How can I climb into something so small?"

"Hmm," said Rhodilan. "My son can handle that, and he can fix it so this won't happen to the next candidate to receive Rimon's legacy."

I can?

His father told Lexy reassuringly, "Rimon put too much into that coffer. Each person should find only what they're able to absorb, not everything that's there. With good shielding installed, it should only destroy a few candidates, but only those who couldn't survive the burden anyway. Select and train the next candidates carefully and there should be no problem."

"So I'll have to absorb it all because there's no shielding in there now?"

"Basically," agreed Rhodilan. He made eye contact, riveting her attention. "You won't have to remember anything that distresses you. You will forget what you can't understand, or would prefer not to. You will remember only the one most important message about your, hmmm, House of Zeor. Is that clear?"

"Yes."

His father nodded at him. He reached around and found her cord connecting her to her body, stroked it and sent a tiny charge of selyn into it and the baby's cord, then let go of her and stood back commanding, "Go!"

Her body swirled into the coffer following her hand. The coffer snapped closed and reformed on the mantle.

When the transient ripples that marked the exit of a Farris had settled, his father grinned. "I like her. She's not bad for a Farris. Gritty. Self reliant. Good combination."

"I thought so."

"You're not worried she won't make it?"

"No. I'm just worried about Rimon."

"Ah. I saw him die. Him and that Clire woman together. That's what interrupted me." He gestured to his robes apologetically. "I saw them across. It was a good, clean death for both of them, though how you managed that I can't...well, yes, I can imagine. It seems you have finally come into possession of your own wisdom. Though possibly your warding techniques could use some work." He gestured to the coffer which now resided on the mantle.

"They're dead?" He'd known it but hadn't wanted to admit it. "What about Clire's baby?"

"Alive. Yelling like a newborn. You'll have your hands full the next few months."

"Well, then I'm ready for a warding lesson, if you have the time."

"For you, Solamar, I always have the time, even if I have to come *here* to make it."

"So how do I protect this coffer that Rimon made when I can't even touch it?"

"You've pledged yourself to this House of Zeor, haven't you? This thing contains Zeor, so it can be yours as well. That's brilliant, you know, a children's game! That is so impressive. How did you think of it?"

"I didn't, Rimon did. Or actually, he just listened to the children. Really listened. Then he got lost in time, as you saw, and when he came back I'd blocked all his memories. He retrieved the memory of the coffer. It was the one thing he couldn't bear to forget because it was his legacy for his child."

"I've underestimated your Farrises, I see. Well, then have you married his child yet?"

"Only in the heart, not by ceremony."

"Bring her here and call me. I'll be glad to officiate. For now, marriage of the heart should more than suffice if you did the pledge to Rimon correctly."

"With absolute intent."

He nodded, accepting that declaration. "Then change the portrait. Fix it so that it always displays the next heir and the symbol of this House. Then take the coffer, open it and insert veils of misdirection keyed to respond to individual capacities. And don't forget the final veil to protect the memories. Your Farrises are still much too delicate for their own good."

"They are."

His father turned and began to depart.

While his father was treating him as an equal, Solamar seized the chance to ask, "Why have you changed your mind about channeling and Farrises as the key to survival of humanity?"

Rhodilan Grant paused and half turned, confessing over his shoulder. "I saw everything Rimon saw. I know what you've committed your soul to with this House of Zeor. And I won't forget any of it." He turned and walked into the mist saying, "I'll see to it that we help them, no matter how everyone argues." He was gone.

Solamar didn't let himself think about what his father had just said. He set aside visions of Lexy awakening to find her father dead and his aching to be there holding her when she first cried.

With all the discipline that he had ever learned, he applied himself to following his father's directions, carefully testing each step to be sure he'd done it right.

* * * * * * *

Six days later, Solamar, crept up to Rimon's office door carrying Syrus Tuzhel Zeth Farris, the future Sectuib in Zeor, asleep over his shoulder.

Inside, Lexy, almost eight months pregnant, had kicked back in her father's office chair and propped her muddy boots on his desk. She was sound asleep.

Her face held a beatific smile. He had not seen her at peace in the last six days and nights. There had been the three funerals, Clire, Rimon and also Bruce who had given his life attempting to provide selyn for Clire as she voided to death giving birth.

Solamar had zlinned Bruce's body carefully and concluded he had died of a stroke. It had been his first sign of ill health or age. Privately, Solamar believed Rimon's death had triggered the stroke, not Clire's natal draw.

Syrus, though small and irritable, was healthy and much admired by all his caregivers. Solamar's concern was for Lexy. She had cried, blamed herself, smothered her emotions and buried her most beloved, comforted Bruce's family, and then gone through an entire replay of the massive pledge ceremony as everyone pledged to her.

She had given herself wholeheartedly to the House of Zeor and accepted every pledge as Rimon had, with full attention on each person, sharing their grief over Rimon and offering comfort in her hope for their future.

Through it all she had never faltered. Not in public. Only when they were alone, did she cling to him, letting her field control disintegrate and her uncertainties reign.

"Is this just because I'm pregnant, or is it real?" she kept asking him and he kept reassuring her things would look much better after the baby was born.

Now it seemed she'd found a moment when things didn't look quite so bad. Letting his eyes go unfocused, he saw her hovering over her sleeping body and above her head in glowing transparent colors hung Zeor's symbol as if it were an extension of her non-physical body.

As he watched, she gradually sank back into her body and

roused enough to zlin him. Eyes closed she said, "Jor Esren said he'll marry us, Church of the Unity style, but Shaddyr said that as his wife, she wouldn't allow it, just simply would not hear of it, until the women had time to make me a dress fitting the occasion. This she declaims in the middle of the steaming Laundry for all to hear. I'm very sorry, Solamar, but this thing is going to get huge and complicated."

He laughed. "I can deal with it."

That woke the baby. Syrus Tuzhel Zeth Farris howled with hunger.

EPILOGUE
THE LAST SECTUIB

Xigram Klairon Farris, Last Sectuib in Zeor, closed the narrative account and gazed out over the assembly of all of Zeor. Those who had wandered off had all returned.

"When Del Rimon Farris visited this future moment, he gathered us up along with the countless Receptions of Zeor by each Sectuib candidate between us, all leading to this moment. He placed all of that meaning and emotion in a coffer for his heirs. We must now gather up all the memories that each of you have recovered of your previous lives in this House and its daughter Houses.

"Close your eyes and come with me to that other place where Rimon left his gift for us all. See the large transparent cube we have carefully prepared there. Place your memories inside it, so they will be there for those in the future to find when they require them. This will be the legacy of Zeor to the galaxy, for all its species, for all time. Pour your most precious lessons here for our posterity, and I will close and seal this new, larger coffer."

He paused as he felt memories not his own pour into the great cube.

Gradually, the colorless cube began to glow. When they had finished, he sealed the lid into place and left the coffer there before the ashes in Del Rimon's hearth.

"The House of Zeor is not gone, not lost, but it ends here because it has succeeded."

Klairon took a large ring that had been prepared with the necessary sensors and turning toward the bubbling fountain with its selyn-glowing Lamp, he tossed the ring. It settled around the Lamp, whirling in a circle. By the time it had settled to the bottom of the fountain, encircling the post that supported the Lamp, the light had sputtered out.

"Out of Death Was I Born, Unto Zeor, Forever!"

Here Ends The Beginning

NAME THE VILLAIN CONTEST

When Jacqueline Lichtenberg came to the first mention of the villain, she asked the fans to name that villain.
   The Winners tied:

Villain Name: CLIRE FARRIS (Janet Coleman Sides)

Villain Name: RAVEN STONEDRAGON (Deborah Thompson)

So the Villain is named Clire Farris, and nicknamed Stonedragon.

THE NAZTEHRHAI
AMBROV ZEOR
THE FOUNDING 400

(Blanks are anonymous)

1 Donna ambrov Zeor
2 Sibiella ambrov Zeor
3 Hajene SaySha ambrov Zeor
4 Hajene Veraik ambrov Zeor
5 Ray ambrov Zeor
6 Hajene Enidan ambrov Zeor
7 --- ambrov Zeor
8 Karen Farris ambrov Zeor (Farris Gen)
9 Anton ambrov Zeor
10 Eskalie ambrov Zeor
11 Ronniebob ambrov Zeor
12 Meg ambrov Zeor
13 --- ambrov Zeor
14 Gethelwain ambrov Zeor
15 --- ambrov Zeor
16 Hendel ambrov Zeor
17 --- ambrov Zeor
18 C'Reyl ambrov Zeor
19 --- ambrov Zeor
20 --- ambrov Zeor
21 --- ambrov Zeor
22 --- ambrov Zeor
23 Patir ambrov Zeor & unborn Tianjin
24 --- ambrov Zeor

25 Jancie ambrov Zeor
26 Chayuta ambrov Zeor
27 Nora ambrov Zeor
28 D'Vorah ambrov Zeor
29 Larissa ambrov Zeor
30 --- ambrov Zeor
31 Colin ambrov Zeor
32 Pearl ambrov Zeor
33 Anne ambrov Zeor
34 Frevven ambrov Zeor
35 Lady Sirona ambrov Zeor
36 Judy ambrov Zeor
37 Terry ambrov Zeor
38 Rebecca ambrov Zeor
39 Lynda ambrov Zeor
40 Ruth ambrov Zeor
41 Dione ambrov Zeor
42 Aislinn ambrov Zeor
43 Torun ambrov Zeor
44 Marliss ambrov Zeor
45 Larry ambrov Zeor
46 --- ambrov Zeor
47 Jayne ambrov Zeor
48 Julie ambrov Zeor
49 --- ambrov Zeor
50 --- ambrov Zeor
51 --- ambrov Zeor
52 --- ambrov Zeor
53 --- ambrov Zeor
54 Ffrann ambrov Zeor
55 --- ambrov Zeor
56 Gillian ambrov Zeor
57 --- ambrov Zeor
58 Warren ambrov Zeor
59 Ann ambrov Zeor
60 JoEllen ambrov Zeor
61 Phoenix ambrov Zeor
62 --- ambrov Zeor
63 Seanara Farris ambrov Zeor (Farris Gen)

64 --- ambrov Zeor
65 David ambrov Zeor
66 Sandra ambrov Zeor
67 --- ambrov Zeor
68 --- ambrov Zeor
69 Leora ambrov Zeor
70 --- ambrov Zeor
71 Aliana ambrov Zeor
72 --- ambrov Zeor
73 Marens ambrov Zeor
74 Elektra ambrov Zeor
75 DarFishbaum ambrov Zeor
76 Christine ambrov Zeor
77 Bruce ambrov Zeor
78 Jirelle ambrov Zeor
79 --- ambrov Zeor
80 --- ambrov Zeor
81 Samuel ambrov Zeor
82 Shani ambrov Zeor
83 --- ambrov Zeor
84 --- ambrov Zeor
85 Rhymers ambrov Zeor
86 --- ambrov Zeor
87 --- ambrov Zeor
88 --- ambrov Zeor
89 Lyn ambrov Zeor
90 --- ambrov Zeor
91 --- ambrov Zeor
92 R'jeeb ambrov Zeor
93 --- ambrov Zeor
94 --- ambrov Zeor
95 --- ambrov Zeor
96 Nova ambrov Zeor
97 --- ambrov Zeor
98 Ken ambrov Zeor
99 Bonnie ambrov Zeor
100 Hajene Judith ambrov Zeor
101 Levana ambrov Zeor
102 --- ambrov Zeor

103 Jasmin ambrov Zeor
104 Klon ambrov Zeor
105 --- ambrov Zeor
106 Jackson ambrov Zeor
107 Heidi ambrov Zeor
108 Laplor ambrov Zeor
109 Kandy ambrov Zeor
110 --- ambrov Zeor
111 Goral ambrov Zeor
112 Melita ambrov Zeor
113 --- ambrov Zeor
114 Kelly ambrov Zeor
115 Suzanne ambrov Zeor
116 --- ambrov Zeor
117 Minnal ambrov Zeor
118 Merliana ambrov Zeor
119 Rothesis ambrov Zeor
120 --- ambrov Zeor
121 --- ambrov Zeor
122 Arretana ambrov Zeor
123 Cherale ambrov Zeor
124 --- ambrov Zeor
125 --- ambrov Zeor
126 Caline ambrov Zeor
127 Murphy ambrov Zeor
128 Kennet ambrov Zeor
129 Eirelle ambrov Zeor
130 Sardula ambrov Zeor
131 Lucy ambrov Zeor
132 Hal ambrov Zeor
133 Kara ambrov Zeor
134 Celina ambrov Zeor
135 --- ambrov Zeor
136 Carol ambrov Zeor
137 Frances ambrov Zeor
138 William ambrov Zeor
139 T'Khula ambrov Zeor
140 Elyse ambrov Zeor
141 John ambrov Zeor

142 Codi ambrov Zeor
143 ValerieRose ambrov Zeor
144 Chantal ambrov Zeor
145 --- ambrov Zeor
146 Ernest ambrov Zeor
147 Eric ambrov Zeor
148 Christian ambrov Zeor
149 --- ambrov Zeor
150 Dancer ambrov Zeor
151 Lilith ambrov Zeor
152 Joan ambrov Zeor
153 --- ambrov Zeor
154 Jeffparker ambrov Zeor
155 Irmtrud ambrov Zeor
156 Deborah ambrov Zeor
157 Phoebe ambrov Zeor
158 Tori ambrov Zeor
159 Oberin ambrov Zeor
160 Yukio ambrov Zeor
161 Pat ambrov Zeor
162 Fiona ambrov Zeor
163 --- ambrov Zeor
164 Ylynn ambrov Zeor
165 Darkwing ambrov Zeor
166 Jory ambrov Zeor
167 Katherine ambrov Zeor
168 Bill ambrov Zeor
169 Lexy ambrov Zeor
170 --- ambrov Zeor
171 --- ambrov Zeor
172 Jayelithe Laneff ambrov Zeor
173 --- ambrov Zeor
174 --- ambrov Zeor
175 Liz ambrov Zeor
176 Sosu Su ambrov Zeor
177 Freya ambrov Zeor
178 --- ambrov Zeor
179 ANNonymous ambrov Zeor Donor
180 Debbie ambrov Zeor

181 David ambrov Zeor
182 Margaret ambrov Zeor
183 Lancha ambrov Zeor
184 --- ambrov Zeor
185 --- ambrov Zeor
186 --- ambrov Zeor
187 --- ambrov Zeor
188 Janice ambrov Zeor
189 Renee ambrov Zeor
190 Janet ambrov Zeor
191 --- ambrov Zeor
192 Dione ambrov Zeor
193 Zeitlin ambrov Zeor
194 --- ambrov Zeor
195 --- ambrov Zeor
196 --- ambrov Zeor
197 --- ambrov Zeor
198 --- ambrov Zeor
199 Bekka ambrov Zeor
200 --- ambrov Zeor
201 Don ambrov Zeor
202 Merlyn ambrov Zeor
203 --- ambrov Zeor
204 --- ambrov Zeor
205 Jasmine ambrov Zeor
206 Ola' ambrov Zeor
207 Iudita ambrov Zeor
208 --- ambrov Zeor
209 Brek ambrov Zeor
210 Aylinn ambrov Zeor
211 Kaires ambrov Zeor
212 Todd ambrov Zeor
213 Llyn ambrov Zeor
214 Wade ambrov Zeor
215 Muriel ambrov Zeor
216 --- ambrov Zeor
217 Markay ambrov Zeor
218 Kimra ambrov Zeor
219 --- ambrov Zeor

220 Marliarna ambrov Zeor
221 Kimberly ambrov Zeor
222 Ginevra ambrov Zeor
223 --- ambrov Zeor
224 --- ambrov Zeor
225 Rinda ambrov Zeor
226 Jeff ambrov Zeor
227 Janet ambrov Zeor
228 --- ambrov Zeor
229 Thorn ambrov Zeor
230 --- ambrov Zeor
231 Ann ambrov Zeor
232 Danee ambrov Zeor
233 Mark ambrov Zeor
234 --- ambrov Zeor
235 Shaddyr ambrov Zeor
236 Eve ambrov Zeor
237 Balu ambrov Zeor
238 Rowan ambrov Zeor
239 Wilma ambrov Zeor
240 Dimitri ambrov Zeor
241 Azalais ambrov Zeor
242 Iriela ambrov Zeor
243 Darlene ambrov Zeor
244 --- ambrov Zeor
245 Marion ambrov Zeor
246 Angela ambrov Zeor
247 Alinor ambrov Zeor
248 Eldrich ambrov Zeor
249 Siri ambrov Zeor
250 Ina ambrov Zeor
251 Patricia ambrov Zeor
252 --- ambrov Zeor
253 --- ambrov Zeor
254 --- ambrov Zeor
255 Aramanth ambrov Zeor
256 Zedros ambrov Zeor
257 Liz ambrov Zeor
258 --- ambrov Zeor

259 Dawn ambrov Zeor
260 Dee ambrov Zeor
261 Louise ambrov Zeor
262 Maia ambrov Zeor
263 --- ambrov Zeor
264 Anwyn ambrov Zeor
265 Sioc ambrov Zeor
266 --- ambrov Zeor
267 Sygnus ambrov Zeor
268 Sharra ambrov Zeor
269 --- ambrov Zeor
270 Shara ambrov Zeor
271 BethAnn ambrov Zeor
272 Michelle ambrov Zeor
273 James ambrov Zeor
274 Amanda ambrov Zeor
275 Joy ambrov Zeor
276 Joel ambrov Zeor
277 Elizabeth ambrov Zeor
278 Dakin ambrov Zeor
279 Connor ambrov Zeor
280 Lynn ambrov Zeor
281 Endra ambrov Zeor
282 N'omiRose ambrov Zeor
283 Amberlynn ambrov Zeor
284 Alorie ambrov Zeor
285 Gary ambrov Zeor
286 Phlis ambrov Zeor
287 Fengal ambrov Zeor
288 Eloise ambrov Zeor
289 Kela ambrov Zeor
290 Shaerra ambrov Zeor
291 Edward ambrov Zeor
292 Shanhadar ambrov Zeor
293 Gisele ambrov Zeor
294 Amandaleigh ambrov Zeor
295 Pamela ambrov Zeor
296 WingedWolf ambrov Zeor
297 Garen ambrov Zeor

298 Jor ambrov Zeor
299 Maigrey ambrov Zeor
300 Doreen ambrov Zeor
301 Marlene ambrov Zeor
302 Laura ambrov Zeor
303 Jessrial ambrov Zeor
304 Alyx ambrov Zeor
305 Greg ambrov Zeor
306 Keith ambrov Zeor
307 Melina ambrov Zeor
308 Henk ambrov Zeor
309 Sinaje ambrov Zeor
310 Don ambrov Zeor
311 Valorie ambrov Zeor
312 Judith ambrov Zeor
313 Julie ambrov Zeor
314 Erin ambrov Zeor
315 MaryAnn ambrov Zeor
316 Mhairin ambrov Zeor
317 Kestral ambrov Zeor
318 Marguerite ambrov Zeor
319 Kyra ambrov Zeor
320 Dejla ambrov Zeor
321 Joelle ambrov Zeor
322 Faith ambrov Zeor
323 Arachne ambrov Zeor
324 Kara ambrov Zeor
325 --- ambrov Zeor
326 Cessair ambrov Zeor
327 Katrinka ambrov Zeor
328 Dixon ambrov Zeor
329 Linnea ambrov Zeor
330 Tigella ambrov Zeor
331 Bejai ambrov Zeor
332 Merie ambrov Zeor
333 Kelvis ambrov Zeor
334 Mongo ambrov Zeor
335 FyreStar ambrov Zeor
336 Keela ambrov Zeor

337 Neal ambrov Zeor
338 Zafaran ambrov Zeor
339 Lynette ambrov Zeor
340 KellyRae ambrov Zeor
341 C'Lover ambrov Zeor
342 Judy ambrov Zeor
343 Evelyn ambrov Zeor
344 Elizabeth ambrov Zeor
345 Karylin ambrov Zeor
346 Tod ambrov Zeor
347 Adam ambrov Zeor
348 Elijahjt ambrov Zeor
349 Susan ambrov Zeor
350 Lisaine ambrov Zeor
351 Talith ambrov Zeor
352 Dinah ambrov Zeor
353 Jason ambrov Zeor
354 Sieglinde ambrov Zeor
355 Cindy ambrov Zeor
356 Litz ambrov Zeor
357 Joby ambrov Zeor
358 Saara ambrov Zeor
359 Lisa ambrov Zeor
360 Bertina ambrov Zeor
361 Tony ambrov Zeor
362 Loriely ambrov Zeor
363 Kelvar ambrov Zeor
364 Lynn ambrov Zeor
365 Pam'la Farris ambrov Zeor
366 Lisbeth ambrov Zeor
367 Emeka ambrov Zeor
368 Karen ambrov Zeor
369 Selene ambrov Zeor
370 Xanon ambrov Zeor
371 Haldane ambrov Zeor
372 Sian ambrov Zeor
373 Ferren ambrov Zeor
374 Ravenisa ambrov Zeor
375 LeXara ambrov Zeor

376 Dayyel ambrov Zeor
377 Stanley ambrov Zeor
378 dbard ambrov Zeor
379 Leona ambrov Zeor
380 BanSha ambrov Zeor
381 Eshala ambrov Zeor
382 Herbert ambrov Zeor
383 --- ambrov Zeor
384 Cat ambrov Zeor
385 Defiance ambrov Zeor
386 Sheryl ambrov Zeor
387 Corrvin ambrov Zeor
388 --- ambrov Zeor
389 Gary ambrov Zeor
390 Ironwood Ferris ambrov Zeor
391 Tani ambrov Zeor
392 Nancie ambrov Zeor
393 Millisa ambrov Zeor
394 Silvia ambrov Zeor
395 Margie ambrov Zeor
396 Martz ambrov Zeor
397 Yavanna ambrov Zeor
398 Patricia ambrov Zeor
399 Timothy ambrov Zeor
400 Robert ambrov Zeor
401 Lalique ambrov Zeor
402 Caspian ambrov Zeor
403 Pim ambrov Zeor
404 Totoq ambrov Zeor
405 Callia ambrov Zeor
406 Dahna ambrov Zeor
407 Lorri-Lynne ambrov Zeor
408 Sara ambrov Zeor
409 Kristen ambrov Zeor
410 Debby ambrov Zeor
411 Carma ambrov Zeor
412 Charles ambrov Zeor
413 Denise ambrov Zeor
414 H'jh'rhan ambrov Zeor

415 Jana ambrov Zeor
416 Alisa ambrov Zeor
417 Irene ambrov Zeor
418 Dale ambrov Zeor
419 Samya ambrov Zeor
420 noitcelfer ambrov Zeor
421 Deborah ambrov Zeor
422 Cinder ambrov Zeor
423 aeryn ambrov Zeor
424 Alexis ambrov Zeor
425 Ketlin ambrov Zeor
426 lea ambrov Zeor
427 Elorie ambrov Zeor
428 Bertha ambrov Zeor
429 Stephanie ambrov Zeor

ABOUT JACQUELINE LICHTENBERG

Jacqueline Lichtenberg is a life member of the Science Fiction Writers of America. She is creator of the Sime~Gen Universe with a vibrant fan following (http://www.Simegen.com), primary author of the Bantam paperback *Star Trek Lives!* which blew the lid on Star Trek fandom, founder of the Star Trek Welcommittee, creator of the genre term Intimate Adventure, winner of the Galaxy Award for Spirituality in Science Fiction with her second novel *Unto Zeor, Forever*, and the first Romantic Times Awards for Best Science Fiction Novel with her later novel *Dushau*, now on Kindle. Her fiction has been in audio-dramatization on XM Satellite Radio. She has been the sf/f reviewer for a professional magazine since 1993. She teaches sf/f writing online while turning to her first love, screenwriting focused on selling to the feature film market.

Currently available e-book and paper novels featured at

http://jacquelinelichtenberg.com

Can be followed on twitter.com/jlichtenberg

Or facebook.com/jacqueline.lichtenberg

Or friendfeed.com as jlichtenberg